STEALING WORLDS

TOR BOOKS BY KARL SCHROEDER

Ventus

Permanence

Lady of Mazes

Sun of Suns

Queen of Candesce

Pirate Sun

The Sunless Countries

Virga: Cities of the Air

Ashes of Candesce

Lockstep

Stealing Worlds

STEALING WORLDS

Karl Schroeder

A TOM DOHERTY ASSOCIATES BOOK
New York

This is a work of fiction. All of the characters, organizations, and events portrayed in this novel are either products of the author's imagination or are used fictitiously.

STEALING WORLDS

A Tor Book
Published by Tom Doherty Associates
175 Fifth Avenue
New York, NY 10010

www.tor-forge.com

Tor® is a registered trademark of Macmillan Publishing Group, LLC.

The Library of Congress Cataloging-in-Publication Data is available upon request.

ISBN 978-0-7653-9998-4 (hardcover)
ISBN 978-0-7653-9997-7 (ebook)

Our books may be purchased in bulk for promotional, educational, or business use. Please contact your local bookseller or the Macmillan Corporate and Premium Sales Department at 1-800-221-7945, extension 5442, or by email at MacmillanSpecialMarkets@macmillan.com.

First Edition: June 2019

Printed in the United States of America

0 9 8 7 6 5 4 3 2 1

ACKNOWLEDGMENTS

Much of this novel was inspired by conversations I had with members of the crypto community on the Ethereum forums in 2014. Particular thanks goes to Stephan Tual for seeing the possibilities at such an early stage and for encouraging me throughout this effort. Thanks also to Cassius Kiani for his work in making the Deodands project succeed, and to the many others with whom I consulted over the past couple of years. Most important, as always, I owe my inspiration and greatest support to my wife, Janice, and my daughter, Paige. I am grateful to all of you for your trust and faith in me.

PART I

THE PRECARIAT

CHAPTER ONE

On a warm night in June, Sura Neelin walks past the homes where her friends once lived, past her old high school and the corner store where she used to buy Popsicles. She turns down a gravel-surfaced alley canopied by black trees, and before she's ready she's standing in the backyard of her old house. She hesitates under its shadow, flashlight in one gloved hand, screwdriver in the other.

The cicadas are winding down, the sounds of traffic and police drones not so frequent this far from the main roads. She enters the backyard through the same old rickety fence that she used to use as a chalkboard. What light there is comes from neighbors' windows peeking from behind silhouetted branches. She can smell but not see the grass, yet this yard is where she learned to walk, and her steps are sure as she makes her way to the back porch.

The screen door didn't have a lock on it when she lived here, and it doesn't now. It eases open and she pokes her head around the doorjamb. Right over there is where Nick McAllister kissed her, when they were scrunched hip to hip in Grandma's orange beanbag chair. It had been hot weather like this. Dad used to keep cartons of beer stacked next to the window; Mom didn't want the stuff cluttering up the kitchen.

There's an Ikea shelving unit where the beanbag once sprawled. Sura straightens up, realizing she's still got her feet on the porch steps. Afraid to commit. With a muttered curse she forces herself on; she knows where the boards creak on this floor, so she zigzags to the brick-framed kitchen door and puts out her hand to feel for its lock.

It's been changed. But that's what the screwdriver is for.

She jams it into the keyhole and bumps it with a practiced hand. The knob turns, she eases the back door open, and steps inside.

It smells like home.

And just like that she's hit with a wave of memories from the first months after Mom died. Dad flew home, and they spent whole days cooking just to keep each other company. Those images lead to others, of birthday parties, late-night snacks, and that day the water sprayed out of the faucet and she couldn't stop it, had to phone Dad and he'd told her, annoyed, about the cut-off valve under the sink.

She has no excuse for being here. She's here on a rumor. Like as not she'll get caught and things will get infinitely worse for her; but how much worse? They're bad, sure, but bad like everybody's life is bad. Debt bad. No future bad. Broken promises and bitterness bad. She can put up with that. She doesn't know for certain that she'll die if she walks away right now.

Sura takes a ragged breath, looks around herself, and sees that the kitchen's been repainted. Even in the dark she can tell that the shade of sky blue is relentless. Mom would have hated it.

One more deep breath, measured now, and she moves to the dining room.

Everything was fine this morning.—Fine, that is, in the sense of only being fucked up in the usual ways. At ten o'clock Sura was out riding her bike, because jittery nerves and annoyance at being let go from yet another short-term contract had her pacing the kitchen. She was trying not to look at the bills—those made of paper that are piled on the table, and the many imminent cancellation notices piled up in her inbox.

She reassured herself that everybody is in this position. It's even true, at least for those of her old friends who'll still talk to her. The economy is roaring ahead, growth is up, and the GDP has never been higher; it's just that nobody's getting by.

The white slab of warehouse which was Sura's last shit job is a couple of miles southwest of her apartment. "Forward warehousing" has finally come to Dayton: all round the city dozens of cars have rented out their trunks, which contain cigars and scotch and stuff. Every now and then one of these trunks will pop open, seemingly at random and often while the car is driving, and a drone carrying a bottle of Talisker's or Oban will zip off at right angles, delivering the package to a waiting customer and justifying the company promise: *Five minutes or it's free.*

Of course, the trunks need to be restocked, from slower drones that originate here. And while the public face of the operation is relentlessly high-tech, the warehouse is staffed with minimum-wage humans, mostly immigrants and kids fresh out of college, who are run off their feet. Sura wore a tracker badge because the fetchers' movements are optimized to the second, like the drones'. If she stopped walking for a minute, they docked her pay. Longer than a minute and, well . . . here she was.

The bike took her through Hillcrest, a neighborhood she's known since she was a kid. Everything looked fine on the surface, though with the city's aggressive deroading program in full swing, half the streets are blocked off. Their asphalt has been torn up and grass and trees planted in its place. Still, the houses she passed seemed well-kept and delivery drones came and went. There's money somewhere, for somebody.

She glided along winding paths past the beautiful homes, peeking through living room windows while calculating how far that last paycheck would get her and wondering what came next. The last of Mom's savings have run out; her buffer is gone. Nobody who knows her will let her couch surf. Time to go online and hunt for some stranger who needs a roommate.

It's six years since Mom died. The echoes of that still chase her, in the form of crushing debt and memories of Mom's long slow decline. Toward the end Sura's whole waking life was consumed with taking care of her. The trauma's still with her but she'd go back to that time in a heartbeat because, despite the awfulness and the sense of them being abandoned both by the world and by Dad, her life had meaning. The tightly structured days, the narrow focus, the complete impossibility of going out; it all hurt. So many movies missed. Yet she'd kept Mom's music playing for her right up until the last day.

She still listens to the old tunes, but the life behind them is gone.

The warehouse job felt like her last chance at a lot of things—income, purpose, some kind of dignity; with it blown sky-high, a long, dull period in her life seems to be ending. She'd put her head down and peddled harder but the anxieties built and built, chasing her like leaves in her wake. She wasn't going to make it. In desperation, for the first time since Mom died Sura gave herself permission to reach back to a coping mechanism from before that time. She'd had a trick for dealing with shit once, an effective one. It's been years since she used it because in the old days, it usually ended with her doing a B&E. Mom never knew, and in her last days, Sura had promised never to disappoint her. Still . . .

She calls this maneuver the *fuck-you.*

The bills, the dead-end jobs, the nervous exhaustion of living in a country that's in a state of perpetual, low-grade civil war—all of these things nag and peck at her, all day, every day. Really, there was only one thing to say to all of it.

Fuck you.

She smiled. Yes, this is exactly what she needed.

Money problems: *fuck you.*

Nobody likes you: well, *fuck you.*

Dad's an asshole, and Mom is dead: then, *fuck you.*

The rush of anger was exhilarating—but it's just the primer. Now some old neglected engine caught, a power she'd built for herself as a kid in those many evenings spent in her room listening to Mom and Dad fight. Cycling down these familiar streets, canopied by green and awash in the roar of the cicadas, Sura shouted screw you to all the baggage of her life and kicked it overboard.

Her imagination broke free at last. Lifted by fantasy, she pictured herself rising to visit the treetops. She felt the tentative touch of millions of leaves as she turned and gyred above the maze. She looked down upon herself and from here it was plain she was being observed, but not by the neighborhood-watch drones. The cicadas were taking note of her, and the squirrels, skunks nesting under the porches, raccoons in the garages. Even the trees must feel her presence, as they breathed her exhalations. None were spies for some dark extractive power. Rather, she moved in the embrace of her neighbors and friends, a family she'd been born into.

She glimpsed it then, the web of exchanges holding this family together. True, the flowers traded their nectar, there were markets in the bushes, but there were also gifts being bestowed, such as the oxygen sighing from the leaves, the flows of nutrients in the ground as older trees gave of themselves to nurture the younger. Light flooding everything, heat making the air tremble, and everywhere little leaf factories banging on incoming molecules with their trip hammers, infinitesimal welders on microscopic scaffolds throwing sparks as mitochondrial cranes lofted newly minted proteins to tiny workers assembling new cells. All these trillions of projects ran independently yet were somehow nested in harmonious circles, invisible to the old man mowing his lawn, to the worried drivers, the delivery guy hauling boxes out of the back of his van. A secret known only to her.

On the bike path, at the eye of this hurricane of motion and industry, a small woman, earbuds in, sped along to a soundtrack of digital beats and pygmy chants.

For a few minutes, she was actually and miraculously herself. She could do anything, and maybe she should . . . And then her phone rang.

She had her smart glasses on, so she replied in hands-free mode. "Hello?"

"Sura, thank God I got through. Listen, it's me, Marjorie."

Marj. The *fuck-you* collapsed. The bike wobbled. "What do you want?" She'd spoken to Dad's new piece exactly twice since he and Mom split up. Why the hell was she calling now?

"Sura, I know you've got—I don't know how to say—Listen. Have you received any packages lately? From your dad?"

"What? No, what?"

"Okay. Um. Sura." She heard Marj take a sharp, half-caught breath. "He's dead, Sura.

"Your father's been murdered. And the people who did it may be after you, too."

Jim said if something like this happened, to look in that spot you signed, Marjorie had told her. *He said you'll know what he means.*

Now, she crosses her old dining room in three quick steps. She's all focus and knows exactly where she's going. Whatever furniture these new homeowners may have put in the way, she can push it aside, she can even smash things if she has to because looting this place is literally only going to take a second.

She was eleven when they renovated the house. Dad brought her in one day, and she was fascinated to see how the interior walls had turned skeletal. The living room's outer wall was now exposed brick.

As she traced its roughness with a finger, Dad grinned and pulled a Sharpie out of his pocket. "Why don't you sign it?" he said. "They'll be putting new drywall up tomorrow. Nobody'll ever know it's there. Nobody but you and me."

SURA NEELIN she wrote on the brick. The rest of the gutted interior barely registered on her. She had signed her house!

She has her phone out and ready, the NFC reader app glowing on its face. Dad used to tease her by asking if she remembered where her signature was. She was always proud to show him: just step into the living room and turn right, go to the wall and slide the phone along it at the height of her solar plexus . . .

She steps in and turns—and there are bookshelves on the wall.

Sura just stares at them. Dad had been so clever, after all: how could he hide a file storage chip so nobody can ever find it no matter how many drawers they rip out or light fixtures they unscrew, yet have the information literally at your fingertips? Simply slap an NFC sticker on the back of the drywall, right where his daughter had signed the bricks it would rest against. *Snap snap snap* said the nailgun, and then the new wall was up. The NFC tag was Dad's secret stash, so secret that she was nineteen before he told her about it—and by that time, the house was sold.

The new owners haven't gutted the place the way the Neelins did. And why shouldn't they screw two sets of bookshelves into the studs? They don't know that this was the wall the couch was against, the one Mom spent her last weeks on as the cancer killed her. The shelves are about three feet tall and start about three and a half feet up from the floor. Hipshot in a slab of streetlight that leans in from the front window, Sura contemplates the steps she's going to have to take to get through the one that's covering her signature.

She pushes back on the memories of kneeling by the couch, mashing Mom's food for her; *Think, think*. With luck, the shelves are just open frames with the drywall exposed behind them . . . She pulls out some Nora Roberts hardcovers and puts her hand out to find faux-wood particleboard where there should be wall. The shelf's got a back. Hopefully that's not too thick, you can only read an NFC from an inch or two away, and the drywall drastically thins the signal. She slides the phone around for a while, but the backing of the shelf must be blocking it entirely. She can't be sure she's even swiping the phone over the right spot.

Shoulders hunched, feeling the ghosts now and the presence of sleepers in the master bedroom directly overhead, she begins pulling books with trembling fingers. She stacks them carefully but quickly until the shelving unit is empty, then feels for the heavy screws that must hold it up. There they are. Lucky she still has her screwdriver.

The first screw doesn't pretend to budge. "Damn fuck shit motherfucker cunt shit . . ." She lacerates her palms twisting, but it's no use. The whole plan's gone south, she should bolt out the back, find some alternative, except she can't because Dad's sins are being visited upon her, and if it were just the cops coming after her (and her sitting calmly on her couch, arms held up for the handcuffs) then that would be okay. It won't be the police or the FBI, though. The FBI care, but they don't *care,* not to the point of murder. According to Marj, the people who do care aren't going to be nice about asking for whatever it is Dad put behind this wall.

For the very first time she knows that if somebody comes down the stairs, bleary-eyed and demanding to know what's going on, she's going to have to hurt them. She can't leave this spot, is trapped to run as long as it takes in a tight circle around this one damned screw—

Leaning in, teeth grinding and her whole body a ramrod, she finally feels it give. She keeps folding herself around it, as with a series of groans and creaks the thing loosens and comes out.

That was the top left one. A little clear voice in her head comments that she should have begun at the bottom.

Fine fine, whatever, she goes for those screws. The lower right one is easy, and that leaves the lower left. As she starts on it, she hears footsteps on the stairs.

It really, really doesn't matter at this point. She keeps cricking her hands around the screwdriver.

"Who are you?"

It's a little girl's voice.

Sura glances back. There's a silhouette on the stairs.

"I'm just fixing the bookshelf," she whispers. "Go back to bed."

"Oh. Okay." The figure turns and starts back up.

Cindy-Lou Who, thinks Sura and she nearly laughs out loud. The third screw pops out and the shelf becomes a pendulum. She grabs her phone off *The Cambridge History of China* and slides it along the wall, swinging the shelf this way and that to get at the smooth white surface behind.

Ping.

Now it's ballet time but with no soundtrack she can imagine; somehow Sura's turning on her toes as she threads the stacks of books, then she pads through the dining room, the unfamiliar kitchen and porch. She's unreeling her whole life, bye-bye Momma, bye-bye Dad and grief-cooking, bye-bye Nick and your kiss, and she's on the lawn pocketing an unknown legacy, and walking raccoon roads under the darkest trees and burnt-out streetlights, out of a neighborhood that's no longer hers.

* * *

She spends twenty minutes standing in the bushes across the street from her apartment block. She's cased buildings like this dozens of times; it's almost refreshing to be doing it again after years away from the craft.

When she's satisfied that nobody else is lurking around her place, Sura jogs from the shadows to the apartment's bright lobby. Her heart is pounding as she approaches her own unit, it's absurdly like she's about to break into her own home. But there could be someone there.

Nobody is, there's only the depressing bills, the useless knickknacks she's accumulated over the years. She doesn't turn on the lights.

The apartment is small enough that the only place she could find for her 3-D printer was on a stand in the walk-in closet. Leaning under jackets and blouses, she calls up one of the files she took from the NFC tag. The file's name is SURA PRINT ME. She shoots it to the printer.

It's a good machine, it makes the paper as well as the ink, even reproducing the folds in the birth certificate, school records, and so on. After all the docs are done, she reaches down to clear the printer's memory. She'll break it, just to be safe, but then she notices the other file names.

Fuck! For a long minute she just drinks in the sight of them. Tears have started at the corners of her eyes. Then she hits *print* on one.

Layer by layer, a tiny statue of Ganesha emerges from the 3-D printer's bed. It comes up in full color and with every detail picked out perfectly on its elephant trunk and tiny belled hands, and of course she remembers it. If she wants, she has a dozen more files she can queue up—files containing everything from a hairbrush to a family photo in a picture frame.

It was Dad who taught her how to do this. One day when she was sixteen, he'd said, "Hold still! Just like that!" He'd walked around her three times, waving his phone up and down slowly like it was an airport security wand. When he was done, he gave a fist pump of triumph and walked off without a word. Days later, he showed her the 3-D–printed mannequin of her, eight inches tall, made of colored resin. He'd scanned her, and now he had a copy of her standing hipshot, hands on hips, looking skeptical.

"Now you can come with me on my trips," he'd said.

"That's creepy, Dad."

Sura's burgled many houses, but she never stole a thing. In the dark of a sleeping home, she'd find some trinket that summed up the place and wave the phone around it, turning the thing over once or twice. And it was hers.

Her career in non-theft ended a week before her eighteenth birthday. She was standing in the darkness, staring up at the lit windows of a house, when a voice behind her said, "Who do you know here?"

It was her father. Hearing a noise after midnight, he'd found her bed empty and the window open, and just glimpsed her skedaddling along shadowed fences. He'd followed her, watched her check her list of candidate buildings one by one. Finally, his curiosity got the better of him.

That was a tough moment. Not because James Neelin was shocked that his seventeen-year-old daughter was breaking into places; he wasn't. It was because he insisted she tell him *why* she was doing it. Standing with him in the damp dark bushes, she stammered and talked in circles, about anything but him and Mom.

Growing up in Dayton, she and her friends had explored all the yards and boulevards on her block. She told him how, when she was fourteen and old enough to be out in the evening alone, she would peek across the hedges and lawns, fascinated with what was revealed in other people's homes as indoor lights came on. She could watch them going about their lives, see houses with the same plan as hers but realized in entirely different ways.

The people in those placid tableaux seemed so comfortably snuggled together. With no fights, no sullen silences, no anxious subtext to every conversation.

By the time she was sixteen, she was all too familiar with the view from the sidewalks, and had to become more daring. She penetrated the alleys and ravines near the school. From under leaves, or on a log or a broken piece of concrete, she could look further. She carried a Taser now.

Seventeen and Mom was sick, Dad was rarely in town, and Sura had taken to standing in backyards at two in the morning.

One night, she pried open the window of a house she'd babysat in years ago. She'd heard the family was away for the weekend. She crammed through the window and unraveled herself awkwardly onto the dining room floor, heart hammering. She thought she was going to faint when she stood up, but it didn't happen, and now she had the whole place to herself.

Overlaid on her mental map of local driveways and paths, fences and hedges, Sura slowly drew another map, of broken latches, vulnerable windows, and substandard locks. While she still lived at home, they spidered around her, an invisible overlay on the ordinary night.

"So what have you stolen?" he demanded.

"Nothing!"

His face was a play of light and shadows, but his incredulous expression was obvious. "Dad, I never took a single thing! I—look, I'll prove it." She took out her phone and showed him the scan files. When he saw, and understood what she'd been doing, he seemed to accept it.

"It stops now," he'd said.

It had. Sura had self-control, she could do it. It was enough, by now, to know that she'd once defied the world by standing in the living room of a girl who taunted her at school, knowing she could smash or steal any of her stuff. She'd needed that proof, but now she had it. She could walk away from burglary. The only thing that really hurt was that Dad had confiscated her phone, and the tangible proof of what she'd done.

She'd stolen without stealing, but when Dad took her phone he also took all her trophies; the only copies of her scan files were on it. That had felt like a theft. All this time, nearly ten years, she's been sure he deleted the things. And all these years they've been stashed behind the wall in her old living room. Right there with her signature.

Her finger hovers over another file. She imagines the proof of her daring and skill all piling out of the closet while bad guys kick down her door. Obviously doing this is a terrible idea. Yet she doesn't move until Ganesha finishes rendering and is shunted to the pickup tray. Sura drops the warm god in her backpack and turns away.

After smashing the printer she comes and sits in the dark kitchen. Crouching in the closet with a hammer has done more to make her situation real than breaking into her old house. *Dad, what did you do?*

One evening, six months after he caught her, Dad offered to go for a walk. Two blocks away from home, conversation petered out; he seemed nervous. Finally he'd said, "Sura, those . . . skills of yours. You haven't been using them, have you?"

"No way! Dad, I promised. Don't you trust me?"

He raised his hands in apology. "I do, and I believe you. It's just that, well . . .

"What if I had a thing I needed you to do? One that involved . . . those skills?"

What little light filters into the kitchen from the curtained living room isn't enough for Sura to read the details of her new identity. Her fingers stroke the papers and cards, the rest of her still as a statue. When she's ready she rises again, and for a silent hour she moves through the condo, wiping away her fingerprints. It's a dance of subtraction, a peeling away of herself from all the surfaces that have been hers, and after a while, she finds herself back at the kitchen table, standing now, aware of the waiting door.

She aims one word into the place that's been her home for six years—and further, at the person she's been all this time: "Goodbye."

Eyes down, she crosses the threshold, blurring and fading in the shaded streets, turning down the volume on Sura Neelin until she's a rumor, an uncertain hum, and finally, gone.

CHAPTER TWO

"Can I help you with that?" Sura spots the woman unloading her car as she's walking between the river and the yellow, girdered 16th Street Bridge. There are converted lofts in this part of Pittsburgh, and most are chic and unaffordable. Some of the buildings near the railway sidings, though, have a certain down-at-heel look, with cracked, grass-strewn parking lots and haphazard air-conditioning arrangements in the big square windows. This one is the fourth of five old warehouses jammed up against the railroad tracks. As she figured, they've been subdivided and rented out to painters, poets, design students, and . . . well, this one's wearing black leather.

"It's okay, I've got it," says the woman, who has the whole strict-teacher vibe down pat. She snaps her fingers and a man in a business suit and a dog collar gets out of the Fiat and gathers up her grocery bags. She grins at Sura. "Getting a senior partner to carry your shit is one of the perks of the job."

Sura and the dominatrix watch the eager lawyer work. They're sharing a moment, so Sura lets her explain how lots of men in high-power, high-pressure jobs come to her for a holiday from responsibility.

She holds out a hand to shake. "Jeri."

"Britt," says Sura "I'm looking to rent down here. Are all the units taken?"

"Yeah, sorry. Mine's big enough I've got my own machine shop in the back."

"Machine shop? Not dungeon?"

"No no, machine shop *and* dungeon! Want to see?"

"Actually, right now I'm looking for a secure mesh gateway." She taps her glasses.

Jeri nods. "Got that too. Come on."

This and helping carry the groceries gets Sura in the door, and the next fifteen minutes are really interesting. After checking out the machine shop and dungeon they end up in Jeri's living quarters, which are a comparatively tiny slice of the place. Just room for a little kitchenette, a toilet and shower stall, and a narrow little bedroom. There's a chopping-block table in the kitchen, and a young woman in full Goth regalia is sitting there, reading a large hardcover textbook in a pool of sunlight. She glances up as Sura and Jeri come in.

"New client?"

Jeri eyes Sura, who despite herself has been casing the windows and door locks. "What do you say?"

Sura eyes her back. "Naw."

Jeri pouts. "Can always use some help, though. How are you with ropes?"

"Never tried 'em."

"There's a first time for everything. Nothing quite like paddling the backside of a blindfolded CEO."

Sura thinks about it. "It's still kind of male gaze-y, though, isn't it? He's still objectifying you from behind the blindfold, in a way?"

"Oh ho!" The Goth lays down her book. "'Male gaze'! How sophistricated."

"Down, Maeve, the nice lady brought in the asparagus."

Only now does Sura see the titles on the stack of texts. "Philosophy, huh?"

Maeve nods briskly. "Summer school. Object-Oriented Ontology? Like, Levi Bryant, Tim Morton, and Quentin Meillassoux?"

"I found Maeve in a strip club," says Jeri, nodding out the window. "She paid her tuition with cash she pulled out of her G-string. But I made her a better offer. She's great at role-play."

"Let me get this straight. Guys'll pay more to get yelled at than a lap dance?"

"Yeah," says Maeve. "Plus all our business was getting eaten up by this VR-porn shit. They don't even have to leave the apartment anymore."

Jeri rolls her eyes. "Here comes the rant."

"They started doing full 3-D motion-capture on us while we were on the pole!" Maeve throws down her pen. "They *recorded* it. After you've danced a few times they don't need the real you. Half the dancers on the website don't even work there anymore, they're *in virtua*. The only reason people were coming to the bar was because you can't scan beer."

Sura looks her up and down in all her lace and leather glory. "They have no idea what they're missing."

"Well, thank you." There's a tiny pause—just an instant—as she and Sura lock gazes. Then, smoothly, Maeve goes on: "This is only temporary too. Jeri doesn't have enough work for me. Something's gotta give. I just hope I graduate."

While Jeri stocks the fridge and Maeve reads, Sura goes online to continue shutting her various accounts. There's a strong cell signal, but if she were to use it, the unstoppable surveillance machine that's replaced the Internet would paint personalized ads over every blank surface in the loft. The sky would become a billboard, and tags and touchable interfaces would spring up everywhere, pointing out nearby coffee shops, suggesting restaurants and clothing stores and social services. Tall thin stalks would appear in the streets—tappable connections to available cars that can take her anywhere she wants. There'd be news, weather, and sports, and if she had any friends, their photos and chats and favorite music would spill out and swirl around Sura, a cloud of friendship.

Instead, she connects to the mesh. It's not the Internet, but a parallel pirate network that's built with anonymity and privacy in mind. The few apps are open-source and maintained by paranoid libertarian hackers. Their tags do things that are useful to someone in Sura's position: flags hovering over the neighborhood show where and when there have been rapes, gun incidents, and robberies. Meridional lines on the sky outline gang territories, heat maps highlight where the police usually patrol, and skulking neighborhood-watch drones are revealed as red dots. There may be fewer services, but there are no ads—and most importantly, the mesh is not set up to track your every click and eyeblink like the Internet is.

She had to trash her desktop machine back home, so here she has to do with a virtual keyboard projected on the tabletop by her smart glasses. The glasses fill her visual field with other objects and windows too. Some of the sites she has to visit are glasses-ready, but many are still screen- or phone-oriented and just put up annoying little rectangular windows that she has to poke at. To Jeri and Maeve, she'll look like a total spaz, scabbling on the blank table and jabbing at thin air.

She transfers money from her bank account into the supposedly untraceable cryptocurrency NotchCoin. She messes up her name and addresses on various sites, and when she's done she thanks the dom and her protégée. It's only when she takes off the glasses that she notices her eyes are wet.

A few nights after arriving in Pittsburgh, she'd finally summoned the courage to delve into her backpack for the documents she printed before leaving Dayton. Her hands shook a little as she turned over the birth certificate. The name on it was *Britt Birch*. Britt is twenty-seven, born and raised in Dayton just like Sura. There was a sheet of notes accompanying the certificate, printed in an anonymous typeface; she knew it was from Dad. He seemed to have spent more time planning Britt Birch's life than he did Sura's. The notes say that he bought this ID on the dark web ten years ago—well, that makes sense, given the timeline—and ever since, he's been putting money into an anonymous NotchCoin account that pays for Britt's various online memberships.

Sura can't help it. She's jealous of Britt. Dad nursed the ID along, kept her alive in digital terms, for a whole decade; it hardly matters that he ultimately intended to hand her over to Sura. Sura is Britt now, if she wants to be. But what does it say about Dad that he spent more time making plans for his virtual daughter than his real one?

That Britt exists at all should be a revelation; that Sura wasn't blindsided by the big reveal really is one. It's only now that she realizes how, in subtle ways, Dad had been prepping her for this moment for years. Disappearance was a game he insisted she learn, and being young and naïve she'd played along all unthinking. "You need a backup for everything," he'd explained, and it seemed reasonable. "And you need to know how to delete your data, your job, where you live . . ." And your name. And never a breath about why.

She'd taken the lesson to heart, and it's proven valuable. It's only by having backup skills and job prospects that she's kept her head above water in recent years. Backup jobs, backup social networks, backup relationships . . . Yeah. All so reasonable.

She wipes her eyes and Jeri notices that she's done her work. "What was all that?"

"Running from my ex," Sura lies.

She gets the address for Building Management from Jeri, then Maeve walks her down the industrial-gray staircase to the untaped-drywall, ceilingless front lobby. At the door there's another moment outside time, as she notices Maeve and Maeve notices her noticing. Feigning innocence, Sura examines the mailboxes. As she'd hoped, the unit is a standard three-by-six set of bays that can be opened from behind the wall, or individually from the front. That makes eighteen boxes. There are thirteen apartments in the building.

"Thanks," she says. "See you around."

"Come by any time," says Maeve with a sphinxlike smile.

Building Management turns out to be a white stucco house, incongruously nestled under a pillar of the nearby bridge. It's seen better days, its cracking skin scarred with various mounting points for signs that might have advertised it as a coffee bar, back when there was coffee, or a massage parlor or pawn shop. Now there's just a business card in the glass of the front door. Inside, in what was once a tiny living room, Sura finds a mountainous mop-headed woman seated behind an orange Ikea desk that's covered in recently emptied fast-food containers.

"Hi, I'd like to know about Building Four—"

"They're all taken."

"I figured," says Sura with an apologetic smile. "I was actually wondering if I could just rent a mailbox."

She's dressed well for this and rehearsed her story, which involves Britt Birch living out of town but having to make unpredictable visits to her mother, who's in a nearby long-term care facility. Sura thinks somebody at the place is opening its residents' mail. Checks have gone missing.

Ten minutes of commiseration and shared outrage later, Britt Birch has a postal address.

Suddenly giddy, Sura pumps her fist in the air as soon as she's out of sight of the place. It's been so long since she did anything like this. Breaking into her own house doesn't count; that was home. But *here*! Here she is, on her own, getting shit done.

She tries her glasses in the parking lot and discovers that Jeri's repeater signal reaches this far. It shows her the city in a whole different way, and she has to pause to take it in.

Past the buckling lots, a thin screen of trees tries to hide the river. There, some people are dodging in and out of the foliage, laughing and waving sticks. They're the distant descendants of the *Pokémon Go* fans—larpers, living out some fantasy in a gameworld only they can see. The mesh has them tagged as players so you don't think they're lunatics or terrorists on a rampage—a useful feature when the cops are around. The game this group is playing is called *Rivet Couture*.

Sura sees but doesn't notice all these signs and signifiers. Her eyes turn back to the fire escape outside Jeri's window, where the mesh antenna is clamped.

She remembers hanging from somebody's gutter in the rain. She thinks about the sensual click of a lock releasing itself to her practiced hand.

She follows the chain of memory, and the hard angles and black peeling paint of the fire escape lead her straight to Dad.

"What if I had a thing I needed you to do? One that involved . . . those skills?" Dad had asked on that evening walk, years ago.

She'd eyed him askance. "Yeah?"

"Well. The thing here is, stealing, it's not *always* a bad thing."

The conversation went into a gawky spiral as he talked about how you sometimes have to break the law to do the right thing. He brought up Watergate and cases of investigative journalists breaking into people's offices or homes to gather evidence. Sura can't remember saying a word; she probably just stared at him as he worked up his courage. Finally, when they were nearly home again, he said, "Do you think you could steal one actual thing? Just a hard drive from a computer?"

Two weeks later she found herself standing on the roof of a building in downtown Boston, tying a rope to an air-conditioning unit. Two floors down was the office of a legal firm that represented some of the biggest oil companies on the planet. In that office was a computer that had never been connected to the Internet. That computer wasn't special in any other way—it was supposed to look normal, to be overlooked. Security through obscurity, a gambit that hadn't worked.

Her heart was pounding and she was sure she was going to be sick. To sort herself out, she went to stand at the edge of the roof, where the city revealed itself in glorious patterns of light and blackness. Somehow the fire escapes on the building across the street made a particular imprint on her memory, every detail in their wrought-iron angles picked out with photographic clarity. Staring at them, she drew deeply on the night air, listened to the traffic, and then, as she had so many times before, she summoned the *fuck-you* feeling.

She was Catwoman. She was Black Widow. She was every badass heroine she'd ever watched or read about, but she was *real*, she was actually going to make a difference tonight. She spread her arms, imagining that she held an invisible net of power, into which treasures would fall. Two floors down they awaited the gloved hands that would own them.

The *fuck-you* is that moment when you redraw the boundaries of the world in your own favor. It's not always an act of defiance, it can be the ecstatic reimagining of any idea that's supposed to stay unquestioned. The *fuck-you* may start out in the imagination, but if you let it push you . . .

Power and confidence rose through her in that of summoning. When she had her rope secured, she flung herself over the vertiginous edge as easily as stepping into the street.

Having succeeded in her mail-drop mission, she heads back to the Pittsburgh motel where she's been staying. The place seems built to remind her of inaccessible pasts. She walked by the big, faded, round sign five times before recognizing that mottled surface and the strange spider-like thing perched on it. The Tranquility Motel was built during the excitement of the Apollo era. The dejection of the peeling moon is matched by the interiors, where faux wood paneling bows out slightly from the walls, the bathroom window has plastic curtains that once might have had a cheery flower pattern on them, and the bed has a flocked cover. She's half-sure that if she looks hard enough she'll find a coin-operated Magic Fingers unit built into it. If it weren't for the truckers and squabbling families who come and go in the neighboring units, she'd think she was living in some ironic art installation.

The whole mail-drop thing feels like an epic win, and she's light on her feet. Balanced. At the end of the day, though, she has stuff she has to face. So, reluctantly, she sits down at the motel room's little table and opens the news reports Marj emailed her, looking for some detail she didn't spot last time.

The official story is that Jim Neelin was participating in a protest at some abandoned oil wells in Amazonian Peru. The multinationals deforested the entire region, stripped it of its treasures, and left improperly capped wells leaking poisons into the soil and river system.

Dad and his crew were looking for suspect wellheads, and they spotted one in a low area by a stream. They didn't notice the carcasses of several animals near the wellhead, nor the fallen birds; they were too busy getting the shot. All five of them collapsed simultaneously, poleaxed by hydrogen sulfide. They literally didn't know what hit them.

If Marjorie is to be believed, the official story is not the whole story. Police found recent prints leading to and from the wellhead. Somebody had been there and survived; how was that possible if they weren't equipped for it? The footprints leading away were widely spaced, as if whoever had left them had exited at a run. Marj is sure someone sabotaged the well the night before and that this was a deliberate hit on James. She couldn't explain why anybody would want him dead, though. For that, Sura is supposed to talk to the last living member of her dad's team, someone named Remy Heath. He'd avoided dying by not being with them that day.

Remy told Marj that Sura was their next target. Sura has been wondering what to ask him ever since; somehow, those tracks in the dirt of eastern Peru and this motel room share some causal link. They're both inscriptions on the world, innocent in themselves, that hint at something terrible. She keeps thinking about those footprints; otherwise, she wouldn't be here. If not for them, she could laugh off Remy's paranoia, just go about the business of telling the last decade to fuck off, and beta a new version of Sura Neelin.

But she needs to be sure. She's tried calling Marj several times, but all she gets is a female bot voice saying, "We're sorry, this number is not in service."

Oh no you don't, Marj.

She'll try again tonight.

There's a knock on the door. Expecting the motel manager, she pops up without a thought and opens it.

Black hair with a few white traitors in it splays out from under his brown leather hat. His oval face is landscaped with stubble and wrinkles, and even in this heat he's wearing a jean jacket over a black T-shirt that he fills out in all the right ways. Eagle belt buckle, cowboy boots. A holstered pistol.

"Sura Neelin?"

For a moment all she can think is *He didn't say "Britt Birch."*

While she's standing there he's squinting at the air around her through his smart glasses—a characteristic gesture of somebody looking at augmented reality images that only they can see.

He grins, nods. "Gotcha."

Sura blinks at him while something like a cannonball plunges down her stomach. "Seriously? And if I—oh, fuck it." She backs into the motel room.

"Don't try nothing fancy," he says. "Let me see that bag. You got anything in the bathroom?—I'll get it," he says when she makes a move in that direction. "You just stand there where I can see you. Oh, and I'll take those glasses, thank you very much."

She's no fool; before she takes them off she starts a data-wiping app she installed at Jeri's. She's long since uploaded her personal stuff and the data from behind the bookshelves to a secure IFS pod. Still, there could be some trace left in the glasses. The app will reset them to the factory defaults.

She watches while he efficiently tosses the room then jams the glasses and all her other belongings into her bag. He slings this over his shoulder.

"You're not police," she ventures, her voice husky in her own ears.

"Duly deputized," he says. "But no, I'm not." He motions her toward the door.

She kind of floats out of the building; parked outside is a very old gas-powered Plymouth with rudimentary sensors bolted to it. She looks from it to him incredulously. She needs words, harder words, some way to summon courage in herself. "Is this piece of crap even street legal?"

He raises an eyebrow, but as he hustles her into the back seat he says, ". . . Which is why you got caught." He's got a grille between front and back, like a squad car.

"What do you mean that's why I got caught? I'm dissing your car." The words are helping, but she's still acutely aware that she's just let a complete stranger lock her in the back of a vehicle.

He climbs in the front, slams the door, and turns to grin at her. "No. You were failing to understand my car. Quid pro quo. Or whatever.

"Some ground rules. One: I don't care. I don't care what you did, or that you did it because your momma needed an operation, or any of that shit. If I came after you it's because you broke the law, period, end of story. Everything that's going down is on you.

"Two: I don't take counteroffers. I don't take money, I don't take blowjobs, I don't take condo time-shares in Florida. I just don't. If I did, I wouldn't last ten minutes in this business."

He glares at her, as if she personally has tried all these gambits on him. "Three: I'm not gonna read you your rights or any of that shit, because I don't work for the police. I work directly for the people you done wrong to, so you ain't got no rights. Right?"

She looks him in the eye, trying to think of what to say. She needs words to defend herself right now. The more, the better.

"What's your name?" is what she manages.

"You can call me Jay. My friends call me something else."

The car's archaic engine is loud. After he's started it, Jay says, "So. The car. This beater's so old all the self-driving stuff is bolted on. Which means I was able to mod it. Fer instance: if I'm not in sight of another car or a cam or drone, then as far as the traffic routing system is concerned, I don't exist." There's a big yellow toggle-switch mounted on the dashboard next to the radio. He flips it. "Now it can see us." He drives them off the lot, the car wallowing like a boat in a flood.

More words come to her, but they're a random jumble hopping about in her head. Trying to pull herself together, she watches houses and signs slide by. "You're saying I didn't have an off-switch. I get it."

His gaze flashes to her in the rearview. "Smart girl. I'll tell you how you fucked up if you tell me what you did."

"So *they* didn't tell you? Interesting." She feels she's rallying, a little.

"No reason they should."

"Still. Makes you a bit of a gofer, doesn't it? A delivery boy?"

"Delivery boy is exactly what I am," he says smoothly. "I take it back. I don't want to know what you did."

"But I want to know how you found me."

"Tough shit."

There's a long silence. He's heading out of town. "We going to Dayton?" she asks.

"Got it in one."

Another long silence. Sura fidgets. He took away her glasses; with them, she could be recording this whole encounter, uploading it somewhere. She could call the real police, or go on social media and broadcast her situation to the world. But to what end? Boarded-up car dealerships and gas stations rise and subside along the road as she imagines the deluge of useless platitudes that would fill her inbox if she did appeal to her few, shallow friends. She sees self-storage signs. Strip malls with falafel shops and unaccountably open hair salons. "They're going to kill me, you know," she says.

"Rule one," he points out, finger in the air. "And oh, by the way, everybody says that. It's just a fucking collection agency that's after you. They're assholes, but they're not the kind of assholes who'll stash you in a culvert when they're done with you. So, I say to you, fuck off with that shit. Like your momma said, if you can't say something nice, don't say nothin' at all."

"Momma. That's adorable."

For some reason the next silence stretches. To an hour. They've left one city behind, now following a string of nearly-towns signified by truck stops and minor industrial parks. Lank grass and lopsided trees struggle to make a living on the edges of empty concrete lots. There's a kind of visual rhythm to it all, and in a brighter moment Sura might find some inspiration there, some liftoff of the imagination that could help her stand above the situation.

Instead, she's getting the reverse, the fat ass of universal existential despair descending on the world. Everything's gray. She can't see any busy people or open businesses out there, just failed attempts passing one after another in an endless stream. Just as the illusion has been laid bare that she might have some ept-ness in her, the landscape beyond the still-living urban heart shows the failure of America's domestic arrangements. Nobody's working, everything's owned by somebody else; there's lots going on, but all that activity is done by driverless vehicles and drones. They thunder indifferently past the walkers by the highway, the kids sitting in the cracked, weeded basketball courts.

"I guess it was never real," she says suddenly.

"What?" Jay's reading a tablet while the car drives.

"The future. It was just another *fuck-you.*"

He eyes her in the mirror. "Losing it, are we?"

"No." She sighs heavily and turns back to the view. "Just being too deep for you."

Another silence, as if they've lost their common tongue.

CHAPTER THREE

Dayton enfolds Sura, a ruin of memories.

Her whole life has been lived here, but as she watches the familiar boulevards and skylines slide by, she's acutely aware of the glass that separates her from it. She's already in jail, gazing at might-have-beens.

They skirt the edges of the city, stopping once for a pee break at an unmanned automat before coming into an area where new concrete factories and warehouses are crammed alongside old, decaying houses. The block-and-avenue pattern of an earlier city is visible here, but written over by the efficiencies of the new age.

Efficient it certainly is. Industry is booming, art and design studios have taken over downtown. The only problem is the factories are completely automated, and to work in an art studio these days you have to have spent half a million dollars on your education—and it has to have been at the right school. Dayton advertises itself as prosperous, and it is. It's just that none of that prosperity will ever reach Sura.

Jay turns onto a street lined with turn-of-the-century low-rise office buildings that combine pale coral facades with green windows. He pulls into a side lot next to a five-story tower indistinguishable from the others. Sura's mouth is dry, her heart is thumping as Jay turns to her and says, in an ironic tone, "So let's take care of those bills, 'kay?"

She thinks about running, but he's got a gun. She follows him inside, where they discover the elevator is out. Jay curses in a way that would be charming were he not the enemy. She has to watch the back of his sagging pants as he trudges up the stairs. About two floors up she sees people ahead of them, just standing there. It's a lineup.

They're a cross-section of visible minorities, at least one representative from every immigrant demographic that might make white folk uncomfortable. She's certainly uncomfortable, feeling their eyes on her as she walks past; do they want to be here? The line isn't moving and the air is stuffy.

They ascend two more levels and squeeze by an exhausted-looking guy in a walker on the landing of the fourth. This floor's carpets are worn in blotches that clearly indicate where to go. Half the old fluorescents are out. There's a strap cordon that's trying to keep the line in order, and people are shouting names and waving tablets at both ends of the hall. Near the door is a welcome robot, pink and green plastic with a cute abstract face on it. Motionless, it stands facing the wall.

"Come on." Jay bulls his way through the crowds to a large room that looks like a gym. People are being made to walk a line on the floor. Near the windows is an open area where they take three steps up a box horse and then step down again. All of these activities are watched by cameras bolted to poles.

At the desks, eyes are being scanned, finger- and palm-prints being taken. Sura's skin crawls as they pass a swab station.

"Fuck, they're doing DNA!"

Jay shrugs. "It's a biometrics lab. Of course they are."

The people in the stairwell do want to be here. They want to be middle class, and the middle class can just walk into a shop, pick out what they want, and walk out without talking with a clerk. They'll be recognized by the cameras, their accounts billed automatically. It's really convenient.

Sura does all her shopping online. There's a reason she wiped down her apartment before leaving. She's carefully avoided letting the system trap her irises, her face, hands and fingertips, DNA and gait. The camera, it steals your soul.

"You can't just leave her here," some lady behind a desk is protesting to Jay.

"Look, Galen Bester said he'd be here," says Jay. "He's supposed to sign her in so you can scan her."

"Not my problem. Look at this place." She nods at the crowds. "This ain't a jail. What do you want me to do with her?"

Sura's staring at the pole-cameras and terahertz booths. Are they recording her now, out of the corners of their eyes? The phrase *male gaze* comes to her; they might as well get her to dance on a pole. The sum of all those gazes will construct a puppet version of her on the Internet and

she'll be stuck in amber like Maeve, forever recognizable to every car, shop front, and parking lot gateway.

She has a sudden, startled thought: these particular cameras, and only these ones, are specialized and hyperfocused on learning each person, one at a time. Of all the watchers she's likely to encounter, these are the only ones that won't see her until they're supposed to see her. She is invisible for the moment precisely because this is where she is expected to expose herself.

She scans the rest of the room, looking for lenses that belong to ordinary security cameras. There aren't any.

Sura's on full alert now and it's a welcome feeling. Only half-aware that she's doing it, she starts casing the place.

"Actually," says Jay suddenly, "I think there's been a mistake. I wasn't supposed to bring her here." He makes to grab Sura's arm, but she backs away. The look he shoots her is intense and urgent. If she didn't know better, she'd think he's scared.

The clerk steps between them. "If you sign at the front desk, you can get paid," she says to Jay. He lays her backpack on the counter, with an odd slow reluctance as if he's just realized something. Meanwhile the clerk's turning to Sura. "Come on."

She leads Sura into the hallway; glancing back, she sees Jay frozen in place, a weird expression on his face. That, though, is just one of the details flooding Sura's attention; Jay has to compete with the black plastic baseboards peeling off the wall, the grime on the acoustic tiles that hint of an airspace above them. She's judging sight lines and counting personnel as they pass the stairwell door then an open copy-and-print room. The clerk drops her backpack on a shelf in the copy room, then goes next door and unlocks a supply closet.

"Guy's gonna come for you in a bit, get your biometrics, read you into the system," says the clerk. "Then somebody's gonna pick you up and take you downtown. Make sure you pay those bills or whatever. Thanks for not being a shithead."

"Go to hell," Sura says, and steps into the closet.

Thankfully it's more of a storage room, of the same rectangular dimensions as the print room. Sura ransacks the gray metal utility shelves as soon as the door's closed. There's oodles of paper, naturally, and felt markers and pens. Lots of boxes that have to be opened and therefore . . .

"Ha!" She raises the yellow box cutter over her head, imagining a shaft

of holy light flaming from heaven to pinion it. Then she starts tapping her way along the wall that separates her from the print room.

Turn-of-the-century design means thin aluminum joists, and generally poor-quality construction. She scratches, looking for the drywall tape that signals a row of nails and hence a joist. When she's found a pair of these she crouches between them and etches a square into the wall with the box cutter.

She draws the lines again, cutting deeper this time. Any second now the door may open and then she's screwed. It would be pointless to try to jam it so she focuses on what she's doing, and this is just like those damned shelves at home . . .

Eight cuts around the square and she's far enough in that she can stand up and start lightly kicking it. It's noisy enough outside that she's not worried about anybody hearing. The square gives way. She yanks it out, exposing the gray back of the printer-room wall. Rinse and repeat. As she gets into the rhythm of it, an old Frankie Rose song pops into her head. The driving beat of "Trouble" coordinates everything she does in the next few minutes.

There might be somebody in the printer room. If she's calculated it right she's behind the big machine and out of sight from the hallway. Even so, she doesn't kick this time, but cuts and cuts until she's all the way through, then reaches down to peel and lever out the powdery sheetrock.

The square is tiny; she'll have to wriggle. It's behind the printer as hoped, and nobody's standing there pointing and screaming. About to drop the box cutter, she thinks *fingerprints,* and holds onto it. Awkwardly, she jams herself through the wall. Crouched behind the printer, cut and scraped in a dozen places, she slaps herself to dislodge the Sheetrock powder, and gets ready.

It's always a fight. Part of her is imagining cops or Jay or monsters just on the other side of the printer. That part is strong. It's stopped her many times, right on the verge of sliding up a window or easing under a half-open garage door. "Fuck you," she mutters to it. "Fuck you, fuck you, fuck *you*!"

She's on her feet, grabbing her backpack and strolling out of the printer room and about to turn left for the stairs—when she looks across the room and locks eyes with Jay.

He's talking to a short man with a buzz cut. She sees his eyes widen in surprise—she's frozen in place—and then he turns his head away, laughing, and moves so that the man turns away from her to follow him.

What the—? She finishes her left turn, walks five more feet and eases past the knot at the stairs. She heads down, while Frankie sings "trouble follows you" over and over in her head.

—And she'll be stopped with this next step, she knows it, and she'll be stopped with this one, or this one; each time her foot falls it's accompanied by a wave of certainty that there is no fucking way this is going to work. And then she's gone a whole floor and nobody's looking at her, and it's two steps between certainties, then three, and two more floors.

She emerges, blinking, from a side door. A glance each way shows no visible cameras, just gray clouds above and flashes of traffic crossing the mouths of the alley, left right left right.

Sura has gone about a block when she hears a conspicuously loud car pull up beside her. Jay's voice drifts over: "That was fast."

Sura considers running, but before she does she glances over. He's got the passenger-side window rolled down and she expects him to be wearing the same shit-eating grin he had on when they met. Instead he looks worried. "Get in," he says.

She stammers, but he raises one hand. "I'm not taking you back there. I did my job, I delivered you, and I got paid. But . . . something's not right. You gotta tell me what's really going on—but not here. Get *in*!"

Sura thinks about it. This bounty hunter is her only link to Dad. But she's no fool.

"Why'd you do that back there?"

"I'm not telling you here. Don't you get it, they could come out at any second—"

"I'm not getting in that car again. I'm going to flag down my own share and then, *maybe*, follow you. You go near a police station or anywhere suspicious, I peel off. Okay?"

He shrugs. "Not your best option, but all right."

"Whatever," she says past a clenched jaw. "I'll give you my side of the story.

"But you have to tell me how you found me."

Apparently Jay likes Chinese food—or at least, that combination of nostalgia, cultural appropriation, and outright fakery known as "Chinese-American" food. Chicken balls in red sauce. Lemon chicken. Lots of noodle dishes. This particular restaurant is on the edge of town, and Sura doesn't fail to notice that there are no cameras here, either outside or in, and the parking lot has hedges that obscure it from the street. The wait-staff are all human.

At her insistence, Jay left his various phones, smart glasses, wearables, and trackers in his car. The elderly waitress hands them laminated blue menus, Jay blows out a breath, glowers at her, and then he says, "What the *fuck* did you do?"

"Me!" She half rises. "What the fuck are *you* doing? Why are we here? Give me one good reason why I shouldn't scream 'rape' at the top of my lungs and run right out the door?"

"This ain't about school debts, or your mom's medical bills." He slaps down the menu. "Once we got in there I seen this guy. I knew him, 'cause I spent weeks tracking him down a couple years ago. For who? For the FBI. That lady who stuffed you in the closet, she called him 'Galen Bester' but that's not his name. He's a contract killer. For the mob."

A cold flush washes over Sura. "You . . . he what?"

Jay shifts restlessly, shrugs inside his jacket, and says, "So I stalled. When she put you in the closet I walked over and just said the first thing came into my head. Said had we met at a concert or something. Tried to keep his back to the hallway. Then I look over and there you are, sauntering to the stairs like you just went shopping."

She has to grin. "That was pretty good, wasn't it?"

"I tried that closet on the way by. It was still locked! How'd you get out of a locked room?"

"Mad skills," she says. "Anyway, why do you care?"

"Because if it gets out that I turned somebody over to the *mob,* who then got *killed,* what do you think would happen to me? Least of it would be, my career would be over."

"Oh," she says. "Imagine the lack of sympathy that's slopping around inside me at this very moment."

"Help me out here," he says. "I wanna know what I got myself into."

"How can you fail to know what you got yourself into? You're a bounty hunter—"

"Skip-tracer," he interrupts.

"The fuck is that?"

"Not a bounty hunter. Usually." He looks shifty, grabs up his menu again. "But business is bad. With facial recognition cams everywhere, people can't just walk away from their old life the way they used to. It ain't enough to just close your bank account and move to Minneapolis. First time you go into a store, your face'll be captured and in two days the cops'll be at your door."

"So you've started taking side gigs," she says.

"Which I've got the license to do. Usually it's working directly for the feds. This time, it was an insurance company."

"Really? Which one?"

"I'll tell you if you tell me what you did."

"Nothing," she says, staring down. "Simply and utterly, nothing at all."

"But you ran away. Innocent people don't do that."

"They do when their father's just—" Her voice catches. "Father's just died, and people think it's murder, and whoever killed him was after something and they think she's got it, only she doesn't but how the fuck is she ever going to explain that one to them—"

"You like to order?" says the waitress.

There's a lull while they do that.

"I had legitimate reasons to think my life was in danger," she says eventually. "And now you've actually gone and put it in danger. Get that I'm mad about that?" He has the decency to look away. "So," she says, "why don't you start to make it up by telling me how you found me?"

Jay thinks about it for a while, then sighs. "Regularity," he says.

"This alias of yours, Britt Birch, always renewed her online memberships on time, down to the second. Always bought the same shows, on the same schedule, never any impulse buys, and never anything physical, no Coke or donuts. Any botnet scanning the books of a hundred million people would flag it as suspicious. No variance, never buys lunch or tampons, you must be another bot. Even a really smart one is going to show patterns that deep data mining can pick up. So, they been watching Britt Birch for years but they could never connect her to a real person. And then suddenly Britt's buying habits change the day that Sura Neelin goes missing.

"After that, it was just a matter of hiring a good skip-tracer to find the hand in the puppet."

He pauses a beat. "So should I call you Britt, or Sura?"

"You can call me Britt. And you? What is it your *friends* call you, Mr. Jay?"

He grimaces. "Actually, it's just Jay. I hate aliases."

"I'm not a fan of them either, but . . ." Sura feels that she's gained the advantage; how far can she push it?

"You told me how you found me. Now how do we un-find me? I want to disappear. For good this time."

Jay takes his time. There's food to be eaten, and between mouthfuls he complains, mostly about the deadbeats he has to find, and the deadbeats he has to find them for. He's gathering his thoughts, and eventually he says, "The problem with you is money."

She snorts. "Tell me about it."

"No, I mean the problem with *you,* is money. With you being you, whether you're Britt Birch or whoever. It used to be that money was cash. You could spend tons of it and be completely anonymous. But money's not cash anymore. It's information."

She nods. "All numbers in the bank."

"Worse. It *was* that—credit cards, bank accounts. They're all just containers for cash, right? Except the container's gotten more important than the thing in it. You don't pay for things with cash anymore, you pay with your personal information. It's worth way more than whatever's in your bank account. You trade bits of yourself away day in and day out and don't even realize.

"You thought you were being clever, using cash and anonymous services and shit. Some of what you did was good; you've got mail drops—fake postal addresses?" She thinks of Jeri's loft and nods cautiously. Jay hops up and down in his seat, making the whole cubicle jump. "Yeah! Good stuff, I never found those. But everything else—anything at all that wound back into the Net, it left a trail. Even the cash, 'cause there's patterns in withdrawal and deposit. And like I said, you being missing from your old life has left an information hole that's gonna be as visible as your online trail was. This whole goddamned economy runs on your diary entries. All you got to buy and sell with, is you."

Sura remembers movies and shows from when she was a kid, in which sinister government forces are watching everybody through cameras on the street corners. Well, they are—but what if the government's not the real problem?

"So what all that mansplaining adds up to is, I'm fucked."

"Well, not necessarily. 'Cause I said *this* goddamned economy. There are others."

"It's not that easy to move to Costa Rica. I mean, I checked—" But he's shaking his head.

He holds up a finger to signal a pause as he shovels up rice, a couple of spring rolls, and some dumplings. Then he says, "Y'know, when I started in this business, there was just one of everything. One government of the United States, one police force per city. One tax department, one army, one conspiracy of socialist liberal media and one conspiracy of alt-right proto-fascist Christian fundamentalists. One dollar, one local grocery store, and only one job or career at a time.

"Now we got online citizenship in virtual nations. We got Notch-Coin, Bitcoin, and a hundred other e-currencies; we got military contractors, sanctuary cities, and fascist enclaves. We got distributed autonomous corporations with no humans in the loop that buy and sell and hire and fire. Nobody can afford just one job anymore, we all do mechanical turking, gigs, internships, and goldfarming in global larps. There's the gig economy, the attention economy, the Eastern Standard Tribe, and the fucking Antarctican Terraforming League. Everything there ever was one of, now there's two or five or ten of them. And that means if you're not satisfied with one version of something, you can use another.

"The problem with your identity is only a problem in a world where people have one final, official name. That was the world you and I grew up in, but it's not the world now. And your problem with money is only a problem in a world where there's just one kind of money. You know that's not where we are."

There's a long silence as Sura stares at him. "I have no idea what the fuck you are talking about."

He leans back, looking tired. "It never mattered to me either. But you know how I said it's getting harder and harder to disappear? That's true for most people—but lately, every now and then, one of my targets will just . . ." He sweeps his hands together and apart and says, "Poof. Gone gone. They're not just moving to another city and changing their names. It's like they're erasing themselves, like they never even existed."

She puts down her cup. "How? Have you found any of them?"

Jay knows he's got her hooked and grins. "Just hints—enough to know they're alive and free. But I did track down a . . . kind of gatekeeper, for however it is they do it."

"Can you introduce me? Is he in town? What does he charge?"

"She doesn't charge. Not that I've heard, anyway. And just your luck, she's in Pittsburgh. Britt Birch can go home."

Sura snorts. "She's burnt. They found me once, they can do it again."

"Hopefully not," he says, "once Compass is done with you."

CHAPTER FOUR

Naturally, it's not that simple. Jay wants something in return for introducing Sura to this Compass person. He wants to know how her disappearing trick works.

"You know that's not a deal you can enforce," she tells him.

He grimaces. "I chase bad people. Deadbeats, guys who stole their grandparents' money, grifters, and con artists. Some of them used this underground railroad. So it's not a deal. You'll be doing me a favor."

The fact is, he owes her one; so after a stay in a seedy hotel he swears is safe, she's back in Pittsburgh the next afternoon. Jay drives her, and along the way she pries out a few details about him. Enough for her to cautiously think that this contact of his might actually be real.

Threading their way through Pittsburgh, they pass the Strip District, where Jeri has her loft. Well beyond the redbrick warehouses with their big square windows, and past the suppuration of outlet malls and plazas, the jutting billboards and fast-food signs, lies the Millennial Warehouse District. These buildings are windowless, mostly white contoured-cement facades with one stripe of green glass window beside the front door. There are dozens of these places, and since most are abandoned, they've become the new artists' colonies.

Every now and then Jay exchanges a few cryptic words with somebody who's not here. Suddenly he turns to Sura and says, "Hey, are you self-sovereign?"

"Am I what?"

"I'll take that as a no. No, she's not," he says to whoever he's talking to. After a minute he nods. "We'll be there."

"Where are we going?"

"She just gave me an address," he says, tapping his glasses. "It's not far. So you're not self-sovereign. Big mistake."

She ransacks her memory, and comes up with, "I know it's a way to own your own information online. I just . . . never did it."

"Okay. You know what a key party is?"

"Yeah." She's defensive. "What, do I look forty? It's where people exchange crypto keys."

"*Tattoo* key party?"

"Er. What the fuck."

"Forty it is. The tattoo's a special kind of self-sovereign ID. It's quantum encrypted or something, more secure than the old public-key codes, and most of all it's geographically based. Compass says you'll need one if you wanna play."

He sounds a bit smug; Jay has this theory that Compass runs some kind of sophisticated goldfarming operation, where people get paid for playing online. He thinks his theory's just been confirmed. The problem is goldfarming's an old if not exactly respectable profession, and it's as taxed and regulated as any other business. Sura can't see how Compass's operation would give her any more anonymity than she already has.

He wants her to find out if it does, and as for her, she has no choice in the matter. If whatever it is works, she'll have found a safe haven. From there, maybe she can figure out who's after her—even, if she's lucky, turn the tables.

"Okay, this is it," he says suddenly, taking the wheel to drive manually. "Uh, one thing. Compass is . . . a bit weird. Harmless, though. I mean you can trust her. I trust her."

"Oookay." He's giving her a look that seems to say, *It would take too long to explain.*

Early-evening traffic is still heavy as Jay stops in the middle of a long block; there's nothing but chain-link fence and oil tanks here, not even a sidewalk past the curb. "Uh . . ." says Sura, but Jay points across the street.

"Compass."

Somebody's there, so Sura gets out. She lifts a hand; the figure cocks its head. This moment is just one more unknown in a sea of unknowns, so Sura walks over.

Cargo pants and sneakers; a T-shirt and a utility vest patterned in Desert Storm camouflage. Baseball cap. She's shorter than Sura, a few years younger, her eyes eclipsed by a very high-end pair of smart glasses. As she turns her head to watch Jay drive away, Sura sees that her black hair hangs down her back in a braid, the coils drawn obsessively tight as if it's a personal demon she has to fight and subdue every day.

"Compass?"

She looks Sura up and down. "What would you like me to call you?"

"Jay didn't tell you . . . ? Oh, okay." Who should she be today? "I'm Claire. Claire Belanger." A little hint of Montreal never hurt anything.

"Th-This way." Compass sets off across the weedy grass, heading for a big gap in the chain-link fence. One of the large windowless warehouses lies beyond. There are no cars in the cracked lot, but Sura hadn't really expected there to be. Anybody here who actually owns a car will have it out cruising for fares.

"How do you know Jay?" Sura asks casually as she ducks under the sagging galvanized steel pipe that's trying to hold up the fence.

"Found him f-floating in a lifeboat at the end of the war," says Compass. *What war?* Sura thinks but Compass is hurrying ahead with, "I was his nurse in the rehab center. We had a w-whirlwind romance b-but his gunrunner friends caught up with him and we had to make a break for it. Ended up here."

She stands there looking at Sura, perfectly calm, until Sura says, "You don't want to tell me, I get it."

Compass tilts her head, seemingly puzzled. "But I am t-telling you. Wait—what?" She cocks her head again, as though listening to somebody. She probably is, Sura realizes: another person is in her smart glasses with her, a friend or boss.

Oh. Maybe this Compass is just the messenger. Jay can't find out how she runs her operation because it's not her operation. She's just the courier.

The way her face is drawn, with a small mouth turned in a perpetual frown and very dark eyes under aggressively drawn eyebrows, she looks perpetually angry, but she doesn't sound it, nor did she seem to be bullshitting Sura just now. Weird.

Impatient, Sura says, "What are we doing?"

And just like that, Compass transforms. Sura's glasses overlay her with the image of a taller, blonder, and more busty woman in a Chanel suit; she stands straight, looks Sura in the eye, and in a clear, confident voice says, "It's sometimes called goldfarming. You can be an avatar for people. You can also play NPCs." Her stutter is gone. "Try it, you'll be great!"

Sura stares at her. "Who's feeding you these lines? Who am I talking to? How do I know I can trust them?"

"Chain of attestation," says Compass. "I trust Jay. My contacts trust me." She doesn't make eye contact as she says this. After an awkward pause, she turns and walks up to an open loading dock bay. In the early-evening light, this side of the building is casting a long blue shadow across the cement. The loading bay is a square of gold cradling the complex geometry of some interior space; it's actually kind of welcoming. Compass wrestles herself up onto the concrete dock and walks in, not looking back or lowering her hand to help Sura.

Inside, she can feel the walls vibrating to throbbing music. "Rave?" she calls to Compass, who's passed through the cinder-block-walled staging area into the building proper.

"Yes," Compass calls back. "That's not where we're going."

The warehouse has been subdivided in crazy ways, as if four or five architects had drawn their own plans and the builders executed them all at once and in the same place. The beams that indicate a ceiling on the right side of the roofless hall are at a different height than the ones on the left. Is that a closet behind that open door, or a thirty-foot-long corridor to nowhere? The burglar in Sura instantly responds to this cubist chaos. Everywhere she looks, there are intriguing hints that door, floor, ceiling, and stair are not being used for their intended purpose, or that a creative person could reimagine their function, declaring a passageway to be a living room, or a room to be a corridor. She likes this a lot.

There are no signs, but Compass is probably navigating with her glasses, and without hesitation pulls them through the labyrinth to one particular metal door. The rave music is quieter here. Now Compass does pause. "You need an app for your g . . . for your glasses. Can we sync?" Sura gives permission and Compass looks at her; an orange icon appears over her head, indicating she wants to share. "Everyone behind that door is wearing," she adds.

"So?"

"Glasses cams." Compass taps hers. "They can all do facial recognition. You want to hide, right?"

"Oh." Yet another thing she's forgotten to take into account. It's not just the stop signs, store displays, and police drones that do facial rec. It's every other person she passes on the street. Why not download that free NSA app that pays you a bounty if your glasses spot a wanted felon? You won't just be a good citizen, you'll be The Man. So naturally everybody's doing it. A wave of hopelessness hits her as she realizes that there's no way to stop her image from being captured, passed around, and sold.

"Readme," says Compass suddenly. "—Sorry, I'm r-reading the readme file for the app. 'FaceStorm is a free, open-source app designed to render crowd-sourced Mixed Reality–based facial recognition useless to law enforcement and criminal organizations. How does it do this? Just hold out your glasses so they can see you. Once FaceStorm has registered your biometrics, it will encrypt them and pass them around the mesh to every other FaceStorm instance. Then, every pair of glasses with FaceStorm on it will pretend to recognize you every now and then, at random intervals. If several users are in the same location, they will all pretend to see you simultaneously. In jurisdictions where FaceStorm-like apps are illegal, FaceStorm will do this once or twice before deleting itself.'"

"Shit," says Sura. She loads the app, holds out the smart glasses and says, "Cheese." Then she puts them on, and follows Compass through the door.

This room's about thirty feet on a side, and just as tall. Angled skylights at the top show the turquoise sky but no longer cast any light down the unfinished Sheetrock walls.

About fifty people are milling around, some of them privileged WASPs of the sort she's seen larping in the parks, but a surprising number are Latino and black. A good ratio of women to men, too. Many are clustered in one corner watching three big dentist's chairs. A shirtless guy is sitting in one of these while another, bald, tattooed, and studded, presses a cinder-block-sized machine into his shoulder. The one in the chair is wincing and saying "Shit shit shit." Somebody hands him a can of beer.

"Tattoo key party," says Compass, who's suddenly standing next to Sura.

In Mixed Reality, the place is full of signs and signifiers: SIGNUP FOR METALGEBRA hovers here, SIGNUP FOR RIVET COUTURE over there. There are public interfaces (transparent, floating menus) but nobody's using them. Everybody's wearing smart glasses, and at least ten of them have little flags over their heads—indicators that they're running FaceStorm too (there's a toggle that lets you share with other users or hide from them).

"Compass!" A tall slender man spreads his arms wide to enfold Compass in a quick embrace. His skin's a gorgeous mahogany and his hair's in tight cornrows, almost as obsessive as Compass's ponytail. He's very well dressed, in a pale pink shirt, a gray jacket and slacks. His shoes are polished mirror-sharp. "How are you?" he says, stepping back to appraise her.

"Great!" says Compass. "There was a d-dinosaur outbreak in Sector

Six, b-but I got out with the power core so no harm, no foul. Malcolm, this is Claire. She's come to p-play."

"You and I, we are Charon boatmen for our latest passengers, no?" Malcolm's got a French accent. Continental. He grins at Sura. "I'm poling six people to the other shore. You're Compass's only charge tonight?"

Sura nods. "You NPC in these games too?"

Malcolm rolls his eyes. "No! I am an architect. Procedural architecture, that is my thing. I came to America to study it, become better. Now I make cities for people like Compass to play in."

"Dinosaur cities?"

"Sometimes."

"You're from France?"

"Morocco. And you are from here."

Behind him an aging hipster in a black T-shirt steps up on a chair and calls for silence. "Okay, you want to know what to do!" he shouts. He's got an Australian accent. "Unless you're chaperoning somebody, this will be the first and last time you ever attend a tattoo key party. We expect you to be confused."

"You take people to these?" Sura asks Compass as Malcolm waves goodbye and goes to find whoever he's brought.

"Y-you can't play l-live-action unless you h-have."

"So all those kids in the parks and stuff—"

"Different kind of game."

The hipster is saying, "You're here because you want to roll a character and play in the most sophisticated Augmented Reality games going. Or, you're here because you're a snitch for DHS or the tax people or the Trumpists. That's okay, in fact in that case we highly encourage you to get yourself tagged, because then we can keep track of you.

"Keeping track of people, that's what it's all about, right?" He grins round the room. "How can you adopt a role, do work and help people, and be helped yourself if you don't have a single, stable identity? It's no problem in the real world. You're you, you can't be copied. On the Internet, identity theft is an issue. And it happens in Alternate Reality Games too. This system solves that problem. You can use the ID you're getting tonight in all the games and still keep your privacy.

"How's it work? I'm gonna use one big technical sentence here specially for the geeks out there, so the rest of you can tune out for the next fifteen seconds if you want. Here it is: what you're going to do is create a non-transferable token in a homomorphically encrypted position-based provenance blockchain that tracks your path through the world and allows people to query that token without revealing anything about *you*.

"Whew-ee, right? In plain English, you can prove all kinds of facts about yourself without sharing anything you don't want to. Like, for instance, you could show that you weren't at some place at some time without having to say exactly *where* you were at that time. You can also buy and sell anonymously. And you can parcel out bits of yourself, like your health records or criminal background check, and not give away everything else.

"The key to this, and I mean the literal key—is the tattoo."

It seems that the tattoo is a 3-D–printed circuit embedded under the skin. It's mostly invisible; the hipster shows his, which is on his shoulder. Sura can just make out some kind of shield-shape. The circuit runs on body heat and has just enough power to maintain a position-based ID that's tracked on a public blockchain.

"So the mesh sees you as this uninterrupted thread, one unique path through space and time. Any command you issue or email or text you send, you can prove it came from you because it's signed as coming from the tip of the worldline. In other words, from you."

Without this elaborate protocol, peoples' identities could be copied. Sura gets it. "You own and control your encrypted identity," he goes on. "This is called self-sovereignty. You can encrypt all kinds of things so they can only be opened using your ID—things like bank records, cryptoassets, game characters, and tokens for all the swag you own. You've got total control over what you reveal about yourself. So feel free to lock your medical records, anything secret you want, using your tattoo. It's yours for life."

A guy next to Sura raises his hand. "What if somebody cuts it off?"

"It shuts down," says the Australian crisply. "Also does that when you die, by the way."

"All I want to do is roll my character!" whines a teenager.

"Well, go get your tattoo, then!" The hipster makes shoving motions. "Don't worry about me."

There's a rush on the dentists' chairs. Sura leans in to Compass. "What do the tattoos look like? Bar codes? The Mark of the Beast?"

Compass turns and pries down her belt. Just above her hipbone is a faint constellation-shape. "Lyra," she says.

"So I can have anything I want?"

"The shape doesn't matter."

They join the lineup. Sura's thought about getting tattoos, but every candidate went out of favor after a month or two. How can you tell what image you'd want to wear for life?

For a while, when she was in her late teens, there was a fad among the girls at school to get Pokémon tats on their ankles. When Sura finally gets to a chair and sits, the gum-chewing girl hoisting the 3-D-printer-cum-tattoo-gun says, "What'dya want and where d'ya want it?"

What the hell, she thinks. "I'll have a Purrloin." She raises her leg. "On my calf."

Purrloin is a thief Pokémon, half cat, half burglar. It's a no-brainer, really.

The girl clamps the heavy machine to Sura's leg and for a few seconds it feels like a horde of fire ants is stinging her. "Holy shit!"

"Hold still, you'll smear it."

Sura hisses and clamps the arms of the chair. The burning subsides, leaving a raw soreness. "All done."

"Thanks." Ankle smarting, she limps away, looking around for Compass. Visually herself again, she is standing and staring off at nothing, or more likely something in her glasses. But there's also Malcolm, who's hoisting a Beck's at a bar on the other side of the room (physically, it's just a vending machine next to a table with plastic stools, but *in virtua,* the table has a padded leather counter and the stools have red felt seats). Sura heads over there and when Malcolm sees her, she turns her ankle to show her sly, purple and gold Purrloin. He barks a laugh.

The bar takes NotchCoin, so she orders a beer to match his. "How do you know Compass?" she asks.

He laughs again. "Everybody knows Compass! She's in all the games. One day she'll be a zombie hunter; the next she's the zombie. She is a fairy princess, or a Prohibition gangster. Or the gangster's moll." He talks with his hands, waving his bottle dangerously. "She is everywhere all the time, and if you've got your glasses on, and you're totally immersed in the game, you might not even notice that it's her next to you. She becomes her roles more completely than any other larper I've ever seen."

"Like an actor. Does she also avatar for people?"

"Well." He's watching Compass, who's walking over. "There's the rub. You will never—and I mean ever—meet Compass-in-herself. She's only ever an avatar, whether it's for a game engine–driven NPC, or just some kid who's lying on his couch in his parents' basement, eating chips and playing in VR.

"Everybody's met Compass. But nobody knows her."

In Sura's glasses, Compass is haloed by virtual game portals, each one confined within a hexagon of light drawn on the floor. Behind her, dragons and porn stars, Disney princesses and rampaging kaiju swirl in turbulent clouds in the room's middle space. This vision of her, framed like some postmodern Botticelli goddess held aloft by clouds of advertisement, drives all thought from Sura's head. When she remembers that she wants to ask Malcolm who's riding Compass right now, it's too late: Compass is morphing again, this time into mirrorshades and Mohawk cyberpunk eye candy. Her breasts have grown again. In a clipped, urgent voice she says, "Come roll a character."

Sura frowns and deliberately takes a long slug from her beer. She nods goodbye to Malcolm and steps away from the bar. "I'm not here to play games. I'm trying to hide, not put myself out there."

"Naturally." Compass/cybergirl grimaces impatiently. "That's how you're going to do it."

"I don't understand."

"Come!" Compass strides over to the pillars of color and motion that advertise this season's Augmented Reality Live Action Role Playing games.

"These are just the commercial titles," Compass continues, still in that edgy voice; surely these words she's speaking are not her own. "They've got billions of dollars of development behind them. Very slick. But there are lots of free indie games, built by larpwrights like Pax."

"Pax?"

"He's a larpwright. Really good one. Here." She reaches up, closing her fist on thin air, and pulls. Game titles and floor hexagons fly by, faster the farther she extends her arm. As she does this some of the people in the room dim and virtual versions of them slide away with the hexagons.

"What do you want to play? Romance? Political thriller? Resource management? Shooter?"

"What's this one?" It's called *Lethe,* and the image being displayed is the street-level view of a modern city. There are a lot of people in the picture, dressed normally except that all are wearing Mardi Gras masks.

Compass shakes her head. "Never go to *Lethe*. What about *Rivet Couture*?" That one's title looks stamped, elegant yet blotchy in a kind of Victorian-print way. The image below it is of a leather airman's cap hovering in front of a crossed brass telescope and riding crop.

"Steampunk alternate-Earth," says Compass. "It's the biggest open-source indie game. Pax does scenario-design in it. It's global, has millions of players. A great place to NPC." Her voice lowers. "I d-do it all the time."

Compass walks into that hex, and Sura follows.

"Try it." Compass taps the title. Sura does too, and suddenly the Sheetrock walls melt away, the ceiling flies off, and sunlight floods the crowd. Most people are grayed out, but others have appeared in the distance. Sura stands in some city square, the cobblestoned space surrounded by tall, crowded buildings with leaded-glass windows. Smokestacks loom behind them, and overhead four or five intricately painted zeppelins stand next to white puffy clouds.

A woman passes close by, her severe black dress broken by puffs of white lace at the throat and cuffs; the dress has a bustle. She's lightly holding the arm of a man in a garish yellow suit and top hat. Another man stands a little ways away. He's wearing buckskins and is dark-skinned and heavily tattooed.

Compass points at this man. "*Rivet Couture*'s an alternate reality game where colonialism wasn't as successful as in the real world. In *Rivet Couture,* the American Revolution never happened, and the lands west of the Adirondacks were never annexed by European settlers. We're in a trade town in New Cahokia. There are Indian and Chinese empires, free African nations, and places like Dreamtime, which is unexplored Australia. Players are diplomats, explorers and spies, traders and smugglers."

"So what do I do? Be an NPC here? How does that help me?"

"*Rivet Couture* desperately needs non-player characters." Compass's voice has changed again, and looking, Sura sees that she's adopted yet another skin. This one's strictly Victorian, hair pulled back in a bun, waist cinched within an inch of its life, but her skirt short enough for Sura to see that she's wearing heavy work boots. Welding goggles are pushed back on her forehead.

"You're NPCing right now," Sura accuses. "These words you're speaking, that's some advertising bot feeding you the lines, and you're getting paid to recite them to me?"

Compass nods. "We could create a virtual avatar to be your tour guide, but alternate reality games are all about human interaction. And virtual people can't touch things or carry them or open doors for you. NPCs are usually servants or secondary characters, or bad guys. (We g-get run through and shot. A lot.)"

Sura laughs, covers her mouth with her hand. "So you're getting paid right now, in what, NotchCoin?"

"Gwaiicoin. Real-world Haida c-cryptocurrency. B-better than Notch-Coin. You can't use it unless you're self-sovereign. Now you are, you can join th-the in-game economy."

"And what, buy food? Lodgings?" To Sura's amazement, Compass nods. "But that's crazy."

"Why? Game economies have been real for decades. You can start here, or would you like to see some of the other games?"

Sura shakes her head. *Rivet Couture*'s clothing styles are fantastic, as is the architecture. And the idea of a world where colonialism never happened is intriguing, to say the least.

"I still don't understand how all this is going to keep me *safe*."

"Jay did say," Compass admits, ducking her head. "Sorry. You should still roll a c-character for *RC*, b-but maybe you need a safe gateway to it."

"Gateway? What do you mean?"

"A-a way to lay low, and still be a player."

"Yes, yes I'm sure that's what Jay meant."

"Then we need to start . . ." Compass points across the room. "There."

The one hexagon everyone is giving a wide berth contains a sign that says *The White Rose*. Behind the words is some kind of banner. As this turns slowly into view Sura feels her breath catch in her throat.

The red banner contains a white circle and in that is a swastika. Fluttering before it like a leaf in a storm is a yellow Jewish star.

Compass reaches out and taps the star, and *Rivet Couture*'s towers swap out for those of some central European city. The lurid banners of the Third Reich hang from the hard stone facades; blue smoke stutters from the tailpipe of a passing motor car, and on the sidewalks, men and women hurry past, swaddled in thick woolen coats. Their suspicious eyes are hidden under the brims of their hats, their hands clutch bags or their lapels. Halfway down the block, a man in the striking black uniform of the SS is standing in the street. He's inspecting the people as they pass.

"Jesus! Is this a game?"

"'Game' was never the right word. Larps can be very serious." Compass is a young blond woman wearing a tan greatcoat. Sura holds out her hands and sees that she's skinned the same way. They should blend in here, yet Sura still feels exposed. "I don't like this. I don't want to be here."

"Good. That's how you're supposed to feel." Compass's voice has changed again; her words are now crisp, cold, and with a sensual, slightly smoky accent to them.

They hurry away from the SS officer and down a maze of twisty alleys; belatedly, Sura realizes that they are leaving the warehouse. In the parking lot—half-real, half-obscured by the hellish vision of Nazi-occupied Europe—Compass points out a game waypoint far down the avenue. It's within walking distance, the path measured by pools of streetlight. As they walk she says, "There are two kinds of players: those who run *The White Rose* railways, and people like you, who need to be smuggled about. It's mostly liberals hiding illegal immigrants from ICE.

"So illegals are our bread and butter," says not-Compass, "but *The White Rose*'s really here for a different kind of refugee. See, if you can build a detailed behavioral profile of somebody based on their purchasing habits, you can also build a political one. Some such people drift, unknowingly, into the awareness of the authorities. They're watched, harassed, threatened, and fired from their jobs not for what they have done, but for what their profile suggests they *might* do. We try to find such people and shelter them."

"My dad used to talk about this sort of thing," says Sura. She half laughs. "Mom always told me not to pay any attention to him. 'Your dad's kind of a conspiracy nut,' she'd say."

"If you're one of the sixty million Americans with a steady job in a safe neighborhood, then that's how it'll look," says the avatar. "For the other three hundred million of us, it's very real."

Dad had theories about what might trigger just the sort of unwanted attention that *The White Rose* persona is talking about—it had to do with which books you buy, movies you see, nightclubs you visit. But he wasn't sure how subtle the searches are. Nobody is sure why some people get repeatedly stopped by the cops, why cruisers sit outside their houses at night. It just happens. If you're poor, black, Latino, or Muslim, it happens a lot.

Sura and her blonde guide meet a woman in an alley. (In reality a car has silently pulled up and the player has gotten out. They're standing by the side of the road.) She whispers that she can get them across town safely, and hands them both shopping bags. They drive downtown, and get out of the car in another alley. From here they proceed on foot, being very careful about which streets they walk down. Sometimes they switch from one sidewalk to the other, and Sura is instructed to look in the shop windows, turning her head so that some camera on the other side of the street can't make out her face.

You can't avoid them all. They meet with another partisan, a kid behind the counter of a retro vinyl record store. In *The White Rose,* this is a haberdashery. He gives Sura a hat and a fine veil that's printed with a faint pattern. It's designed to confuse the cameras' facial recognition systems.

"Wait, is this a Rorschach veil?" Sura slides the material through her fingers. "These are incredibly expensive, aren't they?"

He smiles. "You're only borrowing it." He and the woman show her how to drape it over her hat. "Obviously anybody looking at you can tell you're wearing a veil. That'll be suspicious to any human cops, so try to avoid those. But the cameras won't see the veil, and they won't recognize you."

Veiled, taking carefully vetted routes, and timing their journey based on telemetry from *The White Rose*'s own network of police-watching cameras, they take pedestrian ways and bike paths through the quiet, deroaded central business district. Past the Strip and Bloomfield they come to Shadyside and a region of low-rises and small businesses that's fairly camera free.

"This will do for now," Compass says. "We've obfuscated your trail, and this neighborhood has safe houses and restaurants. But here, there's a *White Rose* plugin for other games. I'll transfer it."

She takes back the veil and sends an app to Sura's glasses. Warsaw melts back into *Rivet Couture,* but the new overlay remains visible. It grades the local area according to threat level. Now, suspicious men hang about in the alleys of certain ill-lit streets (these represent neighborhood-watch drones), and dark carriages roll down the cobbles (autonomous cars whose dashcams are licensed ICE feeds). "The plugin's not as reliable as actually playing *The White Rose,* but it should do for most uses," says the blonde partisan before she flickers and is replaced by Compass.

Sura is exhausted from lugging her heavy backpack all over town. "But what do the players get out of this?"

"Aside from helping real people evade real incarceration? Game achievements. P-points. Gwaiicoin for epic wins." Compass shrugs. "Just avoid the dark alleys. Here, this bed and b-breakfast is safe. And they take NotchCoin. Goodbye."

"Wait, what—?" Through some trick of Mixed Reality, Compass vanishes, leaving Sura standing on the sidewalk in front of an ordinary house on a residential side street. When Sura takes off her smart glasses she finds the young woman is actually gone.

"Oh, shit."

She looks around. Defeated, with no choice, she walks up to the house and knocks on the door.

CHAPTER FIVE

"The Society for Creative Anachronism was the first time I got to wear full-plate armor," says Walter. Sura's sitting with him and his husband, Dan, in their backyard. Dan's set up a barbecue next to the garage.

The house is a bungalow with white aluminum siding and a gravel driveway leading to the garage, which is just big enough for one car. The rest of the yard is a plot of rather sad yellow grass, with a gnarled crabapple tree in one corner. It's midafternoon. Saturday.

"So we're having an epic SCA battle in some poor shlub's field, and there they go, dozens of guys in period armor waving rubber swords as they run at each other. Plenty of women, too, you know, warrior maidens and elf princesses and on. I'm going *oh boy this is it* and I raise my sword over my head and I scream raaaawr! and start running." Walter is no longer young but this part he has to tell with his whole body so he hops out of the lawn chair and flings his arms above his head.

"And I'm running and running and hell this is going to be great and the lines are coming together, I can sorta see that through the tiny little slit in the can I'm wearing on my head. It's all I can do to keep myself pointed in the right direction but I can hear the battle straight ahead.

"And I'm still running and running and damn! I'm getting tired. And I stop for a sec"—he puts his hands on his knees and mimes panting—"and then I think *what the hell?* and I pull off my helmet.

"I've gone twenty feet."

Walter dissolves into peals of laughter, scoops up his lemonade glass and sits back down. "Well you try running in full armor some time, see how you do."

"Tell her about the bells," says Dan. Walter laughs again.

"Oh yeah so the guys who aren't wearing all that crap are coming straight for me. I mash down the helmet and swing the broadsword, but these assholes aren't weighed down like me so they just start wailing on me, and it's *bong bong bong* on the helmet. I mean, I know they're hitting me, but I can't feel a damn thing. It's like I'm a human drum kit."

Sura nearly snorts her lemonade onto the grass. She is having a really great time with these complete strangers—the best time she's had in a long, long while, to the point that her laughter is starting to skid close to tears. Dan and Walter run the *Rivet Couture*–themed B&B where Compass dropped her off.

That was two days ago, and she hasn't heard from the strange girl since.

"Back then none of us knew a damn thing about Nordic larp," Walter is saying. "Which is where it really took off. Here, I want to show you something." He bolts out of his chair and goes inside. Dan shoots a fond grin after him and turns back to Sura. "We've done some crazy stuff in *RC*, but going larpabout the way you are is . . ." He shakes his head. "Pretty hard-core."

Sura picks up her lemonade, a kind of talisman to hide behind, and says, "If I was hard-core, I'd be cinched into a fourteen-inch corset."

"We have those! You have to see the shop," says Dan, but at this point Walter returns. He's cupping something small that he gives to Sura; it's a coin. "Real Duvrike money from *Trenne Byar*," he says reverently. "Stamped by the same guy who engraved the Swedish krona. They made eighteen thousand of these, tin and copper, and they used 'em for a week. Over a thousand players, in Sweden. 1994. *Trenne Byar* means 'three villages,' and they literally built three villages for it! Holy crap, I wish I'd been there."

Sura turns over the coin in her hands. Aside from being suspiciously light, it looks like real money, with beautiful elvish-style script around the outside and a crowned swan in the center. "Why have I never heard of this?"

"There was no media coverage," says Dan. "How would you cover something like that? The audience is the participants. That's the key to larps. That's why *Rivet Couture* is going on all around us all the time, and nobody notices."

"*These* take it to the next level." Walter nudges his Mixed Reality smart glasses, which are sitting on the wrought-iron garden table next to the half-empty bottle of Cab Sav. "You don't need real plate mail anymore, though some people still craft it. You can have virtual armor and weapons—well, swords and guns and shit can't be physical, or the cops'll shoot you first and ask questions later. We can easily find other players, and locations and such, without the mundanes noticing."

"Still." Dan shoots Walter a warning glance. "It can be dangerous, because there are no boundaries. But you know that, you're on larp-about."

"Actually I'm pretty new to this," says Sura. "I just find the idea of, you know, *being somebody else* for a while, it's irresistible."

They nod. "So in the beginning was *Trenne Byar,*" says Walter, taking back his coin, "and of course the Stanford prison experiment, though those guys had no idea what they were actually doing. After *Trenne Byar* there was *Ground Zero* and *Europa, inside:outside* and *Luminescence, The White Road* and *Delirium.* Rules-based or sandbox, combat-oriented or about political intrigue, or just philosophy, or historical or all about intrigue or therapy—or about sex. It just kept going and building, and then one day somebody built a blockchain that could keep track of all the intangibles. Suddenly you could scale a world infinitely. So now"—he spreads his arms again, this time like he's doing a benediction—"we have *Rivet Couture, Gaea Ascendant, The Paved Earth, Cyber Iris,* and all the rest. Global. Permanent. With millions of players."

Each has its own economy and ways of tracking identity. Sura's not Sura here, nor is she Britt Birch or some other stolen persona. Walter and Dan have just helped her roll her first *Rivet Couture* character: Countess Vesta.

Somebody shouts "hallooo" from in front of the house. Dan sighs and picks up his glasses. "Back to the fray."

"It's the Grand Market for you today?" asks Walter as they rise. Sura nods.

"I've got a fireteam invitation. But I have stuff to do here first."

"Well, knock 'em dead." They walk Dan out to the street. There's a perfectly ordinary driverless van paused at the curb. In the game, though, this is an elaborate stagecoach with a tall, sepulchral driver perched up top. It already has several passengers, other players headed for the market.

"Don't let me forget to show you the store," says Dan as Walter helps him into the van. "The corsets are divine."

* * *

There's this thing she's been putting off. Sura retreats to the little kitchenette in the basement, and with her glasses on starts positioning virtual windows around herself.

It's time to investigate Dad's death.

The pleasant afternoon, lemonade with Dan and Walter, and not thinking about what she's about to do, are the only things that get her over the hump and into reading the news reports. There's a little galaxy of them, and they need to be sorted. One, which the global journalism blockchain has tagged as most reliable, is an eyewitness report by an Iquitos-based journalist who arrived on the scene with the first responders.

She needs to email him.—No no, if he's not on the mesh, the whole exchange is going to go through the Internet, and every word will be scrutinized by government agencies and maybe the very people who killed Dad. She's going to have to phone him, but she's not ready for that yet. She turns to the other reports.

Eastern Peru is speckled with abandoned oil and gas wells, and many of them are leaky. The sour gas is instantly deadly, and sometimes it wafts across the highway. Cars are found upside down among the denuded stumps of the former forest. Would-be rescuers are parked neatly on the shoulder, dead at the wheel. Supposedly there are sensors on the well caps to register leaks, but if the gas does escape, somebody's liable. Not the oil companies, they've all been liquidated, their trillions of dollars of assets having been stranded by the rise of renewables. It's generally locals or the *federales* left holding the bag. In Peru, the locals would rather shoot you and bury you in the bush than pay an unfairly inherited fine. Just getting to Iquitos, and on to the well sites, had involved an elaborate human smuggling operation comparable to *The White Rose.*

If Jim Neelin was murdered, there doesn't have to have been a reason. All that's needed is opportunity.

Still, after some browsing she finds a glasses-cam video taken by someone at the death site. Men wearing bulky breathing masks cluster around a bright yellow well head; the cameraman is walking an earthen embankment that surrounds the wells, probably to keep back floodwaters. Emergency vehicles and men in bulky fireman's gear cluster up on the road.

The camera suddenly swerves down and to the right. When the shot stabilizes, Sura sees the footprints: several sets of them. Deep and crisply drawn, they lead down the embankment towards the well head. The camera zooms in on two other sets, coming back; several of the incoming prints overlay outgoing ones. Since it rained the day before her dad came out here, this means that somebody was here between then, and the arrival of Dad and his friends.

Jay gave her the name of the insurance company that hired him; now she just needs to connect the dots. But this is all she can manage for today. She has to track down Compass, and find out how to make a living in the games, as Walter and Dan seem to. Is that all she has to do, to disappear properly? Somehow she doubts it.

She should go; instead, she sits for a while, pensively scrolling through the photos. She stops at one, unsure why it's caught her eye. It contains a photo of the well head, but this one taken from far away. The well is half-visible past the deeply tangled, moss-covered roots of some great tree. Shadows of the forest lean out onto the clear-cut ground. It's dark and deeply atmospheric, and just the place she can imagine Jim Neelin tromping through, head held high.

Dad carried a gun. Sura has a very early memory of watching it bob on his hip as they walked in the woods somewhere. Sometimes, Sura would go with him on his "business trips," and then Mom would come too. He called them business trips, but they visited no offices; instead, they would walk in the countryside, where Dad did mysterious things with sample containers and GPS. They weren't a religious family, so for Sura the only times she felt herself in the presence of grace was when she was walking among these grand, silent trees, in the deep maze of the forest. Until one day, when she lost it.

"Sura! Keep up, there might be bears!" They were somewhere in Michigan, she doesn't remember where now. She'd been transfixed, staring down some corkscrewing tunnel of green and tree limbs and now hurried to catch up to Mom and Dad. It was only years later, when she saw her first Emily Carr painting, that she realized other people saw the forest the way she had. Now, she clutched Mom's hand.

"Daddy, is it true? Are there bears?"

"Maybe." He shrugged. "But they'll be more scared of you than you are of them. And they can hear us coming a mile away."

"Is that why you carry a gun?"

He glanced at Mom, smiled, and said nothing.

Every fifteen minutes or so, Dad would say "here" to Sura. As he'd instructed, she would take a little plastic spike out of her pack and jam it into the ground or a fallen log or in the split of a rock. She'd thought these were environmental sensors, but when she proudly said that she was helping the world by adding to its eyes and ears, Dad had laughed.

"Actually, these are just for us. I tag everywhere I go so I can prove I've been there. These tags give a little radio chirp when I come near—but only when it's me." He knelt on the loam next to her, poking the spot where she'd planted her latest spike. "Tell you what. I'll give you the key too, and then if ever you want, you can follow in my footsteps. Deal?"

"Deal!"

They had come under the silent green cathedrals to a crystalline stream that meandered beneath an audience of ferns. Dad bent to take a sample and, delighted, Sura cupped her hands and drew some of the perfect water to her lips.

"Stop!" The water spattered her shoes. Dad was glaring at her. "Do *not* drink that!"

"Wh-what?" She fought back tears.

"This whole aquifer is contaminated," he said. "That's why we're here." He pointed upstream. "Lead and heavy metals have been leaching into this stream for years. It's poisoned, Sura. The whole forest is poisoned."

She blinked and hurriedly dried her hands on her pants. They walked on, and came to a region of dead trees, where Dad took another sample. The gray trunks jutted in crazy, random angles. Past them, she could see a cleared lot and some portables and, beyond that, a road.

Her father pointed it out. "That's a remediation center. We're working to heal the forest, Sura. That's what we do."

"But I thought this was all . . . isn't this the wilderness?"

He shook his head. "There is no wilderness. Get that through your head. We have to manage all the land, everywhere, now. Nothing can survive without our help anymore."

"Shush, Jim. Let the girl enjoy the forest."

But Dad wouldn't have it; and so now as they went on he pointed out the invasive species, and lifted pine canopies to show her where native plants should be but were not. He took her to see where summer students had been planting. He talked about the political maneuvers, enemies and allies that were the underbrush he cut through every day, and were all he could see of Nature now.

They walked on, but now when Sura looked down those green tangled avenues, she no longer glimpsed a realm of magic where possibilities beyond the everyday shimmered. Instead, she saw the managed categories of a project.

The lesson was that wonder leads to disappointment. She would learn it well in the coming years.

"Vesta!" Walter shouts from upstairs. "Visitor!"

Sura emerges from the house to find Compass waiting. She's wearing the same clothes as the other day—not that Sura is doing much better. She owns three pairs of pants right now.

"Hi! Thanks for—well . . ." *For coming back* just sounds pathetic, so instead she says, "Listen, for the other night—the tattoo party and that larp we did—do I owe you anything?"

Compass shakes her head. "P-P-People are investing in you. R-Right now you're trending on th-the market. Come on." She pivots like a marionette and heads for the front of the house.

Walter is watching her go. "Do you know Compass?" Sura asks him.

"Everybody knows Compass."

Hurrying to catch up, she finds her guide waiting next to a minivan. It's much like the one that picked up Dan, except it has a bird logo on its side, with the slogan *Proudly Eagle Owned!* under it. There are several people in the van, all wearing smart glasses. She loads the *Rivet Couture* overlay in hers, and Dan and Walter's Shadyside dream is overwritten with Victorian-styled row houses. Pillars of smoke are rising above the slate shingles, and Sura hears a deep irregular thudding that she suspects might be artillery fire. The minivan is now a carriage drawn by four skittish horses.

Compass is no longer Compass. She's labeled *Mad Scratchie* and *he* is squat and wide, with a bowler hat on his head and suspenders strapping his gray linen shirt. He's a ginger and even has a stubby cigar jammed in the corner of his mouth.

"Get'n the carriage, mum," he commands. "It ain't safe here." It's Compass's voice but transformed into a Cockney rasp. Startled, Sura complies.

There are four other passengers. Compass takes the driver's seat but doesn't drive; the van seems to know where it's going. "Hi," Sura says as she tries to buckle herself with a seat belt she can't see. Once she's done that, she finds herself facing four fantasy archetypes: an Aviator, a Soldier of Fortune (who looks much like Scratchie), a Gambler, and an Inventor. She is Countess Vesta in this game, a Spy, and though in reality she's dressed normcore, in a gray hoodie and blue jeans, in *Rivet Couture* she's sporting leather pants, a pistol in a belted holster, a corset/bandolier, and a loose white blouse. Atop all of this is a felt hat penetrated by hat pins that, like the rest of the gear, she purchased with character-building points. The hat pins are infighting weapons, and Vesta has a high skill rating with them.

She taps the arm of the glasses and the overlay disappears. Sharing the minivan with her are a young bearded guy in a plaid shirt, a mild-looking middle-aged black man; a rather handsome and elegantly groomed young Latino; and a grim-looking skinhead.

"Listen up!" snaps Scratchie. "This here's your fireteam! The player-matching algorithms put you together because you have complementary skills." All made-up, those skills—though Vesta has one, burglary, that Sura's willing to defend.

"Also," and suddenly it's Compass speaking, "you're all here for th-the same reason."

Suddenly the van's passengers are eyeing one another in a new way.

"You haven't played before," Compass continues in her voice. "So we're going t-to start you out as NPCs. You'll get your instructions from—well, you'll see. B-Best part is, you get paid to do this."

Sura raises her hand. "What about, you know, cameras and . . . stuff?" Soldier of Fortune nods in agreement.

Compass speaks in a third voice—the one she used at the tattoo party. "You can hide in Walter's basement if you want. But then how can you act in the world?

"You'll be p-playing in a camera-safe area. Your overlays should warn you about exceptions. You should g-get to know each other, you'll be relying on the person next to you for the next few hours."

"Hendge," says the Inventor, extending a hand for Sura to shake. "Vaughan, actually, but you won't find me in the games by that name."

"Rico. I am pleased to meet you." The Latino Aviator's accent is thick, though not Mexican. His handshake is firm.

"K.C." That's all the middle-aged Gambler offers. He keeps his hands to himself.

The skinhead Soldier of Fortune is silent. "Vesta," says Sura, offering her hand. "And you are . . . ?"

"The fuck does it matter? None of us are using our real names."

"Yeah, so?" She looks outside, and the glasses show her a town in ruins. Trees have been broken in half and lie across the road. Houses lean drunkenly, missing walls or a roof. Smoke is still drifting from burnt-out shop fronts.

"What happened here?"

Compass is Mad Scratchie again; he laughs. "Whaddaya think? God-damned Martians is what. They didn't all die after the invasion. Some're still hidin' in their tripods, mostly lurkin' in the woods and exsanguinatin' deer. Now and then they need things, like metals and chemicals. Then they knock over a chemist's, or a train station. You ain't lived till you seen a tripod carry off a passenger carriage full o' people all screamin' and fallin' about."

Sura turns to the skinhead. "So," she drawls, "if, say, a tripod's about to step on your head, what do I say other than 'hey you!' to get your attention?"

He hesitates, then shrugs. "Call me Cutter."

Nobody talks for a while. Sura knows what they're thinking, it's the same thing running through her mind. *The White Rose* has convinced her that these games aren't *entirely* useless; maybe Jay's right and they can help her get around unnoticed. But that doesn't solve the basic problem of how she's supposed to survive when she can't work or even rent a motel room under her own name. These guys seem to be in the same boat, but how to even raise the subject, much less pool what they know?

The cityscape has been getting more and more torn up. Soon they're surrounded by smoke, and the sound of machine-gun fire comes from up ahead. When the van stops, Scratchie bolts out the door, shouting, "Over here!" They pile out, momentarily lost. Then K.C. points. "That way!" He runs to join Scratchie, who's hunkered down behind the low remains of a pulverized wall. Sura lowers herself carefully next to him; she reaches out, expecting to touch brick, but instead finds her fingers tangled in a tennis net.

Muting her glasses she finds that in reality they're bivouacked in an empty tennis court on the edge of a public park. "Shit." She unmutes the glasses and the devastation returns.

A big icon appears in the air above the wall; it looks like a spinning coin. "You should have an NPC job offer," says Compass. "Accept it and your identity will morph, maybe more than once. If you're a red shirt, expect to b-be blown up and stuff. Just g-go along with it, but if you wanna scream and thrash about, use emotes instead. Non-p-players get creeped out when players go b-bonkers in public. And the police . . . might just shoot you."

". . . Right."

"Here they come!"

Pandemonium breaks out as a hotel collapses, fire blooms as screaming people run by, and then through the veil of smoke something long and spindly sweeps the sky. Haloed by a yellow smudge of sun, a Martian war machine steps daintily into the street.

Straddles it, rather. The thing is huge.

Scratchie stands up, turns into a thin man in a black suit, and runs off. Sura accepts her quest offer and words appear in front of her: CIVILIAN, FEMALE. YOU ARE LOOKING FOR SOMEONE TO RESCUE YOUR EMPLOYER, WHO IS A BANK MANAGER. Arrows show her a path through the chaos. Red crosshairs are centered on a live player standing nearby.

Sura thinks for a second, then runs over and grabs him. He practically jumps over the tennis net; he probably had no idea she was real.

Her own arms and hands are clad in long sleeves with ruffled cuffs. Her fellow player is dressed as a steampunk soldier, his torso crossed with bandoliers. He's got a pith helmet on his head.

"Please!" Sura screams. "He's going to die! You have to help me!"

He scrambles away, swearing. "The fuck? Get away from me!"

INCENTIVE: MONEY IN BANK VAULT.

Ah, now she gets it. "Please, sir. Mr. Braithwaite is an esteemed member of the chamber of commerce. I'm sure the chamber will reward you if you help."

He hesitates. "What do you mean? Where's this guy?"

She looks where the arrows are pointing. "We took shelter in the back of the bank when the horrible foreign apparatus began its assault. Mr. Braithwaite adjudged the bank vault the safest place, but no sooner had he opened it than the foreign machine kicked in the wall!" She's just bullshitting here; from what little studying she did last night, she gathers that Malcolm's level-design systems can improvise landscapes and building layouts on the fly.

There's a thermometer graph in her right peripheral view that bobs up and down as she talks, and it's now rising into the green.

She leads her player through the carnage. Other soldiers are firing volleys at the war machine; at one point its round metal foot, big as a car, thumps into the cobbles not ten feet away.

"Wait!" Her player grabs her arm and pulls her into a doorway. Everything goes to hell outside. "Thank you," she stammers, but pulls her hand out of his. There must be physical rules of engagement here—boundaries. She didn't think to ask Compass how they work.

"There you are!" Four more soldiers crowd in with them. They're a truly motley crew including a Gurkha, a Chinese man with a braid like Compass's, and a New Cahokian. They slap her player's back and laugh in relief.

"We gotta help this girl," says her player. *Girl,* thinks Sura in annoyance. *As if.* He's describing the situation and their eyes light up when he says the words "bank vault."

"We'll help you, miss!"

As the dust settles she leads them across the street and through the shattered front window of the bank. Dead tellers litter the floor. Sura follows her guide arrows into the back, where a little light from a tiny window high in one wall shows the half-collapsed interior. Bricks almost cover a man lying by the open door to the vault.

"Oh, Mr. Braithwaite!" She crouches by the imaginary body, but then gets a message: INCOMING PARCEL TRANSFER. META CONTEXT.

Suddenly she's in the park, all augmented reality gone except for one blinking arrow that bounces by its point on the head of a woman strolling up the grass. She's dressed in casual clothes, looks relaxed and happy. She's carrying a shopping bag. As Sura stands she stops, smiles, and says, "Here."

She hands the bag to Sura and walks away.

Blink! and she's back in the bank, where the players are cheerfully looting the vault. One of them is K.C.; she imagines that the other players in this fireteam could be anywhere in the world, and they might have their own accompanying NPCs to provide physical realism. That's a pretty cool idea, but new instructions appear: DIPLOMATIC POUCH MUST BE DELIVERED TO THE HUDSON'S BAY OUTPOST.

She looks down. What she feels as a shopping bag looks, in the game, like a leather satchel. Ah.

She reaches for her currently assigned player. "Please, sir, I know there's no more hope for Mr. Braithwaite, but his mission, it could be salvaged."

"Mission? What mission?"

She pushes the bag into his hands. "This diplomatic pouch must be delivered to the Hudson's Bay Company. Mr. Braithwaite would see no one but himself do it, but how are we to accomplish it now? Please, sir, can I trust you?"

"Well, missy, sure." He takes the bag. Sura's thermometer graph has blown its top. Mission accomplished, she supposes.

"—Can't let her live," she hears K.C say. "She'd identify us."

Awash in sudden adrenaline, she turns to see her player's friends eyeing her levelly. The Chinese one is being played by middle-aged K.C. He's got an Aussie or South African accent he can't quite disguise, but even with the corny voice she finds herself acting like this is real; she starts to back away. "Wait, I—I swear I will tell no one—" K.C. raises his pistol.

"Are you crazy?" Her player tries to push her out of the way, but a shot rings out and everything goes transparent.

NPC DEATH, says her prompt.

Sura paws at her player, then falls over, careful to check that there isn't any actual dogshit on the actual grass. Her player howls in outrage.

"Why, Neil, I didn't think you was that soft," says the Gurkha. "Maybe you lack the spine for this sort of thing."

Her player looks at them, looks down at the satchel in his hands—and runs.

DISENGAGED. The bank disappears. Sura's now in the ruined street, wearing the dusty body of a man. She stands up, watches her player bolting out of the bank. His backdrop is flames and a distant, whirling tripod.

"Hey, that's not fair! They're gonna kill him!" She wants to intervene, but her game-body disappears when she takes a step after him. Meanwhile, her heads-up display is showing that her character has acquired some cryptocurrency. There's an option to email it as Gwaiicoin to an account of her choosing. She has no idea how much sixty Gwaiicoin is worth.

There are also options to NPC again—or to begin playing as Countess Vesta.

Later, she can't remember making the choice. She feels swept along, knowing somehow that this is *not* a game, not in any way that she's ever understood that term.

When she finds her player, his back is to an alley wall and his erstwhile friends are closing in a semicircle around him. He's holding up the bag, as if it can shield him from what's to come.

Vesta fires her pistol into the air. As the soldiers dive for cover, she plants one booted foot on a fallen cornice and aims the weapon at them.

"Gentlemen," she drawls, "this is that moment they talk about, when discretion becomes the better part of valor."

CHAPTER SIX

Jay squints at Sura as he enters the diner, then grins. He collapses more than sits on the bench opposite her. "Great to see ya!"

She cocks an eyebrow at him. They haven't spoken since he handed her off to Compass. "You're not used to repeat business, are you."

"Frankly, no."

"How's your car?"

"Still street legal, if that's what you're asking." He cranks himself around to look back at the door. "And as far as I know, nobody's following me today." Planting his elbows on the table, he returns his attention to her. "You look good. Got a job? Or did that game thing work out?"

"As a matter of fact it did. But it's a little weird."

He bursts out laughing. "If I'd told you what you were getting yourself into, you'd never have believed me. Compass helped you land on your feet?"

"Yeah. But I was wondering, how do you know Compass in the first place? You don't seem like you'd . . . run in the same circles."

He waves vaguely. "Everybody knows about larpers, you see 'em everywhere. But the third time somebody I was chasing just disappeared, I mean, *financially,* while people would swear they saw him just the other day and he's well-dressed and well-fed . . ." He shrugs. "You assume he's being paid in cash by the cartels. So you hunt him down on foot, the old-fashioned way, and yeah he's running all over town delivering packages, making deals of some kind with people in parking lots, but he's also wearing these damned *glasses.* And he's hanging out with this girl . . ."

"So that's how you met? She was a job?" He doesn't answer. "Come on, Jay, I know enough about you to know that everybody in your life is a job."

"Ow, stings, girl, stings." His Coke arrives. "You really are entirely in the games?"

She sighs. "Yeah. I'm getting paid in Gwaiicoin. It's not even worth converting it to NotchCoin much less cash. I buy food and stuff straight with it. I haven't seen a dollar bill in days."

He looks so impressed that a horrible suspicion crawls into Sura's mind. "You didn't know! You had no idea this was going to work, did you? When you gave me that whole song-and-dance in the Chinese restaurant about 'identity is money' and how the only way I could properly disappear was by larping, you literally had no clue whether I was gonna survive, or crash and burn! You fucker!"

Shrug. "It was a long shot. Looks like it paid off."

She slumps back, looks away. "No wonder you have no friends."

"I have plenty. And what are you complaining about? You said it yourself. It worked." He crosses his arms. "So is it hard? Do you have to stay in character all day? Are you, like, part of a clan or something? With, like, matching bowling shirts? Have you told anybody your real name?"

"I don't even know where to start." She's been on the steep part of the learning curve since her first time NPCing.

She can't explain or justify her conversion into Countess Vesta. She's done VR for years. Surely having further to walk while you're playing isn't going to enhance the experience; if anything, it'll just make adventure into a grind. But when she plays this way, she's no longer the chessmaster, but a combination chessmaster and pawn. It's exhilarating and terrifying.

She's replayed that first day in her mind, trying to find the lintel of whatever magic door she stepped over. All that afternoon, K.C., Vaughan, and Rico had appeared and disappeared, playing hapless citizens, looters, or soldiers with varying degrees of enthusiasm and success. Other players and NPCs were entirely virtual, as were most of the places and obstacles. Sura knew in a vague sort of way that the long chain of ruined street corners she'd traversed didn't exist, that in reality she was running in tight circles in a park. It didn't matter. She was *there*.

Now and then Compass joined in, always with a perfect grace note to make the moment beautiful, thrilling, or heart-wrenching.

"Well, are you making connections, at least?"

"The players mostly seem like ex-professionals. I met a woman who used to be a paralegal. There's lots of out-of-work truckers. Accountants, notaries, you know, anybody who got replaced by automation or a blockchain."

"Anyone you think is hiding? Like you?"

Both Rico and K.C. could be illegals, for all she knows. She shrugs. "There are as many reasons to hide as there are people."

Every day, Sura visits a game hub called the Grand Market. In *Rivet Couture* it's a town square ringed by tall Cahokian houses. Virtual Mississippian warriors are keeping order in a lively marketplace that parallels the real one. The stalls and vendors are mostly but not all virtual. Some of the real stalls look the same whether you've got your glasses on or not; others mutate into RC equivalents, or simply have digital goods on them as well as real stuff. Still others are entirely virtual and the vendors are game sprites or players who are here only *in virtua*. Most of the real shopkeepers take Gwaiicoin; some of the virtual ones take dollars.

In reality the Grand Market takes up half of the park she usually plays in; it's a farmer's market that's allowed game-oriented augmentations. The *Rivet Couture* part of it isn't always in this place or even geographically situated at all—and it has a VR presence. On rainy days her game play is an entirely VR thing as she hides in Dan and Walter's basement. But wherever the Market is, there's bound to be work, even if it's only NPC-ing as a foul-mouthed fishmonger or sly money changer.

"Well, that's damned cool," he says when she tells him all this. "So how does it—"

"I don't want to be doing this!" She slaps down her menu. "Jay. I do not. Want. To be. Here. I need to find out why those shitheads who hired you are after me. I need to get them off my back and go back to being a real girl, not some gamer imitation."

"Right." He nods briskly. "So, here's the scoop. I went back to them. Told them I'd heard a rumor that you got away, and offered to find you again."

"You *what*?"

"Don't get your panties in a twist." He holds up his hands. "Can you think of a better way to get the inside scoop on them than by being on the inside? It's no risk to me, if I'm careful. I just can't find you. Meanwhile, I've been asking questions to, you know, narrow my search."

"Oh." She sits back. "That's actually kind of brilliant."

"Jesus, how do you think I make my living? I do it by faking out people who think they're cleverer than everybody else. It's not just the people I chase, half the people looking for them are just like that. These assholes, well, they say they're a collection agency working for the insurance company you owe for your mom's medical expenses. Those debts, they're real, right?"

Sura shrugs. "Yeah. No way I'm ever going to pay them off, and they know it."

"Right, so they think the plan is to record all your biometrics, go way beyond facial recognition so you can't even take a shit without them carving off their share of it. You'll be paying them a big chunk of your income for the rest of your life and you can never escape them. Pretty standard situation."

". . . Except?"

"Except for this 'collection agency.' It's called Summit Recoveries, it's Detroit based, and I tell you, it has some pretty shady people working for it. Like that 'Galen Bester' guy who nearly got you at the biometrics lab. Some of these jerks are ex-military contractors—there's a glut on the mercenary market since we pulled out of the Middle East. I'm tracing the employment histories of two of them. Should be able to tell you who they're connected with in a couple of days."

"Really. You asked to meet just to tell me this? I mean, it's good, but you could have just called."

"I told you, finding people in the real world isn't a trick anymore. At the rate things are going I'm gonna be out of work. I told you I want to keep up with the times, expand my territory into online worlds. But now I'm thinking I want to do more than just find people who've used Compass's underground railroad."

"More? Like what?"

"Find things as well as people. Do general investigation. *In* the games."

"You're offering me a job as, what, some game equivalent of a private detective?"

"I'd think anyone would jump at the chance to be the world's first virtual dick."

She chuckles at that, then frowns. "I'd been wondering; your plan was to take apart Compass's operation. She trusts you, and you wanted me to help you screw her over."

"Simple moral calculus," he says. "Some people can't be allowed to get away.

That's the Jay who locked her in the back seat of his car. She hasn't seen him in a while. Then he says, "But I believe we can find better things to do than chase down Compass's lost boys."

She thinks about that. Investigating for Jay is still not a real job, as she understands them, but something about it appeals to her burglar side. "I'm in."

"Don't say it if you don't mean it. Seriously, I get it that you want to go back to your old life. It would be great to be debt-free, able to walk into any shop anywhere in the country without worrying that the feds will be waiting when you step outside. But you already *are* working, in a way, aren't you? I mean, these games, they're paying you."

"It's not a job! It's the total opposite of a job. I'm not even laying around on my ass all day collecting GI, I'm actually . . ." Dare she say it? "Having fun! It's the ultimate in slacking off and I'm getting paid to do it."

"It costs to play the game, though, right?"

She shakes her head. "That's the weird part. *Rivet Couture* is free. *Star Wars* and *Middle Earth*, the big franchise worlds, those charge."

"Damn straight. So you've already got a job, and a safe one. It's just off the books. Would you really work for me too?"

She broods on this while they order. Why should she feel guilty about not having a "real job" when there's no work anyway? God knows she tried, like everybody does. The waitress that just served Sura is probably an unpaid intern, building her reputation as a diligent worker in hopes that somewhere, to someone, that will someday mean something.

"I'll admit, somehow, it is a living," she says after a while.

"But it doesn't feel like a life."

A zeppelin hangs above the ambassador's palace, its Hudson's Bay Company flag blazing in the rosy light of early evening. This proxy sun casts troubled red and blue reflections over the palace. Countess Vesta and her companions stop to take in the building's decadent glories: sides tiled in intricate patterns, windows latticed and reaching their arches to Heaven. A marble staircase leads up to the tall bronze doors, where footmen in red silk graciously bow to the bejeweled women and uniformed men who swirl in and out in the ancient dance of diplomatic privilege.

It's mid-July. Three weeks have passed since Sura entered the world of *Rivet Couture*, two since she spoke to Jay in the diner. She's starting to get the hang of *RC*.

Unlike the older generation of computer games, missions in *RC* can't be repeated. Each event is unique and pushes the gameworld's multi-threaded intrigues forward in some way. Sura quickly found that she couldn't play NPCs without picking up on the politics, high gossip, and, well, sheer maniacal fun that's to be had as a player. She started playing as Vesta, at first just to blow off steam. After a few days it became clear that having a reputation—and a reliable fireteam—can turn you from a simple pawn into a plot driver that adventures can be built around. That can be even more lucrative than NPCing.

Today, for the first time, she and her fireteam are playing as their main characters in a scenario that could have a real impact on other plotlines. It's a great opportunity.

"Damn," says K.C., who's Vesta's second in command on this mission. "This is a fine, fine place."

She laughs at his accent. "I see what they meant about not being able to enter through the front door." It isn't just the doormen who'll accost them if they try that, but the whole cream of Company society is likely to come ravening after them. Vesta's got the credentials to walk here—or, at any rate, nearly so—but since a recent "incident" with a visiting Marquis she's been a bit of a pariah of the Great Game. This is partly why she's not the one dressed in a formal ball gown tonight.

"The place does back onto the river, like they said," points out Vaughan. "There's a window ajar around back—if our man has done his job."

"I'm to be crawling through windows in this?" Ajanta, the runaway Indian princess, crosses her arms and pouts at the golden building. Her gold-patterned silks leave little to the imagination; if she tears them on a nail, it'll be nothing.

Vesta is in practical leathers, with her hair tied back and a rapier at her side.

"I'll give you a helping hand." K.C. leers.

"I don't want your hands anywhere near me!"

Vesta bows to her. "I'll cover the lintel with my jacket." She's still amazed that Compass accepted her invitation to play. Compass never plays, she only NPCs; even Mad Scratchie is just a sock-puppet she hires out. Since she agreed, Sura's been looking forward to having wall-eyed, foul-mouthed Scratchie along for the ride—so it was a complete surprise when Ajanta showed up instead. As Ajanta, Compass looks nothing like herself, except for her ponytail.

Staying to the lengthening shadows, they pick their way down a plank-walled alley a stone's throw from the palace. Rats, lazy dogs in the trash, and some dockmen on a break watch them pass, but there are no fences or other obstacles between them and the slowly drifting waters of the river.

"Be extra careful," says K.C. "Remember the Jack Pine Murderer's still not been caught."

"Urban hysteria!" protests Ajanta. "Surely a giant, tree-like monster cannot be stalking the city."

Rico shrugs. "There are Martians. Why not killer giants?"

Where the river takes a bend about a mile north, great Cahokian mounds sit watchful in the deepening light. The far shore is mostly tree-lined, but lamps are coming on under those brows of green, and beyond, the city rolls away in smoke-capped mazeways.

"There's our way in," Vesta whispers unnecessarily as they peek around the corner of the yacht club. The piers end a good twenty meters from the waterline, so they're good for little more than sightseeing. Clearly the Company has made the best of the deficiency, since the wooden bridge-like structures are currently festooned with lanterns. An old man is tottering along, lighting these one by one. He doesn't notice Vesta's team as they approach the lower level of the Hudson's Bay building where a row of more modest windows should provide access to the kitchens.

"Right, let's review this one more time." She spreads her map against the yellow bricks. "Rico will land the ornithopter on the roof and make sure the door there is unlocked. K.C. and Vaughan will create the diversion in the grand salon. Pick a fight with the richest man you can find, as long as he's British. You must get the Company's thugs after you and lead them on a merry chase. I'll have escorted Ajanta upstairs, where her job is to keep the spectronomer out of his laboratory, giving me a chance to sneak in and plunder the wall safe."

K.C. scowls at the paper. "You're certain your friend in the Home Office can make bail for us?"

"K.C., have I ever led you astray?"

"This is not the time to be bringing that up."

"You'd better not take too long," snaps Ajanta. "The ambassador's appetites are famous."

"All I'll need is five minutes. If the combination we were given is wrong, we won't get another chance." She peers around at them. "Anybody want to back out?"

They're all with her as she cautiously peeks through the half-opened window that leads to an office off the kitchens. Vesta can hear muted conversations, the clank of pots being cleaned. "All clear!" She goes first, and as promised lays her coat down for Ajanta, who in the end does accept a boost from Vaughan. A minute later they're strolling the white marble floors of the palace's west corridor. There are mustachioed men in stark white uniforms here, and women in fabulous dresses, some local, but most in a debauched Victorian style that favors tight corsets and ample cleavage. A few rakes in airmen's leathers similar to Rico's, goggles pushed back on their flying caps, stand in a knot from which sword sheathes jut like thorns. If they join in the chase after K.C. and Vaughan, as they're likely to, their little diversion could be over too soon. She's just going to have to trust the legendary swordsmanship and gymnastics of the Briton and his American friend.

The palace's grand salon isn't papered in gold but there's still enough silk, jade, and jewelry among the lolling elites to ransom an airship-load of the stuff. Vesta takes a quick look and is relieved that she recognizes no one. She glances up. Polished black pillars support a second-floor gallery, which should transmit the sound of the diversion to the ambassador's office. At least the blueprints seem to be accurate.

Without a word she and Ajanta separate from the other two, and Vesta cocks an arm for her to take. Compass's actual fingers twine around Sura's arm as they ascend to the second floor; the touch is electric. At the top, Ajanta takes a deep breath and brightens. "How do I look?" She twirls for Sura, who has to laugh.

"Beautiful! Now go get the bastard, while I make for the safe."

Ajanta's feet are noiseless on the soft carpet. Vesta takes one last look after her, then heads the other way. She has a few minutes before the diversion.

In a long corridor, she picks the lock on a tall wooden door and eases into a large chamber. The place is lit only by the moon, which is peeking down from the edge of a big ceiling dome. The wan, cross-hatched fan of silver sketches the spectronomer's work benches, kilns, and intricate glass devices. Still shadowed, the center of the room is hidden behind a circle of drapes hung from the beams ringing the dome.

The safe is either a metal box, or it's built into the wall. Sura pads around the perimeter of the room, looking high and low.

When she's about halfway around, she passes an equipment stand and *click!* A light comes on about ten feet in front of her.

The sudden pool of radiance reveals the spectronomer, sitting in a red leather armchair near a tall window. How long has he been half-curled here in the dark?

"I knew someone would come," he says smoothly. "You're interested in my machine, I know I know."

He looks to be about eighty, with a fringe of white hair around his bald skull and sunken cheeks. His spectacles have multiple interchangeable lenses, three of which are splayed out over his right brow, like a glass wing. He's wearing a white lab coat and a stained leather apron. Steepling his hands, he stands as Sura reaches for her pistol.

"Oh, tush, dear, there's no need for that. You see, there's nothing here that's portable enough for you to take. And all the notes and diagrams I use are stored . . ." he points at his temple, "here."

Vesta considers, then says, "Well, that's a disappointment."

He laughs in apparent delight. "Oh, don't be! In fact, be prepared to be amazed. I admit some of my recent tests have been . . . disappointing . . . but it's ready. It's finally finished and working to my satisfaction."

She eyes the exits. "What is?"

"Allow me to show you." He's pretty fast for such an old man; he nips over to a pulley rope and hauls on it, furling the circle of drapery hiding the center of the room.

The rising moon reveals a spherical machine, perhaps ten feet in diameter. It glitters faintly. As the spectronomer walks around it, Sura follows, but stops and gasps when they reach the flank illuminated by lunar light. The machine is apparently made entirely out of stained glass.

"Behold the kaleidoscaphe!"

With the emerging colors as his backdrop, the spectronomer throws out his arms like an impresario. "The culmination of my life's work! By cunning art, this sphere's six layers of carefully pigmented crystal can pivot 'round one another, concentrating light of precise spectral requirements on the center sphere—nay, removing that central sphere from all influences save that of an exact, chosen hue!"

"Nice," says Vesta. "But, um, what's it for?"

"Bah! Philistine." He gazes lovingly up at his contraption. The creeping moon has uncovered a hatch in its side. "Just as a bathyscaphe is a vehicle for exploring earthly oceans, the kaleidoscaphe travels through the dimension of color. We explore the seas with our devices and there discover many new and amazing forms of life; with the advent of the kaleidoscaphe, we can now seek out the wondrous denizens of orange, chartreuse, teal, or even—heaven forbid!—*beige*!"

He sidles up to her. "Have you never wondered what fabulous or monstrous creatures might inhabit royal purple? Or emerald? How vastly different the province of sapphire might be from its ostensible neighbor, ultramarine? I have thought these things, nay, I have dared the trip myself! And the things I have found, the things I have b-brought back . . ." He's no longer seeing Vesta, but gazing at nothing, his features shifting gradually into a rictus of horror.

It all clicks together suddenly, and Sura backs away. "The Jack Pine Murderer! That was you!"

"Me! Not me, no, but a, a mistake. Don't you see," he yammers as he paws at the cluttered top of a workbench. "One mistake cannot be allowed to silence decades of work. The potential! The possibilities, it can't end here. And if you've figured it out, that's unfortunate, because—" He rounds on her, a large pistol in his hand.

Vesta dives for cover, and—

"Hey! What th'fuck you doin' here?"

The voice rakes away the lab's carefully built soundscape, revealing an entirely different space around Sura—somewhere huge but empty.

The voice comes again. "Yeah, you, fucker!"

Sura mutes her glasses.

She's standing on a crumbling concrete gallery above an abandoned factory floor. The old building has roughly the same dimensions as the ambassador's palace, but it's a hollow shell. The tall rectangular windows are so begrimed that the river isn't even visible outside them. The slanting, dusted light picks out long parallelograms of cracked cement punctuated by up-thrusts of rebar and iron brackets. Vaughan and K.C. are standing down there, elbows jutting in surprise, as three men in overalls and yellow hard hats swagger toward them. Big and burly, they could be laborers or city inspectors—or something else entirely.

K.C. bolts, Vaughan right behind him. Have the hard-hats seen her up here? Sura takes a step back from the edge of the gallery and looks cautiously about. Compass is hunkered down behind a tarpaulin-shrouded heap of boxes. She's tapping frantically at the arm of her glasses, eyes focused on nothing.

The cold wash of adrenaline comes with a little interior voice that's saying, *They'll catch you and turn you over to* them. *Maybe these guys were sent here to find you. Maybe Jay got bought off. Maybe—*

She spares a glance at the real layout of the building, judges where the other available exits must be, then drops the glasses over her eyes again.

The spectronomer's lab, yes. The spectronomer hasn't found her, in fact he's on the far side of his device and heading for the door she came in. "It's all right," he's crooning. "Just fine. If I can't find you, I'm sure that pretty young distraction you sent to my office is still available. Jack must be fed, after all, mustn't he . . ."

The level still exists and the quest's still running. And Sura's just spotted the safe, which is against the wall under a large portrait of Queen Victoria.

She mutes the glasses and, hunkering down, scuttles over to the old factory's outer wall. This puts her out of sight of the floor below. Compass has taken off her glasses and is squinting at them; Sura will get to her in a second. She unmutes her own glasses. In the palace, she's just a couple of feet from the painting. Victoria is sending her a decidedly disapproving look.

Fuck you. Sura quickly enters the combination she was given back at the Grand Market. From inside she takes a large leather-bound book (which weighs nothing, it being virtual) and then runs for the lab's second door.

From Compass's point of view—glasses off, that is—what happens next must look bizarre. She'll see Sura take an odd, roundabout route to the edge of the gallery and then over to her. Sura mimes tapping something (or someone) at about shoulder height, and then throws an extravagant punch at empty air. "So much for the spectronomer," she says as she reaches for Compass's hand. Together they race down the rickety cement-and-iron stairs and out the factory's side door. They've gone half a block before Sura stops and mutes her glasses again. She grins at Compass and pats her jacket where, in *Rivet Couture,* Vesta will be patting her satchel, which contains the spectronomer's book.

"No need for the whole evening to be a waste," she says. It was the old *fuck-you* that drove her just now, which was utterly unwise. She can't explain to Compass, but instead peers into the deepening twilight. "Look, the guys got away too."

Vaughan looks spooked, K.C. is panting. Rico is unruffled. "Did you see?" he says. "I called the gamer protection service and their drones showed up in two minutes! The assholes took off as soon as they saw them."

"Some local gang, maybe?" says Vaughan, peering back the way they came.

K.C. leans over to put his hands on his knees. "That was awful," he says around gusting breaths.

Vesta tilts her head and purses her lips, gazing back at the brooding, black-windowed factory. "Oh, I dunno," she says with a shrug. "I think it went rather well!"

Then she notices how Compass is standing a bit apart, muttering and twisting her glasses in her hands.

"Compass? Are you okay?"

Compass takes a deep breath, puts on the glasses and shakes her head. "Th-They broke or something. Not working. I j-just need a, a character. I need . . ." She sits down on the ground, shaking, and wraps her arms around her knees.

"Hey . . ." says Vaughan, stepping forward.

"Are you hurt?" asks K.C. "I can call—" Compass shakes her head.

Sura kneels next to her. "How can I help you, Compass? Do you need to go home?"

Compass's braid bobs.

"And where is that?" Sura asks gently. "I can call us a car."

"Yes, a car," says Compass.

"I'll call one, but where are we going? Compass? Where's your home?"

"Cars."

"I know, I'll get one. Where do you live?"

". . . Cars," mumbles Compass. She raises tear-streaked eyes to match eyes with Sura for the first time over the frames of her glasses.

"I live in cars."

"Here," Sura says, and offers Compass her glasses. Compass's shoulders slump as she puts them on and they register her irises, switching accounts instantly to load her presets. Sura feels a sympathetic flood of relief, and something else, too: joy at being helpful to someone in their time of need. Like she used to be, for Mom.

But now, from the cardinal directions they come, Compass's guardian angels. First, a buzzing, canted, and obviously overloaded quadcopter appears above the factory skyline to the north. It wanders drunkenly in their direction, descending in lurches, and finally bombs them with a big oval package. The sack hits the sidewalk and doesn't bounce.

Another buzz and another drone arrives from the south. It's more sprightly and comes to hover over Compass, who reaches to pluck a plastic bag full of toiletries—and a replacement pair of glasses. Feet dragging, Compass retrieves the bigger parcel. It's got a sleeping bag and pillow in it.

From the west comes a change of clothes, and from the east, food. Vaughan and K.C. watch openmouthed. Sura stands with her arms crossed, glowering at the little helpers, whose very presence proclaims that she's unnecessary. Then, guilty that she's being selfish, she turns back to Compass, who's moving like she's drunk.

Vaughan says uncertainly, "Maybe she needs to go to the hospital?"

Of course that's ridiculous. Nobody can afford to do that. There are plenty of black market clinics, and maybe Compass even has insurance for them through the games. Sura finds herself stepping forward confidently. "I'll make sure she's okay."

K.C. and Vaughan will report the incident back at the Market; while they're calling their own ride, a car pulls up beside Compass. The vehicle's a hatchback with tinted windows. Compass stares at it listlessly for a while, then raises her hand. Its back hatch pops open.

"This is yours?" Sura looks inside. It's anonymous and clean. Looks like the rear seats fold down, and sure enough Compass climbs in and lowers one.

"No," she says. "It's just a car."

"A share?"

"Yeah, a share. Lots of people share for sleeping."

"I did not know that." If a car's got nothing better to do, it might as well make itself useful. But to sleep in one?

"I guess it can run the AC or heat or whatever?" She tries out the idea, as if tasting an unfamiliar dish. Compass unrolls a foam pad and lays out her sleeping bag. She looks miserable as she hauls her stuff in after her. As she's reaching to close the hatch Sura blurts, "Wait! You want company?"

Compass hesitates, shrugs, and flops back. Sura slips in, shuts the hatch, and the car starts moving. "Where are we going?"

"Somewhere near a public washroom."

"Oh. I guess that . . . makes sense." Sura watches the street slide by, the steering wheel turning by itself. Compass is curled up with her eyes closed.

"Compass? How long have you lived like this?"

Compass cracks one eye open. "I dunno. Few years."

"But why?"

"Cheap. Versatile."

"But I mean—don't you *own* anything?"

Compass shifts irritably. "I've unlocked lots of achievements. I have rights to things in my inventory. This is one."

Sura lies next to her, staring at the ceiling as the world turns this way and that. The lulling stop-and-go of light traffic could make her sleepy. "Have you got anybody? Family?"

Compass closes her eyes, and Sura knows the answer is complicated.

"My dad died recently," says Sura. "Mom a few years ago. Mom had cancer. We sold the house to pay for the treatment. It didn't work. And Dad . . ."

The car stops at a light. Motionless silence descends. Sura sneaks a glance at Compass. She might be asleep.

Sura purses her lips, tracing the edging around the windows with one outstretched hand. She wonders how you'd break into this particular brand of car.

She wants to help, but Compass is too self-contained. Everybody is, that's the lesson. Dad left. Mom didn't mean to leave, but in the end she was barely aware of Sura. Understandably so. But others . . . Over the years Sura's school friends have become strange to her, Jan's and Lindy's and Caroline's eyes no longer transparent but as opaque as metal, their smiles aimed not at her, but at best, at some memory of her that's now her substitute. Maybe the whole world is leaving, as climate change eats the coastlines, depression and isolationism pull the United Nations apart. America's divorcing itself too, like a giant tearing off its own limbs.

Sura left Dayton, and her last loyalties to place, which somehow felt like breaking a promise to Mom. Compass just left Sura. It goes on and on.

She frowns, looking out, and sees where they are. "Car?" she says. "Pull over, please."

Sura presses the buzzer and waits. After a minute a woman's voice comes through the speaker. "Who is it?"

"Hi. Um. I'm not sure you remember me. Asparagus girl? I helped Jeri with her groceries—"

"Oh, sure! What's up? Did Jeri invite you?"

"No, I was literally just in the neighborhood. Got dropped off here by—it's a long story. I dunno, I just thought—"

"I'll be right down."

Sura gnaws a fingernail, wondering why she's here. Compass's car left her near the bridge—that part's true. She's restless, she doesn't want to go home, and she remembers a certain excitement she felt on her previous visit. Maybe that's all the justification she needs.

Still, she's just about to walk away when Maeve appears behind the wired glass of the loft's inner door. She's dressed in full Goth gear: white pancake makeup, black eyeliner and ironed hair, leather, and even a dog collar. She looks Sura up and down, says, "Normcore Barbie? Kinky," and opens the door.

Sura glances back, aims a little fuck-you at the judgmental world, and follows her in.

Upstairs, they perch on makeshift seats in Jeri's kitchen, as thumping bass vibrates the dried herbs hung on the wall.

"Jeri's working?"

Maeve nods. "You look like you ran a marathon. What happened?"

"I was larping."

Maeve brays a laugh. "You're shitting me. I thought you were cool."

"I get paid for it."

"Naw. Really?"

"We should talk," says Sura, suddenly sensing a possibility. "But man, it's hot in here! Doesn't Jeri have air-conditioning?"

"Yeah, in her bedroom and the workshop." Maeve's fetching beers from the fridge. She shoots an arch look back at Sura. "Sweat looks good on you. But if you're dying, we can retire to the shop."

The long space, one wall windowed, the other backing on the kitchen, reminds Sura of the spectronomer's lab. There are workbenches; most of what Jeri does is custom leather work. And, oops, she'd forgotten all about the bed that's jammed into the far end. Or maybe she didn't. Maeve sits on it, her back against the painted brickwork, and Sura joins her. It's quieter here.

Her frustration's turned into quite something else. "Larping, huh?" says Maeve. "Tell me how that's cool."

Sura considers. "Sure, I'll tell you all about it. But if it's all right with you, I didn't actually come here to talk."

Maeve just smiles, tilts her head to let Sura know that she too hears the sounds coming from the dungeon. They share that for a long moment. Then she puts down her bottle.

Sura does the same, then reaches out.

CHAPTER SEVEN

Days pass, marked by the wallowing advent of a heat wave, and an influx into the city of tornado refugees. A feeling of tension settles onto the streets, yet somehow Sura is still eating, and still has a roof over her head. She commutes to different parts of town, and strange things happen. At the end of each day, she manages to have enough Gwaiicoin to pay for a little more life.

Lately she's been playing more as Vesta and doing less NPC work. Vesta's escapades have been limited to tricking rich old men out of their gold, distracting guards while a master thief climbs through a window, and generally making connections in the local underworld. It's fun, but she feels like she's treading water.

Despite the tension, or maybe because of the energy it adds, the fireteam seems to have coalesced into a tight unit. They get a lot done together.

She doesn't always go out with them, but she always looks for Compass when she comes to the market. Sura worries about her, a bit, and after the incident at the ambassador's palace, just wants to keep tabs on her. She has no other way to find her than to show up in person, since Compass has no presence in the games' social media.

One day Sura's browsing in the stalls under the fiery hammer of the midday sun, when a sunburnt older woman wearing a combination of beaded regalia and European dress approaches. Sura has not yet learned to read regalia, so she's not sure how important this Cahokian elder is; just to be sure, she bows deeply.

"There is something you could help us with," says the elder. She looks

Vesta over—or is it Sura? "You're young, we need that. You've got a good reputation *in virtua,* but how trustworthy are you in person?"

"What's the job?" A raid? An infiltration? Maybe some burglary? Local gym climbing walls sometimes substitute for Gothic facades that she and other second-story specialists have to scale.

"It's apples," says the old lady.

She turns grandly, indicating the four points of the compass. "When your people first saw this land, it puzzled them. The forests looked wrong. The trees were widely spaced, you could drive a cart between them. There was little underbrush. The trees themselves were almost all edible kinds—walnuts, right? They did not know that what they were seeing was not a wilderness, but one single, vast orchard stretching from the Great Lakes to Florida. *Our* orchard. After the Invasion, you turned the forests into a real wilderness, but some of the orchard remains. Your task today, Countess, is to find a piece of it.

"I hear you have companions. Go with them and find us some apple trees."

The old lady is virtual, but Sura has to resist the urge to mute her glasses to check. The uncanny feeling has come over her of a vast presence looming, of something speaking these lines in a whisper penetrating enough to pierce her layers of cynicism. She mumbles something incoherent and staggers away, hurriedly pinging the fireteam. "Apples," she blurts. "Meet me in the market."

While she waits, a Cahokian runner brings her a large satchel that turns out to be real. It's heavy. When she opens it she says, "What the shit?" and starts pulling out strange objects. Luckily, they're self-describing in Mixed Reality. By the time K.C., Vaughan, and Rico arrive, she thinks she knows what to do. "Let's find a carriage and head on out," she says to them. "This is a different kind of mission."

One of the many cars parked along the avenue is a late-model Hyundai with the *Proudly Eagle Owned!* logo on its side. There's just enough room for the four of them to cram in.

"After expenses," says the car in a warm voice, "all proceeds from this trip will go directly to Eagle Family 155 in the Northern Cascades clan area. By driving with us you're helping preserve our habitat and breeding area!

"If you want air-conditioning," it adds, "that will be an extra four Gwaiicoin."

"What kind of a quest is this?" asks K.C. "Apples? What the fuck?"

"The elder sent me a map," says Sura. "They've been flying drones around the city, identifying apple trees in empty lots and railroad easements and such." She hoists the satchel. "We're supposed to tag them with these Internet of Things sensors."

"What the fuck for?"

Vaughan gives a surprised laugh. "You're shitting me. They're gonna make these apples into an in-game *resource*?"

"Looks like."

The car drops them off at a thin slice of woods that cowers in the heat between two interstate overpasses. This land is totally useless, you can't put up a building here, not even a billboard. The arms of wild bushes jut up as if to ward off strangers. There's one cardboard-box hutch which was probably some homeless guy's habitat for a while, but it's drooped from the rain, tenting down as if trying to clamber underground. Sweating already, the fireteam ducks under and around the obstacles until they achieve the trees at the core of the space.

"Over here!" shouts Rico. "Here too!" comes from somewhere off to the right.

The satchel contains a nailgun. Vesta presses it against the trunk of one of the apple trees, and there's a *thunk* as something gets embedded in the bark. She thinks of Dad, and his trail of breadcrumbs.

They make several more trips around the city, and each time they do, the car they're riding in morphs into a cart loaded with apples. When they get back to the market they drive the virtual cart right past the main *RC* stalls, to a buzz of comment and even some appreciative applause.

"It's like we did something," she mutters to Vaughan. "Something mysterious."

"I kind of think we did," he says. He seems really excited, but she can't imagine why. "I'll tell you later."

When they line up and hold out their haul of virtual apple baskets to the Cahokian elder, the old woman nods gravely. They each receive two hundred Gwaiicoin; Vaughan's jaw drops, and K.C. mouths "Holy crap" to Sura.

As the ceremonial moment ends, the elder motions Vesta to walk with her. "We've been watching you," she says. "You have a rare skill set, much more physical than most players. And you've been recommended by one of our finest."

Compass? "Recommended? For what?"

"We call them 'frames,'" says the elder. "You've been playing in gameworlds, but there are frameworlds too. They take the games to the next level, and they use your imagination in a different way. You seem to have the right gifts for them, so we may call on you, once you've got a more stable identity. Meanwhile, I have a gift for you." She reaches into the haversack at her side and brings out something small. She hands it to Sura.

It's a virtual broach, carved out of turquoise in the shape of a bird. Is it regalia?—No, Vesta's a colonial, she has no right to wear regalia. Still, it's something more than decoration. As she goes to clip it to her jacket, the elder raises her hand.

"Not yet," she says. "Wait until you are ready."

Puzzled but intrigued, Sura bows and steps away. "That was cool, but weird," she mutters to Vaughan.

He scans the crowds, as if expecting spies, and then hauls on her arm, waving the other two along. "Shit!" he says when they've found a marginally less boiling-hot spot under some trees. "Did you *see* that? I mean, did you take it in?"

"I took in way too much sunlight," she says. "I think I've got heatstroke." Groaning, she lies down on the grass and pokes at some virtual menus above her head.

Despite the heat, Vaughan is pacing on the grass. "What we did today—I've been checking. *Rivet Couture*'s part of some kind of global resource commons. It gets players to tag things that can be shared, like people's services, say if you've got an electrician's certification. Or cars, tool libraries, you know? And then it uses game scenarios to bring all those resources together to accomplish something."

"Apples," says Rico wearily. "You're talking about the apples." He too is on his back, an arm flung over his eyes.

"Not just apples. They intercept and repurpose food that's not pretty enough for the supermarkets. Otherwise it's often just thrown out. They're doing this worldwide!"

"Surely that's illegal," says K.C. "Who're they taking it from?"

"That's the point, it's like those apple trees. Not owned by anybody—or if it is, it's being ignored and wasted. They get to use it because nobody else cares."

K.C. looks uncomfortable. "That doesn't seem right."

"But I've been wondering about it—you know, how so much of what we get as achievements is *real,* like that free meal I got yesterday for breaking up the Salusa gang . . ."

Sura mutes her glasses and stares up at the tree branches, which are all stuck in mid-writhe in the heat. She thinks about the mysterious packages delivered, the people ferried here and there, the documents and the conspiratorial meetups. They're all part of a made-up world, and yet, so many of those deliveries are physically real. So many of the meetings involve difficult decision-making for stakeholders. Conflict resolution. Legal fine points. Urban planning in the Cahokian frontier . . .

"Naw," she says, and throws her arm over her face in imitation of Rico. "I don't believe it. I don't think we did shit today.

"Wake me up when something real happens."

Leaning in Jeri's doorway, Sura says, "Listen, there's another reason I came by. I want to make a call over the mesh." Maeve arches an eyebrow. "I know I could do it through the game network, but that's usually overloaded and, the fact is I don't completely trust it."

Maeve twists her purple lips. "Must be a hell of a call." Sura nods and Maeve tries out some more banter, obviously hopeful about why Sura's here. They've hooked up three times now, but it's clear to Sura that for both of them the sex has been a pressure-relief valve more than anything serious. Maeve shrugs and says, "Come on." They go back to the workshop. Sura sits on the familiar bed, looks at distant gulls wheeling, and thinks about all the things she can no longer say to her parents. Lost words, like birds dwindling over the horizon.

She unmutes her glasses and makes the call.

"Yeah'llo?" It's a voice-only connection, not surprising if he's still in eastern Peru.

"Hi, Remy Heath? You don't know me, I'm Sura Neelin. I'm Jim Neelin's daughter."

There's a long pause. "Jesus. Sura, yeah, he talked about you. Sorry about what happened."

One thing Sura learned after Mom's death is that words really do fail you; you have to forgive people for saying too little, it's all they're capable of in the moment. She nods, realizes he can't see that, and says, "Thanks. It must have been hard for you. Taking care of all the arrangements . . ."

"You should have been the executor! Or, or at least next of kin. But Jim always said he wanted to keep you as far away as possible from what we did. I think that's what he was up to. Not that he had much to will you anyway . . ."

She longs to follow that thread, but instead, with difficulty, says, "What exactly *were* you doing down there?"

"At the site? Following up on a lead. The companies and the government, they rely on the monitoring equipment, but we'd been getting calls about leaks that weren't showing up in the data. Thing is, the data's on a blockchain, it's supposed to be tamper-proof. Jim—your dad, he figured it was, but GIGO, you know?—garbage in, garbage out. If the monitors were feeding crap to the system to begin with . . . with blockchains, they call that the 'oracle problem.' The smart contracts that coordinate the monitoring system, they're totally trustworthy, but they rely on data from the real world. Corrupt that data, you corrupt the contract."

"So you went out to test the monitors?"

"Jim did. I'm not a field man, I wouldn't have been any good. But just before . . . Jim called me. Said there was no evidence of tampering, but he'd found one leaky well and the sensor next to it, it was right in the plume of sour gas. He asked me to go online and check the blockchain record for that sensor. I did—and it didn't show the gas at all. He . . . actually seemed pleased. I asked him to bring the sensor back."

"Do you have it?"

"Yes. I've got the stuff he had on him. Frankly, didn't know what to do with any of it. You want me to send it to you? I've looked at it but I don't have the resources here to take it apart, you know, forensically. And, well I don't trust the local labs . . ."

"Yeah! Yeah, could you ship it back? A-All of it. I can't take anything too big . . ." The mailbox she rents three floors down from here won't hold a box of clothes. "But whatever he had on him, that would be great."

"Listen, there was more. He went everywhere with this orange backpack. It wasn't with the body. A couple of days before he died we were talking, and he sounded worried. Said he was scared the local police were going to shake him down, confiscate his stuff. Said . . . something odd, I'm trying to remember the words . . ."

"What?"

"Ah, that was it: he said he'd been on a snark hunt, and had proven something important, but that he was afraid someone was following him. Said he'd found something important but had to 'hide the key down a borehole.'"

"Key to what? Down a borehole? You mean, like a wellhead?"

"I guess so. He never told me where. I don't know if it really means anything, but that conversation, I keep thinking about it."

"Yes, we need to follow up on that. Can I give you an address to ship out his things?"

"Once I know you are who you say you are," he adds, suddenly cautious. Did it really take him this long to get paranoid? She shakes her head in disbelief.

"Right. I'll get Marj to vouch for me. That be good enough?"

"Sure. The address?" She gives it, in a bit of a haze, and rings off.

As she drifts out of the workshop, Maeve asks, "How'd it go?" It's all Sura can do to say "Fine." Instead of the loft and Jeri's absurdly painted dungeon, all she can see is Dad's coat, his boots, overalls, in her mind stained with oil. Evidence of a man where none now remains.

"Hey," she says, her voice rough. "You want to hear a crazy story . . . ?"

She calls Marj but can never get through so leaves a message about Remy. More days pass, each one bounded by the fear of bounty hunters or the FBI or the border police hauling her into a dark car. Between these bookends, her time is spent in a succession of worlds, each weirder than the last. Yet however fantastical they become, Sura is always reeled back, in the end, to one place: sitting on a sagging bed in Dan and Walter's basement in Shadyside, paging through the mesh's game gossip by the light of an Ikea lamp.

It smells of mildew down here. The drywall is painted olive green and has no baseboards. Aside from the bed and a side table just big enough to hold the lamp, there's nothing in the room but Sura's backpack.

On this particular night, at Maeve's urging, she's spent half an hour making herself a character for a game called *Encounters*. You can skin yourself however you want in the sexual games—even scan your naked body and use that. *Encounters* is a world of subtle innuendo and voyeuristic moments and can be activated within a number of other games, including *RC*. Supposedly you can safely find compatible partners and hook up; or just sexually browse your fellow players. Maeve is sure this is the cure for what ails Sura—and theoretically Purrloin will give her anonymity she could never have had before—but at a certain point she realizes that for the past five minutes she's been ignoring the slowly rotating doll-version of herself, just staring at the wall behind it.

She dismisses the *Encounters* character room. A little digging in her backpack and she puts Ganesha next to the lamp. If she wakes later in total darkness, she can reach out to put the contours of his head under her hand and, for at least that moment, feel watched over.

All across the city other people sit as she is, all dropping equally empty activities to stare at blank walls. A million people in a million rooms, aimless as abandoned toys. This is a night feeling, though more than once in recent years it's flooded Sura during daylight hours too.

Her world's a waiting room. She goes from one chair that's not hers to another chair that's not hers, trapped in between destinations, maybe forever. *Rivet Couture* and its relatives are the ultimate airport lounge, where millions sit together yet remain alone.

Mom? Dad? If only she could feel their presence—and she tries, longing her way through the walls, up the garden fence, above the soughing treetops and wary streetlights. Remembering again the trail of breadcrumbs that Dad used to leave wherever he went, she imagines following it, in astral form, across continents, down lost rivers. This is something she's never really done because in reality his trails lead to brown, stained oil disasters, leaking wellheads, post-apocalyptic clear-cuts where forests have been slaughtered.

If she was any kind of daughter, she'd be in Iquitos now, tracking down whoever killed him. She could follow his trail, maybe find that backpack Remy said he'd hidden. More likely, though, Dad's breadcrumbs would just lead her to one particular clear-cut, and one wellhead. She sees herself walking up to it as if it were Dad's tombstone, but it's more than that, it's also the weapon that killed him, an iron avatar of the angel of death.

She opens her eyes with a shudder. The aftermath of the vision stretches, a minute silent and basement-cold.

She's up and moving, in the hallway with no destination in mind. Half the floor is taken up by Dan and Walter's store, which is closed but whose wares are still visible behind the glass door. She cups her hands and peers at the typical steampunk gear: aviator's caps, corsets and Edwardian skirts, women's felt car coats and bomber jackets, brass belt-buckles, and on and on. It all looks tawdry, but when she retrieves her glasses and looks again in Mixed Reality, the artifacts come alive with individual histories and significance. As if they have been given souls by Story.

Is Vaughan right? Is this some new mode of economic life? A replacement for the feckless drudgery she was taught to accept? Or just a new training wheel for the rats in capitalism's maze?

Whatever it is, it's made her feel more alive than anything has in a long time. More than memories of her lost family. She roves outside of *Rivet Couture* now. There's *Encounters.* Other games are art happenings, or giant self-help groups, a reassembly of AA and other step programs around a new paradigm where one's recovery from crack addiction becomes the noble and fiery quest of a hero. In these scenarios, she's no longer living her life, she's performing it, with these capes and gloves and riding crops as guides and talismans.

In such a world, shoveling garbage on the edge of town becomes meaningful where carting boxes around a warehouse wasn't—and it's only then that you realize that somewhere along the way, the whole grand epic of Progress and Civilization that you were born into must, correspondingly, have lost its meaning. Maybe it happened while your attention was elsewhere; maybe it came after the thirtieth or thousandth hypocritical pratfall by the larpwrights of Globalization.

Sura's smart glasses permit many overlays on top of normality—gaming, celebrity spotting, news; she can paint a weather map on the sky and count the isobars and pressure gradients. She craves what *Encounters* promises, but it seems too contrived and she's not sure she wants to parade herself—even a virtual version of herself—around town.

She can find no overlay for what she needs tonight.

Quietly, she goes upstairs and eases open the back door. It's a clear night, but hot, as all nights are these days. For a while she stares up and out, toggling different views over the indistinct city.

Then she remembers the broach the Cahokian elder gave her. She loads it and makes the motion that would pin a real ornament to her T-shirt.

Oddly, its overlay demands she shut down all her other ones before it will activate. Sura hesitates, then shrugs. She's safe for the moment, rounded as these streets are by drone patrols, license-plate cameras, and police. She darkens a dozen skies and pins the bird to her breast.

Sound—a vast cry pouring in from the horizon.

"Shit!" She snatches off the glasses, but there were words there, written on the air. Cautiously, she puts the glasses on again. The noise isn't loud, but it's . . . full, tumbling over all frequencies.

The words a few feet in front of her say *This is what this place sounded like before humans arrived.*

Sura puts her hands to her ears as the chirping, warbling, and chattering of a million lives washes round her, a chaos overtopped with whistles and underpinned by the dark *ziz-ziz* of cicadas. She can't identify even a tenth of the voices, but the night is fully aroar with them, everywhere in every direction. She staggers back, stumbles on the step, and sits down. The night cries. So does she, suddenly, but silently lest Walter or Dan come upon her. She doesn't know those men, they don't deserve to see her like this.

Eventually, she takes off the pin and, drained, moves quietly and smoothly inside. Already half dreaming, she lays down to sleep.

CHAPTER EIGHT

Over the next week, as Vesta networks her way through *RC* society, Sura is occasionally blocked from entire areas of town by big virtual walls. When she mutes her glasses she can see smoke, burnt-out storefronts, black people standing around. There's nothing on the few TV news stations and websites that are left after the lawsuits and the Truth Bill. It's clear though that the heat and tension of the summer are building up to something—probably exactly the same something that's been going on since before she was born. Rioting, marching, inexplicable outbreaks of violence, all papered over by the blinded normalcy of reality TV, goofball comedies, and movie star gossip. And meanwhile, fewer and fewer jobs, more and more scapegoating, the inexorable draining of America's lifeblood through an unstaunched wound.

In the games it's different. Her overlays tell her what streets she can safely walk down and where to detour. They tell her what stores to avoid because they're connected into the facial recognition cameras of surveillance capitalism. They pinpoint traffic cams, police drones, bodycams, and known gang members who are also working hard to avoid being seen. Half the city is lurking, it seems, deploying measures and countermeasures, trying to figure out who's who and who to trust. The very geography of the place bows under the weight of all these gazes.

A bit of relief comes when, one morning, Maeve shows up at the market.

They hug, then Maeve pulls her top off-shoulder to display a leaping tiger tattoo. It's pretty red and raw. "Ouch!" says Sura. "Good thing that's not your flogging arm."

"Ha! Jeri doesn't let me whip anybody. Mostly, for insurance reasons. There's not that much good old-fashioned beating goes on anyway. Domination is almost entirely psychological. Jeri's a licensed psychiatrist."

"Really?"

"Well, and a registered member of the Boilermakers' Union." Maeve smirks. "Hey, thanks for telling me about the games. Not sure they're not all bullshit—I'd just rather not have to pay my way through school by pandering to the perversions of rich perverts. If you want to get in touch with me, my tattoo's name is Knife Fairy. I'm Annabelle in *Rivet Couture.*"

"Knife Fairy, cool. You know I'm Countess Vesta. I'll show you around. I was serious when I said I could use another woman on my fireteam."

She shows Maeve the market, darting enthusiastically from sight to sight. "Yes, Germany! After we board the zeppelin, this market's going to be closed to us until we get back. We'll have three days where only the zeppelin will be real in *RC*, but naturally it'll be packed with intrigue. When we get to Europe all kinds of locales will be visible that are locked for us right now. Europe's all over town so, like, I hear Prague is bigger than this—Oh! There's Compass!"

She waves, but Compass is Mad Scratchie today and won't answer to any other name. He's lurking around a craft stall, and as usual has the look of somebody caught doing something they shouldn't. "Cousin Annabelle, meet Scratchie. He's a denizen of the underworld, and a great source of information."

"Charmed," says Scratchie, leaning hard and long on the *R* as he bows before the Knife Fairy. "Countess, I seen some'f yer mates yonder. Ye might be lookin' for them?"

"I might indeed. Scratchie, Cousin Annabelle and I are trying to bury the hatchet in a very old family feud. I'm hoping she'll come with me to Germany, and meanwhile I promised to introduce her around to Cahokian society."

He leans in. "Do you think that wise, ma'am?"

They find the boys and Sura introduces "Cousin Annabelle." Her lads are building a vast pile of steamer trunks, satchels, kit bags, and crates—almost entirely virtual—that they'll be taking to Europe.

Maeve shrugs. "Well they're not real. Why not store them online in, like, a bag of holding or something, and pull them out when you need them?"

Vaughan shakes his head. "It doesn't work that way."

"Why not? Like, why this elaborate pretense that you're actually traveling? If Prague is literally right next door, why not just teleport there?"

"Some worlds you can. But they have to stay consistent for everybody. There's no teleportation in *Rivet Couture*'s universe."

Scratchie's eyes are darting everywhere, but for once he seems to be listening to the conversation. Shading his beetle-brows with one hairy hand, he says, "M'lady, where do you think we *are*, exactly?"

"Trick question," says Maeve. "Pittsburgh.—But the nineteenth-century steampunk version."

"Aye. And since this be a game, we could just as easily be in Tel Aviv, or Cairo, or Johannesburg. Right?

"'Cept you can't just jump around in *Rivet Couture*," he goes on. "This ain't yer ordinary gameworld. It's open-source, built on a public blockchain, and everythin' in the game is nailed to an encrypted set of GPS coordinates. Pittsburgh can't be moved or duplicated, and yer Annabelle is unique, too."

"So what?"

Scratchie does the impatience dance, but all he can say is, "But it's important!"

Vaughan steps in. "It used to be, data could be copied infinitely. There was never such a thing as a 'unique file.' If it's data, it can be copied, by definition. You remember file sharing, DRM, piracy, all that bullshit?" Maeve frowns and shakes her head. "Well, point is I scan a painting or make a piece of software or a will, and boom! anybody who gets hold of the file can upload it onto the Internet and suddenly there's millions of copies floating around. Nobody can say which is the official one."

"Yeah—"

"But that can't happen in a blockchain. A blockchain lets you say which copy is the *real* one. In *Rivet Couture,* that means there's just one Pittsburgh, one Cousin Annabelle who can only be in one place at a time, and—"

"One Mad Scratchie." She smiles at Compass.

"One Mad Scratchie. And *that* means that here, the digital world behaves in critical ways like the real, physical world."

"Ooookay, but how does this—"

"It means that *Rivet Couture*'s Pittsburgh is, in some senses, like a real place. And the things in it, even the virtual ones, share that reality."

Maeve crosses her arms. "O . . . okay, but you guys play with a lot of real stuff. What's to stop me smuggling one of your real bags into Prague?"

Vaughan shakes his head. "Have you got something small and portable? In the real world, I mean with you."

Sura digs into her fanny pack, comes up with lipstick. "It has to be expendable," says Vaughan.

"Oh," says Maeve. She looks around, and dives on a crumpled Coke can near one of the park's overflowing garbage bins. "This do?"

"Perfect. Hold it up." Vaughan sets his glasses' camera to hi-res mode and leans in. "Now turn it around . . ."

A few turns and he's scanned in the can. With a magician's flourish, he makes its digital counterpart visible in MR; Sura fully expects that to be a virtual version of the can, available now to any player in *Rivet Couture*'s alternate Pittsburgh. It's not—instead, the virtual thing he's showing Annabelle is a small leather purse. "It's like biometrics," he says. "Like measuring the contours of somebody's face, except we measured the 'face' of the can. Just like you can use your face to unlock something online, I can now use the can as the key to a virtual thing. So. I've just put five Gwaiicoin in this purse—that's about fifty bucks if I were to exchange it for NotchCoins and then dollars. It's all registered in the blockchain—the wallet's position in Rivet-land, and that it has five Gwaii in it. But you can only get at that five Gwaii with a scan of the can."

"So?"

He tosses the can in the trash. Maeve stares after it for a second, then yelps "No!" and runs to retrieve it.

"Exactly," says Vaughan dryly. He fishes in his pocket and comes up with a ten-dollar bill. "I could just as easily morph this into a promissory note to pay me five Gwaiicoin and get you to put your digital signature on it."

"Not sure you can turn a dollar bill into a negotiable instrument," comments K.C., but Vaughan waves him away.

"*Point* is," he says, "we can transform a thing into another thing. Give value to an object, or negative value. Make hybrids—half-real, half-virtual, like game houses whose rooms correspond to real ones in buildings scattered all over the world."

A light is dawning in Maeve's eyes. "They've digitized performative utterances! But what good does it . . ."

Sura has no idea what a performative utterance is, but she's made a connection herself: "The apples! I get it. That Coke can, it was like printing money. Money's just paper, until the government says it's something more. And then it's . . ."

"Something more." It's Mad Scratchie, but he's looking at Maeve as he says this. "There's only one thing that can change a c-crumpled can into something worth d-dumpster diving for. It's *power.* Used to be only big institutions had this power. But Vaughan just turned a p-pop can into five Gwaii, and no government nor bank could have turned it back without the can."

Maeve looks from Vaughan to Compass and back again. "This is crazy shit! Tell me more!"

Vaughan starts to speak, but Scratchie smoothly steps between them. "M'lady, in any world, power comes from being able to name things. Name them new, and you disappear from that world. That's always been true, but there's a new force at play. A kind of amplifier. You just caught a glimpse of it.

"If you'd like a guide . . ." Scratchie bows. "Consider me your white rabbit, Alice. Come with me. Wonderland awaits."

This is totally a line, and the corniest of lines at that. Sura and Vaughan glower at Compass, but it's too late. She and the Knife Fairy exit, stage left.

The heat rises and rises, and as one more boiling night descends on the city, the people break before the weather can. The TV and Internet news sites don't cover the riots that spill into Polish Hill and Upper Hill's streets, but suddenly Jeri's messaging all her friends, warning them to stay away from the Strip. She sends a direct message for Sura: "A big package is jamming up your mailbox. But it's not safe to come by here. Can you wait a few days?"

Antsy and frustrated, Sura steps out into the saturated evening air and sees nothing unusual. When she puts on her glasses, the mesh lights the city up with warning flags. She stands there for a while, pulling in video feeds and messages. Only gradually does she become aware that some of the sirens she hears are reaching her through ordinary air, and not through her earpieces.

Her landlords come out to share the ambience. "It's '68 all over again," says Dan glumly. Walter shakes his head.

"It's not about race this time. It's the goddamn GI Act."

"Which is still about race."

The Republicans have been messing with the Guaranteed Income Act. Sura had lost interest when she found out that you'll have to give up your full biometrics, plus DNA, to get the supposedly "no-questions-asked" government handout. Now Walter tells her that the Act has been changed to exclude anyone with a prior felony conviction. Since poverty's been effectively criminalized for decades, a huge swath of the underclass stands to be disenfranchised from both the vote and the GI. And that underclass is disproportionately African American.

Dan and Walter sleep with the lights on, and Sura barely sleeps at all. In the morning, there are troop carriers downtown, and *The White Rose* has gone into full-blown paranoia mode.

In *Rivet Couture*'s Germany, Countess Vesta, her cousin Annabelle, and their lads build reputations among players who actually live in Europe. They compare common pool resources in Pennsylvania and Berlin, and start conspiracies and intrigues that are thinly disguised trade agreements. When there's no progress to be made in *RC,* Sura finds herself volunteering in *The White Rose* and its sister world, the feminist protection league known as *The Movement.* It's easy for her to think like a partisan, since she's no stranger to lurking in the shadows; besides, configuring and reconfiguring paths across the city is fun.

When she encounters Compass, they play other games, in which the goal is to find out who hasn't eaten today, who's living under a bridge, and who—like Sura Neelin—is running from forces too big to fight.

Surprisingly, she finds herself opening up to the one person she would never have expected. Jay knows who she really is. He seems genuinely not to be judging her, despite dissing the rest of the world vocally and all the time. Their conversations are almost entirely by secure mesh email, but it's a conversation, nonetheless, with someone who's met *her.*

So the worlds come and go, crises rise and fall in reality and in their imaginations—and in late July rain finally comes to the city. With its passing, the landscape's dark mood seems to lift, at least for now. In real life, roadblocks disappear, and in *The White Rose*'s Warsaw, roads and alleys morph back into being, eventually forming a maze that will allow Sura to safely visit the Strip District.

Sura finds a big enough dumpster a few blocks from Jeri's loft, and hurls the box into it. She can barely see past tears, so she sits on the curb. Clubbers drift by, some noting her, nobody asking how she is. She imagines the tides and ebbs of humanity that fill the city, all of them surging around her, no one seeing.

Damn Remy Heath for sending her everything. If she can't have her dad, what good are his clothes? Their emptiness just mocked her. She didn't recognize anything in his water-damaged wallet except the face on his driver's license. She didn't recognize the shirt and shorts he'd been wearing. Stained and dried to a kind of cracked patina, they said it all: some man she didn't know had been alive, and then he'd fallen in his tracks in a foreign country and is gone. Mom wasn't there to know him. Sura wasn't there. He died alone. That she's also alone doesn't create any commonality between them.

Remy did come through on everything, though. In a zipped pocket of Dad's nylon windbreaker is a little metal rod with a grille on its end. It looks like a microphone, but she's seen its like in her online searches for environmental sensors. Someone (Remy or Dad) has wrapped it in the kind of metal mesh that's supposed to block radio signals.

The sensor, and the wallet, are all she'll keep.

When her eyes are finally dry, she looks up and realizes where she is. *The White Rose* has declared this street safe, although this is a part of town that should be fiercely surveilled. It's close to where the riots happened, but the residents have pushed back against any cameras. She spots one drone hovering above the roofline, but her glasses tell her it's a neighborhood-watch hawk that's there to keep others out.

This is Lawrenceville. She's heard a rumor about this place—and Compass.

Flipping back through the years she finds other incarnations of the area. Where she is now, sandwiched between tall glass condos, there were once car-oriented shops with quaint names like Midas and Goodyear. She doesn't even know where cars go to get serviced these days; they just send you a text to tell you that they're doing it and disappear for a few hours.

Due to the lack of surveillance, her MR overlays are more sparse than usual—but part of the rumor at least, is true. The number of *Diminuendo* hotspots around here is crazy.

Virtual flags stand over the cityline, proclaiming the kind of music you'll find in renovated storefronts, back alleys, house porches. She can hear Appalachian bluegrass drifting on the night breeze. She's been told about an empty discount clothing store that's near the river. In the larp called *Diminuendo,* it's currently a rather posh house in Leipzig.

The rumor is that Compass can sometimes be found in this place, or others like it. Not NPCing, but actually playing.

It's not some *Encounters* lounge; with all that she knows about Compass, this virtual house is a somehow more enticing mystery.

Emotionally drained, she lets her feet steer her and soon finds a real-world building that fits the description. It's surrounded by a palisade of plywood cladding that proclaims the imminent construction of a fifteen-story tower that, from the virtual model her glasses insist on thrusting in front of her, seems indistinguishable from the one across the street. It might be a condo, but none of the owners will live in it. Despite its appearance of wealth, each one- or two-bedroom suite is likely to have two or three families renting it, or it'll be shared round-robin, like cars are.

That the same is true for the houses on the side streets is just a sign of how invisible poverty has become these days.

She's been afraid of *Diminuendo* because of how strongly music and memory intertwine for her. She should go home. But home is a basement, and she'll be even more alone there. So, Sura dials herself back to 1828 and dons a Regency version of Countess Vesta, though you don't have to roll a character to visit here. In *Diminuendo,* the building is indeed an old mansion. Vesta nods imperiously to the (virtual) footman at the door and is let into the home of the director of the Colditz Castle lunatic asylum. It's immediately apparent why she's here.

Something extraordinary is flooding the air of the tall, stuffy rooms. A-dance, alive in an almost inhuman way, rolling and crashing tides of piano music are chasing each other about the place. The servants have paused in their duties, stunned. Even a giant old hound, sprawled by the fireplace in the sitting room, has raised its head to look.

The sound is coming from further within; Sura finds her way blocked by the backs of men and women, who are jammed in the hall, oblivious of anything except what's happening in the music room. She walks through the virtual and around the real, and stepping inside the amber-lit cube at the heart of the house, discovers what all the fuss is about.

A little girl is attacking the piano, like a wolf trying to savage its way through the hide of a downed buffalo. She lunges, flings herself from side to side, and her hands hammer the keys. Her arms can barely span the octaves. An arresting and deeply emotional tower of sound soars above her. Her name is Clara Josephine Wieck, and she can't be more than eight years old.

Sura mutes her glasses and sees the real performer: Cargo pants, sneakers, a T-shirt, and a utility vest patterned in Desert Storm camouflage. There's a baseball cap on the piano bench next to her (and it's a real piano, incongruous in this abandoned store). Bouncing behind her as she plays is a very long braid. The muscles in her arms and the nape of her neck bunch and slide as she attacks the instrument with the same skill and ferocity as her avatar.

Nobody watching her is able to move, either in reality or *in virtua;* in *Diminuendo,* the shock on the faces of the mustachioed burghers and black-gowned dowagers is delightful to behold. It's as if a squad of Mormon missionaries had taken a wrong turn and wound up in the spit-zone of a death metal concert.

Mom would have loved this.

Sura hangs back until Compass is done. As she raises her hands, the last chord hanging in the air, the audience erupts in calls of "bravo!" and "hear hear!" The burghers are overcome, and while they wipe tears from their eyes, the performer looks up, sees Sura, and smiles.

Sura bumps her hip against the piano, twists her hands together. "Hi! That . . . that was amazing!"

"Thanks." After that initial smile, Clara/Compass's face goes back to a neutral expression. Sura hesitates.

"I . . . I didn't know this place was here." Sura looks around the crowd, which is about half virtual. "You never talked about it."

"I don't come here for money. You said you needed money." Compass nods at the man who's playing the old, bald owner of the house. "Want to watch me p-play through? Clara is about to meet Robert Schumann, who's nine years older. He'll wait until she's eighteen and then p-propose. His love letters are the music he writes, and she'll play it and write her own, and they'll be the darlings of Europe until one day, Robert starts hearing a sound—a single note—that he can't get out of his head. And he'll begin to go mad."

This is Compass talking. *This is Compass!* Sura realizes she's grinning and mutes herself a bit. Impatient though she is, she steps aside and watches for the next hour as Compass plays through the drama of Clara Schumann's first meeting with her future husband.—And it's the strangest thing: Sura can feel the ghost of her mom standing with her, enjoying Sura's enjoyment of everything that's happening.

Why didn't I do this before?

As the larp winds down, Sura approaches Compass. She's telling a small crowd about Johannes Brahms, whom the Schumanns will take under their wing, and who will later console Clara in her grief.

"So you like Schumann," Sura says when Compass runs out of breath.

She knows a tiny bit about romantic composers—mostly, that they all died young.

"I like Schubert better," says Compass. "And Haydn more th-than either."

"Haydn?" Sura vaguely remembers listening to interminable, identical symphonies at home—sonic wallpaper that Mom used to put on when she was working. "He's boring."

"Boring? Because he was never a b-bad boy like Mozart or a star like the Schumanns?" For once, Compass's face is lit up with some spirit that's not borrowed. "But you can actually meet him in his music. C-Connect what's on the outside, with what's inside."

Sura senses something very important to Compass in that statement. Is it like the way Sura meets Mom through her music? "Meet him? What do you mean?"

"The music . . ." Compass looks a bit embarrassed. "It's a light. F-Follow it, sometimes you f-find the man."

Sura nods, though she's not sure she understands. Maybe music is Compass's fuck-you. Maybe it's like Mom. She wants to know more.

"Hey, did you give some kind of testimonial for me to the Cahokians?"

Compass's attention snaps back to her. "Yes. You do improv well."

"So what's the business with these 'frames'? They let you trade in real assets or something?"

"They're where game economy tokens meet real world commodities. You d-don't see many of them here. Not yet. Some p-places, though . . ." Compass gazes away again for a moment. "I want to move to Oneota. Lots g-going on there."

"Oneota?"

"*Rivet Couture*'s making a cloud country. It's being instantiated in D-Detroit. It's a place where your in-game assets c-can get you real services. Health care. Marriage and property rights and stuff like that."

This kind of makes sense since Detroit's already a sanctuary city, and a member of the Urban Alliance. They're wildly progressive, and have stepped in to provide benefits the feds used to.

Compass eyes her, a speculative twist to her brows above the light-filled glasses. "In some places, the only work is in-game. In some, the *best* work is in-game. Countess Vesta might think about moving too."

"Oh. Well . . ." Detroit is where Summit Recoveries is located. Sura's not sure whether moving next to the headquarters of the mercenary outfit that's trying to find her is such a good idea.

Compass does a tiny hop, once, with both feet. "H-Hey, you want to meet Felix Mendelssohn? He's sixteen, his little sister is doing an amateur production of Shakespeare's *Midsummer Night's Dream* in their b-backyard, so Felix has written some music for it . . ."

Once again Compass is Sura's boatman to another shore, only tonight their destination is music. If anything can erase the hollowness she feels, the box of clothing she didn't even recognize, and the dumpster she threw it in, then it's this. Music defies death like nothing else, for it lives in the present moment. Her last days with Mom, when symphonies and songs filled the house, taught her that. Somehow, she'd forgotten.

Guided by this girl who makes her remember, Sura takes the journey.

CHAPTER NINE

"I can't meet you at the diner," she tells Jay. "It's not safe."

It's night in *The White Rose*, the sky is bisected by roving searchlights, and she's lurking behind a trash bin while the SS does a house-to-house sweep near the previously safe restaurant. Depending on who you are, this is not an illusion, but a metaphor. It's true that outside Mixed Reality it's morning, the air is clear, bicycles are purring and skateboards are rattling by; an old lady is walking her schnauzer and Sura can see Jay sitting in the diner with somebody. She's not actually crouching, she's just sent that emote to the game, which has told her where to stand to remain out of the sightline of whatever is watching the place. But she knows the real street isn't the *real* street. She's been playing this game long enough.

"Sorry for the inconvenience, but you know what's at stake. Why don't you meet me at the Water Steps?"

She can see him lean back, running a hand through his mullet. "Are you kidding me? That's a public plaza. It's, like, festooned with cameras!"

"Yes, but the facial-recognition ones are owned by a private security contractor that cut too many corners. The algorithums generate so many false positives that the feds have taken to charging these clowns for every one. So right now, the cameras at the Water Steps are face-blind."

"And all the tourists wearing cameras, with their own Interpol connections and—"

"Got it covered, Jay. Just meet me there, okay?"

She finds them seated at one of the crescent benches near the hurrying streams of the Steps. Jay always looks exactly the same, he's as constant as a stone, so she notices that his smart glasses are new, and high end. The sandy-haired, goateed man he's with is also wearing. This guy has on a plaid shirt over a white T, a uniform as specific as a *Rivet Couture* waistcoat. He's at least forty, an MBA or a programmer or something else equally obsolete.

When Jay called her yesterday and suggested this meet, he'd used the words "client" and "contract." These two words are the only thing Sura remembers about their conversation. They're why she's here.

"Hi," says the hipster. He's clearly not sure whether to shake her hand or stick his own in his pockets. "Jay says you know your way around the games."

"I do. Would you like to share a world?" Really, she knows enough to know that she's barely scratched the surface of the open-source universes—and has never visited the commercial ones at all. She plants an offer in the air, and both Jay and his guest reach for it—Jay awkwardly, the hipster with smooth familiarity.

Some of the local buildings are replaced by Parisian equivalents, and the Water Steps morph into fountains. They've relocated to Paris's Tuileries gardens. Airship masts like miniature Eiffel Towers jut up from the Fer a Cheval, a dozen of the brightly painted craft jockeying for position overhead. The Eiffel itself is ringed by them, an aerial mandala. *Rivet Couture* players in their hundreds come and go. The Tuileries are a hub and center of commerce that utterly dwarfs its Pittsburgh equivalents.

"Huh." Jay is trying not to look impressed. "Trey Saunders, this is . . ."

"Vesta," she says.

". . . Vesta. If anybody can track down Bill, it's her."

Sura channels Countess Vesta and smiles at the lads. "How can I help?"

"Have you seen this man?" Jay fumbles his way through sharing a photo. When it finally comes to hover between them, it shows a man about Saunders's age, with a wing of raven-black hair falling across his brows, piercing gray eyes, and the confident, direct gaze of a politician or businessman. Sura squints at him.

"Nope. He's disappeared into a game?"

Jay glances at Saunders, who says, "We think it's one called *Lethe*."

Sura sits down just up the curve. "Oh."

"What's wrong?"

"Nothing's wrong. *Lethe* is just hard-core, that's all. Who is this guy?"

"Bill," says Saunders. "Bill Duchene." He pauses, expectant, but Sura shakes her head. "The founder of Conjure Industries," he continues. It's pretty obvious that Sura *should* know what this means, but she doesn't.

Trey Saunders might be relieved or disappointed; maybe it's a bit of both. Sura's annoyed, because this is all feeling like a job interview, and she shouldn't have to defend herself. She wants to turn the tables. "He's missing? Or he's hiding from the law? Or," she adds, just to see Saunders's reaction, "he just doesn't want to talk to you?"

He grimaces. "Missing. He has no reason to hide from me. I kind of feel responsible, is all. It's because of me that he dropped out." He blows out a breath. "We made a stupid bet."

"Bet?"

He talks about his life with Bill. They met in high school; neither could afford university so they lived with six other guys in a hacker collective, a little house. They spent half their time doing programming sprints, and the rest gaming.

"We'd get hepped up on Red Bull and Adderall and code for sixteen hours, then climb on the roof and scream at the city lights. We were good—really good. Built apps and did corporate espionage. Two of the guys were building a game, another was into quantum cryptography.

"Bill was the loser.

"He got into cryptocurrencies right around the time that every country on Earth was cracking down on Initial Coin Offerings. Bill wanted to free money from government control. He kept pushing me to read Ayn Rand, talked about how *The Fountainhead* changed his life; but he didn't make anything useful, he just played around with smart contracts.

"Then one day he showed me this platform he'd put together. It was a system for transitioning a standard business into a distributed autonomous corporation—replacing its CEO and other senior officers with disputed applications."

Sura nods. She knows how DACs have eaten up the whole white-collar world.

"Ah, you know the idea. Bill's genius was to build the system so that anybody in a company could start transitioning their role; they didn't have to ask permission, they could just use it as a cloud service for whatever they did. But whoever did this first would get the biggest payout when the system took over all the jobs. It rewarded early adopters and punished holdouts."

"And he sold it?"

Saunders shakes his head. "Investors hated the idea. Thought nobody would sell out their coworkers just to get a bigger severance package. Me, I'd been optimizing code for Internet of Things devices. That was huge.

I'd done my research, I'd figured out a way to save a micro-satoshi for each transaction between your smart fridge and thermostat and so on. Could be worth billions.

"Some VCs knew about us and one day they asked us to come in and pitch our work. All of us. We had the games team, the cryptographer, me, and Bill. And I had the most solid pitch of them all.

"Except the night before, I got food poisoning. Not a surprise, really, considering the fridge." He stares into the distance for a moment. "So I wasn't able to go. And you know Bill had the weakest pitch of any of us, but it turned out one of the VCs was a fellow Randroid and he just loved the incentive model. So they funded Bill."

He leans back, crosses his arms. "Which is how Bill got to surf the DAC wave and become a billionaire. Somebody else came up with an algorithm a lot like mine and scooped me on my work, and that was that."

"Oh . . . kay." Sura can't see where this is going, and flicks her eyes to Jay, whose own are half-closed. He's waiting for a punchline he's already heard.

"Bill and I stayed friends. I worked with him on the DAC thing, then for him. I did okay, got my own company now, but Bill, he just soared. And he started getting arrogant about it."

It's not exactly a tirade that Saunders launches into now, but maybe a spirited illustration of the verbal brawl that he and Bill were to engage in for the next five years. Sura's got the sense that neither of them likes to back down and both are always sure they're right. What they fought about was the role luck had played in their lives.

Specifically, when all was said and done, in Bill's success.

"Sure I envied him! Who wouldn't. But if I hadn't been barfing my guts out at home during the pitch session, and if that VC hadn't been a big Rand fan, I would have been funded, not Bill. He'd tried to sell his ideas a dozen times before, nobody was biting. And he knew how important luck was, we talked about it all the time. But after, he wasn't lucky anymore, see. He was destined. His success was entirely his own making. The implication being that my lack of success was my own damn fault."

"Okay," says Sura. "So you snapped and murdered him and stuffed him in a culvert somewhere?"

Saunders scratches his goatee. "Thought about it. But no, I went after him where he lives. I got statistical."

Saunders managed to dig up mountains of research on the role that luck plays in financial success. "The big rule," he says, "is that in a perfect game of chance played by equals, inequality is the inevitable outcome. The butterfly effect amplifies random initial successes until one player comes out on top. That's what happens when you play Monopoly. Monopoly was invented to educate people about that very point. There's no skill to winning at it, you don't win the game because you're *good.* You win because of tiny differences in luck that snowball over the course of the game. The problem is, nobody ever gets that. Everybody who wins at it thinks they won because they were smarter than anybody else, because *success flatters you*. The game totally backfired.

"I could prove, mathematically, that Bill's success was accidental, and I did. By that time he'd surrounded himself with other hacker billionaires who all thought they were geniuses, just like him; he insisted everything was his own doing even though he couldn't actually deny the math when I showed it to him.

"Last fall he sold off his controlling interest in Conjure. Spent six months traveling the world, trying out the billionaire playboy lifestyle. He didn't like it much, kept getting restless, looking for something new, a start-up, an investment.

"I caught him in the right mood a couple of months ago and bet him that he couldn't start over from scratch—with *nothing,* not even his reputation—and become successful again."

"Oooooh." They both look at Sura. "I mean that explains why he chose to play *Lethe*."

The premise of *Lethe* is that everyone on Earth has been hit with sudden total amnesia. Nobody can even read. People riding the subway one morning emerge downtown not knowing whether they're baristas or stock brokers. If you were flying an airplane when the amnesia hit you'd figure out you were a pilot, but the game excludes such obvious roles.

Lethe is a chance to start over, building up a new you complete with a new history, skills, and relationships.

"You have to actually surrender some of your property to play," she says. "What did he give up?" Players put entire houses and their contents into escrow; those on true larpabout walk away from their day jobs and sometimes even their families. There are no stakes for the unemployed and for those who own nothing. Those who do take the big chances tend to be poor, retired, or wealthy. The game is biggest in Japan.

Saunders shrugs. "A house. A car. Nothing he'd miss. I already tracked those down, they're being used by other players. None of them remember meeting him."

"Well, they wouldn't," she says. "They wouldn't know him as Bill Duchene, not if he's playing properly. He's got a new name, a new job, maybe even a new wife. Is he married in real life?" Saunders shakes his head.

When Sura first looked into *Lethe* she'd wondered why Compass hadn't taken her there. It seems tailor-made for people who want to disappear, but Sura had to admit there was something about it that sounded unhealthy. *Lethe* is sly. Its designers expect people to default to whatever work they already know. It anticipates that they'll try to use their hard-won badges, so it randomizes skills. If you're a pilot in real life, you can be one in *Lethe*—but the skill required to fly an airplane in *Lethe* may be entirely different from the ones you use in real life. In order to pilot an airplane, *Lethe* might demand that you knit a sweater. Or cook a soufflé. Or sing.

In *Lethe,* your skills are no longer your skills. Being a cop might require pharmacist's training; being a teacher might require that you change tires. Compass is the only person Sura knows who'll admit to having played it, but when Sura asked, she refused to talk about the experience.

"You might be right if he's really trying to hide," Jay says to her. "But he isn't, is he?" He looks to Saunders, who shakes his head. "He's not covering his tracks, he's just not phoning home. As far as we know. He's probably right in the middle of everything, actually. Mr. Saunders just can't find him from outside."

"Can *you* find him?" Saunders asks her. "If he's not trying to hide, I mean?"

Her fingers go to her fanny pack, where something's burning a metaphoric hole. "I can. Thing is, I'm looking for somebody to answer some questions about an Internet of Things problem. You said you used to program IoT. Could you help me with this?"

Saunders grins. "Deal!"

Sura gives the decisive nod that seems to work for Vesta. "Great. I can't guarantee anything. He could be anywhere in the country. Or the world. *Lethe* is global."

"We know he hasn't left the USA."

She thinks about where *Lethe* is big right now, and another perfect puzzle piece falls into place. "If he's determined to make it big in *Lethe*, there's only one place he'd go. The center of all things *Lethe*-ish. In America, anyway." They look at her expectantly.

"Detroit," she says. "Cloud country."

Oneota.

"Detectives?" She's never seen Vaughan look so surprised. "A detective agency *inside* the games?"

"Why not? Shit happens here as much as the outside world. People lose stuff. Lose . . . other people. And crap gets stolen . . ."

"It's a fine, fine idea," says K.C. He's got that grandfatherly manner on that makes her want to punch him.

"But—Detroit? I can't go to Detroit," says Rico. "My mom's here."

"I'm in," announces K.C. "Detroit's the fulcrum. We can accomplish more there than here."

While they're having this conversation, the fireteam is inching its way between ruined office towers that barely shield them from sandblasting winds. They're in the post-apocalyptic comedy *Tarnation Alley*, delivering packages from a tribe of zombie Oompa-Loompas to an enclave of runaway sexbots in the badlands. A normal workday, in other words.

"Get going!" shouts the package behind Sura. "It's not safe out here." Its pipsqueak voice is barely audible over the soughing of the wind. The satchel is strapped onto her velobike's cargo rack, along with a spare energy cell and her rifle. Caretaker 124 can hardly see her destination, three dunes down, behind curtains of blowing sand. The boys have similar targets, and similarly grumpy parcels.

She reaches back to casually slap the satchel. "You be quiet, or I'll sell you."

"You can't! I've freely chosen my new owner. You can't change that."

"Maybe not." She leans back. "But I can eat you right here."

Silence from the package.

"How about you guys?" In this world, Vaughan and Maeve are Caretakers 237 and 519, respectively. They're completely swaddled in rags and bandages, with makeshift helmets above their sand goggles. "Oh, fuck this." She mutes her glasses, and there they are, each straddling a city share bike. Big white plastic bags are tied behind their saddles.

"Sure," says Vaughan. "All the coders are moving to Detroit. Something big's going down there. We should be part of it."

"Jeez," says Rico. "Are you not even paying attention to what we're doing today?"

Sura turns to Maeve, who is looking everywhere but at her. "I gotta finish the summer term first," she says. "It's true there's no work here . . ."

Sura expects more, but the moment drags. Finally she shrugs. "Just . . . think about it. I don't want to split up the team. We'd be good there, I know it."

"We don't have to split up," says Maeve. "Most teams have at least one remote member."

That's her answer, then. Sura's going to wait until she actually says it, though. "Let's roll." She unmutes her glasses and kicks the velobike into gear.

"About time!" says her package. "I'm dyin' back here."

"Tell me again why I care?"

"You care because I am a self-sovereign object, able to declare who gets to use me. You care because some of me is perishable and in case you hadn't noticed, it's hot out here! And you care because my chosen owner needs me."

"You forgot the part about you paying me to deliver you."

"I thought you caretakers were above such things."

The dunes disappear while she's pedaling along the street, but when she pauses in a safe spot, her destination emerges, like a fever dream, closer each time.

If it weren't for the fact that some of the black rectangles of its blown-out windows were curtained by burlap, and that there's a cluster of velobikes around its entrance, she couldn't have told this ex-office building from the others huddled in the dunes. There are reavers about, their presence visible in the caretaker's HUD goggles as bright lozenges of body heat. Two are crouched atop a nearby dune, plainly arguing over her. They won't touch her. The rules against interfering with a caretaker run generations deep—and everybody enforces them.

Ignoring the rifle barrels, she makes it to the hive's entrance just as the wind picks up and erases the horizon. Somebody has crudely spray-painted THINK LOCALLY, ACT GLOBALLY beside the glassless doors. Caretaker 124 tosses back her hood, blows out a dusty breath, and follows a foot-worn path through the darkness to a stuffy stairwell.

Well, fuck that. Sura turns, mutes, and takes the elevator.

"You'll lose points for that."

"Don't sound so happy. I'm tired is all." The chatbot assigned to her package is really good, in an annoying-sidekick sort of way. The games are rife with beings just like it, and she knows she can ignore it if she wants.

The doors open. Fifth floor, suite 507, right where it's supposed to be. She knocks, suddenly nervous. As she tilts her glasses up and covers them with her baseball cap, she hears, "Hold your horses, I'm coming, I'm coming," from behind the door. It opens a crack, chain still on. "Can I help you?"

"Mrs. Glover? My name's Terri, I'm with the church. I've got some groceries for you, if you'd like 'em."

"Oh, my." The chain comes off, and Mrs. Glover waves Sura inside. "Oh, I tell them I don't need the help, but what can I do? They keep sending you folk anyway."

"I'm sorry if I'm causing you any trouble."

"Pish-tosh! Come in, please, here, let me clear the counter."

Sura puts cans of corn, bread, a bag of milk, and some fresh apples onto a faux-marble surface that's scratched and peeling at the corners. She lowers her glasses so they can register the delivery; just above her sock, Purrloin will be registering her location. Next time she passes an active mesh point, it'll upload this and the rest of her recent trail to her permanent record. Somewhere, sometime soon, a process in *Tarnation Alley* will poll that record to complete the transaction. The answer will be an irrefutable yes, and the Tarnation Life Points associated with the groceries will be transferred to Caretaker 124.

These groceries are part of a large stash that's had a distribution algorithm attached to it. The stash is splitting itself into semi-autonomous parcels, each with a delivery address and experience points, game items or Gwaiicoin held in escrow for the deliveryman. They're gathered by Caretakers in *Tarnation*, smugglers in *Rivet Couture*, and half a dozen other games; by fairies, by ghouls, by clue-hunting detectives, and vaccine-toting soldiers; by diplomats, treasure hunters, and spies. And, by horse, by spaceship, by rail or by helicopter or on foot, they arrive at their destinations.

"Oh, this is too much, too much," says the gnome-like old woman as she sorts through her windfall. "I don't know why they say such awful things about young people today, you're really too kind."

"Oh, it's the church you should thank, not me," says Sura. Despite her protestations, it takes her twenty minutes to disentangle from Mrs. Glover's hospitality. When she finally emerges from the building, glasses still back on her head, it's to find the boys and the bikes gone, and Maeve waiting.

"Listen," Maeve begins, but Sura holds up a hand.

"You don't owe me anything. Besides, if this is your town, it's your town. You're not rootless, so why start?"

Maeve grins at Sura, then hugs her. "I still want to be in your fireteam. And I still might come. The real world won't be the same without you."

Sura realizes she's blushing. Nobody's talked this way to her in . . . well, ever. "I mean, all I did was carry Jeri's vegetables for her."

Maeve snorts. "You introduced me to a world I didn't know existed. Jeri got me out of dancing, and you got me out of Jeri's."

"I guess that would count for something." They share a smile, because there's so much more to it than that and they both know it. Maeve's a natural at the games; maybe it's all that Object Oriented Ontology she's been studying. She can juggle identities in multiple worlds all at the same time in a way that Sura envies. Sura's proud of her.

She's got a car waiting, and makes an offering gesture. Sura smiles and nods, then spots something.

"Oh, hey. Actually, I'll catch up with you later. Back at the Tuileries, okay?"

Maeve's car pulls away and, putting her hands in her pockets, Sura strolls to where Compass is leaning on the hood of a nearby Tesla share, her backdrop a 7-Eleven, McDonalds, and a strip mall containing a laundromat. She's got her arms and ankles crossed, her glasses rakishly down on her nose. Her tightly wound braid is draped down her right shoulder.

Sura unmutes her glasses and Mixed Reality replaces the mall with a dunefield. Compass is a ridiculously big leather-clad *Mad Max* warrior perched atop a tank. "Hail," he says in an unsuccessfully low voice.

"Wotcher," says Sura in her best British accent.

"I hear . . ." Compass pushes herself into a standing posture. Ghostly past the warrior, Sura can see the real woman clutch her braid. Compass says, "I hear you're moving."

"I am. To Detroit. I've got a contract."

"Rivet Couture?"

She shakes her head. *"Lethe."*

Compass looks around at the dune-scape, thinking. "Are you working for Jay?"

"Maybe."

"He's important to you."

"I am not into Jay. Fuck, I don't even know his last name."

"You d-don't know mine either."

"I don't trust the sonofabitch as far as I can throw him. No, it's not that."

"Then why do you care?"

She does like Jay. Once he found out that she was actually in trouble, he bent over backwards to help her. She loves his easy banter and no-bullshit attitude, but to say that now would seem trite. A few nights ago she thought of an image for how she feels about him, but she's sure it'll only make sense to her: she pictured the golden thread that's supposed to connect an astral traveler's virtual self back to their real body. Campy new-age books would show that body lying on a bed, drawn in black-and-white, with the golden thread curling up to the vividly colored image of the astral form, surrounded in light, flying among postcard clouds. She, identity-less, a laborer in hallucinations, is the brightly burning traveler.

Jay is the thread, or at least the last link in a chain—

—And somewhere, that thread has to connect to a sleeping form, some monochrome, real Sura Neelin, some place in the real world. That woman, and that place, is still anchored to Mom and Dad, to her old neighborhood and her friends; to America and careers and the world as she was taught to understand it. If the thread snaps, will that connection be lost?

"I have no good reason," she says.

"No, fuck that, I need him. He's an investigator, hell, he's a clue himself. He may know more than he realizes."

Compass spends some time staring at the vehicle next to her. "I d-don't like living in cars."

"Oh. I know what you mean. Ha! I'm making just enough as Vesta to flop at Dan and Walter's. This job for Jay could lead to better stuff.

"And I want to pay you back for the time you've invested in me. So." She screws up the courage.

"You could come along? I, uh, kinda need a roommate."

For a while Compass is just a silhouette against the yellow sky of *Tarnation Alley*. "Okay," she says.

"Really? Uh, perfect! Then it's set? You'll come?"

Compass nods. Sura gives a little cheer and says, "Thank you so much. This is going to be great, you'll see."

A little smile, rarely seen, drifts across Compass's face as she says, "You might want to wait until you see how much c-crap I actually own."

Trey Saunders said he would help with her own little problem, so Sura sends him the sensor she found in her dad's jacket pocket. She doesn't know what she's looking for, but he promises his people will investigate every possible anomaly. That'll have to do for now.

Jay is still investigating Summit Recoveries, and she's doing the same in her own limited way. Between this and disentangling Vesta from her European gambits, the next few days are a little crazy. Suddenly, one evening, she finds herself standing on the curb saying goodbye to Walter and Dan, as two *Proudly Eagle Owned!* cars pull up. One has K.C. and Vaughan in it, and all she can see in the other is the top of Compass's head.

"Keep in touch!" says Walter. "And if you know anybody who's playing into Pittsburgh, in any world, send 'em here!"

She joins Compass, and they drive. For a while their glasses are all in range and they sit together in a velvet-upholstered shell from an *RC* moon cannon. Rico and Maeve are here *in virtua*. They all talk about new beginnings, opportunities, and how the fireteam is going to transition to detective work.

None of them are in character except Compass, who insists on being Scratchie. This is normal for her so nobody minds. She seems happy to be leaving, but as the cars draw farther apart, the mesh connection fails, and the fireteam dissolves. Sura frowns nervously at the passing countryside. State troopers will pull over anyone these days, particularly any car from an Urban Alliance city. Intercity travel is dangerous.

The bigger problem is that while Scratchie is happy to talk, Compass is not. By now Sura's tried about a thousand conversational thrusts designed to disarm the player and touch the girl behind him. Lines like "Are you from around here?" definitely don't work, nor does "Do you have friends in Michigan?" Compass seems to eat up details about Sura's own life, so after a little silence she tells her about growing up in Dayton. "It was my mom who loved music," she says. "She introduced me to classical, to indie, everything. Used to dance to Frankie Rose while doing the housework."

Compass smiles.

"What about you?" Sura asks. "Did you grow up with music?"

"The lapin' of the waters on the barge," says Compass, deadpan. "That's me first memory."

Sura sighs. "Fine, be that way." *What have I gotten myself into?* She turns away, crossing her arms, and watches the countryside for a while.

It seems redundant to be asking why the hell she's doing this; why the hell is she doing any of it? She should be grinding in a warehouse or clothing store back in Dayton. Would it be so bad to pay off the family debts a dollar at a time, so long as she's not harrassed? Even those shitheads who killed Dad, maybe she could convince them she knows nothing about what he was up to. She pictures herself standing there in full shrug, open hands up by her shoulders.

Well. Maybe *they* could leave it alone. She can't. From what Remy's said, and based on Dad's movements over the past few months, he was chasing down false reports from pollution monitors all over the globe. This is hardly a new thing; everybody lies. What seems to set Dad's investigation apart is that he wasn't going after lying people. It was the sensors themselves that interested him.

She's got one, but is it the right one? What about his backpack? If Remy's right, he hid it somewhere in the abandoned oil fields. Remy knows roughly where Dad went in the days leading up to his death. The backpack, if it really has been hidden, can only be in one of a dozen or so places.

Remy won't go back there, he's afraid. Sura . . . Sura can't go, and not just because she's broke.

The one person who could step up is Marj. Marj is a celebrity, known for her work in AI; the University of Lima, say, would jump at the chance to host her for a few days. She could go down, nose around, hire people. Sura would even ask her to do this, but Marj is still not answering her phone. This is not the kind of request to make by message, and Marj's public email address is too risky.

The car turns out to be a better conversationalist than Compass. Sura talks to it and discovers that these vehicles really are owned by eagles. Somebody set up a distributed autonomous corporation as a B-corp and, once it was running, handed signing authority over to an AI charged with protecting the eagles of the Pacific Northwest. The cars work as taxis, pay for their own upkeep, and any profits go to the birds. No humans are involved—at least, not anymore.

"Wow!" Sura says to Compass. "Did you know about this?"

Compass gives her an enigmatic, satisfied little smile.

There's a long silence after that, until Sura turns on the radio. It comes on to hip-hop and Compass snaps at the car to change it. She demands a classical station and settles back, clearly relieved.

Sura's glasses could find out what the music is, but instead she asks, "Who's this?"

"Massenet." Compass says this as if it's obvious and Sura's an idiot. There's the tiniest hesitation and then, as if she just can't stop herself, she launches into the biography and now Sura can't shut her up. The trip turns into an episode of *Lives of the Composers* with this week's show about abusive fathers. Sura finds this both fascinating and disturbing because of what it implies about Compass. After a few hundred miles the bastards all blur together, Clara Schumann's dad who drags her into the public eye at age six; Wulfie Mozart's father who builds the family business around him; Beethoven's alcoholic pater who would command him to play piano all night. If Daddy woke up and didn't hear the piano, he'd come in and beat little Ludwig.

The compulsive way Compass tells these tales, her tone and mannerisms—somehow they feel like an apology. It's like these anecdotes are all that Compass has to give. Puzzled, Sura listens as well as she can. As Compass weaves stories about the nineteenth century, she finds herself dreamily imagining palaces, broad cobblestoned avenues, and tall houses. She's seen many such places in the last few weeks, traveled into the past and alternate Americas. At a certain point, she realizes that the overlays in her glasses are presenting the countryside to her in a way utterly different than she's seen before.

That terrible drive with Jay wasn't like this one, for then all she could see was the palpable decay, the air of exhaustion to the industrial heartland. Glasses on and tuned to other worlds, she beholds something quite different:

Where Balkan Europe and Cahokia meet, a cautious cultural exchange is happening. European colonials are learning the indigenous history of the countryside they've moved into and are starting to see it in a different way. Where before there were jobs and gas stations and strip malls, now there are woods and plots of land, and vast resources—like the apple trees they tagged—that aren't yet owned by anybody. Through treaties between the Cahokians and Europeans, logistical chains, storehouses, and rules for distribution are being negotiated. Old and poor people are getting food, and it's the neighborhood kids delivering it. Beyond this, the supply lines and arrangements sprawl into the outer world, changing games and names, but scaling up in ways she can't yet see.

Other frameworlds overlay the land, idealist's maps, and each comes with a logistics package, cryptoassets, and exchange rates. The different realities trade, and what was a bleak vista of cracked and abandoned parking lots becomes the New World, its vales resettled and its borders redrawn.

Past the horizon but approaching is a great knot of activity. All the worlds converge in that distant glow, where imaginary monies, underused tools and vehicles, common-pool resources, and a shifting, half-virtual army of officially unemployed people have come together to build something new.

Each individual drop on the windshield is insignificant. Gradually they grow, and soon it's apparent that some new rain is falling on America.

PART II

CLOUD COUNTRY

CHAPTER TEN

"What's it like?" asks Maeve.

Sura frowns at the street. "It's this weird cross between cohousing and hackspaces."

Compass laughs—or is she relaying Maeve's laugh? Maeve's riding Compass, an arrangement way more flexible than talking on the phone because she can look through Compass's glasses and steer her around. It's confusing, though, because it's Compass that Sura is house-hunting with.

The row of semi-detached homes is based on European plans, but squeezed through the magic machinery of Malcolm's procedural architecture programs. The old-city water pipes are corroded, and the last power lines drooped and fell years ago, so the houses capture rain and recycle gray water, and are solar powered. With all that, they'd be too expensive if they weren't being built by and bought by larpers.

"Which one is it?" Maeve asks through Compass. Sura points to the third floor of one unit. As they come up the newly poured walk, Compass/Maeve skips ahead but stops as the door opens by itself. "There's no doorbell," she calls back.

Compass (you can tell it's her because of a slight change in tone) says, "No need for bells or locks. The door recognizes players." Maeve hesitates, so Sura goes in first.

The real estate agent is waiting upstairs. She's tagged as a *Lethe* player, but when she sees Sura and Compass/Maeve she immediately curtsies and says, "Countess Vesta Kodaly, it's a privilege. How can I help you?"

"We'd like to see if these rooms are suitable."

"Of course. You know that you haven't purchased a specific unit, but a *right* to occupy one unit, here or anywhere else in the frames?" Sura nods. The agent shows them a set of brand-new, sunny rooms, the drywall still unpainted. There are three bedrooms, one of which has a beautiful old tree outside it. Past that lies the checkerboard of half-rebuilt Brush Street.

"I love it!" Maeve is steering Compass from room to room. Compass herself hasn't said anything yet. "But how can you afford it?"

"It's not a traditional purchase, it's a set of smart contracts. Vesta's earned part of an estate in Balkan Europe; well, a couple of rooms only, so far. But Compass could take over the whole house if she wanted. She's accumulated this ridiculous pile of game property in her inventory and all we have to do is instantiate some of it as this place." She aims her next words at Compass. "If I can have the big bedroom, you can have the rest."

These housing units are like the crumpled Coke can Vaughan showed Maeve. They're partly physical, partly virtual. Instead of buying with traditional money, players can attach an equivalent cryptoasset to the real one. The advantage is that you can do the same with all the contents and swap them at any time for somebody else's. Vesta can shuffle her assets to any qualifying space; anybody can. Any room, street, or house in Oneota and the neighborhood known as Not in Service can instantiate in Detroit, Shanghai, Berlin, or Toronto.

She understands the blockchain part of the deal. It's like that can: each real thing here has a virtual component. It was only after talking with Trey Saunders that she understood the rest of what makes this kind of arrangement possible. Everything in this place is tagged in the Internet of Things. Dent a wall here and the system registers the damage; break or lose an appliance and it drops out of your inventory. Your cryptoasset degrades, and if you stop contributing by playing, the size and quality of place and fixtures you have rights to will also degrade. There's a floor to how little you can have, though, just as there's a ceiling to how much you can instantiate.

There's something else, too—another layer, plainly visible but too strange for her to figure out. Like the talking groceries in *Tarnation Alley*, anything, real or virtual, can be given a little game-personality. And why not? If the system can designate Compass as a particular NPC and feed her lines, why can't it feed those lines to an inanimate object? And then why not give those objects ambitions appropriate to them? So, bricks and piles of boards can suggest to passersby how they might be used. Cinder blocks dream of joining up with other cinder blocks to form walls. It seems sometimes that all the rubble and ruin of Detroit is tossing in its sleep, murmuring dreams of a transfigured future.

Somebody used the term "self-allocating resources" the other day. That might be what these things are, but right now she can only talk about what she understands.

". . . So if we get tired and want to start, oh, say, living in a car," she tells Maeve, "we can put all this crap back *in virtua*. Compass has tons of stuff in there."

Naturally there's haggling involved. In that sense this is a market. "What do you think, Compass?"

Compass looks around, frowns, and (as expected) shrugs. "Sure."

"We'll take it." Now for the fun part: cross-checking the labor, material, and time that went into building this place, and will go into its upkeep, and comparing that to the work and social intangibles that Sura and Compass have contributed to the games since they started playing. All these things are tracked and stored in their tattoos. Sura is herself a crumpled can.

"There are three rooms," Maeve interjects at one point. Sura grins at her through Compass.

"The third's for you, when you finally decide to join us."

"I can barely hear you," says Trey Saunders.

"Sorry, I'll go in the other room." The mumbling and ka-chunk of the printer has become the background hum of Sura's new life, just as the discarded feedstock boxes in the corners have become the scenery. It's making a side table or something right now, who knows? She's lost track.

Sura sits on the floor in her bedroom, knees apart, arms on knees. "Is this better?"

"Yeah. How are you?"

"I'm fine. Just settling in," she says, glancing at her burglary trophies, now all printed and sitting on the windowsill. "I'm sorry I have nothing to report about your friend yet."

"That's okay. Tit for tat, I guess," he says with a slight laugh. "I have nothing to tell you about that sensor."

"You haven't had time to—?"

"No, I mean there's nothing to report. It's generic. 3-D printed and it could have been made anywhere, at any time in the past five years. It runs the same open-source IoT software as half the sensors in the world. Pays for its data uploads with standard crypto. The ID says it's owned by Bolivarian State Oil. They were heavily into the Peruvian fields when the bubble popped."

"So how would you make the thing lie? Report clean air when it's actually smelling of sour gas?"

"You could," Trey says. "But this one hasn't been lying. My guys checked, and there's not much to it to begin with; it just takes a reading and uploads it to the IoT blockchain. It's open-sourced hardware and software because it's an oracle. It has to be trustworthy."

Remy talked about oracles. "What does that mean, though, really? What's an oracle?"

"The world runs on smart contracts. I do X for you, you do Y for me. They only go through if I do what I say I'll do. You have to be able to verify that I did it. That's easy when we're human beings dealing face-to-face, or if we're two computer algorithms that can check each other's work. But if I'm a smart car and you're a human passenger, there has to be some way of proving to both of us—or to a court of law—that I picked you up at Eight Mile and dropped you downtown. *That* is not because the program can't look the way we can. It's like it needed some kind of all-seeing, infallible oracle to say, 'Yes, it happened.' But there really is no such thing."

She opens her mouth to object that it's actually easy, then realizes that part of her mind is already thinking about how to trick a *Proudly Eagle Owned!* You feed in fake data, and how's the car to know? All the elaborate shenanigans that go into her Purrloin tattoo are designed to minimize such spoofing.

Trey continues. "That's why what you're saying about this sensor is really, really disturbing. It's an oracle, so it's the weak link in the chain. We expect some oracles to lie now and then. I figured when you gave it to me that we'd find the hardware had been tampered with. That's normal, happens all the time. The problem is the hardware's working fine. We did find traces of hydrogen sulfide inside it. Get what I'm saying? The *oracle* isn't lying.

"But the oracle reports to the pollution-monitoring blockchain. And that *can't* lie. It's within the cryptographic circle of trust, where all the carbon counting and pollution auditing goes on. Billions of dollars in penalties and offsets are traded there every day, trillions per year. If even one of the transactions inside that circle could be shown to have been corrupted, then they *all* could be.

"If there's been deception, and if it isn't the oracle that's lying, then the global pollution-monitoring system is, itself, a lie."

At first Jay's car stays safe and clear on the Chrysler Freeway, whose barriers keep away the gap-toothed light of the Detroit skyline. Distant towers stand sentinel over the roil of black trees. Past downtown, Sura (who's riding the car's cameras remotely) says, "Turn here," and the car spins off a cloverleaf and west on the Davison North service drive. There are no streetlights in this area, just sodium lamps yellowing the parking lots and storage yards. For a while, only these warehouses and their barbed-wire fences slide past. Jay has to weave to avoid frost-heaved pavement and potholes.

"You didn't have to come," she says for the fifth time. "I'm fine."

"Sure," he says. He glances at the console when he speaks to her, as if he can see her in there somehow. In reality, she can see him through an interior cam by the review mirror. "I believe you. It's just, I don't want you poking the hornet's nest while I'm not around."

"I can't *not* do something. Those fuckers murdered him, Jay! And they're right here!"

Trey's revelation about the sensor has provided motive for murder—even if, as he's pointed out, you have to believe six impossible things before breakfast to buy it. "It's not about whether you or I think the auditing could be compromised," she'd said to Jay during their weekly call. "It's whether Dad believed it and pushed the wrong people."

"As to that," Jay had replied in a reluctant tone, "I found out a little more about our friends at Summit Recoveries."

He'd sensed that Summit guarded its privacy more than most firms, so Jay hadn't investigated them directly. Instead, he'd used the social engineering of a good skip-tracer to impersonate or invent personas, and asked Detroit city utilities, mail carriers, and even people who lived nearby a series of seemingly innocent questions. Gradually, he'd built up a profile of the place, and of the people who came and went. Online, people hired by people he'd called in favors from were doing similar, cautious investigations.

"So, let's say you're in an industry whose assets are just one public announcement away from being stranded," he'd told her. "Like fossil fuels were ten years ago. Everybody knew, kinda sorta, that we couldn't get away with burning any of the oil and gas that was still in the ground. Do that, and the world cooks. But the stock market valuations of the oil companies were based on those very reserves. If they could never be used, the companies were overvalued by eight to nine hundred percent. Nobody *said* that, not publicly. We all whistled past the graveyard, until it just got too obvious. I forget who it was divested and tipped it over, but when the bubble popped . . . well, you know."

Government collapses, revolutions, war, and a paroxysm of right-wing isolationism—sure, she knew about it. That was her childhood.

"The thing is, though, that the oil guys did succeed in putting off the inevitable, long enough for a lot of them to pull out their own investments and retire rich. And how do you think they did that? Partly it was the Trumpist fake news machine—the same advertising firms that whitewashed tobacco back in the day got paid billions to do the same with global warming. But when that wasn't enough—when some whistle-blower cropped up, about to lay down the facts on WikiLeaks or the *Financial Times*, then they needed a different kind of fixer."

"Oh my god," she said.

Summit Recoveries' employees are mostly ex-military. They get paid to shut people up, not for the mob, but for legitimate companies that want to buy time, for one reason or another.

"And . . ." He'd paused a long time before going on. "Thing is, I traced two of their guys to Iquitos around the time your dad died."

"This way," she says now.

The warehouses fall away and he turns left onto a wider but empty road. Here and there are houses. The car's headlights sweep across a sign: Brush Street. It's brush*land*, really, almost denuded of buildings, though sidewalks, hedges, and picket fences await their return. Then comes a region where there are only bare fields guarded by pickets of garbage and debris. If the horizons didn't glow pale blue, you'd think you were in the country. A side street to the left is choked with trash. Ahead, there's more confident light.

Something white sails past the car, startling Jay. "What the—" Sura rotates her view to see, was it an owl? No, just a quadcopter, a drone with the span of a dinner table. With a determined sense of direction, it lofts a box between the goalposts of two ragged pines and vanishes in the blackness.

"This is the place," says Sura. She stands and walks out to meet him;

he's seeing a large brick building that's lit by brave little LEDs on stakes. There are white wooden letters above the door.

GR FIELD P RK
ELE EN RY

Jay pulls around the corner and into a parking lot that's full of cars of all models, ages, and makes, including a city bus whose destination sign says NOT IN SERVICE. As he parks she mutes her glasses for a moment to see him as he really is. He's real, and somehow she feels huge relief.

Through her glasses she can still see through the car's cameras. She herself is a silhouette in the doorway. She mutes again, finds herself on the step enfolded by layered sound: a basement of thumping hip-hop with happy talk and laughter built on top of it. She takes a deep breath and walks out to meet Jay.

He's turning circles, saying "shit" over and over. He probably hasn't guested in *Rivet Couture* since that meeting with Trey Saunders at the Water Steps. She knows he's not seeing a devastated Detroit neighborhood, but rather the mounds of the Cahokian capital, their tops adorned with torches and bonfires. Instead of empty lots, here is a busy city walled with wooden palisades, its broad streets crowded with men and women on foot as well as horses and carts. Aside from the mounds there are hundreds of thatched houses, their central fires glimpsed past their open doors. Families are cooking supper or settling in for the night. Here and there European-style shapes poke out incongruously and there are English road signs for visitors like Jay. A constant murmur of voices and music enfolds them.

Jay looks up. "Holy crap!"

The sky is full of aboriginal forms, and lettering and glowing lines that join the mounds and arc away over the horizon like ley lines. European symbols sit side by side with the native glyphs—crosses, pentagrams, signs for pounds, dollars, and other currencies.

MR has not erased the abandoned school, but has refaced it as an Indian palace in the grand style of the Raj (a partnership in this world, rather than an imperial property). Two vast zeppelins bearing the insignia of the East India Company hang above it.

Glasses muted, it's a different story. Somebody's erected a newer sign over the door to Greenfield Park Elementary. This says NOT IN

SERVICE. Light spills through the doorway and the glassless windows that flank it.

"It's just a metaphor," she says. "Hi, Jay."

He takes off his glasses, grins at her. "You look great. Not starving or scruffy at all. No track marks . . ."

"Thanks for the vote of confidence."

He's frowning at the darkness past the parking lot. "What's really here?"

"Oh, everything you just saw. Just, not as flashy in real life. Come on in."

They've just made it inside when somebody shouts "Jay!" and runs over. It's Compass, a big grin on her face. Jay opens his arms and to Sura's surprise they hug for a second.

"It's great to see ya, kid!"

Sura unmutes and can almost ignore the smell of the fire-gutted school and imagine that the vast, lantern-lit and gold-chased entrance is real. Uniformed footmen bow as the three pass. One of the footmen is a real person, some new player who's just learning the mechanics of larping in MR.

"Yay," says Compass. "Are you moving to Oneota?"

"No," says Jay. "Just here on business."

Sura looks away, hiding a frown.

From the roof of the school, you can just see Summit's offices, five miles away. Jay's come to Oneota because Sura admitted she's staking the place out. Wending her way there at night through the labyrinths of *The White Rose,* she'll crouch in shadow a block away, taking photos. Thinking like a burglar. At home, she's sketched out the entry and exit points, made a rough guess at the building's internal structure.

She doesn't know what secrets she might find in the place, but she's determined to find *something*. Or, had been.

"Jay, I don't think you've met my fireteam." She introduces K.C. and Vaughan, then has to say "The others are in *RC*." Jay remembers to flip down his glasses, and then he can say hello to Maeve and Rico.

The school's former gymnasium is decorated as a raja's audience hall in that particular game, but MR icons indicate that it's also a place in dozens more. Tables, machines, and huge plastic bins sprawl over much of the floor, and people are working there under the pinpoint light of LED spots. The clear central space is a combination mosh pit, dance floor, and performance stage. There's work going on, and dancing and laughter. Drones fly in and out through the broken windows, depositing small packages and picking up more.

"Pittsburgh's nothing like this," says Jay. "At least, not the parts I saw."

Sura nods. "We're rebuilding the neighborhood. There's the matternet"—she points to the drones—"and you can see we've got a lot of printers going. The municipal government's supplying some of the feed-stock."

"What're you making?"

"Houses, right now. Me and the team helped locate a lot of the resources. Some of those drones you see are building walls, one recovered brick at a time. It's pretty cool; you go to sleep and there's an empty field, you wake up and there's a new house."

Sura shows him how to flip through the parallel worlds; each reveals part of a larger, coordinated activity. Half the people in the room are having conversations with thin air or are moving virtual objects around. The duelists and dancers are typical of anybody wearing glasses: each sees a slightly, or sometimes entirely, different scene. This one building is a gameplay hub, a factory, a warehouse, office space, dance hall, and classroom for the players' kids. Somebody ripped out the sinks in the bathroom but ranks of solar panels are lined up in the former playground, and there are portable toilets in the parking lot.

"Used to be prostitution and drugs all through Wayne County," she says. "Then the militias moved in, and some evangelicals bought in a private police force. There were artists' collectives and biker gangs. Weird mix. We supplied the matternet and twenty-four-hour drone surveillance and started making deals with the banks and municipality. Now we get dibs on every other lot we can revive, if there isn't an owner who refuses to sell."

"And the houses are just for players?"

She shakes her head. "The games are just one interface to the frames. Non-players can lease them, and they also work with us."

He smiles. "Us. You said 'us.' And 'we' just now."

"Um. Really? That's weird." He laughs, but Sura feels defensive. She doesn't really buy into all this bullshit, does she? Certainly she doesn't feel a real sense of belonging here. She's still hiding. There are killers out there, and her dad's murder to solve. If anything, she's on pause, caught in midstep, the foot that lifted from the threshold of the house she grew up in not yet having touched down despite adventures.

Anxious to change the subject, she says, "The team's been helping look for Duchene. K.C. here's got a history with the alt-right, he's been making inquiries with the preppers."

"Really?" Jay's expression hovers between impressed and skeptical. "You're not giving away that you're looking, are you?"

"Son," drawls K.C., "I am an old hand at discretion."

"We know Duchene's been through town," says Vaughan. "He's been playing a game called *Lethe*. One name he's used there is Cradle. We lost track of him, though; he seems to have Aliced into a subworld."

"So Duchene's not in *Lethe* anymore? But he is in Detroit?"

"No, he's not in *Lethe*." Vaughan smirks. "He ain't in Kansas anymore, either.

"None of us are."

Jay is eager to tour Oneota, so she takes him on a walk the next morning. It's beautiful and clear, and the heat has retreated for now. She shows him how the new layout of buildings de-emphasizes roads, focusing instead on self-contained, walkable neighborhoods.

"And all this comes from playing games?"

She laughs. "I don't visit those much anymore. Or—I do, but only when we're following leads on Duchene. People don't know who we're looking for, but word's getting around that we've started a cross-reality detective agency." She grins. "Most of my time is spent in the frameworlds now."

Jay's puzzled. "You talked about these 'frames' before, but what are they? Settings for the games' quests?"

"No, they're their own thing. I don't know how to—oh, wait. There's Johnson's. That'll show you how it works."

Up ahead, alone on a block stripped of any other buildings, sits a corner store.

"When the larpwrights first came into this neighborhood, they found a lot of angry people, and no work, and no social services. So guess what they did?" He shrugs.

"They handed out smart glasses and showed people a virtual building. That one." She indicates the tall, narrow brick store, which has a typical 1960s-style painted glass sign, windows showing various sale items, and a deeply inset door under a grumbling air conditioner. People are wandering in and out.

"It's real," Jay points out.

"Not at first. It started out virtual, overlaid on a ruined building. See where the brickwork is new? There was nothing here—except Johnson, who used to actually run a corner store when he was younger. Inherited it from his dad, lost it in the crash, but never left the neighborhood. They camped him out here, made an MR store with virtual items to buy, and told everybody in the area that they'd started a new game. People could come and buy online items from Johnson, using tokens they got by signing up for the game."

Jay laughs. "Why the fuck would they want to do that?"

"They made it into a social media meme. They made it cool. But what you really got cred for was for figuring out a *step*. A step was a thing that had to happen or had to exist, to make a path from the ruin of the now, to a future where Johnson's store was *real*."

She tells him how people started remembering the way things used to be. They filled in details in the simulation: how many people had lived here, what they had done, what sorts of goods they would have bought at a local outlet. The virtual store's virtual contents began to flesh out. Somebody had the idea of putting a set of courier lockers outside the ruin, so people could pick up drone deliveries here. They began getting Johnson to handle their online orders. Then, they started preordering groceries and milk, and some guys reinforced the building's wall, got rid of the vermin, and put solar panels on the roof. By degrees, the pretend community became a real community.

"It was all about this progressive replacement of the virtual with the real," she says a few minutes later, as they're walking away from Johnson's with a couple of ice cream cones. "And finding the right seed—a kernel to grow something new without using *money*."

Explaining what she does in the frameworlds is a bit harder. "I've earned an apprentice reframing badge! I'm a cross between an event planner and a building inspector. I get hired into various teams and go around to empty lots and rail yards and abandoned car factories, and I look for new ways to use them. The real inspectors have to pronounce them safe, and there's this huge list of things we're not allowed to do in them. We rent them short-term from the car company liquidators; they're desperate for any source of income . . ."

She tries to describe reframing—how she'll stand in the vast, echoing cavern that used to house a Ford production line and, using an interactive CAD program in her glasses, invent different floor plans. She changes the walls to amber and imagines a grand ball. She subdivides the place into a

thousand little cells and pictures a crafts fair. It's not random, she does have customers: larpwrights with spare players or spare commodities and no idea how to use them; players needing work; and self-allocating resources that are equally restless. Engines looking for a job. What do you do if you've got two hundred idle people, a flatbed truck loaded with defective wind turbine generator windings, and three days? Add a building, make up a culture where all these things are meaningful, and let them play it out. Brainstorming and problem-solving algorithms are built into the scenario rules, and connections run around the world instantly. Suddenly the place may have a virtual annex that's a corresponding space in south Asia where complementary resources have been found. Instant machine translation means no barriers to communication; half the people on the floor are *in virtua* or avatars being ridden by foreign players. Some are players NPCing for the actual machinery, and they walk around telling people what it can and can't do. Out of nothing, a temporary business appears, refurbishing turbine parts using the expertise of Cambodian ship-breakers riding American ex-factory workers.

Shipping is arranged, other stakeholders brought in. Engineers, lawyers, and prospective customers arrive at an expensive brownstone downtown. Deals happen. Millions of real dollars come flooding in as the turbines go out.

Next day, the factory is empty again, ready for Sura and her gangs to imagine it into another world.

"Apparently I'm good at it," she adds, a little defensively. "Reframers are in demand."

Jay mashes the last of his ice cream cone into his mouth, thinking. Then he says, "What about this team of yours?"

"Hmm." She arches an eyebrow. "I do trust them. But they're like puzzles, and not all the pieces fit yet. They may never."

Now that he's in Detroit, K.C. is missing in action half the time. He too is hunting someone but won't talk about who or why. Vaughan is loving Oneota. He trained as a computer programmer, and now he's actually getting to use his skills. Mostly he dismantles the complexity of the smart contract systems for Sura, and he's pretty proficient with MR interfaces and 3-D printing. She tells Jay this, but not that Vaughan is obsessed with cryptocurrency markets. She's heard rumors that he's got some kind of ill-gotten gains wrapped up in Bitcoin, and can't get at them because the addresses are being watched by some very bad people. The

value of his BTCs is draining away before his eyes, and he lacks the courage to grab them and run.

"Speaking of printing," says Jay. He looks around carefully, but they're alone in the checkerboard of half-ruined houses, empty lots, and grass-stitched streets. "Do you have a gun?" She frowns and shakes her head.

"Dad never used one."

"Here." He pulls a small, heavy-looking pistol out of one of his utility pouches. "Its bark is worse than its bite. It's just a .22. I printed it myself, there's no serial number."

She eyes it like it's a scorpion. "You think I need that?"

"I think you can't be trusted to leave well enough alone. Sura, those guys at Summit are killers. I agree that we have to bring them down, but there's literally nothing you can do about it right now. *This* is a reminder of just how dangerous this shit is." He holds out the gun, and reluctantly, she takes it.

"Oh, and this." He reaches around, comes up with a little Taser. She snorts.

"What next? A bowie knife?"

"I'm serious. If you go near those guys, none of this is going to help you. Fact is, I'm not comfortable with you being in the same city as them."

She hesitates. "I want to go to Peru."

He does a double take, then shakes his head violently. "You'd be scooped up at the border. Fuck, you wouldn't even get out of Michigan, much less get to Lima."

"Would you say that if I was a man?" She takes the Taser. "I'm not helpless." She looks around, judging the setting. "Watch."

Sura drops her bag, runs into a yard full of waist-high grass, and in one, two, three lunges has scaled the brick wall of a house. She perches atop its collapsed roof, twenty feet up, and smiles at his astonished look. "I do parkour, too."

"You think that's going to reassure me," he shouts up. "All you've done is convince me that I'm right, and you"—he jabs a finger at her to punctuate his words—"have an over-inflated sense of your own abilities."

As she swings her way back down, he says, "Parkour isn't going to get you to South America or save you from the crazies down the fucking Amazon. Promise me you won't leave Detroit. And promise me you won't do something stupid at Summit Recoveries either. I mean it."

"What I have," she says levelly as she brushes off her palms, "is a murdered father and a price on my head. Don't expect me to take that sitting down."

"I don't. But I expect you to be smart about it. Fuck, Sura, I catch people like you every day for making the kinds of shitheaded mistakes I see you getting ready to make."

This hits home. She scuffs her way along the street, not looking at him.

"All right," she says eventually. "I promise. Satisfied?"

He adjusts his hat on his head, tries to figure out how to react, but can't keep a smile from creeping in as he gives her a gimlet eye and says, "I'll be watching you.

"Now, about Bill Duchene . . ."

CHAPTER ELEVEN

Jay heads back to Pittsburgh, and Sura steels her will to do as he says. No peeking, no matter how angrily she paces her room, thinking about Summit Recoveries and Dad.

Staying clean this way means she has to focus on other things. Gradually, over days that turn into weeks, she finds herself settling into something like a domestic routine with Compass. Adventures with the fireteam can be crazy, as personas are adopted, plots ripen, realities merge or come apart, but her bed's always in the same place when she gets home. There's no putting a price on that.

She and the boys spend part of their time NPCing in *Lethe,* and the rest in other games, or reframing resources and situations. Her work has earned Sura a lot of badges, some of which equate to real-world goods and services. What she hasn't earned a right to, she can print or buy. She can even browse the high-end shops downtown—the ones that have no regular staff, and use facial recognition and IoT sensors to let you just walk in and take stuff. Players like her can visit them by riding avatars. This is a trick she learns from a local player named Tamara, who's black and who explains that in some stores, despite the law, prices change depending on the color of the buyer's skin. Tamara rides white girls when she wants to go shopping.

Sura joins the Oneota Gym and starts using the climbing walls. She gets a microwave and a little fridge. For a whole week she agonizes over whether to blow a considerable wad of NotchCoin on a digital piano for Compass, and finally does. Compass is thrilled, and the condo fills up with music and finally feels like home.

Just to have the luxury of thinking about buying somebody a present, much less doing it, signals massive change. Somehow, in Oneota, Sura has stopped living like a refugee.

She's even started playing *Encounters*—though not yet as a contact sport. She likes that it can be subtle, just exposing a flash of skin here and there or bringing her glances from handsome NPCs at interesting moments. It's not porn, rather it's designed to sense and heighten sexual tension. You can get haptic bracelets and garters that help the system tell when you're in the mood. It can use your glasses' iris scanners to register who and what you're noticing, and it'll refine its match-making algorithms accordingly. It heightens eroticism, as opposed to just hooking you up with sex partners; she appreciates that.

One evening Sura's walking home with some of Tamara's fireteam, who lately feel like more than mere acquaintances. "Who's that?" somebody says, pointing.

The Cahokian elder who gave her the broach in Pittsburgh is standing on the newly repaired curb. She's dressed in jeans and a T-shirt, with a nice hand-crafted shawl draped over her shoulders.

"You guys go ahead," says Sura, and walks up to her. "You're in person this time. Who are you?"

The old woman laughs. "Surely you've figured it out by now. I'm a larpwright. My name is Binesi."

"Oh! Do you know a wright named Pax?"

"Pax and I don't see eye to eye on some things," says Binesi. Then she smiles. "But we get along. Listen, I have a gift for you." She digs in her haversack.

"For me? Well, thank you." The elder hands her an oval of translucent amber. At least it looks like amber, but it could be plastic and it doesn't matter; it's physically real. There's a machine-readable glyph of some kind carved into it.

"What is it? And why are you giving it to me?"

"Call it a graduation present. For mastering the games and moving on to the frameworlds. And," she adds with a more mischievous smile, "as a hint of what the *next* level looks like."

"What does it do?" Her glasses show an interface, hovering just above the glyph.

"It gives you the ability to recognize the faces," says the elder, "of animals."

With another enigmatic smile, she walks away.

Sura hefts the faux amber. Aside from the occasional whine of a distant drone, it's eerily quiet. Cars don't make much noise these days. And the end of coal has meant the horizon's not smeared with yellow anymore. She can smell grass and flowers and hear crickets. The Cahokian bird broach, which she still wears, has made her more aware of these things.

That thing is somehow more insidious than *Encounters*. She doesn't wear the broach during the day, but as the shadows lengthen Sura will often find somewhere outside to sit—braving the mosquitoes—and activate it. Just for a few minutes, mind you; this isn't like listening to music. The tsunami of animal noises, pregnant and deep, isn't something you enjoy or even meditate to. If anything it's a rebuke, because the world no longer has these riches in it. She recognizes the sound for what it is: it's the *fuck-you* of the natural world, an imaginative pole-vault over all the categories and assumptions of the workaday. Somebody thought of making the broach. Somewhere out there someone thinks like her.

Though Sura hasn't told anybody about the broach, she shows the amber to Compass when she gets home. "A larpwright gave it to me. She said it's 'facial recognition for animals.' No fucking idea what that means."

Compass doesn't touch it but holds her face close (or maybe her glasses' camera), tilting her head from side to side. She's playing some sort of June Cleaver housewife tonight, complete with apron. "The nice lady twinked you?"

"What'd me?"

"Sura, don't they teach you kids anything these days? Twinking is when a high-level player gives a high-level item to a low-level player." Compass frowns at Sura. "Facial recognition for animals, you say. Are animals players, too?"

The words hit Sura like a little lightning bolt. "Oh shit. I guess that really is a question, isn't it?"

"Don't swear, dear."

She's seen a few raccoons in the neighborhood, a rabbit or two, and even a fox way off in the distance. There are always crows. If she activates the amber and looks out the window, what—or who—will she see?

Compass looks up at her. "Are you going to try it?"

Sura closes her hand over the oval, returns it to her pocket. "Not tonight."

Maybe not ever. The bird broach has already become heavy with significance. It's also higher-level than she is, she supposes, which may explain why it scares her a bit. The frames still work on the ordinary world, built as they are on hackneyed fantasy stories and inhabited, for the most part, by happy idiots playing at remaking the world. If Binesi's showing her a new door, what's it a door into? The thought is disquieting; and too much of her life has been disquieting.

"What about you?" she asks brightly. Compass is laboriously unwinding her braid, a nightly ritual that signals she's winding down for bed.

"Got a gig," she says. "Playing a c-company."

This isn't nearly as odd a thing for her to say as it should be. "How so? You're avatar for a rep?" There are plenty of those around, but Compass shakes her head.

"You've heard of Brim?" Sura nods; they're a major clothing line. "They're clo-clos—shutting down most of their outlets. Instead they're sending avatars into the gaming community. I d-dress in their clothes and the company scouts people to sell to. It talks through me, calls up a virtual store, that sort of thing."

"You're a model?" Sura cracks up. "That's so you—*not*!"

Compass yanks at her ponytail. "I'm still an NPC. They call it a Non-Person Character. I get to be the whole company. Sales, scouting c-customers, returns . . ."

Sura nods. Compass needs connections to the world. Feeling that she's participating so deeply in a company must be satisfying for her.

The job itself is just the logical next step in dematerialization. Why have stores at all? There are probably vans lurking about, loaded with plastic-wrapped garments, just waiting for someone to ask her, "Where'd you get that?" Minutes later the customer can be holding a similar dress, unaware until that moment that they *were* a customer. "It's sort of outside the game economy, though, isn't it?"

Compass shakes her head. "Haven't you noticed? The games *are* the economy now."

Sura opens her mouth. Closes it. It's been a long time since she had that feeling of guilt about not holding a "real job" that she'd so clumsily tried to describe to Jay. What they're doing isn't entertainment, though it can be damned entertaining. The frames themselves are something else—modes or perspectives she steps in and out of while trying to solve larger problems. There is no other name than *reframing*, that she's heard of anyway, for what she does.

"Right, I'm going to check my mail and go to bed." She leaves Compass curled on the couch, proud that she's here and not sleeping in a car somewhere. Compass is one of her real-world accomplishments, even if she sometimes feels like another high-level item, given into Sura's care with no instruction sheet to explain what she's for.

K.C.'s been missing for two days when he suddenly calls. "Meet me in Delray," he says, with no other explanation. "Jefferson and West End."

Sura's taking the day off; you have to enjoy the summer while you can. Reluctantly she puts herself into motion, locking the condo and stretching while she heads down the stairs. While she's waiting for a game-owned car to get her out of Not in Service, she checks her team's status. Maeve the Knife Fairy is in mid-quest inside *Tarnation Alley.* Vaughan is doing some design work in the traditional economy. Mostly, her other new friends and acquaintances are online and buzzing about an external event: there's been a global stock market crash.

She feels insulated from it all here, but in what she used to think of as the "real world," the media are going nuts. What is interesting is that some of the press are talking breathlessly about a socialist (or, according to some, anarchist) collective that's partnered with the City of Detroit to rehabilitate its brownlands. The frameworlds are being touted as an economic miracle, and suddenly, everybody wants to know how they work.

Maybe they're onto something. She regularly meets players who are being ridden by people from Korea and India; the discovery and sharing process has penetrated far into global logistics and supply-chain management. With over fifteen thousand shipping containers lost every year just from toppling over the side of container ships, the global logistics system has a surprising amount of flex and slop to it. The frameworlds are harvesting some tiny fraction of planetary capitalism's rounding errors, everywhere and all at once. It's becoming clear to Sura that what's happening in Detroit is just a rounding error on *that.*

The game car lets her off in what looks like the set from a post-apocalyptic movie. There's water at the end of the street, and across it squats black, deathly Zug Island, a forbidding forest of refinery towers and off-gassing stacks. Nobody goes there anymore.

In an empty lot next to her, gangs of men and women are getting their exercise by playing robots in an AI future. Some have formed an elaborate bucket brigade that, for a few minutes or an hour, is sorting an insanely varied pile of packages being disgorged from four eighteen-wheelers arrayed around them like the blunt arrows of a vast compass. It's an impromptu postal service, FedEx-for-a-day, and only about half of what's being sorted is fully real, many of the boxes being visible only in MR. Their physical presence is felt only to those players wearing haptic-feedback gloves. Nothing that's being moved is stolen, nobody technically owns any of it, and much of it is entirely useless outside of some esoteric sub-reality in some game or other. Dozens of currencies, real and imagined, pay for, lease, or establish credit based on the junk and bright virtual shimmers floating above the shoulders of the crowd.

K.C. is waiting to one side. He looks nervous. "What the hell, K.C.," she says as she walks up. "Why'd you drag me down to this shit-hole?"

"I've found him."

"Duchene?" She spins and peers into the scrum of players. "He's here?"

"Not here. But nearby."

"What have you been up to?"

"I told you," he says, "I have my own contacts. People from . . . another life. Some of them were gamers right from the start—back in the PC and console days. They went straight to VR and took to MR like they'd been born for it.

"You know *The White Rose*? They found out about it. First they infiltrated it, then they built their own version—one where they get to be the SS and hunt people. The frameworlds don't want to have anything to do with them, but they've copied our systems, made their own paradise."

Ever since Trump promised his wall, it's been obvious that what the white supremacists really want is their own reality. Now they can finally have it. K.C. describes their *America* game, in which the South won the war and everything now has the misty, color-saturated quality of *Gone with the Wind*. The men are all gentlemen—and white—and the women wear skirts with flounces when they wear anything at all.

There are no other countries, there is no "rest of the world." There are no other religions than the one where a blond, blue-eyed Christ gazes benevolently down upon his people. But there are always traitors, and the congenitally inferior to ferret out and destroy.

"But you wouldn't even be real to them. You're black!"

"Oh, they need us to be real, or there'd be nobody to look down on. I couldn't play as an equal, but as long as I acted the way they expected . . ." She's hearing his accent again, and concludes that it must be South African.

"So you went in. Why?"

"Partly to take 'em for all they were worth. You didn't want to know about that either."

"Why haven't you told me about this before?"

"Because it had nothing to do with our investigation. And right from the start I heard talk of players so extreme that the doxers, Tea-party loyalists, and Trumpists wouldn't have anything to do with them. Too dangerous for you. People home-schooled in Pizzagate metaphysics, who believe Hillary Clinton was a baby-eating demon running a global child-snatching ring from a fast-food outlet. They've built their own fantasy-land in MR, and it's really well-funded. Their founders made billions from the Bitcoin bubble and now they run an international doxing and swatting operation. Online intimidation, kompromat, reputation-ruining, threats, and denial-of-service attacks, for a price."

"Why did that mean anything to you?"

K.C. looks away. "I have a . . . special insight into that sort of thing. I thought I could use my connections to look into their links more safely than . . . other people."

"What other people . . . ?" He stares at her in reply, and slowly it dawns on Sura. "Me? You thought they might have some connection with me?"

"You try to be tight-lipped, but you're not very good at it. I mean, the whole fireteam knows you've got problems with some company of fixers. You won't tell us its name, but it wasn't hard for me to find. Summit Recoveries is one of these guys' customers."

"Holy shit. K.C.? You've been working my case?" He looks down bashfully. "That's sweet, but—"

"So anyway," he hurries on, "this is how it went down: A while back, this guy shows up, says he wants to join the Community. He's got this crazy scheme to sell Decision Architecture overlays for preppers. To help them plan for The Day. Well, that's not going to work, these folk aren't actually into planning, they've already decided what's going to happen and when. They were laughing about him, didn't take him seriously. They sent him to talk to the doxers.

"A couple days ago, the laughing stopped. Somebody said a billionaire had shown up in the Community, but he hadn't been recognized until too late. Somebody'd pushed him on the doxers for a joke, but the doxers knew who he was, and well, they didn't let him go. They've got him. In their troll factory."

They've been sidling down the street, using all their resources to avoid cameras and sight lines. Up ahead is a crumbling tire factory that her security overlays have forested with warning flags. Its fence is topped with barbed wire, and there's a big metal gate. The place is practically a concentration camp. Hovering over it in MR is a giant Confederate flag rendered in hyperreal Socialist Realist detail; it's even waving in time to the real-world breeze.

Sura scowls. "Do you actually know that it's Duchene they've got?"

"No. But they've got somebody." He looks her in the eye. "Are we going to abandon a brother in need?"

She groans and rubs her eyes, thinking about Jay's visit and how well she's been keeping out of trouble. "No, no we are not.

"But we do this carefully, hear me? No *Die Hard* shit."

K.C. nods approvingly. "At my age, that's not even an option."

"Good. Let's call the team."

Jay's reaction is predictable. "I'm coming to Detroit," he says when she tells him. "I'll bring Trey. Don't do anything until we get there." He hangs up.

She called him from a mildew-infested upper room in an abandoned Venetian blind works, two blocks from the troll factory. She's made the place into a command center, setting up a secure mesh connection and some battery packs. When Vaughan shows up with a satchel of microdrones, they send an unending stream of spies to reconnoiter the place.

The apocalypse-porn incels in the factory (all of them are men) are living out their *Mad Max* fantasies in the only way possible: with the full support of the twenty-first-century economy. They have solar panels on their roof but suck a prodigious amount of power from the city's grid. They aren't allowed to touch the cell phone tower next to the panels; it's probably an FBI stingray and is intercepting all their calls, but what do they know? They patrol the roof, armed to the teeth, but don't notice her tiny drones hovering behind the barbed wire.

It takes a day for Jay and Trey to show up, and when they do, they're not pleased. "You haven't got enough to even warrant a drive-by from the cops," Jay complains as she and the team lay out their evidence. "If they did believe you, they'd be as likely to go full Waco on the place as anything."

"Jay, we have to do something. There's a lot of activity, more than K.C. has seen before, right K.C.? Cars and trucks going in and out. They might be getting ready to move him. If we're going to do anything, we've got to do it now."

Trey is fanning through the drone photos. They show a heavily guarded, small building in an inner courtyard. Baskets of food are brought into it every now and then, and there's blurry movement behind the windows. "This is really all you've got?"

"We've got K.C.'s testimony. I trust him."

Jay and Trey look at each other. "Even if we did believe you," says Trey after a while, "I'm not sure there's anything we can do right now. The place is a fortress."

"Ah. Well, as to that." She calls up some windows. "While you were driving up here, Vaughan stitched together a few thousand pictures from the drones and made a 3-D model. We started doing walkthroughs of the place last night."

Trey looks mildly impressed. "Nice, but—"

"Oh, it gets better. We retextured the model as a *Rivet Couture* airship factory and built a VR infiltration scenario around it. Not larpwright-quality stuff, but good enough for casual gameplay. We put sentries on the rooftops where they are in real life, and Vaughan got mean and added pressure plates in the corridor floors, locks and barriers everywhere and lots and lots of dogs all around the grounds. Then we uploaded the scenario to the public *RC* quest board. And waited."

It took about six hours for some insomniac player to crack the level. She and Vaughan rearranged the defenses and uploaded that version, and then another. "By this time we had a pretty good idea of how the blind spots in the building and grounds fight against their own security. The vulnerabilities are built into the architecture; this is usually the case."

She brings up the model in MR as well as the overlay that highlights all the lessons learned. "A frontal assault isn't going to work," she says. "But one or two people could literally just walk in and out, as long as they get their timing right."

"No!" Jay throws his hat on the table. "Sura, that is just batshit crazy! You are not going in there like this is some game level! Those assholes have guns!"

She protests that she hadn't intended for any of them to go in; they could give this information to the police tactical squad. Jay's not having any of it. Consensus is they're not going to do anything until there's some kind of concrete evidence that it's Duchene in there, and that he's in trouble. Something like a ransom demand. "Until then, you do nothing!" he commands.

Yer fuckin' bastard, you can't order me around! she fumes as she stomps down the sagging stairs. *We found him. My team found him.*

Duchene's there, somehow Summit Recoveries is involved, and Jay wants her to wait? *To hell with that.*

She tells herself these things as she walks out to hail a car. It's late, there are a lot of suspicious characters about, but nobody's going to mess with a lady who's got her own drone swarm. When the car arrives, she collapses the cloud into a large bag; the walk has already taken a bit of the edge off her sense of urgency. By the time she reaches the border of Not in Service and the car announces its owner won't let it go any further, she's just tired.

Maybe Jay is right. They need to be sensible, wait for better evidence. If the doxers bundle Duchene into a car, her drones will register their license plates. Besides, Trey has his own resources. It'll be fine.

She's turning onto Brush Street when one of her alerts goes off. A virtual servant she based on Mad Scratchie appears, looking spooked.

"Don't go home," he says. "Neighborhood is crawling with cameras."

"What? Cops?"

He shakes his head. "Press and bloggers and people with their glasses on *record*. Dee-scended on the place after news that people are pumping their money into Gwaiicoin. Gettin' self-sovereignty tatts is the new thing."

"Wait, people are investing in Gwaii?"

"It's currency that's backed by ecosystem services, so it's stable right now. It's keepin' its value while the fiat currencies are crashin' left, right, n'center."

Looking up the road past Scratchie, Sura can see a flutter of dots above the old elementary school. News drones. They'll be dive-bombing the neighborhood taking filler shots and, sadly, they're between her and her house. Any face they record will be run through the security databases of a hundred countries and other, more shadowy groups. She can't count on her Rorschach veil to protect her from that level of scrutiny.

At that moment a call comes in. It's K.C. "Lots of movement at the troll factory," he says. "Cars going in and out. Something's up."

"Is Jay still there?"

"He and your client left a while back. Said not to bring him in unless we have 'something definitive.' Like a photo of Duchene tied to a chair."

"Thanks," she says. She stands there for a few seconds, wondering where to go.

A photo—that's all Jay needs. She imagines the grounds, the windows and plastic blinds she's seen in the drone images. Jay doesn't need heroics. All he needs is somebody to pull back those curtains . . .

Sura decides, raises her hands, and summons her powers.

"K.C.?"

"I'm in place."

"Maeve?"

"Overhead and seeing everything, Countess."

"Vaughan?"

". . . You sure you want to do this?"

"This is my specialty. You'll see."

She checks her inventory as she pauses under the canopy of a collapsing gas station. The structure she's looking for is an administrative building/garage nestled against the outside of the former tire plant and surrounded on three other sides by a ten-foot-high brick wall. This compound, in turn, is inside the plant's chain-link fence. Dobermans are patrolling that.

Sura is ready with her Taser, a rope and pitons, shivs and lockpicks. After some consideration, she decided not to bring the gun Jay made for her.

There's a stiff breeze from the west tonight, which should mask her scent from the dogs. Just to be safe, K.C. is about to make a lot of noise on the far side of the complex. Maeve is piloting the drones, and her job is to bob around making them visible to any Dobermans that don't go after K.C. Vaughan is monitoring everything from the Venetian blind factory.

She waits a few minutes, and when she hears a clamor of barking moving away from the main building, she sprints across the street to a gnarled tree that interrupts the chain-link fence.

She waits until the men on the roof walk away to yell at the dogs, then scales the tree and drops inside the fence. A quick dash to the courtyard wall and she starts up the brickwork. They'd identified good finger- and toe-holds by shooting the wall with a telephoto lens and enhancing the image in a photo-manipulation program. Now she sees each of these spots as a glowing green line.

Broken glass tops the wall, but she's mapped that too and knows where there's a gap. She levers herself up and peeks into the inner courtyard.

The troll factory is all lit up, and slots of sickly yellow sodium-lamp light lean through the gate to the south. The bars sketch a gravel driveway that leads to a garage with a second floor.

Three times since they've been watching, men in suits have been let into the compound. Vaughan stashed treasure all over their game levels and she knows that there is absolutely no reason for people to be going in and out of this yard unless there's something important in the garage. If Duchene's not there, she's not looking any further.

The garage's second floor has faded plastic curtains on its windows. Those curtains are the problem. All she has to do is get the drones a view past them. This is not a rescue mission.

Sura's hooked a leg over the wall, and every muscle in her body is now screaming. She lets her knotted rope down the inside wall. At this time of the evening, shadows occult the bricks. She rapidly slides down the rope, and she's in.

It's a sad little lot, the only distinguishing detail being stacks of shipping palettes that have been here so long that trees have sprouted through them. The snout of a car is visible under one tilted door of the garage. If it can drive itself it can also be hacked to be an effective watchdog. She'll just have to hope the doxers don't have the resources or gumption to do this.

It'd make a great scene, though, to screech out of here in the thing, somehow having overridden its ownership locks. She has a momentary vision of herself, Duchene duct-taped in the back seat, smashing down the gate, chain-link fence unraveling behind them as she hits the road and accelerates into the night . . .

No. Cars can be shut down remotely, if they'll obey you at all. She sidles along the inside of the wall, notes that the only way upstairs is past the car, and sucks in a deep breath. The little *fuck-you* vision has helped, but there's one last ritual to do before she goes in.

Purrloin has been tracking her movements ever since he was tattooed onto her leg. Sura murmurs her password, composes an email to the police, and pastes a permission into it. She's not going to send it now, but keeps the email open, visible in MR as a white square floating just in front and to her right. She'll send it the instant things go south. The police will receive a blockchain-proven link to her current GPS location, and as long as Purrloin has a good satellite signal, it'll keep updating.

Presumably, Duchene didn't do something like this. But then, he seems not to have paranoia as one of his achievements.

The car doesn't stir, so she strides up the cement stairs behind it. At the top is a door. There's really no other way in, unless she throws her grapple through a window, so she gingerly turns the knob. It moves easily. She steps into the second floor of the garage, heart pounding.

No self-respecting level designer had a hand in building this place. The stairs open into a little kitchen area with a table and two chairs. It's done up in strip-paneled wood that's painted mint green. This takes up a quarter of the floor space; a narrow toilet and an equally small storage room take up another quarter. The other half of the floor is all one room.

Two voices, both male. Under that another sound that might be a television from the way it dopplers in Sura's ears.

"Fine," says one voice, "but he'll hear about it." Suddenly footsteps are coming her way.

Decide: Duck back down the stairs or into the storage room? Sura darts across the kitchen and hunkers down in the closet.

A man enters the toilet and slams the door. It's surreal; this is such a classic game trope—the distracted guard—but she can't question it. Horribly aware of the boards creaking under her feet, she eases past the toilet and comes to stand in the doorway to the main room.

It's a creepy little boudoir, the walls and ceiling covered in chicken wire over red felt patterned wallpaper and acoustic tile. Frayed silk pillows cover the abundant if sagging couches, and there's a big-screen TV, a time-traveler from the early twenty-first century visiting the worst dregs of the twentieth. And there he is, sitting slumped way down on one of the couches, feet planted wide on the floor, arms crossed as he glares at the box. Duchene's right pantleg has been cut off below the knee, and his ankle is swaddled in bandages.

Sura steps in front of the screen and puts her finger to her lips.

Duchene's reflexive jerk practically carries him over the back of the couch. "Jesus Christ!"

"All I'm gonna do is open these blinds here. You smile for the cameras. I was never here. Got it?"

"What the fuck?"

"Shut up!" she hisses. "You wanna get out of here or not?"

Duchene looks from her to the chicken wire–covered window, where the shadow of a drone is passing; he grins.

Then his eyes slide past her and the look in them tells her all she needs to know.

She goes for her Taser but there's a big guy in her face suddenly, swinging an open-handed slap that sends Sura's glasses flying.

As she stumbles her backpack mashes the doorjamb, and the doxer's unholstered a pistol. Behind him Duchene is hanging a sock over a small camera mounted on a pillar.

Sura can't handle this so Countess Vesta takes over and dives for the guy, ramming the Taser into the center of his chest. The gun goes flying as they hit the floor with her straddling him.

He grabs her wrist. "That fuckin' *hurt*!" So much for Tasering him a second time. His rabbit-punch catches her in the solar plexus and then he's rolling them both over, him on top now *oh shit*—

His head jerks to the side; Duchene's kicked him. This just makes him mad but Duchene does it again, leg in full extension and using his heel now. The guy windmills, knee-walks backward and Duchene does him again, right in the nose. Sura hears cartilage crunch and he goes down.

Sura nods at Duchene's bandaged calf. "Guessing that's not busted," she gasps.

"Fuckers burned off my tattoo. You got a plan B?"

"We run for it." She retrieves her Taser and glasses, which are broken. Fuck, did she send the email? She can't remember.

Duchene doesn't have shoes but keeps up until they're out of the garage. When he sees the climbing rope he says, "What, are you going to carry me? I can't make that!"

She races to the courtyard gate, which is loosely chained but not padlocked. "Unravel that! Then it's a straight run to the fence."

"You got a car waiting?" She nods. Vaughan should have one circling the block, starting about now.

There's shouting from the roof. Men are boiling out the factory door, and the dogs are going nuts. "Get that chain off!" she shouts, and he unreels it. Then it's a sprint to the outer fence with howling men right behind them.

He staggers to a halt under it. "I can't climb!"

"You have to!" She's not waiting, just goes up and over, perching atop for a second and lifting her legs high as she jumps over the barbed wire.

He goes under instead, ripping and scraping as the dogs come up. Sura looks to the road, desperate to see what she wants—

The sign on the side of the car says *Proudly Eagle Owned!*

Laughing hysterically, she hauls him to his feet and they pile into the car. "Drive!" she screams at it.

"What's your destination?" it asks politely.

"Where do we—?" starts Duchene. Then he and Sura both say, "Not the police!"

"Huh." He stares at her.

"Huh." She stares back. They've fetched up like a human dune in the back seat. Sura lets herself wash back a bit and turns to the dashboard. "Car: Do you do virtual destinations? In larpworlds?"

"Where there is an overlap with the real world," says the car, unfazed. "There's an additional fee—"

"Take us to the nearest *White Rose* safe transit point."

"This is never going to work," Duchene points out. "Self-drivers don't do car chases! How are we going to get away?"

A gunshot sounds somewhere nearby, then another, and the shouting is getting nearer. "My people are on it," she says. She has no idea whether this is true, but she's seen Vaughan and Maeve improvise in tight corners; if nothing else, Maeve can dive-bomb any pursuing cars with the drones.

The I-75 on-ramp is only six blocks away and by the time there are cars after them, they're sailing up it. Sura lets out a whoosh, slumps back, and squints at Duchene. "You don't want to take this to the cops?"

He crosses his arms. "I will if you will."

"Uh . . . no."

And that's the end of that.

CHAPTER TWELVE

Passed from partisan to partisan, slipped through camera shadows, and watched over by deeply hacked drones, Sura and Duchene eventually fetch up in a *White Rose* safe house. It's the middle of the night when a grim-faced Latino woman in a print dress makes up cots for them in the back of a former cell phone outlet. The front of the shop looks into an abandoned shopping mall.

A retired nurse redoes Duchene's bandage, and then the *White Rose* players retreat. Duchene limps to the till to look out at the sad plazas of the mall through the shop's security mesh. "Creepy," he says.

Sura comes to stand next to him. "Places like this were never meant to be empty." Bereft of people, the mall's interior is just an exercise in geometry, no one present to admire the orange tile floors and rectangle benches. The shop interiors are like the eyesockets of a dead god.

"What did the doxers want?" she asks him. "Ransom?"

He nods, looking down. "I guess I'm not the badass I thought I was. They got all my accounts and passwords out of me the first day. Fuckers, I . . ." He runs a shaky hand through his hair, grins weakly at her. "You know."

Both of them threw up earlier, a few minutes after they left the I-75. Sura had the *Proudly Eagle Owned!* pull over and they'd knelt side by side on somebody's front lawn. *That's a thing to share,* she'd thought, yet it felt like it forged a bond in a way that merely breaking him out of his prison hadn't.

"Why ransom you if they've got into your accounts? Just to twist the knife?"

He shakes his head. "Before I went larpabout, I changed my security so everything needs multisig. It takes more than my password to perform any transaction. My lawyers and business partner have to use theirs too. So the bastards can't get into any of my accounts, no matter how cooperative I am. Once they figured that out, they switched to plan B."

She grins. "Think they've got a plan C?"

"Oh, I doubt it. Now I'm gone, they'll be too busy packing to come after us." He laughs, then gazes at the mall pensively.

"Thanks," he says after a while. "I really mean it. You put your life on the line back there. No way you had to."

"I was just there to get a picture. I was gonna upload that, then call in the cavalry. Besides . . ." She raises her jeans cuff, shows him Purrloin. "I'm a walking dead-man switch. If I stayed cut-off in that Faraday cage they had you in for more than a few seconds, all kinds of alarms would have gone off. We'd have been swarmed with game drones in seconds, and the cops'd've been there in minutes."

"Oh." He thinks about it, and shrugs. "Still—"

"—Thanks is still appreciated." They exchange a look. She's shy, he's unreadable in this light.

"But what the fuck were you even doing there?" She crosses her arms, stepping away. "Do you buy into that shit?"

"No. I was desperate. They looked like easy marks."

"And yet you let them snatch you? You should have had countermeasures at least as sophisticated as mine."

"I did, at first." In unspoken agreement they both back away from the front of the store. With dusty racks and displays between them and the doors, Duchene lowers himself onto a plastic chair and hangs his hands between his knees. "I couldn't afford the upkeep. You talked to Trey. You know why I was here?"

"A bet, he said."

Duchene nods. "I'm sure it seems ridiculous to you, but we were dead serious. Listen, when in human history has it been possible for somebody to reboot their life, without actually running away? To experiment with how things would have gone if you'd made different choices? The games let us do that." He shoots her a sly smile. "Tell me that's not why you're here."

"Uh . . ."

"Plus it was important!" Exhausted as he obviously is, he sits up straight. "This country's built on the premise that we all earn what we get out of life. Nothing about America makes sense if that isn't true. It's got to be possible for a man to work his way up from nothing, become as rich or powerful as he wants. Trey says it's not, but if that were true then . . ." He shakes his head angrily. "What's the fucking point? Might as well go all-out socialist."

"You wanted to prove him wrong."

"No! I wanted to prove *me* right." He runs his hand through his hair. "But the first few months were a disaster."

He tells her how *Lethe* scrambled his skills to the point where he had none. "I was the fucking equivalent of a ditch-digging mouth-breather, I had no marketable talents." The game biased his conversations, downgrading his negotiation scores. "It loaded the dice against me."

"Isn't that the point? That the dice are loaded against most people?"

He stands up restlessly, winces. "Maybe. Sure, what the fuck. Point is I lost everything I went in with, and it was taking me more time than I planned on, getting it back."

"Hmm."

He shoots her a look. "What? You don't believe I could have come out on top again?"

"No, it's not that. It's just . . ."

"Oh, just out with it. I don't fucking care how stupid you think I am."

"Seems to me," says Sura, "that the game *you* were playing was *Prince and the Pauper*. You thought this guy"—she taps her ankle—"meant you could play it with just princes, no paupers. But there's always a pauper wanting to take your place, isn't there? This time, it was the doxers."

He stares at her.

"Is all I was thinking." She looks down.

Duchene laughs. "Shit, I never thought of it like that! Fuck, you should have been a genius."

"Gee, thanks."

He lands on the chair again. "What's your name? For real?"

"There is no 'for real.' Let's go with Countess Vesta."

"Bah! Fine, be that way. So you're a, like, what, a private investigator in the games?"

"Exactly." She's absurdly pleased at his look of wonder.

"I mean it makes perfect sense there'd be such a thing, I just never . . . And Trey hired you?"

"Hired . . . us." She really wants to take full credit for this, but she can't short-change Jay. "Me and my partner."

"Is she a bad-ass like you?"

"Absolutely."

The conversation peters out, but in its place she has a moment, not a *fuck-you,* but something like it that for a change isn't fueled by anger. Her consciousness enlarges past the walls of this little shop to take in the downcast thoroughfares of the mall, its fake outdoorsyness, the shabby peeling facades, the silence. Outside, the city sprawls away in tumbles of roof, steaming and murmuring to itself in its sleep. It all wheels around this little corner, and him and her, and the AC/DC hum of the utilities that are keeping the lights on and the air moving. A strange idyll, a pause in her race through life.

"What now?" she asks finally. "Back to *Lethe*? Or are you done with playing games?"

"It wasn't a total waste. I learned a few things," he says ruefully. She's expecting a confession, that he's had some revelation about his own life, but instead he says, "First, you can't learn shit from larps. The whole prince and pauper thing was never going to work. Except I don't know how I'm going to convince Trey of that. He's gonna say I'm copping out because I don't want to lose the bet."

"So lose the bet," she says. "I mean, let him have something. You're the one who took the chances. You can at least tell him never to bring up the subject again."

The chair cricks as he leans back, drawing a finger down his chin, a slight smile on his face. "I could, couldn't I? Specially after the whole kidnapping thing. But I'd rather void the bet."

"Because, kidnapping," she says. He nods. "So back to business, then?" she presses. Sura would love to know how you resume your old life after larpabout.

"Yeah, but I learned a couple other things." He bounces a little in the chair, which complains. "You know about the participatory economics stuff they're doing with the frameworlds?"

"A bit. Don't really understand it."

"It's pretty simple. They're replacing market forces with data mining to set prices and production targets. Like Soviet central planning, only *de*-centralized and emergent."

"Can that even work?"

"Last I saw, it *is* working. It's Pareto-optimal. And it's a really cool idea, but a little, you know, shall we say, communist?"

Sura, who is actually living in a commune now that she thinks about it, shrugs noncommittally.

"You get fooled by the games, you know. They're so local, so specific, you think they must be designed by people right here. But the big thing I found out is that they didn't even originate in America. Can you believe it? And even now, the frames here are just the tip of the iceberg. There's some kind of international movement, a cloud country, an online nation behind it all. The frames are its economy. Here, the games are the gateway drug, but the people who built the frames never used 'em. The frames came first, the games are just a way to serve them up to the yokels in North America and Europe.

"This cloud country thing scares the hell out of me. It's a kind of invasion, an attack on our sovereignty. I started out trying to reboot my life in the games, but I ended up committed to finding out who's behind it and stopping them."

She's never heard of any cloud country, but you can't escape the transnational nature of the frames. "How are you going to do that?"

"I bet a commercial version of the frameworlds will run even more efficiently than this open-source stuff. It's all cobbled together. We can streamline it."

"So that's what you're going to do now? Commercialize the frames?"

He nods. "And I would have bailed and started all that months ago, except that I stumbled on a clue." He tilts his head, eyeing her speculatively. "You a big fan of Pax?"

"I'm on nobody's side," she says, and she can hear in her own voice that she means it.

He looks at her for a few seconds, obviously deciding whether to reveal something. Then: "You ever heard of a game called *The Rewilding*?"

"Rewilding? Like when they brought wolves back to Yellowstone. That kind of thing?"

"No, not *that* kind of thing. More like, if this mysterious cloud country is some kind of conspiracy, then *The Rewilding* is the elite that run it. The secret government."

"Now you're sounding like the doxers."

He shakes his head violently. "This isn't made-up bullshit. *The Rewilding* isn't just a game, I do know that. The frames are a front for something, and maybe what Pax and his people have in mind is a full-blown return to Bolshevism. Get people hooked on a planned economy, then declare that the whole distributed thing isn't working and cut over to central planning. A new Stalinist regime."

She recoils. "That's horrible."

"And God help me I hope I'm wrong. That's what I was investigating when the doxers caught me. I gotta know. *We* have to know."

"How are you going to find this conspiracy, if it even exists?"

"I can work from the outside, but the whole reason I was still there was that I needed an inside investigator, too."

"Oh," she says, and he nods.

"Isn't that what you are? A private eye inside the frameworlds?"

"Not entirely, I mean, it's more complicated than that—"

"But you know the frames. You know the people, you obviously know how to track somebody down, you did it with me."

"You want to hire us to find a conspiracy inside the frames?"

Duchene shakes his head. "Not you and your partner. Just you. Or is that not possible?"

"No no it's totally possible. It's just, I'm not as experienced, I'm like the junior partner—"

"Tonight was a good enough audition for me."

"Yeah. Well." She looks down, bashful. "It was kind of awesome, wasn't it?"

He's really close, grinning, and there's huge energy between them. She hopes he's not going to take it as sexual, although that wouldn't be entirely terrible, the grateful billionaire lover . . . The moment's charged, but nothing happens. And soon, cars arrive, and they go their separate ways.

After a couple of nights in which she can't go home and has to sleep in cars, *The White Rose* adapts itself to the presence of the media in Oneota, and Sura's able to get back to the condo. She wants to just sleep for a week, but the fireteam have other ideas. They throw a party at Not in Service's school and drag her along.

The gymnasium is its usual insane romp of cosplayers, suits, and normcore Kens and Barbies who pay the waitresses in pounds, sovereigns, credits, Gwaiicoin, or a dozen other currencies. Sura perks up the instant she's inside, and when she sees Jay and Trey Saunders—both here in reality, not *in virtua*—she grins and actually runs to hug Jay. He returns it awkwardly.

The fireteam has claimed a spot of floor and made it their own party world. Trey congratulates them all on their good work, and particularly on the daring escape—though he recognizes that it was unsanctioned. "Jay was right to wait, whatever the outcome. You acted in the moment, and for that Bill and I are grateful. I just hope you never have to pull a stunt like that again."

"Where's Bill?" Sura asks.

"Home—back in Chicago," says Trey. "Sleeping it off, basically. This has been really traumatic for him. We've only spoken briefly, but I'm pushing him to get counseling. He sends his best wishes—and he wants to reward you for rescuing him."

"As long as the reward's not in dollars," Vaughan mutters, and everybody laughs. The dollar is collapsing, as are most other national currencies. There's a general run on the banks.

"It's safe to say Bill and I are going to be putting our money in Gwaiicoin," Trey admits. "I don't know what he's got in mind for you, but I do know he's very grateful. As am I."

A while later, with Jay and Trey out exploring the neighborhood, the fireteam sit down together to talk about what's next for their fledgling detective agency.

"This isn't going to be like any company in the real world," Vaughan points out. "Meaning is world-dependent. What counts as theft, or harassment, or manipulation can be different in different games. Even what we call ourselves is going to have to be context-sensitive: investigators here, grand inquisitors there . . ."

"So what are we going to do, really?" asks Rico, who's attending *in virtua* but happily chugging a celebratory beer back in Pittsburgh.

Vaughan stares off into space for a while. "The larpwrights data-mine the game blockchains to look for classic market manipulation, but that's only half the story. The other half of the world is what's inside people's heads as they play. The only way to get at the meaning of the data-mined numbers is to have agents on the ground. I mean, in the games. We can be those agents."

They compare notes and find another growth area. A *replay* is when you do a walkthrough of a larp that developed weird subplots or ended badly. The idea is to find design flaws or evidence of abuse of the rule-sets by larpwrights or players. Usually, things go wrong because of the personalities of the people involved, or because of the law of unexpected consequences. People buy into theories that just don't work—Vaughan uses the example of trickle-down economics—and then are surprised when, well, they don't work.

Vaughan and Maeve keep congratulating K.C. on his infiltration of the doxers, but he doesn't seem to be liking the attention. "I'm not saying you should be our undercover agent," says Vaughan. "Only that we can do more of that kind of investigation. Just, maybe, in less dangerous worlds."

K.C. is silent as Vaughan, Maeve, and Rico happily argue over the idea. Sura watches him.

During a lull, as they're all pondering the possibilities, Maeve says, "You know, there's a bona fide mystery right now. A cross-world one."

"What's that?" asks Rico.

"It's this grand meeting, or conference, or parlay that everybody in every world seems to have been invited to, all at the same time. Maybe we should investigate it pro bono."

"Interesting," says Vaughan, but just then K.C. pops up a private flag for Sura's eyes-only. It means "Can we talk?"

She blinks, then tilts her head at the entrance. He nods.

"'Scuse us, guys," she says, getting up.

"Oh?" says Maeve. "Conspiring?"

"Sure." She and K.C. go outside, where it's cool and clear.

"Thank you for tracking down Duchene," she starts. "I know you may have burned your bridges and I really appreciate the risk you took. We couldn't have done it without you."

K.C. scuffs at the ground, then smiles at her. "It was a small thing. Which is kind of the point."

"What do you mean?"

"Those doxers were nothing. Small-fry. They also weren't about to turn us—me—in to the authorities, at least not the ones people like you and I might be worried about."

She tilts her head noncommittally. "Authorities like . . ."

"Well, in my case, ICE."

"Ah." Not a surprise, really, but she feels she needs to reciprocate now. She points to herself. "You were right about me, I'm hiding. Enemies of my father. It's complicated."

"Yeah." He looks away. "There's a lot going on. A lot you may not know about, and it worries me that you don't seem more curious."

"About what?"

"Well, for instance." He waves his hands about. "Who built all this?"

"We did!"

"The shit. Who designed the game system? Who started them? Don't you think about things like that? I worry about what kind of investigator you'll be if you don't wonder about that sort of thing."

It's lucky they're out in the darkness because she can feel herself blushing. "My mind's been on other stuff." But Bill Duchene was in as dire a situation as her, and he still had time for such questions.

"You'd better ask yourself if your attention is too divided for this kind of work."

There's a long silence. When she feels she has to break it, she says, "It seems like everybody's hunting whoever started the frames. Are you doing it too?"

"Oh, I know who started them," says K.C. "No, I'm only looking for one thing. I'm trying to find a man."

Turns out K.C. is from South Africa, and he's illegally in the US. The reasons, though, are surprising.

"I was a talk-radio host."

"No shit. You do have the voice for it."

"Thanks."

Sura would not have liked listening to K.C. back in the day. He was a provocateur, as nasty and abusive, by his own admission, as the worst right-wing pundits in the US.

He could be funny; he could mask his sarcasm and anger with apparently self-deprecating humor. He'd started out as just another YouTube ranter, but one day a white man with bodyguards in tow dropped by the studio. He offered K.C. money—lots of it—to focus his attacks on Zimbabwean immigrants. K.C. was no fool, he knew this man represented white farmers who dreamed of a return to apartheid; the thing was, he felt the same way about immigration. He hated liberals. So he accepted the money.

Things took off and he found himself in Johannesburg, broadcasting from a church on weekdays. The congregation didn't mind, they didn't come there to praise God anyway, but rather to have their own anger focused and channeled. K.C. discovered he could do that.

"What people want more than anything is to witness a takedown. An unmasking. They want to watch John McClane chase down the bad guy. They'll hang on the edge of their seats, they'll pay anything to be part of that."

But it was in Johannesburg that he'd met Safiya Abbott.

She was the daughter of another preacher, but she didn't approve of K.C.'s show. In fact, their first meeting happened when at a meeting of church elders, out of the blue she walked up and slapped him.

He smooths his cheek with one hand, smiling. "I still feel it. Oh, she told me off! You should have been there. We argued, and I liked it, and she liked it. We started seeing each other.

"Her father was there that night but I didn't actually meet him until we'd been together for a while. My church didn't approve of him, and neither did my financial backers."

Nile Abbott was known as an advocate for immigrants' rights, but as K.C. got to know him, it emerged that he was far more. Abbott had ties to UN refugee agencies, US NGOs, and deep connections into the diaspora of fifty nations. With their help, he was building something. "Best I could figure out at the time, he was a missionary, but he'd staked his tent where none of the rest of us had gone: in Mixed Reality.

"When we finally did meet—oh! it was an awkward dinner, at least for me!—I asked him about it. Was he going after the rich kids, the sons of the landowners and mining barons? He shook his head. His flock was in the refugee camps.

"Can you imagine the awkwardness? I was spending my days calling immigrants vermin and screaming that they should be kept out, and Abbott was helping them sneak in. Or so I thought.

"He talked about solar charging stations for smartphones and mobile apps for organizing refugees; I had no clue. I struggled to be polite though I was seething. I felt betrayed. When we finally got around to talking about politics he smiled and said, 'When I was younger I too believed in left and right, and I was on the right; but then I learned the truth.' I expected him to launch into some Blood of Christ speech, but instead he said—and I'll never forget this—*'How do you control something?'*

"I stammered some nonsense. He smiled and said, 'Whatever does the controlling has to have at least as many options for acting as the thing it controls, right?' When I thought it through and cautiously agreed, he said, 'The controller has two choices. It can either increase its own variety, its number of options, to match or exceed those of what it's controlling. Or it can try to reduce the complexity of what it's controlling to match its own. What I mean is that there are two ways to approach the world: either by learning and expanding your horizons, accepting people who are different and embracing diversity; or by attacking anyone you don't understand, by crushing diversity, by lumping everyone together, labeling and dehumanizing. The first approach,' he said, 'is guaranteed to succeed because it works with what's there. But, because you can't really simplify the world but only fool yourself into thinking you have, the second approach is bound to fail.

"'Since I learned this I no longer see right and left, or liberal and conservative,' he said, 'All I see is Ashby's Law, written on the sky. I know which approach will succeed.'

"I had no fucking idea what he was talking about. I told my backers that I had an ear in Abbott's clique. I became their spy; when I learned that champion-of-immigrants Abbott would be visiting some pro-immigrant leaders in Musina, I told my people.

"And that," K.C. says without a change of expression or tone, "is how my Safiya came to be macheted in a church with a dozen others. Nile Abbott wasn't there. It was his daughter who'd gone, because she was the one who was passionate about immigrants' rights. Nile was involved in something completely different."

"Oh K.C.," says Sura. He lets her come and place her hand on his arm, but she doesn't hug him. Despite their adventures, she knows they're not that close.

He looks away, takes a deep breath. "Abbott vanished after the Musina massacre, but I—I went after him. I had no idea what was going to happen, I swear, but still it was my fault. I wanted to atone, and at first I wanted to throw myself at his feet; but I know now that that was a selfish urge. I was hoping he would excuse my actions, set me free of my guilt. And that's not real atonement.

"After some searching I heard he'd moved to the States. My backers had friends there, they could sneak me in. By that time I'd learned what he'd been doing all along.

"Mass migration and refugee movements are so huge . . . you really have no idea of what a million people on the march means until you see it. In the past, it meant mass starvation, chaos. No distribution of food or medicine could ever be even. Yet nowadays nearly every one of those marching people has a phone. Even the poorest have smartphones, and in any group there'll be one or two who have smart glasses. Backpack solar chargers are everywhere. So everybody in that mass of a million people could be connected.

"What Nile Abbott and his friends had done was build a kind of *Facebook for refugees:* a social media app that would automatically match up people that had skills or resources with those needing them. It had aids and tutorials for everything from digging a latrine to doing throat surgery. The app was called *Zomia.*

"Zomia is everywhere, all round the world, and it's saved many lives. All those millions of users, they have no country of their own. Zomia is their country, if only virtually, and it has a life of its own now; it's unstoppable.

"So Zomia lived; what was Nile Abbott to do next? I think, in his grief, he couldn't stay in Africa. It reminded him of our Safiya. Like me he was driven, but he's a better man than I. He'd recognized a new kind of refugee, which I would never have seen. There's a population of people in the rich nations who've been abandoned by the very success of the globalized, automated world they built. In a clumsy sort of way, without knowing it, they'd been trying to make their own Zomia—and some clever people, mostly in the indigenous community, realized what they were hoping to do and knew how to supercharge it.

"Abbott came to America to help build that new kind of Zomia. He and the other designers knew that this time, what they built had to be more than just an app. There were new opportunities here, new organizational methods and technologies they could use."

"You're talking about the games," says Sura. "The blockchains." K.C. nods.

"So that's how you knew those doxers, through your old contacts. And Abbott's here? Somehow, behind everything we've been doing?"

"Not behind," says K.C., shaking his head. "He's right out in front of it. You've even heard of him.

"His gamer tag is Pax."

There's a long silence. Then Sura says, "You came to Detroit because Pax is here. You still want to atone. How are you going to do it?"

He clasps his hands together and looks down, almost like he's praying. When he looks up again his eyes are wet. "I don't know. The best I can think of, best I can do as far as I know, is just to help him. Help him build this new world."

There's nothing to say after that. They go in and Sura heads to the toilet. When she comes back, she hesitates before crossing the room and joining the team.

K.C.'s obsession is sad; she worries for him. Still, having talked with him, Sura feels empowered. Maybe she really hasn't been paying attention, but she's managed to surround herself with people like him who do. Without her even intending it, a kind of a plan is coming together, and it's a good one: as a private investigator in the games, she can hone skills, learn ropes, and get wise about the streets; and then she can turn her attention to Summit. They'll never know what hit them.

She spots Trey and Jay sitting at a table some distance from her team, and heads over. Jay looks up, says, "I'm going to get some drinks, want one?" Once he's gone, Sura leans toward Trey and says, "Any more word on that other thing?"

He nods. "Whoever gave you that sensor, they're onto something. You know there's a grand old tradition of falsifying EPA data. Everybody used to do it, to avoid fines. But now . . . With global carbon-emissions counting, it looks like the stakes have gone up exponentially. And the payoff, if you're able to hide a megaton of emissions from old wells."

"So, it doesn't have to be anything more than that," she says. "Somebody doesn't want to pay a few extra dollars to clean up an old mess."

"A million here, a million there, it all adds up. And it doesn't have to be the old oil companies, it could be governments, too. They're the ones who're ultimately going to have to pay for all this.

"But that's not it either," he admits.

"Look, these sensors, they're just the start of it. There's similar tech in everything you buy, from printers to shoes. Internet of Things devices that measure how fast your heels are wearing down, so the shoe company can have a new pair ready the instant your old ones wear out—and not a second before. We're past the days when anybody had inventory. Warehousing's dead, and literally every supply chain in the world depends on the truthfulness of these sensors. That's why I told you, they *can't* lie. As in, if the world finds out they can, the whole house of cards comes down."

"Do you think they can?" she asks.

"In theory . . . maybe. Your dumb sensor reports to a blockchain that's secured by something called a zk-SNARK. It's a kind of zero-knowledge cryptographic proof of record. Snarks are unbreakable—unless the system's original random seed wasn't actually random. If you knew the seed's algorithm, you could anticipate results, maybe even control them. Organizations that use snarks bend over backwards to prove that their original seeds are pure. The one your little guy reports to was seeded in an orgy of paranoia. Everybody's confident it's secure.

"Everyone except, apparently, whoever gave you the sensor."

Snarks. Remy said Dad was hunting snarks; at the time, she'd thought it was a euphemism. This is important, but Sura can't think of what else to ask, and Jay's coming back with the drinks. As he sits, Saunders rises, saying, "Just gonna visit the john." He leaves them and there's a momentary silence that somehow stretches, becoming awkward.

"I really didn't mean to go over that fence—" she starts, but he cuts her off.

"We talked about it," he says. "We talked about how stupid it would be to pull a stunt like this, and then you go and pull a stunt like this."

She doesn't answer; after a minute he says, "You know what I hate? I hate watching people deliberately fuck up."

She reaches for her drink. "I am not fucking up. I got you Duchene."

"You nearly got yourself killed." As she starts to protest he raises a hand. "Sure, Saunders is thrilled. We've been paid plus a bonus. You'll get your cut. But what you did is unforgivable."

"It worked!"

"Sura, I've seen this shit over and over. You think you're learning how to be some superhero. What you're really doing is rehearsing. The question is, what is it you're rehearsing for?"

"I don't—"

"I knew a guy once. Watched him go from confronting his neighbors to having a showdown with his boss, then his ex-wife, his parents, building up and up to that day that he pulled a gun on the cops in his front yard. I think your life is a rehearsal, and I want to know what you're building up to."

"You think I'm still planning on breaking into Summit? I told you I wasn't going near that place."

He looks at her levelly. "Based on your behavior, that is exactly what I think you're gonna do. The one thing I've learned about people is to believe what they do, not what they say. I heard what you just said, but what did you just *do*?"

"So what are you saying, you—"

"I can't watch you do this. I'm not going to hire you anymore. I'm not going to help you with Summit. Seems to me you've got a good thing going here and I really wish I could be part of it. But not if you're setting up to be your own patsy. Until you get your shit together and decide where you're going with all your bullshit, you and me are done."

He gets up from the table, and just like that, her lifeline is snapped.

Sura sits alone while laughter and conversation swirl around her, a dark rock in a clear stream.

CHAPTER THIRTEEN

A giant chunk of Greenland's ice shelf breaks off, and scientists are worrying it'll shut down the Gulf Stream, flipping the switch on Europe's climate from temperate to Siberian. Refugees continue to pour into the EU as central Africa becomes unlivably hot. The Chinese annexation of Kazakhstan is made official, and thousands more American soldiers flood back into the US, permanently demobbed from reunited Korea and from Iraq.

Sura sees her first human-shaped robot that's not a PR stunt or gimmick; it's shingling a roof on Telegraph Road. Another sign that the human workforce is obsolete.

She keeps her head down, works, and ignores Summit Recoveries as best she can. Then, one evening in September while Sura's on the couch reading about cryptoassets and Compass is listening to music in the papasan, Maeve walks in.

It takes Sura a second to realize that the Knife Fairy is not just an avatar in her glasses. "Maeve!"

They shriek and hug and it turns into a party, with Sura inviting the fireteam over, in reality and *in virtua*.

"What did you expect?" laughs Maeve. "Summer term is over."

"But you came! Are you just visiting? Or moving?"

Maeve gnaws on a fingernail, looking up past her coal-black bangs. "Moving, I hope. It's either that or back to work for Jeri. That is, if—"

"Yes we have room! Right, Compass?"

Compass draws down her headphones. "Why get another roommate?" She doesn't sound resentful, just curious.

"Fewer chores for you," says Sura.

The headphones go back on again.

Maeve moves into the third bedroom.

Compass has favorites, who would have thought? Sura often hears Beethoven's Ninth and Bach's *Brandenburg Concertos* leaking out from under her headphones. She'd usually put this down to the simple fact that those are the pieces most people know. Compass, though, has an encyclopedic knowledge of orchestral music.

She'll even play Bach on the keyboard, setting it to harpsichord mode. On those evenings, Sura puts down her glasses or e-reader and simply listens. To listen, without something to watch or do, is so rare and odd that she almost doesn't know how to do it anymore. Compass reminds her.

"Why the Ninth?" she asks one night.

"Beethoven was deaf when he wrote it," Compass tells her. "And he conducted the first performance. When they finished he was afraid to turn around, he th-thought everyone would have left, or would be yelling insults at him. Until someone came over and g-gently made him look. And he saw the standing ovation."

That's quite the story, but it's no answer. She tries to triangulate the Ninth with the *Brandenburg Concertos,* and is told that Bach wrote them as an audition piece, mailed them off, and never heard them performed in his own lifetime.

These facts are hugely important to Compass, and Sura can't figure out why. She does know that she likes listening to her play; even enjoys watching her long fingers in the soapy sink water when they wash dishes together. (There is a dishwasher in Compass's inventory, but the kitchen is too small to take it from virtual to real.) Somehow, those times, just standing with her, have become as important as all the games and intrigues that fill the rest of her day.

She puts it down to missing having a family, until one night when Compass isn't around. She and Maeve get to talking about her, and Maeve says, "Does she know?"

"Know what?"

"How you feel about her?"

Sura blinks at her. "How I—? What do you mean?"

"Oh, come on, Sur, anybody who's not totally blind can see how goofy you get around her. She's your catnip!"

"What? No, no—"

"Why? Are you straight now?"

"No." Sura laughs; she has no idea what she is, sexually, but doesn't care; her generation is past the whole labeling thing. "I just . . . she's a compulsive liar."

"Oh, fuck yeah!" Maeve shakes her head. "We were having a great time the other night, I mean really relating, and I, fuck I opened up to her! About my fucking religious nutbar family and the whole preppers-for-Christ thing and how I had to run away. And Compass started talking about her own childhood."

"Oh?" Sura pricks up her ears.

"So yeah, she talked about how her dad was a building inspector who got a gig with the feds traveling around the country inspecting old gate guardians. You know those things, the giant cement donuts and wheat sheaves and whatnot that little towns put up on the drive in. A big turtle and they have an annual turtle festival, that sort of thing. So her whole childhood was her and her parents driving around the country, finding these things, and Compass would play around the feet of a blue ox or in the shadow of a Lady Liberty while her dad walked around and around it with a clipboard, then she and her mom would stand way back and he'd blow it up."

They look at each other for a moment, then both shake their heads. "Naaw!"

"Such a *liar*!" Sura is practically bouncing, she's so indignant. "And why?"

"It's like she can't turn it off."

"I know she's somewhere on the spectrum."

Maeve shakes her head again. "She's not autistic. She's so . . . sparkly, when she's acting. Brilliant, and funny."

"Maybe. But," Sura sighs in disappointment, "acting is all she does. Neither you nor I know the first thing about her, and we live with her. No. Just—no."

They've been curled up on opposite ends of the couch. Maeve gets up and heads for the kitchen; this usually means she's going to fix a drink. "I talked to Jay today," she says, in a slightly teasing tone.

"How is he?"

"He asked about you."

"Really?"

Maeve leans out the doorway. "He'll come around. We're all working on him."

"Thanks, but—hey! I told you, I am not into Jay. That way. I just thought he was becoming a friend, that's all. I helped him out, and he walked away. It hurt."

"Okay, I can believe it's not Jay, but there's something about you and Compass, even if it's not in that way. I mean, like our thing. You won't come to *Encounters* parties with me, you just hide in here like somebody's spinster aunt. And when she walks in the door, you come alive."

"I . . . I dunno, Maeve, I'm not used to talking about this stuff. To . . . having somebody to talk to about them." She looks away, nervous. "I feel like, with me, I have two ways to be. One is selfish, well, no, maybe not selfish, but self-oriented?" She sneaks a glance at Maeve, who's keeping a neutral expression. She thinks about burglary. "But the other—when Mom was, when she was dying, I was the only one who was there for her. And it took everything I had and gave nothing back, I hated everything about it—and yet, while I was taking care of her, somehow I was the best version of myself.

"Since then, I don't know how, I mean . . ." She hugs herself, gazing at the carpet. "How can I be the best of myself without stepping into the fire again? And who could I give myself to that needed me that much, who could also give back? Maeve, I don't know. All I know is that I like taking care of Compass, even if she doesn't appreciate it. Maybe because she doesn't appreciate it. Is that sick? I don't know."

Maeve leans in. "It's not sick, hon. It's just that you and me, all we know is extremes. We just need to find the middle way. Maybe we can figure out how together."

Sura beams at her. "I haven't seen you with anybody lately."

"Actually, I have a date. For the metameetup." That's what people have taken to calling the mysterious cross-game gathering that's supposed to be happening soon.

"A date! Tell me, tell me!"

"Nuh-uh." Maeve retreats to clatter around in the kitchen. "I'll tell you who it is when you find one, too."

Sura hesitates. "Bill Duchene called me. He wants to do lunch."

"Noooo!" Maeve hops back on the couch, almost spilling her drink. "That doesn't sound like business. He's got people for that."

"Maybe. I don't know."

"Is he hot, I mean in real life?"

"Of course he's hot, he's a billionaire." She smirks, pretends to look wistfully into the distance. "I'll always cherish that moment when we vomited together, side by side in the crabgrass . . ."

"You're beginning to sound like one of Jeri's clients. So are you gonna do it? Bring him to the metameetup?"

"I don't even know what he wants to see me about. Maybe I'm getting sued."

Maeve sits on the arm of the couch, rattles her drink. "Or maybe you'll get 'served.' Think about *that*."

Bill offers to send a car around, and names a high-end French restaurant downtown. She'd been anticipating such a problem—the place is right in the heart of the surveillance zone, there's no way *The White Rose* can get her in and out of there—and knows what to say. "I have meetings right before and after our lunch," she emails. "Would it be an inconvenience if I met you near where I have to be?" She names a midrange, but not disreputable, place that *The White Rose* has declared safe for now.

"No problem," he replies. And just like that, it's happening.

Maybe Bill's car would have been a better idea, she thinks the next day as she heads out on the Not in Service bus. Sura was terribly anxious when she boarded, which is silly because she really has nothing to lose by meeting Bill. Compass is along on an errand of her own, and should be a reassuring presence, but the rest of the vehicle is packed with drag queens and a visiting troupe of opera singers who just toured Not in Service. Just another sign that Oneota's fame has gotten out of control, but the singers bother no one, talking in low-key, mid-Atlantic accents. Then the drag queens discover who they are. The queens proceed to serenade the dignified men and women of the arts with cacophonous and off-key rap. To everybody's surprise the professionals are thrilled, reply in kind, and it turns into a contest to see who can be ruder.

Compass has been curled up next to Sura, a little bundle of potential, and suddenly she bounces to her feet and strides into the center of the group. She's morphed into some sort of mad impresario and starts conducting. By the time Sura gets off the bus, she's got everybody on board doing a debased version of Wagner's *Lohengrin* in which bodily functions play a large role:

Heil deiner fahrt! (Everybody bends over and grunts)

Heil deinen kommen! (As one, they give an orgasmic sigh)

Sura staggers to the curb, anxiety gone but her mind empty of all strategies. She simply walks into the restaurant, spots Bill Duchene the billionaire sitting alone at a table, and strolls over. "Hi!"

He grins. "You're looking good. The frames treating you well?"

"Actually, they are."

"They must be, if you've got to fit me in between meetings."

She'd been building an elaborate backstory to explain why they're eating here, but now, in the moment, it all seems ridiculous. This is Bill. She's followed him like a lost child through the games, she feels she knows him. They've thrown up together, so fuck it.

"I'm living in Oneota because it's camera-free," she says. "Remember when you didn't want to go to the police, and neither did I? I've got my reasons to want to avoid the surveillance state."

He crosses his arms. "Yet you insist you're not hiding from the law." He's all cleaned up today and in a very well-fitted suit. She's wearing a new dress that did come from a surveilled shop, but that she picked out by avatar rather than in person.

"The cops use facial recognition, but they're not the only ones," she points out. "I'm hiding from . . . a private concern."

"Like, a security service?"

"Let's just say, a stalker who works for a security service. He's already tracked me down once."

He nods sharply. "I can help with that."

"Thanks, but I don't really think—"

"I'd guess you can't afford the higher tiers of Internet access," he says. "I know what that's like—neither could I, until a few years ago."

She snorts. "That's not going to cut it."

"Oh, there's higher tiers, and then there's *higher tiers.*"

She glances out the window. Out there in the sun, people are coming and going on the sidewalks, their faces turned full to the world. They're well-dressed, healthy, they look happy. The buildings here aren't run-down, there's no gang tagging. She can't see any police cars or drones, and the parks and boulevards are well-kept. It's America as it's supposed to be.

And yet they've all given up any hope of privacy to be able to parade around so openly. She looks down at her hands.

"Have you been here before?" asks Bill. "I'm wondering if the lamb is good."

"I don't know . . . Hey, you never told me if you and Trey sorted out the bet?"

"Neither of us won it. Look, the games are . . . we thought they could somehow be a good model for the real world. But they're not, are they?"

"Good enough to have their own economy," she points out.

"But not good enough to really simulate society, which was kind of the point. I never had a chance in there, and I should have. Trey's being an asshole about it but he'll come around. Anyway, we've got way more important things to talk about."

"About that. Why are you here, having lunch with a private eye from the games?"

"To tell the truth, I've mostly been sitting around on my ass while the bots and PR companies crank out a new version of me. Rebranding is hard work."

She thinks about how her summer's been and has to smile. "It is, isn't it?"

"The fact is, Vesta, I do have better things to do—and then again, I don't. Everything Trey and I are working on now is tied up in the frameworlds—this superstructure on top of the games. You and I talked a little about that in the mall—remember the mall?" They laugh together. "Even then, the stakes looked high, but not immense. Suddenly, they're immense."

He reminds her that there's a world outside the frames, and in that world, the global economy is crashing. "The fiat currencies are collapsing and the only cryptocurrency that's still sound is Gwaiicoin. Little problem: Gwaiicoin is controlled by indigenous tribes around the world and is a kind of bullion. Suddenly everybody's trying to shift all their money into Gwaii, but there are these in-built barriers, like the tribes and the fact that it's self-taxing and only partly fungible. Meanwhile, the games—I mean frames—have people working even when there's no money to pay them. The instant somebody loses his job in the real economy, he gets snapped up by a frame. Hell, people are starting to quit good, stable positions to get into framing.

"Six months ago nobody in the business community gave a shit about this stuff, and I was a weirdo eccentric who'd dropped out of society to wear a hairshirt and beg for his living in some Dungeons and Dragons fantasyland. Now, I'm the one and only expert on them, and I'm prescient and a 'natural leader.'" He laughs. "And you know what? I'm fine with that.

"The irony is, I don't know anybody in the frameworlds. No one I can trust, anyway.

"Which leads me to you."

"Oh."

"I still think the frameworlds are some kind of Ponzi scheme, or a resurgence of Communism. Other people are similarly concerned, and everybody wants to investigate, but guess what? First thing they all do is come to me!"

"And you're coming to me. But I don't know any more than you do."

"Yes, but you're in a position to. Vesta, what do you know about larpwrights?"

"They're designers. Anybody can become a larpwright, all you have to do is win a set of challenge games. Those're open-sourced and are all about applying pattern-language ideas and stuff. The scoring's on a blockchain, it's cheat-proof. Distributed democracy in action. Once you are a larpwright, you basically disappear. Anonymity is a condition of being one, because they don't want you to be pressured. Believe me, I've been looking for them—a friend of mine is going nuts trying to track down Pax, who's the most famous. But they all do this Banksy act and *poof!* they're gone."

"So how can we trust any of them? If anybody can become a larpwright, then the mob can move their own people into the position. So can the alt-right, or the left. Who really runs the show?"

"I don't know."

"I'd like you to find out for me."

"How?"

He blinks in surprise. "I should have thought that would be obvious. Become a larpwright."

Sura's found Binesi and Pax mysterious and intriguing, it's true. But, "What do I get out of it? You asked me to look into this 'rewilding' game—and by the way, I did and haven't found anything so far—but this . . . It's on a whole other level."

"Sure. So I'd be paying you accordingly. In Gwaii, I wouldn't use dollars." They share another laugh. "More importantly, I meant it when I said I could help you with your little problem. Listen, when you're worth a lot of money, everybody stalks you. You think I don't worry about who's watching *me* through the facial recognition system?

"All rich and powerful people have this problem. They're not the sort to take it lying down. So there are services that intervene with the surveillance networks at the camera level. They can add your face to a whitelist that's stored in every camera, or in the IoT network nodes between 'em. The cameras don't even see you, so even if your guy connected to them directly, he wouldn't be able to find you. It's the only way people like me can move around. Otherwise, there'd be kidnappers waiting for us around every corner."

This is worse than being ejected from a busful of opera singers and drag queens; every assumption about the world and her place in it has suddenly been upended.

I could walk out there. Go anywhere.

Bill's still talking. She tries to focus on what he's saying. "Assuming you're not wanted for any major felonies, Trey and his legal DAC should be able to get you whitelisted by end of day. Call it a gesture of good faith on my part—and gratitude too. If this is a way to show you how grateful I am that you saved my ass, then, perfect! Only thing is . . ." He half smiles. "To get you onto the whitelist, I'll need your real name."

"Oh." Jay would tell her never to break her policy of strict anonymity. She doesn't really know Bill (except that everybody does, he's a public figure). But if that's true, and he's a public figure, how can he even be sitting here with her in an ordinary restaurant without the window being crowded with paparazzi? His whitelist, it must exist . . .

She wants to walk in the sun. She wants to walk away from all the shit that's ruined her life this year.

"I have debts," she says. "I haven't been able to pay them. The collectors are after me."

"I'll set up a payment plan. No problem. Let's say," he adds with a mischievous grin, "it'll make us even."

She sits very still for a moment. "Sura," she says. "I'm Sura Neelin." It's like stepping off a cliff.

"Thanks," he says. "Hang on a minute." He taps the side of his glasses. "Hi, Trey . . . ?"

CHAPTER FOURTEEN

October passes in a blur. Sura has a lot of frame-related work, and spends some time playing the games that can qualify her as a larpwright. They're surprisingly easy, at least for her, but she can't devote full time to them, and credentialing is turning out to be a very slow process.

In total contrast, Bill Duchene's gift to her has rocked her world. No more *White Rose* for Sura Neelin. She can walk into a downtown shop, browse and buy with dollars or NotchCoin, just like she used to. She can go to movies. Clubs. It's like the past half year has been rolled back, revealing just how innocent and free she had actually been before.

Meanwhile, the metameetup approaches. There's now a date for it: Halloween. Maeve's decided to blow it off, she has her mysterious date; she's still refusing to tell Sura who it is until Sura gets a date herself. Compass loudly declares she's staying home. She doesn't like Halloween but won't say why. You'd think it would be ideal for her, but Sura guesses that, unanchored by the rules of a game or frame, all those costumes and all that role-playing would be confusing for her.

One morning they're talking about the meetup and K.C. says, "I'll definitely be there."

They look at him. "Mosh pits don't seem like your thing," says Maeve. "No offense."

He nods and shrugs. "The place will be crawling with larpwrights. It's my best chance to find Nile Abbott. Pax is supposed to be the star of the show."

"What do you mean?"

"Haven't you been following the news? They say the larpwrights are going to be online and live, for the first time!"

From what she knows about the event, saying that it's happening "online" would be like calling the Second World War a feud between neighbors. No matter where you are, be it in Cahokia, the radioactive ruins of Nevada, the ice mines of Ceres, or the amnesiac paradise of *Lethe,* you will have direct access to all the frameworlds.

Larpwrights . . . "Okay, I'll go," she says. Maeve frowns, and Sura has a sudden idea.

She smiles at K.C. "I have no date, though. Would you . . . ?"

Thousands of players are descending on a large open field whose facilities Sura helped design. It's dusk as her Not in Service bus pulls up. The thing is crowded with players, all in their glasses and staring off at odd angles, talking to people who aren't there or making strange gestures. Sura imagines a portrait: *Autumn in Oneota.*

Maeve still won't tell her who her date is with; she left the house dressed in something fantastical and futuristic that shows lots of skin. It's Halloween, after all; even so, Sura can't bring herself to do more than wear *Rivet Couture*'s equivalent of anonymous normcore Barbie gear: riding boots, breeches, a linen shirt and vest, and a pith helmet with a Rorschach veil. "The place is going to be crowded with secret policemen," she says to excuse herself. "Bodycams everywhere."

Yes, she's whitelisted, but she doubts even Bill Duchene's magical pixie hackers can protect her during an event like this.

The field turns out to be a sea of aviatrixes; Sura's costume choice is perfect. All eyes are on the better (or more minimal) costumes anyway. Some are their players' daily dress—such as the holographic insects and dragons worn by the *Dhalgren* players. Evil clowns cavort as well, and ghosts and cartoon figures swirl and run and laugh and break like waves on the pavilions and virtual boundaries. With Mixed Reality you can add any kind of detail no matter how physically impossible, so instead of clouds, the sky is filled with drifting Roger Dean plateaus, crowded with players from other countries, real and online.

K.C. stops, daunted by the sheer insanity of it all. "We're never going to find each other in this!"

"It's okay, there's an overlay." She shows him and runs up an MR flag. "See, I can limit its visibility to just my social network; you can see me and vice versa. Now, come on!" Into the mob they dive.

K.C. heads for a tent to get drinks, and while he's gone Sura loiters next to a roped-in space where some acrobats are performing. They're really good, and the spectacle is made even more impressive by the virtual figures they're dancing with. They leap to catch rainbowed birds that shatter into butterfly clouds at their touch. They spawn mirror images of themselves and dodge around them. Much of the play involves rings, virtual and real, that they multiply and color, suspend in the air and leap through.

After a few minutes a woman in a short scarlet skirt strides out. She's rolling a single hoop that's taller than she is, and to elegiac music she proceeds to dance with it. She's beautiful and the ring is her lover. She sets it turning and wafts around it, then steps in and grips its sides, becoming one with the wheel. The pair seem to defy gravity as they spin and gyre across the ground.

Sura takes off her glasses to watch. The woman and the ring are real, she doesn't need special effects to wonder at them.

As the dancer steps out of the ring and sets it to another slow spin, Sura feels a strange pang, a crest of emotion she can't identify. There's something right about what she's seeing, something that's sounding a resonant response from her heart. Tears start at the corners of her eyes.

The acrobat reaches out to caress the ring and it responds with another turn around her. You're meant to think of the ring as a man or woman, but Sura knows that's not what's getting to her. In that gesture, reaching out to the ring, and in its response, she sees something else that she needs, something she's missing.

She turns away just as K.C. walks up with two huge overflowing plastic cups. Sura laughs. "I hope all the porta-potties got delivered. We're gonna need them."

Outside, she can see that much of the sky is taken up with a giant clock, which has been counting down. They find their way to a large stage, and just as they're getting there two things happen simultaneously:

—The entire space is suddenly splashed with light, revealing somebody on the boards.

—Some asshole stomps on the heel of Sura's boot, splitting it from the sole just as she goes to take a step. The whole heel peels away as K.C. grabs her arm and shouts, "It's him! I knew it, I knew it!"

She staggers, looks up to see a tall black man in a white suit looming above them. He has the look and bearing of a preacher, no surprise since according to K.C., he used to be one. As the crowd cheers he stops in the middle of the stage. He peers about. "Pawns," he mutters.

"Knights and bishops, red shirts. NPCs, tanks, campers, lancers, and queens. Raiders . . ." He steps forward, staring searchingly into the audience. "Fireteams, clans, rocket-jumpers—!" He spreads his arms. "Players!" he shouts, and fists go up, people are shouting back.

"And *friends*!" They go crazy, jumping up and down around Sura. The word echoes three times: once through the earbuds of her glasses, once from the loudspeaker stack behind him, and once, more feebly, across the real air that separates him from her.

Even though he doesn't need one, he's holding a large mic. "How many worlds?" he cries to the orbiting multitudes. "How many worlds are *you*!"

The audience roars.

"To all players and all worlds, good evening and welcome to the meta-meetup! My name is Pax. I'm a larpwright. Some of you have played my quests." There's a blast of approval; he ducks his head modestly.

"How did this happen? How did you come to be here with us tonight, in this place? In this real and unreal theater, this new America and this new Earth, composed of nothing but bits and determination? How did you conjure yourself a new life? Because here, with these people, you have! We've brought you here tonight because we have something awesome to reveal to you. A great secret has been playing hide-and-seek in and around the games you've played, the frames you've made. Tonight, it all becomes clear! Tonight, the future comes to earth, and becomes real!" He grins, then slumps a bit.

"First, though, I need to talk about where we've come from. What we've had to run from to get here. I know it's been hard for you. Many of you found your way here voluntarily, but just as many were driven to the frameworlds by grief, and loss. You've been promised a great future before, after all. And you've been betrayed, too.

"It wasn't always a betrayal, that life you left to join us. Your grandparents or their parents, if they grew up in Europe or North America, or emigrated there, then all their lives, they labored to make things better for themselves and their children. And they were confident they could; the system, it worked! They came out of school, got a job right away, and most of them stayed in that career the rest of their lives. Your grandmothers and grandfathers got better at what they did and their tools improved, and around them the world flickered and changed, horse-drawn carriages morphed into cars, letters became telegrams became phone calls, and the more productive these hardworking men and women were, the more they got paid! The more they got paid, the more money they put in to the community. Everybody lifted everybody else. It did work!

"And then, right around 1980, things changed. Productivity separated from income, and from then on, in real terms working people stopped getting raises at all. Instead, they got *credit*.

"*Your* parents were born and they grew up expecting the prosperity they'd been promised. Instead they paid out hundreds of thousands for a college degree just to get into a job their fathers hadn't even needed a high school education for, and for all their work they received flat wages and mountains, whole Himalayas, more debt! Mortgages! Credit cards! Cars! From 1980 to now, their productivity had doubled—tripled!—yet never in their working lives did they ever receive a *real* raise. Where did all the wealth they were making go? You might well ask the question.

"You might well want to call in the bill! Call in those lost wages!" People around Sura are shouting, raising their fists again, but Pax shakes his head.

"Too late," he says. "It's gone, frittered away by idle billionaires while we worked ourselves to death.

"How many possible futures have you lost? How many worlds did you imagine, that never came true?

"How many worlds *have been stolen from you*?"

He pauses for a long moment, letting the words sink in. "The modern economy has been turned from an engine of productivity into a system for extracting wealth, from us and from the planet. It's not enough to call in the bill. You know it isn't! Mother Earth is rotting around us. The rivers are dead, our oceans dying. Extinction stalks the wilds and famine haunts our cities even as we supposedly built The! Most! Productive! Economy! In! History!"

"Shit, my shoe!" Sura tries to get K.C.'s attention, but he's staring at Pax. "Fuck fuck fuck." She grabs at her boot. The heel's totally missing, forcing her to stand with one foot in wet grass.

Cold water—she hopes it's just water—is working its way to her toes. "K.C., I gotta—ah, fuck it." She hobbles away through the crowd. There must be a printer around somewhere. Having helped scope the constraints of the facilities, she knows where the utility tents are and slowly wriggles her way in that direction.

Meanwhile, Pax has changed his tone, slowing down a bit.

"So why not a workers' rebellion? Why not revive communism, all sleek and modded up for the twenty-first century? Why—" He laughs. "Why *games*? What the fuck is up with that?"

"'Scuse me, excuse me—get the fuck out of my way!" Sura pushes and sidles, and with every step another jolt of cold goes up her leg.

Pax is waiting, looking around, letting the tension build. He's got everybody's attention, on the ground, in the air, in all the other dimensions and subworlds.

"Picture, if you will, a room," he says finally. "In this room a young child is playing on the floor. There's a small table, and there, an adult is writing on a pad of paper.

"The grown-up drops their pen on the floor. Instantly, the kid picks it up and hands it back. The adult resumes their work.

"They drop the pen again. Again, the kid retrieves it. And again, and again. Every time, the child gives it back, automatically, with no hesitation.

"The adult drops the pen once more, but this time, when the child gives it back, he gives her a candy. This continues: now, whenever the girl retrieves the pen, she gets a candy.

"And then, it happens: the child gives back the pen, and gets no candy. Can you guess what happens next?

"She stops giving the pen back. Because doing so is no longer a game. It's *work*."

Sura stops, looks back. Pax is staring into the audience, as if his gaze can penetrate all worlds. "They actually ran that experiment at the Max Planck Institute in Germany in 2010," he says. "It's probably the single most important sociological experiment ever performed. Why? Because there, with two people and a table, a pen and some candies, we have the disproof of the idea that people always act for their own benefit, and we have the reasons why people do. We have the origin of *homo economicus*. We can see the Fall and catch a glimpse of what the Garden looked like before it. We have both the source of Marx's dream of a workers' paradise, and the reason why it will never work.

"That experiment is why I'm here speaking to you today. That experiment . . . is why you're here."

Sura resumes her walk. She can see the flag indicating where K.C. is. She won't get lost. The darkened utility tents are visible now.

"Some of you might still think that you're playing a game," Pax is saying. "That what we're all doing here, is playing games. Well, let me show you something. You got your glasses on? Everybody, I'm gonna show you an overlay that you may not have seen before." He does some of the magical-looking gestures that signal that he's using his glasses' interface. Moments later a little flag pops up in the top-right of Sura's visual field. As she reaches up to tap it, she sees everybody else in the crowd do the same thing. A strange, mass salute.

The overlay requests permission and she gives it. Tall, fine lines with labels on them flood in from the horizon. They're like map pins, thousands, millions of them, and when she looks up she sees that, upside down, the myriad lines converge to form the pixels of a map drawn across the sky.

"Look up," says Pax. "What you're seeing up there is *wealth. Our* wealth. As you moved between gameworlds over the past months, you've been tagging resources—people, places, things—and rating and classifying them.

"They are all resources that aren't accounted for in the traditional economy. They're people whose skills were never recognized, even by themselves, until they had a chance to test them in another world; they're idle production lines and wild raspberry patches and parked self-driving vehicles, they're river fisheries and buildings, abandoned, unused, or underused. For years we've been compiling a library—a *global* library—of such resources. In the gameworlds, you played out different scenarios about how to use them."

He pauses to grin at the audience. "You probably knew that each game has its own economy. What you likely didn't know is that all the treasures and obstacles, enemies and friends you encounter and work with and against . . . They all represent *these*." He points up. "And all the ways we could best use them.

"We couldn't have done this without the newest technologies. Just one example—smart *money*—money that makes its own decisions. You all use Gwaiicoin, right?" Everybody screams happily. "Gwaiicoin is a potlatch currency," says Pax. "If you own Gwaiicoin, your own coins do a regular check to see how many you've got, and if you're rich, they redistribute some of themselves randomly, to low wallets owned by other people. Gwaiicoin provides a guaranteed basic income without the intercession of any government.

"That's smart money. It's one way of using information technology to wake up the economy. But there's another way, and that's to build intelligence and, yes, compassion, into the system itself.

"That doesn't happen automatically. Smart money has an AI attached to it, but a smart economy attaches intelligence to all of the resources we've talked about. Imagine that every unit of work, every skid of iron rebar, and every transistor had a little guardian spirit attached to it—an AI dedicated to finding the right place in the world for that one thing." He's talking about self-sovereign objects, Sura realizes—Non-Person Characters like the peevish groceries she delivered to Mrs. Glover in *Tarnation Alley.* "Now every tool, each log and tonne of ore knows what it is and what it can do. They can all talk to each other and coordinate. We ask for the future that we want, and they build it for us. We call these helpers *self-allocating common-pool resources.*

"They could be harnessed to capitalism, or they could be harnessed to communism. You could use blockchain technology to freeze failed economic models in place forever. You could continue with the fiction that you can guide and improve all our social relations by tweaking the flow of money. Or, you could go a different way. There's a third path, a better way, there always has been. You might have heard of the commons, but did you know that at least two billion people worldwide make their daily living outside the money economy? You don't usually see them, because commons arrangements are social as much as they're economic, and they don't scale. They're always local or specific to one resource and one social situation—or they were, until we invented smart contracts. Now, the commons can *scale*!

"By entering into smart and social contracts with people, places, and things, we can dignify the fact that people, on the one hand, and where they find themselves in life, on the other, are different things. Instead of *pricing their labor,* we can let them work out their own local commons arrangements using these contracts. Doesn't matter how many there are, how complicated they are, how many ways they connect or don't connect with their neighbors—we can track it all. We can also build sandboxes, safe worlds where we can do experimental economics and test Utopian social ideas. Together we can find the best and most humane ways to grow our prosperity together.

"We can make a *Third Way*—a Way governed neither by the state nor by the market—a multiverse of nested smart contracts, each one free in its own domain, combining in a polycentric governance system that delivers wealth and equity for all.

"So what have you been building? Let's think about what the components of a new civilization might look like!"

He starts to tick them off on his fingers. "Self-sovereignty? You own your identity, you're beholden to no government or commercial agency for it? Check! A smart economy of self-allocating common pool resources? Check! A self-redistributing cryptocurrency with a minimum possible balance per wallet? Check! Smart contracts instead of money? Check! Instantiation rather than ownership? Check!

"This new civilization is not money-based. Instead, it works to optimize higher-level measures of human well-being, and those metrics are defined by you, the players! This civilization isn't governed by a hierarchy; it's polycentric governance in which each frameworld runs itself according to the rules and smart contracts that its players create locally. It's simulation-based resource allocation, with you running the sims.

"And finally, reframing. Framing answers the question of 'why games?' Because, you see, our instinct to share never went away. We express that sharing instinct when we're carefree, when we *play*. Play is why the Internet flowered, before net neutrality ended and they put a price on everything. Remember Wikipedia, a free online repository of human knowledge created entirely by volunteer effort? It was built by men and women who, in all other ways, had become entirely economically self-interested. They were right in the heart of the fallen world, and yet they gave freely. They built it for free because it was a form of play—and because they couldn't imagine any way they could get paid to do it. Think about it: they thought they *couldn't* make money doing it, *so they did it.*

"What if there were a way to reframe the situations where we find ourselves, such that things we are perfectly able to do, but would previously demand payment to do, we now do for free? Things that have to be done, but that nobody can pay for?—Things like helping our neighbors? Like rebuilding our communities? Making sure that nobody goes hungry? That we all have roofs over our heads?—All those tasks that we lament nobody does anymore, that constitute the core of basic human decency?

"You, my friends, have found the way.

"This! is why you're here," Pax cries. "You're here because over the past year you've helped refine and perfect a new kind of society, one that doesn't depend on disproven theories, like the theory that we're all 'rational economic actors.' It uses a more generous economics that's neither socialist nor capitalist but something bigger and better than both. History will henceforth be divided into two eras: the time before this day, and what comes after. And *you* are the ones who cleaved time!"

Sura breaks out of the crowd just as it goes nuts. People are screaming and jumping up and down. They've actually stopped partying to listen to him. She can't help but wonder how each of the games has primed its players to be ready to do that at just this moment.

Then she stops, because Binesi is standing in the doorway of one of the tents, as solid as a stone in the stream of people going in and out. She's looking at Sura, and when Sura looks back she turns and walks inside. Sura glances around to make sure she can still see K.C.'s flag above the crowd's chaotic tag cloud, then follows.

The tent is lined with old folding tables and on one there's a cooler. Binesi opens it, hands Sura a Budweiser. "This is all going to end very badly," she says.

Sura looks back at the tent flap. "Pax's little revolution?"

"It's too soon. We were flying under the radar quite nicely, even with all the investment, until tonight." She makes a sound that's halfway between a sigh and a growl. "Idiot."

"I have more immediate problems." Sura raises her leg and bangs her heel down on the tabletop, showing her ruined boot. "Walter and Dan are gonna get a call about their cobbler."

"Oh, I see." There are several men behind the table, and they crowd around to admire Sura's foot.

"You wouldn't happen to have a scanner and a printer, would you?"

"No," says one of the men, who has the same wide aboriginal features as Binesi. "But I have these." He flips over a big black stadium speaker and unscrews one of its plastic feet. "I'll carve you a new one."

"You have got to be kidding me."

"Oh, let Frank work," says Binesi. Reluctantly, Sura gives him the boots, good and bad, and he sets to whittling a new sole, with surprising speed.

They listen to Pax's voice boom over the field. "What do you think's going to happen?" asks Sura.

Binesi guffaws. "What'll happen? The usual. As soon as the big interests like government and multinationals realize how threatened they are, they'll find ways to make what we do illegal. There'll be mass arrests. New laws will forbid manufacturers from donating production line time, and so on and on. In the end, they'll shoot us and put the remainder back on reserves. God, what a fiasco."

Pax is still talking. "People say, 'It used to be, we took care of our neighbors.' And it's true. If somebody's fence was falling down, you'd come by on the weekend with some friends and rebuild it. If someone needed a tool, you'd lend it. If someone was hungry, you'd give of your table. It was never an imposition. You did it and you would do it freely because there was no price on helping.

"But now there is a price on helping. Even the so-called sharing economy isn't really about sharing. We don't freely give our tools and cars and apartments and time. We rent them. We rent everything—our attention, our compassion, our approval. We expect payment for everything we do, and look! The grown-ups have run out of candies.

"Well, forget that. Your Third Way *works*! It works because you imagined it into existence! And so today I say welcome to you! Welcome to your new world! *Welcome to the frameworlds!"* As Pax cries these words the crowd bellows and twists around and into itself, and Sura shrinks back into the tent.

Back at the table, Frank is gluing his new, temporary sole onto Sura's boot. Binesi comes to her as she's effusively thanking him.

"You want to be a larpwright."

"So people keep saying. Why is that?"

"Have you used the stone I gave you?"

Sura hides behind the act of trying on her boot.

"Why not?"

"It's, just, too intense."

Binesi grins. "Exactly. You'd *see* something if you used it, wouldn't you? You know that, because you see things. If you didn't, you wouldn't be such a good architect."

"Is that what larpwrights do? See things?"

Binesi nods. "See a new world, make it visible, and invite people in. Gradually turn down the volume on the reality they're coming from, while you turn up the volume on the new one. If they don't like it they leave. Lately, nobody's leaving.

"So. You know I've been watching you for a while. I like your work, and I'd be happy to take you on as my apprentice."

"Wait. Weren't you just saying that Pax has fucked us all over?"

Binesi makes a dismissive gesture. "Oh, we're not going to go away now that we exist. The genie and the bottle and all that. What Pax has done is paint a very big target on all our backs. So there'll be violence. But how is that any different than at any other time since the Invasion?

"What about it? I could use another pair of hands."

Sura walks back and forth, showing off to Frank and his boys. What Binesi's talking about is way more than she expected. More than she promised to Bill, that's for sure.

She wheels and does another catwalk strut, knowing she's going to say yes. Before she does, the old-fashioned telephone ring she's been using tells her there's an incoming call. "Hang on." She makes the universal signal for phone call (fist, thumb and pinky out, tilted against her head); Binesi nods and turns away.

"Hello?"

"Hey, somebody d-dropped off a package for you."

"Package? I didn't order anything. Who was it?"

It's one of those imperceptible things about knowing someone well that tells Sura that Compass is frowning. "I asked if she wanted to talk to you but she said she'd catch up later."

"But what was her name?"

"It was . . ." There's a pause. "Oh—yeah. Marjorie, she said.

"Marjorie Cadille."

CHAPTER FIFTEEN

Her street is lit almost as bright as day, and fantastical figures swirl around Sura as her new heel helps propel her along it. Spotlights jitter about, fog machines dry-heave white clouds over passing trick-or-treaters; costumed kids wearing powerbocks jump over cars. Overhead, the neighborhood-watch drones are trailing LED threads like jellyfish. Sura sent out a griefer alert before leaving the metameetup, which is normally the fastest way to find an outsider who might still be in the neighborhood. There's no way anybody noticed one woman visiting her house. Even Crazy Neal is out, sitting on his roof and waving at the sky.

She tromps upstairs. "You should have kept her here."

Compass looks over from the armchair, then mutes her glasses. "Th-The fuck? How'd I do that? Who was she?"

Sura grimaces. "Marj. The one Dad took up with after Mom died? She's a big name in artificial intelligence research, or she used to be. Famous for claiming that the most important thing about an artificial intelligence wouldn't be what it thinks, but what it thinks it *is*. She and Dad met when they were working on climate change mitigation strategies at the UN. She's the one who told me he was dead. I . . . haven't actually seen her in years."

"S-Sorry, I had no idea. Since when do we get visitors?" Compass toes a cardboard box, about a foot square, that's sitting next to the couch. "Any-way, here it is."

It's not very heavy. Sura shakes it carefully. No clue what this could be. "Well, you gonna open it?" asks Compass.

"Okay, okay." She slits the tape and lowers the box onto the tabletop. Flips the flaps and sees a single sheet of paper sitting on top of something that's been packed with bunched-up plastic bags. "Huh." She raises the paper to read it, but as she does Compass gasps.

"Ohmigod, Sura. I'm so s-s-sorry."

Sura looks past the paper. Inside the box is a gray funeral urn.

She sits down hard. There's a blaze of white light behind her forehead. "Oh, sure, send him back to me *after* he's dead!"

Her stomach cramps and she bends over, holding herself and crying suddenly in gusts. "Oh, oh!" Compass stares in astonishment.

As she's bawling her eyes out in Compass's arms the cold, detached part of her that's always watching at times like these is noticing that she now owns something that can't be swapped out, substituted for, uploaded and reprinted later, or left behind. She can't scan Dad's ashes into her phone. She can't file him neatly with Ganesha and the other trophies; she can't add him to her achievements or item library and delete the original. Other than Compass, the only really real thing in this apartment is sitting in a box on the table.

The doorbell rings. "Trick or treat!" It's a ragged sound, and definitely not kids. Still, going downstairs with Compass to throw candies at drunks helps her pull herself together. Upstairs, after a while she says, "It's not like I don't get ambushed, you know, at least once a day by a memory. I'll be minding my own business and then suddenly I'll think, he's gone, and *boom!* Everything caves in. But it was the same way with Mom. I expected that."

"Did you keep anything of your mom's?" asks Compass, who's sitting with her, just being there.

"She kept knickknacks of mine. Report cards, awful grade-three art. When she was gone, there wasn't anything of *her* in the house." She finally reaches out to trace the side of the urn. It's elegant, the nameplate faceup. She gently pulls it out and sets it upright on the table.

"Hi, Dad."

She cries again, but this time it's not such a shock. Then she picks up the letter. It's handwritten; there's no date on it.

Dear Sura,

I know James would have wanted you to have this. I hear your mother is buried in Dayton. If you want, I can look into financing a plot for your father somewhere close to her.

This is all we have of him now. I'm so sorry about everything. Sometime soon we'll get together and talk. I'll tell you what I know about what happened at the test. Meanwhile, know that Jim would be proud of what you've become.

Marjorie

Sura's beyond calm at this point. She recycles the box, takes the letter and the urn to her room, and puts Dad next to the window. Then she sits down on the edge of the bed. Alone, she contemplates the paper.

There are mysteries in these words. She'll talk to no one about them. Above and beyond the note itself, and the macabre choice to deliver it tonight of all nights, there's a more vexing question.

How did she know where to find me?

Two days later: it's evening, and Compass is looking up from her piano. "Expecting someone?"

There's knocking on the front door.

Sura puts down her book. "Uh . . ."

"I'll get it," says Maeve. She goes downstairs, and in a minute comes up again—with a visitor.

"K.C. What can we do for you?"

"Nothing—well, maybe a glass of water. But, listen." He shifts from foot to foot. "I talked to Jay. He's gonna work with us again."

"You, he *what*?"

Looking defiant, he follows Sura into the kitchen. "He was being an asshole. We delivered Bill Duchene, and it wasn't just you making the decisions. I pointed that out to him. We're a team, and we acted like one. If we hadn't, none of that would have worked."

"Well, holy shit!" She avoids the sink and instead goes for a bottle of red. "What did you do? Use that talk-radio voice of yours on him? Read him the riot act?"

"Actually," he says, smiling slightly, "yes. Basically, I tore him a new one."

"Am I part of this package deal?"

He shrugs. "Not yet. But he left the door open to talk more. We might not be able to use you on his jobs, to begin with, but it's a start."

All she can think is *Maybe he'll speak to me again*. She hates how things were left between them, it reminds her all too much of other friendships and relationships in the broken trail from high school to here.

But she can't remember the last time someone actually stuck their neck out for her, and she finds herself stammering over what to say. She pops the red, pours him a glass, and comes up with an inadequate "Thanks."

He sips, smiles, and for a second she sees the shadow of a younger man there. "I couldn't leave you hanging out to dry," he says.

At that moment, the house's silent alarm goes off.

They all just look at each other for a moment; then Maeve and Compass scramble for their glasses.

Since Sura's wearing hers, she's the first to hear the voice thunder in her ears: *"This is not a drill. The emergency overlay is loading."*

K.C. runs to the front window and teases back the drapes. "It's an ICE raid," he says. "Right on time."

Maeve sputters. "What do you mean, right on time?"

"All the attention the frames are getting, and the financial collapse, there was bound to be harassment," he says in a matter-of-fact tone. "You white girls aren't used to that, are you?"

Maeve joins K.C. at the window, while Mixed Reality makes the walls translucent and freckles the landscape with friend-and-foe icons. "Cop cars," says Maeve. "And there's a big paddy wagon."

It occurs to Sura that they might search the house and find K.C. "Shit, Compass, hide him. The roof, remember how to get up there?"

"Why?" she asks calmly.

K.C. grimaces. "I'm not supposed to be here."

"They'll be suspicious if we don't answer the door," says Maeve. She's strolling for the stairs. "Sura, you and I can talk to them." Sura hesitates, then remembers she's whitelisted. Reluctantly, she follows Maeve downstairs and outside.

The emergency overlay includes a reverse-view of the neighborhood, painted upside down on the sky. She can see everything that's going on, including various escape routes that *The White Rose* has successfully played through. She could get K.C. out of Dodge if they need to, but why bother? If he's on the roof he'll be fine.

The silhouette of a drone eclipses the streetlights. It has no Oneota tags attached to it.

"Oh, crap." It's a police quadcopter, and it's coming closer.

"And K.C.'s on the roof," mutters Maeve. "Now *this* is going to take some 'splaining."

There's a thunderous *crack!*, and the silhouette of the drone becomes a cloud of little silhouettes, like scattering leaves.

Down the street, Crazy Neal, who harasses any woman who walks by, whoops and raises his shotgun over his head. "Take that ya bastards!" he cries.

They watch the ICE rent-a-cops take down Neal with extreme prejudice. "Nothing like solving two problems at once," mutters Maeve. A few minutes later the van drives off; up and down the block, people go inside, closing their doors, and after a minute Maeve and Sura do the same.

Upstairs, K.C.'s lounging in the living room with Compass. "The Angel of the Lord has passed by this house," he says, then grins. There are more sirens, but far off, and distant yelling. The overlay confirms that this was an ICE raid; *The White Rose* is in full crisis mode, hiding people or engineering distractions while those actual illegal immigrants working to improve the community are smuggled out by preestablished routes. Not in Service has realized that this is just a new game to be played and is quickly adapting. Sura comments on this, and K.C. shakes his head.

"It could easily escalate. A lot of very powerful people are unhappy about Pax's big reveal. Those of us who have reasons to hide should probably find somewhere else to be for a while."

She sees that he's holding a glass half-full of red wine, and remembers why he came over. This is a new version of K.C., at least for her, and she doesn't quite know what to make of it.

As the raid winds down, they draw him into the circle of their conversations, and for the first time talk with him about other things than work and games. He's positively bouncing by the time he leaves, but Sura is left to remember his words about getting out of town, and when she walks into her room now, Dad's urn is there on the windowsill.

Waiting for her to do something.

Two in the morning in November is not the time to be standing on the shore of Lake Michigan, but that's where Sura is.

Just up the shoreline is the headquarters of Summit Recoveries. She's burgled it about a thousand times, in hi-res simulations that are as real as she can make them. She knows how to get into the building, what time of night to do it, the path to thread through it, and how to get out. Vaughan has reluctantly vetted her countermeasures and overall plan.

She's pretty confident about being able to slip past the physical security, but that only gets her inside the office space. It's their files she wants to plunder, and that requires a whole different set of skills.

Once computer security becomes unhackable, you're reduced to social engineering and ordinary, everyday spying. So, she's been accumulating good old 1950s-era technology: bugs. They're a little more sophisticated in how they power themselves and hide their transmissions, but really, they're just bugs. She's got needle-thin cameras to embed in the ceiling above workstations, and microphones to slip into the upholstery. She can't break into an air-gapped computer, or crack its encryption if she could, so why try? Just record hi-res video of the keyboard and screen from a corner of the room.

Is that what she should be doing tonight? Dad's murder remains unsolved. She is theoretically still prey for whoever killed him. Yet none of that has mattered for weeks; months, even. Down the road in Oneota, she's been able to forget the person she used to be. Forget all her dead-ends.

Where do her obligations lie? Which Sura, the daughter or the framer, is the real one?

The lakeshore is gray and sullen under the skies of early winter, the waves like aging tin. This water's polluted. There's no environmentalist glamor here, and when Sura stands on the pebbled shore the ghost of Jim Neelin, standing next to her, shakes his head in disgust. This is the landscape of his nightmares, this jumble of wharfs, towers, and crumbling breakwaters.

"That was your problem, Dad," she murmurs. "You only wanted to defend pretty places."

"What do you mean?" she imagines him saying. "What could be more important than saving the natural world?"

Simple. Saving *everything*. But he never thought that big. He died still believing that the solution would be something you could *do*, but everything humanity does just piles more shit on the land. She'd thought for a while that the frameworlds were different.

There'd been a night, just after the ICE raid, when she'd been in VR, studying larpwrighting from a perspective high above Detroit. Wrights often shared this overlay, she'd learned; you could unroll the land below like a literal game map, and lay constraints and options across it like miniatures. Larpwrights doing this sometimes made themselves visible. Sura's video feed was from an actual drone above the city, so the view was spectacular.

She'd spotted another larpwright silhouetted against the sunset. As she glided over she saw that it was Malcolm. Her glasses were doing a nice HDRI mapping over his avatar, so his dark skin was gorgeously highlighted with the rose and ambers of the sunset.

"You always always wear the best suits," she remembers saying, "even in virtual reality."

"Vesta!" He laughed. "How are you? I heard you were joining the larp-wrights."

"I'm trying. It's hard."

He nodded in sympathy. "I like to stick to my architecture. People and their problems give me a headache. Like tonight."

"What do you mean?"

He sighed. "I took on some extra duties after Pax's big meeting. The reframing goes on, but there are problems. See?"

"Oh. Wow, I had no idea."

The system boards showed everything was maxed, to the point that there was a logjam of scenarios and simulations waiting for a chance to be played. "There're no unallocated resources," she half asked.

"And that's not just local." He pulled in a global view that showed a heatmap of the planet. Black areas signified where no or few game-related activities were going on, red was where most tagged resources were currently inaccessible (as when a truck that worked in-game part time was hauling freight for its corporate owner). Many countries were entirely black due to local laws banning or co-opting the frameworlds. When Sura had looked at the system board the first few times, the predominant color had been yellow, meaning that some reasonable percentage of manpower and resource was being used. On this night it was nearly all green.

"But this is good, isn't it?"

Malcolm shook his head. "Only if everybody's needs are being met. Maximum resource use without full equity is what capitalism tends to, and this is not supposed to be capitalism. If this keeps up we either have to grow the frameworlds, or . . ."

Sura hasn't had time to think about that, but she's thinking about it now. Malcolm had given her a front-row seat to a drama in which the frameworlds snap up every last remaining piece of the Earth that the corporate world's been unable to claim.

The planet is blanketed with trillions of sensors. It's not just that there's no wilderness anymore. The grand panopticon of human development has penetrated under every leaf, inside every honeycomb. Before, you could say things were bad because the modern world was destroying Nature. You can't say that anymore, because there is no Nature. It hasn't been destroyed, it's been co-opted, turned into part of the production machine. And the frames are just as much to blame as Surveillance Capitalism. In fact, they've perfected the process.

So there's nothing you can do to fix the world, it seems. The only thing that might work is to somehow start to undo, but Sura has no more idea of how to do that than anyone else.

She's been hiding, and she's been procrastinating. The games were a hole to hide in, and the frameworlds promise of improving things is only an illusion. And the people . . . the people in her life who think differently, no matter how much she may love them, are just keeping her from fixing the only things in her life that she really has control over. She has to accept that.

When her face is numb and her feet feel like cinder blocks, she turns away from the lake, filled with nothing but a clearheaded determination to finish what Dad's enemies started. The rust-stained rebar jutting from the concrete, the tortured lines of half-collapsed chain-link fence, and the colorless lake water do nothing but agree.

"Hey."

It's Compass, standing in the bedroom doorway. Her fingers are running up and down her ponytail as though it were an instrument; she bumps the doorjamb with her hip. "You're really leaving?"

Sura winces. "Oh thank God, I've been trying to reach you for days. I'm not *leaving,* I'm just taking a trip."

"T-To Peru. I saw the maps on the coffee table."

"It's just for a few weeks." She gives a little laugh that's unconvincing even to her. "I can't afford to go for longer."

"But why?"

"Well." She turns back to packing, glancing up at Compass every now and then as she jams socks and jeans into a rucksack. "Jay doesn't want to help me look into what happened to my dad. So, I went ahead and started my own investigation. It's turned out to be surprisingly simple, so far. Remy made it clear that nobody in Iquitos likes a snitch, and violence isn't uncommon around the sour gas wells and leaking pipelines, so you know it was pretty easy to name a prime suspect: it would be whoever owns the equipment Dad was inspecting.

"As it turns out, that would be a multinational called Bolivarian State Oil. They lost out big-time when the carbon bubble popped; they signed these expensive decommissioning contracts when they leased the land, but expected to have earned out fully by the time they had to clean up their mess. With nobody to buy the oil, they're still on the hook to pay for the cleanup.

"Luckily, they're a publicly owned company so I could look up their shareholder reports. Let me tell you, these are a bloodbath in recent years, but somehow, the decommissioning budgets squeak by. They meet their targets, they don't have terrible cost overruns, and they just barely keep getting funded from the renewables and nuclear the company does now."

Compass is standing there, arms crossed, just looking at Sura in a particular, Compass way. Sura hurries on. "I kinda stalled out when I read that. I mean, I could imagine a motive, but it's a petty motive—somebody from town that Dad insulted, maybe. The company's decommissioning costs just aren't so desperate that some extra sour gas would be worth killing over.

"Then a couple of nights back I got jolted awake in the middle of the night with this horrible, crawling suspicion. It was bad enough that I had to get up and start going through the annual reports of some *other* former oil and gas companies."

"Oh?" Compass sounds distantly interested; encouraged, Sura says, "So there were two things:

"One," she ticks off on a finger, "a sizable number of the companies have well decommissioning efforts that also *just squeak by.*

"Two, those companies are all contracted to Norris Trading, this utterly nondescript carbon-trading outfit that's based out of—wait for it!—Lima, Peru."

Norris Trading's website says that it mines the data from hundreds of thousands of environmental sensors. It sells pollution profiles and spending strategies to government agencies and private firms still invested in oil, gas, and climate change mitigation.

Compass isn't saying anything. "Get it? Norris is selling data—laundered data from supposedly unhackable sensors on oil wells all round the world. Data that shows that the companies involved are meeting their obligations. They're avoiding millions, maybe billions of dollars in penalties, and Norris is the broker. I think my dad figured it out, and they killed him. The evidence, he may have hidden it. Nobody else is going to go after it. I have to."

These words make her feel brave and she stands, waiting for Compass's response.

"That's not th-the 'why' I was asking about."

"Oh, what? What 'why' then?"

"Why didn't you ask me to come?"

"Compass." She's still looking down as she finishes packing. "I thought, it's going to be harder than the games, you know. In the back-country—"

"You th-think I'll be a lia—, lia—, that I'll slow you down. Admit it!"

Behind her, Maeve is hovering in the living room, watching.

Sura can't meet her eyes. "I'm not taking Maeve either."

"Big fucking whoop! Maeve *would* be a liability."

Maeve walks away.

Sura retreats too, sitting on the bed and laying a hand on her rucksack. "I've have to make some hard decisions lately. About what the fuck I'm doing. About what I have to do. And yes, about who I'm willing to trust."

"You can t-trust me!"

"Really?" Now Sura does lock eyes with Compass. "Then why won't you tell me the first goddamn thing about yourself. What's your real name? Where were you born? Fuck, how old are you? You won't reveal the simplest thing about yourself, and yet you want me to let you in on a plan that might end up getting me killed?"

Compass stammers, twisting her ponytail. Now she's the one looking down. "I—I don't—"

"How old are you? Well? Tell me! Come on, if you're going to get all high and mighty about trust then show me you mean it!"

Compass retreats under the barrage of words. She's in the hall, backing away, and just for a second their eyes meet again. A million things spill unsaid between them. The moment snaps, and she runs to her room.

Sura grabs the rucksack and pushes roughly past Maeve, goes down the stairs, and closes yet another door.

PART III

FURO

CHAPTER SIXTEEN

"You take the rain like a native," says Theo, Sura's guide.

"I've just given up."

He laughs. "We'd better head back now. The water is coming."

Sura shakes her head, but Theo's right. There really is a path through this Amazonian jungle—it's outlined in friendly blue dots, as clear as anything in her glasses—but those same glasses are beaded with water drops that keep her from seeing anything else. Theo's an outline more than a visible figure, and Sura barely heard him over the godlike roar of the rain.

"Truly," adds Theo. "It would help if you'd just tell us what you're looking for."

Sura smiles, but she's saved from actually having to say something like "not on your life" by the start of the *real* downpour. It's a typical monsoon really, obeying Looney Tunes physics: sky-sized clouds pelt over the mountain peaks and then suddenly realize there's nothing under their feet and plummet straight down. To the hapless people on the ground, it's like having a million buckets of water poured on you.

The other two boys she's hired are huddling under a violently green leaf that's bigger than they are. They are framed by curtains of rain, backdropped by it, canopied by more. They look utterly miserable.

Theo's starting to look nervous. "You know where we are, right?" he asks. He and the other kids are wearing smart glasses, but theirs are cheap Moldavian knockoffs that don't do inertial navigation—and they're not getting any kind of a signal in this dense brush. The boys are peering around, trying to find a landmark, while to Sura the flags and markers are clearer than the real jungle that surrounds them. She can see the thread of lines crisscrossing the rise to the north—though she can't see the rise itself—that shows where she had them tramping around two days ago. A giant compass rose hangs in the sky, defining north and south, and all the local roads, paths, farmed clearings, and major wildlife are dotted and curled around her. Homey, familiar in their presence.

Dad's markers lead through the dense bush to a clearing that, according to the satellites, is rapidly disappearing under new growth. There's a wellhead in it, so there should be an access road, but it's been absorbed by the forest. And Theo's right, this whole area is going to be under water soon.

There's an app for that, too; Sura can see the virtual tendrils of the flood approaching from the east. The overlay says that it's still a day or so away, but her boys can't see that. To them the water is a monster creeping up in the dark. She respects their unease. If they think she's reckless, they're not going to come back here with her, and she'll need their machete-arms to get any further.

So, branch by branch, foot by carefully placed foot, they retreat. The rain's like standing under a waterfall and the noise just goes on and on, so they don't talk. They reach the main road to find that Sura's flood overlay is wrong: the cracked blacktop is already under water. Cursing, Theo runs for the bright orange ATV and the rest of them barely manage to pile into the back before he's off, sheeting wings of brown water behind them and skidding all over the place as they try to outrun the rising Amazon.

"We'll come back," Sura announces after a while. The boys brighten—it's a chance for more money—but Theo shakes his head.

"Not for five months," he says. "This will all be under ten meters of water until *febrero*."

February. Sura looks away, but she knows her worry is written all over her face. This whole escapade is looking increasingly silly. Why is she even here, rather than in Lima, where Norris Trading is located?

Only because Dad's path is here. She is stubbornly clinging to it, as if he really did leave a trail of breadcrumbs just for her. But that's crazy.

"We'll come back," she says again, and when Theo shakes his head, Sura grips the side of the ATV and mutters, "then *I'll* come back." But she doesn't have a clue how she's going to do that on her own.

Ghostly avatars stride like gods over the Placido de Castro. The Placido is a little Peruvian town on the eastern side of the Andes (fabled as they are, those mountains are not even visible from here), with more connections to Brazil than Lima. Start your boat down any narrow, overhung creek and if your motor gives out, you'll find yourself adrift on the Amazon, heading for the Atlantic.

It's normally a sleepy village but there are problems with the locals, and Sura arrived just in time to witness the government response. One of the virtual people hovering over the treetops is a "liaison" that represents the Peruvian army, who have been pouring convoys up the road for days now in anticipation of it disappearing. Liaisons, she's learned, are like game characters whose personalities are tuned by the aggregated social media scores of whatever organization they represent. Aside from the army there are other liaisons standing around like out-of-work giants; they stand for the various NGOs, corporations, and plurinational citizens' councils of the region. There's even one for the drug lords—created without their consent, of course, based on outside observations of their activities. "We're moving into the area," this liaison told Sura three days ago. "The army will tell you that's why they're coming, but it's really because they've been paid off by Bolivarian State Oil. They're here to intimidate the indigenes."

Theo and Sura watch the two boys splash away from the ATV, which Theo's parked under the piers of a local house. All the buildings by the river perch on stilts; the Placido runs along the crest of the embankment, a steep seven meters above the normal water level, yet the locals still feel the need to add another five meters of height to the town. When Sura arrived here the spaces under the gray poles were crammed with crates, chicken-coops and dog-runs, heaps of refuse and vehicles. Now the whole town's turned out to either drive the stuff to higher ground or winch it up into the houses. The frenzy of activity is exhausting to watch, so Sura plods up the half stairs, half gangway to the house she's rented and collapses into a forty-year-old beanbag chair patterned with little Disney princesses.

The house is a shack about fifteen by twenty feet in size, all one room except for the curtained-off chemical toilet in one corner. Wooden bridges join it to the neighboring places. It's wrapped in screen windows that keep none of the local pests out, and is lit by solar-powered LEDs. Sura's taken to sleeping in a hammock, because otherwise she wakes up itching.

Now that she's near her base station, she's able to establish an uplink to a satellite-based mesh portal. News items, emails, and alerts burst like fireworks at the edge of her vision. A few weeks ago these would all have been from and about Oneota and the many worlds of the frames. Now, her feeds mostly contain international reports and the replies in her inbox are from queries she's sent to various research bots. She hasn't talked to Maeve in three days. She hasn't talked to Compass at all.

She stays busy to keep the light of her feelings from becoming too bright. This new unfamiliar sensation—of everything sharp and painfully clear, as if she were exposed under the glare of an overwhelming noon—had come over her as she waited to board the Detroit–LAX flight.

She was acutely aware that she hadn't flown since she was sixteen. Last time she stood in a lineup like this, she'd held Mom's hand. Grief ambushes you, she knows that, but couldn't it have waited? She's barely holding it together as it is.

She remembered what they'd talked about while waiting in line. "I like to listen to music on takeoff." Mom had shown her the earbuds she often wore around the house. "My favorite's 'Shenzou,' from the *Gravity* movie soundtrack."

Standing in this new lineup, Sura found herself smiling suddenly. Hell, she'd try it.

It was absolutely terrifying, and she spent the rest of the flight calming herself down. Only an adrenaline junkie would do that to herself, she decided—or someone who wanted to celebrate their fear of flying? Pondering this gave her an entirely different perspective on Mom, and the things she may or may not have done to battle her own fears. Was one of those things she was afraid of fascinating, unattainable Jim Neelin?

By the time they got to LAX Sura was pensive, barely noticing the various transfer halls that were leading her to her first hyperloop ride. As she lined up for her car, Mom's ghost came back, saying, "I hear hyperloop acceleration's intense. They do a countdown! First time I try it, I'm gonna play Grimes's 'Artangels.'" Sura tried this too, and this time closed her eyes, imagining Mom sitting next to her going "Foooooo!" as they shot out of the station.

She could have talked to Mom about anything, except burglary. Later, because she could talk to him about it, her confidant had been Dad. Then, nobody in those gray years. And then Maeve and Compass.

Now she's alone again. She expected gray, but instead she's getting the pitiless light of memory; her hands shake, she laughs too loudly at Theo's jokes, smiles tremulously at strangers. She knows they're calling her the "weirdo from El Norte," but she can't help herself.

The hyperloop runs all the way down the continent, parallel to the

Andes, with offshoots into Brazil, Uruguay, and Argentina. The hemisphere-spanning Belt and Road system was initially funded by an American administration obsessed with the threat of China and determined to stake a new economic claim on the New World. With Congress bouncing between official openness and xenophobia, and a low-grade civil war between the Reds and the Blues, the Belt's turned into a strictly Latin American thing—but with it, South America's economies are roaring ahead. She's learning that, like her, the rest of her countrymen have absolutely no idea what's been going on down here. Generally speaking, the locals prefer it that way.

Remy was long gone but before he left he emailed Sura a list of activists that he and Dad had been working with down here. Sura reached out to one before booking her flight; despite her exhaustion when she arrived, she headed straight for Graciella Perea's house.

Her car spoke English, which was a good thing; as they sat in traffic in 100-degree heat, Sura felt a wave of vertigo and panic at the sheer immensity of Lima. She was surrounded by twelve million people and they apparently all had somewhere to be. The tourist overlays just added to the visual and conceptual clutter, so she finally tuned herself into a *Rivet Couture* version of the city, and could relax a bit.

Graciella's house is in Bellavista, just a few blocks from the sea. Sura's knock was answered by a tall, bespectacled older woman with an out-of-control frizz of black hair. She wore jeans and a T-shirt; the buzz of a window-mounted air conditioner blurred her words. "Ah, come in, come in!" She shook Sura's hand and waved her through the cool but noisy front room to a little courtyard with tall whitewashed walls and a single, short palm tree struggling in it. The heat there wasn't actually too bad, and they sat at a black wrought-iron table and Graciella served iced tea. She fussed over Sura. "You're James's daughter, that's wonderful, wonderful! He was such a nice man, very, what's the word, he was a gentleman, yes?"

"How did you know him?"

"Oh I've known James for years! I'm an organizer for the avocado farmers. James and Marjorie helped us set up a provenance blockchain so the farmers could prove which avocados came from their land, and who they sold them to and all that. It's really been helpful. When he came to me about the sour gas leaks in Loreto, I couldn't refuse him."

It turned out that the leaks were just the tip of a very dirty iceberg. "The oil companies still own the concessions, and the roads, and the fences. They enforce their rights to the point where ordinary people can barely travel around their own region." Drones patrol the two-lane tracks they hacked through the trees, even though the ruts are quickly growing over. There isn't anything worth protecting in the forest, the companies just want to show that they're in control.

"Now there's talk of drilling new wells, not to take oil out, but to put the carbon from the atmosphere back in. The companies figure on owning every hectare of ground where they might be able to do that. They'll make money on it. The locals could too, if they could get a foothold."

Graciella, James, and some friends had gone Loreto to stage some political actions: marches, videos, live confrontations with the local politicians. When they got into the forest, though, James changed.

"He seemed to lose interest. We were staying in Iquitos and boating into Tamshiyacu, the forest south of the city. It was the start of the rainy season, like now. James insisted on hiring his own boat. And he would take off for days at a time on mysterious errands. He told me he was testing the wells. His friend Remy said the same."

Something about her tone puzzled Sura. "You don't think that's what he was doing?"

"Well." Graciella leaned forward, redraping her skirt across her knees. "Some Quechua shamans came to us for help. They were refusing to perform ayahuasca ceremonies for tourists until the government listened to the people. That was just a cover, though; they were shielding the activities of local boys, who were replacing the environmental sensors installed by the companies with open-source hardware that the people could trust."

"What would they get by doing that?"

"The eyes and ears of the forest! Knowledge of soil conditions, the health of the water . . . oh, just everything! It was important."

"Huh." Sensors again. "And my father was helping them swap out the sensors?"

"No, that's the point! When he found out what the boys were doing, he told them to stop. We asked him why but he refused to say. I heard him give a very phony if you ask me speech to the shamans, telling them that they had to do it to protect the spirit of Tamshiyacu. We . . . argued about it. The last night I saw him alive, we were sitting in a yard in Iquitos around a barrel fire. He talked about where he was planning to go the next day, he said he'd gotten assurances that the well hadn't been tampered with. Obviously it had."

There was a little pause. Then Sura said, "What if it hadn't?"

Graciella blinked at her. "What?"

"What if the wellhead was just fine, right up until that night?"

"But, that would mean—" Graciella shook her head.

"Right after he died, someone came after me. Marj—Marjorie Cadille—told me he'd contacted her, told her I was in danger. And I was! Dad—James—had crossed the wrong people, people with international reach. I know it because they're still after me. So: Who was there, around the barrel fire that night?"

Graciella named names: James. The men who were to die with him at the wellhead the next day. A couple of shaman from east of Iquitos.

And Remy.

Sura sat back. "Oh." It was all fitting together, and the picture was really ugly. "Graciella, did my father have a backpack with him that night? An orange one?"

"Oh, that old thing! He went everywhere with it, but . . ." She stares off into space, thinking. "I don't remember him having it, no. Why?"

"This is very important. Did James talk about me that night? Or at all on that trip? Did he give any reason to think that I might know what he was up to? That he'd been talking to me, for instance?"

"Oh, he talked about you constantly! He was proud of his daughter, he wished you were with him."

Sura said "Uff" around a suddenly cramping stomach.

"He did say you were the 'key to everything.' But by then, every second word he spoke was some cryptic pronouncement! I thought he'd spent too much time with the spiritists, that maybe he'd tried the ayahuasca. What does it mean?"

Sura stared at her feet. "I was hoping you could tell me."

They talked about other things for a while, about James Neelin and how much fun he could be. Graciella had pictures and transferred a bunch to Sura's glasses. She would look at them later, when she felt strong; oddly, when she did, her father's face grinning out at her had little impact. She kept noticing his orange backpack, which lurked in the background of practically every shot.

"One last question," she said as they were giving their goodbyes at the door. "Have you heard of a company called Norris Trading?"

Graciella shook her head. "No. Should I?"

"Not really. Thank you again, Graciella."

Four days later she's here, on the far side of the Andes with the rainy season coming. This is where the oil fields were, and this is where Dad came, and died.

There are traces of him everywhere. She can follow the ping of one of his private beacons to a siding or abandoned petrol tank and dig beside it. There in the palm of her hand she'll cradle a grimy dart, exactly like the ones he'd gotten her to plant along the paths when they went walking. Each time she's done this she's waited for some emotion, but there's been nothing.

Sura's got no illusions about what this place is, and why she's here. Remy sold her dad out to Norris. He must have heard James talking about his daughter, and he told the company about Sura too. After her successful disappearance, he was their only contact with her. So he teased her, sent her one of the environmental sensors. She knows, now, that he did it to flush her out.

Placido de Castro is a trap.

She's walked right into it.

The condo's living room blooms in her eyes. Sura's gone full VR mode, riding a little drone that Maeve borrowed from the Oneota makers. It hovers at head level and has two cameras that let her look around as if she were there.

Maeve laughs, standing in the door to the kitchen, a glass of sherry in one hand; she can see Sura as rendered by her own glasses. "There you are!"

"Hi, sorry I've been out of touch—" The sensation of being back in Detroit is awful. It's homesickness and regret and renewed determination all rolled into one.

Sura feels sticky and vile and overheated, yet the rooftops of Not in Service gleam with snow.

"We were worried sick!" Maeve is saying. "Are you okay? What have you been doing?"

"Marching through the jungle like some lost conquistador. Being bitten by bugs I didn't even know existed. Getting heatstroke and foot fungi with names I can't pronounce. That sort of thing."

"Oh, girl." Maeve half sits on the back of the couch. "It sounds terrible. Still wish I was there with you."

"I know, and I'm sorry. This is just really something I have to do myself."

Maeve holds up a hand and turns her head away. "Don't preach to the choir. If I ever go back to confront my loony parents, I'm gonna want to do it alone. So, I get it."

"Thanks." The rush of relief is so intense that she has to sit down. Obediently, the drone on the Oneota end lowers itself to compensate. "Um, how's everybody? Is Compass around?"

Maeve shakes her head. "Barely ever see her. I'm starting to wonder if she's sleeping in cars again. Oh, I do see her, it's just she's got some new gig, playing some new kind of NPC. She explained it to me but I didn't understand it."

Malcolm walks out of Maeve's bedroom.

He frowns at the drone, disappears back into the room and emerges again wearing glasses. "Oh! Sura, how are you?"

"I, uh, hi Malcolm. I'm fine, we were just talking." Sura's stomach is in knots suddenly.

He comes and drapes his arm casually over Maeve's shoulder. "I hear it's the rainy season down there. It must be quite the contrast to Detroit."

"It is, it is."

"Where are you staying?"

"Oh, you'd love it. It's a shack in the woods." Describing lowland Amazon architecture gets her brain in gear again, and they all chat together for a while. Then, much sooner than she'd intended, Sura rings off.

She bolts out of the chair. "Shit!" Pacing, she gnaws her thumb, accusing herself of being a terrible friend and other things. It's hard to keep that up in this heat; after a bit she wilts onto the Disney princesses.

But she has another call to make. "Vaughan? How's it going?"

"Vesta! It's great." He's sound-only for some reason, but his voice is clear through the satellite uplink. "K.C. and I have been monitoring you, looks like you've hit eighty percent of your search area."

"Oh, tell me about it. My feet hurt like hell. Any sign of, you know . . . ?"

She'd had two choices once she realized that Remy might try to flush her into the open by luring her with the backpack. Maybe Remy had it all along, and there were goons waiting for her in the forest. In that case she should just go home.

The other choice was to go full Rambo on the jungle. The games are global, and there are players even in Iquitos. It's a back channel she's certain Remy isn't even aware of. So, she's hired local muscle.

Like the drone in her condo back home, most of Sura's security assets are stealthy tech of one sort or another. There are actual drones that are supposed to fly ahead of her as she walks; the problem is that this rain just kills them. She's got tiny infrared cameras that she wears on her hat, that are programmed to ping her if anything warm-blooded appears in the vicinity. It's so hot they can't tell a panther from a giant fern.

K.C. and Vaughan are monitoring chatter between militias and the army in the Iquitos area. They've got a good idea of where the drug runners are, and who's chasing whom. "There's been no mention of a white woman in de Castro," says Vaughan. "K.C.'s been playing his connections, looking for any contracts that might have been taken out on you. Nothing so far."

"So far. Well, that's something."

"Yeah, but listen, Vesta, I have to tell you this is all getting expensive, in real Gwaii." He names some numbers, and her heart sinks. At this rate, she'll burn through all her ready cash in a week.

They talk a little about Oneota. Vaughan hasn't seen Compass at all, but then they don't really run in the same circles. K.C. is also becoming hard to find. He's working his way closer to Pax, and spending less time with the fireteam.

All too quickly the conversation peters out, and Sura rings off. It's just her and the Disney beanbag, suffocating in oily heat with a head full of costs and balances that don't add up.

The tropical night comes like the proverbial switch being thrown. It finds Sura still sitting in the shack.

Eventually hunger overpowers her despondency. She levers herself out of the beanbag chair and wanders to the stairs, vague thoughts of dinner in her mind.

There's only black water swirling at the bottom of the steps. For the first time she realizes that, without a boat, she's going to be stranded here.

The bridge next door. She's never tried it, it has its own door and that was closed when she rented the place. She lifts the latch now and sees that it's basically a narrow, railed floating dock currently propped up on poles. It leads twenty feet to the veranda of the next house, and other bridges radiate from that. This must be a public thoroughfare in flood season. She tests the warped planks with her foot before she steps out onto it; it holds.

All she can see is a blur of hot rain and the dull rectangles of the buildings on their stilts. It's black below and black above, yet after she's crept a few yards she spots a bleary light and hears voices. She edges along the catwalks until she can see the local meeting hall, a big open single-roomed building like a larger version of her own house. The place is packed.

Curiosity takes her up to its door; the rain propels her inside. A few people turn to look as the spring-loaded screen door slams behind her, then go back to buzzing conversations at the long bench-lined tables. Another table at the far end of the room has been set up in a position of prominence, and several elderly men are presiding there, watching the crowd.

"Hisst!" Theo waves Sura over. The boys are sitting, obviously bored, at a table in the corner. Normally there'd be food and drinks all round, but something else is happening tonight.

"Town council," Theo whispers to Sura. "They're arguing about who we should be supporting."

Sura nods slowly. "Bolivarian State Oil."

"No no, it's not them. It's which part of Zomia we should join."

"Zomia? I didn't know they were here . . ." She realizes how stupid that sounds even as she says it. Of course Zomia's here. According to K.C., Pax's original cloud country was tailor-made for places like Loreto, where normal government isn't supplying all the services that citizens need. "But what do you mean, 'which part of Zomia'?"

"Here, you can see for yourself." He sends her an invite to an overlay and she loads it in her glasses.

The hall blossoms with light, signs, and new people. There are avatars everywhere, in fact, as if a troupe of ghosts had descended on the place. One is sitting across the table from Sura and the boys; it looks like a pretty young woman. She's labeled *Los artesanos*. Instances of this avatar are sitting at some of the other tables, talking to some of the townspeople. There are two other avatars, one a man and another a different woman. Some are sitting together, apparently arguing.

"Hello, Vesta," says the one across from Sura.

"Uh, how do you know me?"

"You're a player in the precariat. In North America, no?"

"What's the precariat?"

Theo laughs. "You're a player? And from America. How can you not know the precariat games?"

"I think we call them 'the frames' up there. I *am* an apprentice larpwright," she adds defensively.

"Do you know Pax?"

She rolls her eyes. "Everybody wants to know Pax. No, I don't, not personally. I have friends who do."

"Wow. He says he's trying to hold Zomia together, but he's for the precariat. Down here, we don't want the precariat telling us what to do."

"So the precariat, that's the North American frames? Games?"

Theo nods. "And old Europe, and South Asia and Australia. It's people who used to have jobs but don't anymore. The other two you see here"—he waves at the tables—"are the migrants and the indigenes."

"Ah! It all started with the migrants, right?"

Theo nods and turns to the avatar. "This is Mary. She's an NPC for the indigenous. That's who we should be backing."

"Backing for what?"

Theo's not great at explaining these things, and the avatar has limited functionality. What Sura gathers is that there's an argument about how autonomous communities like Placido de Castro should be. Should they keep tight links, including supply chains, with the precariat or the refugees? One promises economic stability, the other flexibility and rapid response to threats such as Bolivarian State and its friends.

Sura can't help it: she feels a bit smug. She'd started to guilt herself over her cynicism when she moved to Oneota. Maybe Pax's grand experiment really was some new kind of worker's paradise. It had certainly worked for her. There's always a serpent and an apple, though. Knowing that Zomia is already splintering into squabbling camps confirms that she was right to bail, right to come here and chase what matters to her.

She pushes back her chair decisively and walks to the back of the place. The reason she'd braved the rain to come here is that the town hall is also a cantina. There's patarashca tonight, made with real paiche, a local fish she's gotten quite fond of. She orders a large helping from the sweat-sheened cook behind the bar, feeling, in an obscure way, powerful and in control.

As she's wending her way back to Theo's table the screen door bangs open and somebody walks in. Sura's got her glasses on, and nearly drops her bowl; only long familiarity with the visual weirdness of Mixed Reality keeps her cool as a whirling vortex of light topped by a fearsome golden mask crosses the floor. Most of the locals aren't wearing glasses and don't react. Those that are, do, some by hailing the newcomer, others by throwing up their arms in disgust or turning away.

"*Carajo!*" says Theo, gawking past Sura as she sits. "It's Tamshiyacu."

Sura frowns, sips at the broth from her substantial vegetable/fish stew. "The town or the forest?"

The indigenous Zomia avatar rises, an angry look on its face. Sura turns, sees all the other avatars standing too. Tamshiyacu takes center stage at the front of the hall, and points a long, green-glowing arm at them. "What," it shrieks in Spanish that her glasses struggle to translate, "is the issue?"

Sura mutes and squints. Where glowing Tamshiyacu towered, a very skinny, nut-brown old woman is leaning on a cane. She's wearing smart glasses.

"Mama," says a man sitting at one of the tables near her. "If we take the jobs the oil companies are offering, we'll be cutting down what's left of the forest."

"That's not true," says a precariat avatar. "If we ally with the companies we can keep them in check. If we don't we have no way to influence them."

Sura leans toward Theo. "Who is she? An indigenous NPC?"

"No!" Theo frowns at her as if she's an imbecile.

"Another Zomia persona?"

"No, it's Tamshiyacu! The forest itself."

"We have to resist," the indigenous avatar is saying. "If we make it impossible for them to monitor their activities here, they'll leave us alone."

"And then what?" demands the refugee. "You'll be joining us, do you really want to do that? And we're overstretched as it is, you should be our stable base . . ."

This back-and-forth goes on for a while. Sura keeps her head down; after all, she's only here for the food. It's becoming clear, though, that things are going to get increasingly complicated, and not just because of the flooding and her dwindling finances. All the work she figured she had a week or two to do, she'd better try to get done in the next few days. After that, who knows how compromised the roads and tracks are going to be, and who's going to be lurking in the woods?

Finally Tamshiyacu raises a virtual staff over her head and shouts, "Enough!" The arguing avatars turn as one to look at her.

"This is the judgment of Tamshiyacu." The old woman's voice is starting to quaver. Sura wonders how long she can keep this up. "Sometimes, letting an invasive species overshoot and then die back is the best way to manage it. In this case, the invasive species is Man.

"We will allow the companies to do their worst. The forest will recover, but while it does, it will be useless to you. Only without you will it return to what it should be."

She wheels and stalks out, leaving a long silence behind.

Sura turns to Theo and the boys, who are staring after Tamshiyacu, slack-jawed. "So," she says, "would you like to make some more quick money?"

The rain refuses to let up, so Sura abandons waiting and makes her way back along the bridges. As she approaches the gangway to her shack, she slows, suddenly wary. Her security overlay says someone is standing outside her door. It's only one person, not a gang, but she can't make out who it is in the darkness and deluge. She wakens all her drones and cameras, makes sure she has a satellite uplink and that her tattoo is registering her exact location. Then she cautiously moves forward.

A small dark figure is waiting for her under the drooling eaves of the tin-roofed shack. It's the old woman who plays Tamshiyacu. She's not wearing her glasses.

Sura wonders if things are going to get even more complicated for her. "Hello," she says respectfully.

The old woman shouts over the deluge. "You're his daughter."

"What?"

"Our protector. You have the same name."

"I'm James Neelin's daughter, yes. Did you know him?"

She shakes her head. "I did not but the forest did. It wanted to talk to you, but I was too tired. It says you walk our paths yet you go home empty-handed. There must be one very particular thing that you're looking for."

"Come in, come in." She unlatches her door, but the old woman steps back. Sura hesitates on the doorstep.

"I'm looking for my father's backpack," she says at last. "Do you know where it is?"

The old woman shakes her head again. "But maybe we could help you find it."

"Oh? In return for what?"

"Come to us tomorrow night. Then you'll see."

She turns and vanishes in the rain.

CHAPTER SEVENTEEN

Morning announces itself with timid grayness. The drizzle is not going to let up, so Sura groans and half falls out of the hammock. She's got four well sites to visit today, and the boys are waiting for her at the end of the connecting docks.

Locals punt up and down what used to be the street—not apparently going anywhere, but getting a feel for their boats and generally larking about after the dry seasons spent walking. A whole new village's worth of floating platforms is rising with the water, creating little islands all over the place. They're reconfiguring the neighborhood. It's kind of like designing a level in *Rivet Couture,* except that the building blocks are real wooden skids buoyed by white bleach bottles and jerricans. Tow a few together and you have a new sidewalk. Sura would find all this rebuilding fascinating if she weren't so frantic for time.

As she's reaching dry ground at the end of the rising docks, she sees an olive-green army boat go by carrying a load of what look like quadcopters. There must be thousands of the things; for once she's grateful for the rain, because nothing smaller than a full-sized helicopter is getting into the air today.

She meets Theo and his two younger friends in the field where the town's parked all their vehicles. They chat happily as they slew down the muddy back road that leads to the oil fields, but as usual she's cautious around them. She knows Theo and the boys need money, and that Bolivarian State Oil has more of it than she does. Sura likes Theo a lot, but she has no idea what he'll do if he gets a better offer.

An hour later they pull into a shadowy cave made by overhanging branches, and Theo says, "We walk from here."

Sura nods, hiding her disappointment. She's decided to skip the fully developed wells, and just visit the unfinished drill sites. If Dad hid something down a borehole, then he can't have done it at a capped well. But she can't see any trace of Dad's breadcrumb trail through her smart glasses. Maybe he wouldn't have marked a path he didn't want anyone else to know about; only he and she should be able to find his markers.

So maybe he hasn't been here at all.

"I wish we could just use the access road," she grumbles. Theo nods.

"They go straight there, but as you say, the companies monitor them. We're trespassers."

"Trespassers, yay!" shouts the youngest kid.

She growls, and they set off. What ensues is another hour of hard slogging, this time on foot through god-awful underbrush, pissed on by trees and sucked at by ravenous mud. The boys are in cutoffs and tough shoes, their glasses in plastic bags hanging off their belts. Sura's finally learned from them, and today she's foregone her rain slicker and is just in shorts, a tank top, and heavy hiking boots.—And a broad-brimmed hat, which doesn't really keep the water off her own glasses.

Theo's constantly pointing at this or that feature of the local landscape. He's teaching the boys. In another life, Sura would be charmed and listen and learn herself. She's too stunned and tired.

She's almost done in when they finally reach the clear-cut. It stretches on for miles, a vast crime scene of stumps and churned-up earth. The roughnecks sprayed oil everywhere to suppress regrowth, and it's worked.

Her heart lifts as she spots the metal frame around the borehole. Unlike the other wells she's visited, this one isn't capped by a tree of pipes. It looks like they didn't finish drilling here.

This could be it. There are probably security cameras but she doesn't care anymore; darting out to climb the frame, she hauls at the round manhole cover. It's way too heavy for her, but with Theo and the boys helping, she manages to drag it to one side. Could Dad have lifted this himself? She doesn't know.

"Buried treasure, eh?" Theo's down on his haunches, peering at her wisely.

She smirks. "Something like that." What's revealed is a round circle of black water. The well's filled itself in. That shouldn't be surprising, and it probably happened long ago. She can't see anything, though, and the prospect of sticking her arm in there is daunting. Finally she looks at the others; they're staring back. Waiting.

"Oh hell." Half-lying, braced on the lid with her other hand, she thrusts her arm into the warm, oily water, and feels around. Her scalp is prickling with fear of monsters in the deep, or just snakes, but her fingers find only smooth metal.

"Fuck. Nothing."

Theo nods. "We go to the next one?"

"Yeah." She frowns into the misty silver that blurs everything. "You know what? No camera's going to ID us in this. Let's just take the access road."

The boys cheer as if they actually have found treasure.

Sura dreams she's a butterfly, lofting through the coiling steamy air of Tamshiyacu. She stops to drink at a flower, or is it a faucet, and continues on through avenues of trees that all have balconies. All this seems perfectly reasonable; these days, any given thing can be a tree and a building, or a street and a forest. The world is a mat of worm-eaten maps laid overtop one another. Butterfly-Sura slides through the holes from map to map, happily grazing as she goes.

The dream changes. She's standing on her mother's feet, holding her hands as they dance in a circle. Sura laughs and twirls, then suddenly realizes what the music is. It's a very old Joni Mitchell song, "Cactus Tree," which is all about that woman who runs from every love in her life, because

She's so busy

Bein' free . . .

She blinks awake to late afternoon. Oh. Right. The morning's searching was utterly fruitless; after waving a disconsolate goodbye to Theo & Co., she flopped into the hammock, and now here she is, as exhausted as if she's run a marathon. The air is like a vaporized dishrag and despite all the water, it's brain-meltingly hot. She feels like she's been glued into the hammock.

The dream still in mind, she hangs there, sleep-muddled. This is not a *fuck-you* moment, it's the opposite, maybe a what-the-fuck, as in "what the fuck am I doing here?" Jay would probably psychoanalyze her, say she's chasing her father's ghost through the rain forest. He'd be wrong, because when she pings Dad's breadcrumb trail, she feels nothing. Dad may have left traces all through this country, but he himself is gone. She knows that.

Contemplating this leads her to think about other relationships. Maeve is with Malcolm now; how does she feel about that? Numb. Compass, Jay, they're like fading fever dreams. Before that, a very short list of other romantic and sexual entanglements, male and female, lead nowhere in the labyrinth of her feelings.

Something's missing. Something's always been missing. She's not going to find it here.

Groaning, she topples out of the hammock. Only this morning did she learn to put the beanbag chair under it so she has something to land on—but somehow she misses and hits the floor. She kicks the princesses around the place, then sits down to prepare for her meeting with Tamshiyacu.

Microdrones, check. It's not raining hard enough to keep them grounded, but for now they can ride in her backpack. Satellite monitoring, care of K.C.'s friends, check. She can afford a few seconds of that at a time, probably not more than a minute. Facial recognition connected to a black-market backdoor to Lima's police database (again, care of K.C.), check. Taser, check.

Maybe Theo's hanging out in the town hall; she can ask him about Tamshiyacu and buy him dinner. She fudges at the facial-recognition confounding pattern of makeup she's been wearing down here, but there's no point in looking after her hair. She just walks into the rain, not even bothering with the hat this time.

The cook's singing. She might even know the song, she can't tell since he mangles everything. Nobody cares anyway. Sura joins the short lineup, even though he's serving exactly the same thing as last night; fuck variety, it was good. As she reaches him he pauses in his recital and says, "You friends, they look for you."

"What? Theo? Where is he?"

"No, not Theo. Two men. Ayahuasca tourists, look like."

Sura goes cold, nearly fumbles her bowl. Cook notices and narrows his eyes. "Not friends. We look out for them, tell you."

"Thanks. What did they look like?"

Tall, well-built, and they moved like athletes. Cook let the man-buns fool him the first time, but now he realizes what he saw. Sura already knows. Summit Recoveries has found her again, probably through Remy. Or, who knows? Maybe this whitelisting stuff isn't as good as Bill claims.

As she's looking for a table she spots the old lady standing outside in the rain. She gives a tiny wave, but shakes her head when Sura nods at her to come in. Sura wolfs down her stew and goes to meet her. The tropical sunset is knifing down and lights are coming on.

Theo told her a little more about Tamshiyacu on this morning's walk. She's a kind of liaison program for the forest. He's not clear on important details, such as who controls that program. Tamshiyacu's agenda seems to be ecological, though. It's clearly not run by Bolivarian or any of the mining companies. It is also, most definitely, not run by Zomia.

"Has anyone been asking about me?" she asks the old lady, who is hurrying away along a dockway that Sura hasn't taken before.

The woman peers back. "And who would I say you are?"

"I mean, me." She gestures up and down herself. "The crazy lady from el Norte."

"Bah." Tamshiyacu hurries on, tapping her cane on the planks with unnecessary force. Sura frees her microdrones before following. The four hand-sized black quadcopters fan out quietly, watching for thermal signatures behind the rain.

They pass a dozen or so houses, meeting no one. The way they're weaving among the floating sidewalks, Sura would never be able to find her way back if she weren't recording the GPS waypoints. Eventually the old lady takes a pontoon bridge that leads back to shore and disappears under the black looming trees.

"Oh, hell, you're not." Sura catches up to her, but hesitates at grabbing her stick-thin arm. "What did you mean when you said the forest knew my father? Did you mean this avatar? Is it a self-allocating resource with a game-sprite attached to it?"

The old lady pauses, turns, and looks up at her. "You have a way of breaking the translation program."

"Sorry. I know it's . . . technical." She shifts from one foot to the other. "Where are we going?"

"Not far." Tamshiyacu starts walking again; now Sura has to unclip her flashlight and turn it on. To make matters worse, irritated grumblings are coming from the turbulent sky.

"Your father made friends with Tamshiyacu. I don't know what Tamshiyacu is, just that it pays me and others to let it play us in this game and that. Hah! Games! Whatever it is, it wants to protect the forest. So did your father."

Sura's jittering flashlight beam shows palm leaves and tree boles, backed by black. "Huh?" She stabilizes it against something like a cave mouth, very big and very near.

CA-RACK! Lightning outlines a vast maw, white teeth jutting hither and thither, trees bowing to it as orgiastic rain dances through the foreground.

Sura finds she's crouching, half-turned to run away. She lifts the flashlight in time to see Tamshiyacu disappearing into a big hole in the aft-end of a beached cabin cruiser. The teeth are frayed fiberglass strips, its eyes are mooring rings on the deck above. This spot must have been high water for some epic flood of the past decade. Sura hurries inside.

The sound changes to an insensate drumming punctuated by thunder. Lightning flickers randomly, showing the old lady making her way past some crates on the bilge floor to some wire cages crammed into the nose of the boat. Sura follows. "What the—oh."

She just stands there, flashlight drooping. The cages are covered with wire mesh that's sadly familiar. She last saw it as she went through the personal effects Remy mailed her. It was wrapped around a small metal object.

The cages hold hundreds of similar sensors, and others in all sizes and shapes. The mesh is to keep them from phoning home. Tamshiyacu stands in the midst of them, turns, and now Sura is sure that it's not the old lady looking up at her from the blank ovals of her glasses.

So this is what Dad was up to. Somehow, it's all so tawdry. Feeling old, Sura sits on a crate. "So you want me to keep up the family business, is that it? Steal more of these for you? Theo said you were replacing them with ones of your own." Environmental monitoring's a trillion-dollar concern, and as Trey pointed out, all manner of supply chains depend on its accuracy. The lowland indigenous splinter of Zomia has been messing with them, and Dad was helping.

"No no!" Tamshiyacu shakes its head violently. "These are not to be taken. They are to be *returned*."

"What?" Sura stares dumbly at the cages. There are dozens more sensors lined up on a tarp on the floor. "These don't even work."

"They do." Tamshiyacu grins. "The indigenes, they figured out how to spoof the GPS on the older ones. Just the GPS, they can't change the other readings."

Sura picks one up, turns it over in her hands. It's really old and trails wires to a transformer and car battery in the corner. Not self-powered, maybe even pre–carbon bubble.

"Your father, he put back some of the sensors for us—but not those old things. He said they were of no importance. It was the others, the caged ones that he cared about. He showed us we could be free, but only if we leave those untouched. You put these back where they came from, then we help you."

Why would Dad assist with a project that he suspected was corrupting the ecological data of such a fragile region? It makes no sense. Sura shake her head in disbelief. "There are hundreds! I don't even know where they came from. How am I going to take them all back?"

"We pay you. Take them out tonight, hide them so the indigenes can't find them. Take them with you on your hunting trips."

She gapes at the little forest spirit. "Hide them? Pay me? Fuck no. I gotta get out of here. There are people looking for me, don't you get it? I had a few days here, just a few, to find Dad's backpack. I failed! Now you tell me where it is or I'll tell Bolivarian Oil about your little stash here. How's that for a deal?"

Tamshiyacu's not even listening to her, she's staring past Sura out the shark's mouth. "Fuck, what are you—" Sura follows her gaze, in time for a luxurious flood of lightning to paint the path outside in perfect detail.

Two men are standing there, black backlit and big.

"This way!" Tamshiyacu's zipping up the steep steps beside the crates. Sura shakes herself and follows. They emerge into a black mildewed horror that might have once been the galley. "No light!" hisses Tamshiyacu.

Without it they'll be blind; luckily there's a trick she learned in the games. Sura sets her glasses to record a panoramic image, fans the light around once and then clicks it off. She calls up a viewer, loads the picture and orders the viewer to synchronize its display with her glasses' compass.

Now when she moves the picture stays still, a smeared, impressionistic surround consisting of yawning cabinets, trailing wires, and debris-choked decking. Two doors are visible. She takes Tamshiyacu's wrist and whispers, "This way!" Actual light is tilting up from the hold as they cross the grit-spalled floor to another chamber.

Lightning's showing the way now, another set of steep steps up to the deck. She lets go of Tamshiyacu, who spiders up it. Sura follows her into rain and noise.

It's pitch dark except when the lightning flashes, but she doesn't have to repeat her little trick with the camera, because her drones are waiting for her. They've already imaged the whole area, in lidar too like a self-driving car, and have converted the boat, the trees, and pathway into a game level. Sura loads it.

"Why the fuck didn't you see them?" she asks one of the drones as it drifts by. Hell, spotting threats is the entire reason she got these things.

At least she can see in the dark now. "Load this." She gives Tamshiyacu permission to view her level and then moves along the deck to the spot where somebody's built a set of rough steps down to the ground out of shipping pallets.

"Another path over here!" Tamshiyacu points and then she's away. Sura follows, just as their two followers appear.

It's hard to be certain through the rain, but Sura thinks she hears one of them shout, "There she is!"

"Oh fuck fuck." Her drones are finding the new path heavy going; it's just an overgrown track and branches and leaves slap and flail at Sura as she pushes her way through. She's lost one drone, the others are retreating, and then she comes up hard against the old lady, who's standing in front of rushing water.

"Now what?" Intermittent flashes light a ribbon of new shoreline, really just half-flooded grass beyond which blackness swirls. At the end of it are the bleary lights of the town. They try to run along the shore, but it's really an exhausting plod through sucking mud. Sura's remaining three drones tell her there are two men twenty meters behind them.

Before they reach the lights, they reach a dockway. "Thank God!" Sura scrambles onto it after the old woman, and now they can run even though the thing's treacherous and pitching in the waves. It connects to others, and then Sura and the old lady are among buildings.

"Where are you—" Tamshiyacu's going right. The town hall, and maybe people, are left. Sura goes left without being able to say goodbye.

Lightning scampers through the clouds, not at all helpful, but now Sura can use her GPS waypoints. Placido de Castro's a maze of floating docks and stable verandas, but she knows where to go now. The men are still behind her. Neither followed Tamshiyacu, so they really are after Sura.

They must have figured out where she's headed, because one splits off to the right. They mean to catch her in a pincher, and it doesn't look like there's anything she can do about it.

Hurrying too fast, she slips and goes down on her stomach, fetching up against one of the thin poles that holds up the rope railing. Her feet trail into water as she spins. Desperately clawing for a hold on the post, she drags herself to her feet again. Thing One is almost on her, and where's Thing Two?

She pelts up the decking to a long low warehouse. Like all the buildings here it has a deck encircling it. "Help!" She pounds on the door, but it's padlocked. Her drones tell her that Thing Two is coming in from his shortcut. There's no way she can keep ahead of these guys.

But how well can they see? Oil drums are lined up along the wall of the building; she doesn't give herself any more time to think, just climbs them and gets on the corrugated metal roof. She runs up it and down the other side.

Now the lightning's back, strobing images of the roof, the town, and an endless plane of terrifying, writhing water. Thing Two is on the deck below her, Thing One on the other side of the building. Two is between her and the next dockway.

Sura stands tall, summons her drones, and points at Thing Two. "Attack!"

Suddenly he's thrashing and shouting and Sura's little helpers are dashing in and out, battering him like angry bees, and she jumps off the roof and Tases him in the back.

He rears up and she dropkicks him into the water.

Snarling, she crouches and runs for the corner of the building. As Thing One comes round it and a blue flash from heaven shows his startled face and the pistol he's holding, she straight-arms him too with her weapon. She puts both hands on his chest and *shoves*, and he, too, is gone.

She can't help it now, she's screaming in panic and in rage, and this fury she's never felt before but she knows it's been lurking there all along. Under exploding skies, she stalks the boards and howls at the water, "Come on, you fuckers! Come on! What are you waiting for!"

Nobody surfaces.

When she realizes she's killed them, she starts gulping and wailing, and blinded by tears, she staggers back to her shack.

A clap of thunder wakes her—or was it thunder? No, it's something just as startling, a perfect silence that rings in her ears like gunfire.

She's on her feet before she even knows where she is. She must have fallen asleep on the beanbag. "Fuck!" She'd intended to stay awake until morning then roust the cook or Theo or just somebody to keep her company until four o'clock, when the boat from Iquitos is due. She packed in the darkness, while her two surviving drones patrolled the dockways. Somehow, she couldn't bring herself to contact K.C. and Vaughan, even though they could help. She knew why: she'd killed people. She was ashamed.

Nobody was getting in or out of town in the storm. But after the fear, grief, anger, and disappointment wore off, exhaustion had come down on her like a collapsing wall. No surprise she fell asleep.

She groans; her entire body hurts. Then she notices the silence again. Somebody's turned off the rain. A silvery light permeates everything. She needs the sun like forgiveness, so she goes to peer out the window.

Birds are ducking and diving in a rose-colored sky.

She scarfs down a Peruvian breakfast—ham and cheese and bread—while reviewing her plan. Boat to Iquitos, plane to Lima, and then the hyperloop. She can make it back to Detroit by tomorrow. After that . . . More men will come. They'll keep coming, she knows that now, and they must also know that she's using the frameworlds for cover. Detroit's not safe. She'll have to move on.

This then is her life: she'll be on the run until they catch up to her. And where will she go? Once there was a wilderness, and maybe she could have gone feral in it, a little ball of wildcat energy in the grasslands. All that's gone now, the whole fucking planet is one big managed plot of land, a global city, and dotted among its towers and freeways, green spaces. Tamshiyacus of one sort or another. But they're not countryside anymore. Tamshiyacu's not a wilderness, and hasn't been for a long, long time. It's just a yard, like a thousand others. And the neighbors will never stop squabbling until they find a way to split it up.

"Missus American!"

She starts out of her reverie to find that Theo is outside, standing up in an aluminum motorboat. His hands are on his hips and he's grinning. "The rain, it stopped!" he shouts.

She steps onto her veranda. The sky is an azure wonder, completely clear. "So it has," she says.

"But it will be back," Theo points out. "We need to take advantage of the good weather. Who knows how long we'll be stuck inside after today?"

"Um. Theo, I can't use you anymore. The forest is flooded."

Theo waves dismissively. "That doesn't mean we can't get around." He spreads his arms, indicating the boat.

"But it's pointless. The paths I need are under water. Besides I . . . I have to leave now."

"Hey!" Theo's angry now. "I didn't come out this morning for money. I thought you might want to get out for a while, is all. But if you don't want to—" He makes to sit down.

"No, wait, wait!" She can't just stand around in the shack, more men will be coming. "I'm sorry, Theo, I'd love to get out. Just a minute." She runs back to grab her pack, throws some money on the table for her landlady. If she can stay away from town until four, maybe she can get Theo to take her directly to the Iquitos boat—maybe even rendezvous with it in the river, after it leaves.

All she had in her little icebox was a couple of guaraná sodas; she hands one to Theo as she climbs into the boat. He accepts the peace offering with a grin and Sura slaps the pier holding up her house as he guns the outboard motor. The water's only two meters below her floor now. "Is it going to get much higher?"

"Not likely. There's a lot of forest to flood. And the level's not as high as it used to be. Global warming. Maybe this will all be farmed someday."

They rattle up the street and pick up the boys, who have been fishing off their front porch. Their mama dismisses them with an indifferent wave. "Where are we going, Theo?" shouts one. He's leaning over the bow of the boat, a brown-skinned figurehead.

"I dunno. Where do you want to go? Across the river? Up to the granite hill?"

"Granite hill! Granite hill!" Theo nods and threads through the pillars of the town. Several other boats are out, early as it is, punting slowly to avoid the treachery of submerged branches.

The place is utterly transformed. The lower halves of the trees are under water, so the landscape is blank glassy water surmounted by mounds and shafts of green-like islands in some strange sea. Suddenly she's fiercely glad that she's lived to see this. The feeling mixes with her sorrow at her failure to find what Dad was up to, and guilt over sending those two men into the water last night; the result is a bittersweet intensity of emotion that's like nothing she's ever felt.

The mounds are isolated near where the river ran, but as the motorboat approaches the forest they cluster more thickly until they form a wall. Theo steers them into a slot where the road used to be, and passing boaters wave as they follow the now-invisible lanes; they come to a crossroads and Theo actually stops because, well, there's an MR beacon for the automated trucks somewhere below them. Though underwater, it's still operating, according to her glasses.

The forest is crowded with chattering, squalling beasts. Everything that used to live on the ground floor has moved up a story, pushing the former residents of the midlevel yet higher. The harpy eagles at the very top have a look that says, "Well, there goes the neighborhood." It's clear from the tone of the place that everybody's happy about the sunlight. The boys laugh and point things out to each other, and Theo leans back as he steers, letting the wind tease his hair.

The flood doesn't slow Theo's people down at all. It's a revelation.

They're motoring along at high speed when there's a sudden ping in Sura's glasses. She's been watching the caverns of green slide by and blinks, looks around—and for just a second she sees a path, laid out in blue dots, deep beneath the dark surface of the water. Then it's gone.

Dad's little beacons are only eight or ten meters below them. She quickly checks her map and, sure enough, that path was one of the ways she'd explored four days ago. They'll probably cross a few more—not that it matters, as they're under layers of treacherous drowned foliage.

"What's this granite hill?" she asks Theo a little later. The boys are chattering on about it like it's Disneyland.

"Outcrop," says Theo. "Rises up out of the jungle, there's nothing else like it for many kilometers. Some say it's the very start of the Andes."

"I don't remember it."

"Oh, you couldn't get there before."

"What do you mean?"

"There's no road, except in the rainy season. Here, you see?" And with that, Theo turns the boat and aims it straight at the chaos of foliage that walls the highway.

Sura ducks as they sail under life-laden branches, and when she looks up she finds that the boat is gliding slowly through a kind of tunnel hacked through the greenery. She reaches out to touch the recently cut end of a bough as thick as her wrist. Now that she's sensitized to it, she can hear the sound of chain saws coming from somewhere.

There are other boats, ahead and behind. Theo's taken them into a well-known artery, it seems. At times they duck and enter bright sunlight between the tall green mounds, then on the far end a dark maw opens and they're inside the trees again.

Inside a tree: this intermittent tunnel has been dug straight through the forest canopy, ten or more meters above the inaccessible floor. Machetes and chain saws keep the branches at bay, and the result is a rounded fantasy ride of dappled light and deep shadow. Sura finds she's laughing in delight at the sheer ingenuity of it.

"How many of these are there?"

Theo gestures expansively. "Dozens. The *furos* are our seasonal roads, they go everywhere."

"Granite hill, granite hill!" the boys chant.

Ping! A blue-dotted road has appeared and then vanished again, two dozen feet below them.—And suddenly, the hairs on the back of Sura's neck are standing up.

"What did you call them?"

"*Furo*. It's Portuguese, it means—"

"Borehole," says Sura, reading it off her glasses' dictionary.

Through a haze of surprise, she says, "Is there an overlay for the *furos*?"

"No, no. They grow over after the floods. We try to follow last year's paths, but they're always slightly different."

"But you know where they are?"

"Most of them, yeah."

"Theo, I'm hiring you."

Theo grins. "What about granite hill?" complains one of the boys.

"I'll pay you for the morning, then we can go to the granite hill this afternoon."

They're unhappy, but they agree. An hour later they're nosing the boat into a lesser-known *furo*, which hasn't yet had the growth of the past year trimmed from it. The boys reach out to cut branches or help Theo steer the boat around the hands of green that splay into the old tunnel. "Why this way?" one complains.

"Because I see something," says Sura. Many of the *furos* end where the land rises above the water; some intersect roads that run along the edge of the uplands. Some of those roads lead to the oil wells. A hundred meters ahead, this one does.

When they reach the spot, Sura leans out of the boat to inspect the branches. The main *furo* continues on to the north, but . . . She stretches out her arm and just barely manages to snag a branch that doesn't poke into the *furo*. She pulls it close. It was severed sometime in the past.

"This way!" She practically hauls the boat into the tangle of overgrowth. Theo curses and ducks, but moments later they're in a dark tunnel whose jutting beams have half regrown. It's a little *furo*, but it's real.

They cut through the tangles and hunt for old smooth ends where branches have been chopped away, and the *furo* goes on, two hundred meters, four, into unmapped territory—dense growth with no paths below, real or virtual. And then Sura's glasses give a ping. She reaches for a long vine and pulls the boat into a cradle of twigs that, in dry season, must be sixty feet above the forest floor. Nestled there is a bright orange backpack.

She gathers it in her arms.

CHAPTER EIGHTEEN

Lima glitters like all the stars have fallen. "It sounds beautiful," says Maeve, who's in her ears but unable to see through her glasses tonight. "When are you coming home?"

"Ah." All the things she wanted to say and should say train-wreck in Sura's mind. "Here's the thing—"

"We miss you, Sura. You found what you went down there for, why stay there? Or is it too dangerous to travel?"

Sura hasn't told her about the two men in the storm. Maeve is just putting two and two together from the fact that Sura's staying in a game-hotel under the name of one of her characters.

"It is dangerous," she admits. "I think it's bad for me everywhere, now. Maeve, I—I don't know whether Detroit is safe for me anymore."

There's a long pause. "Detroit," says Maeve. "Not Oneota?"

"Not either. They tracked me down, Maeve! They know I'm here! And these fuckers mean business, what am I to do?"

"Have you talked to Jay about this," asks Maeve coldly.

"No, but I will. Maybe he can help, start up his part of the investigation again. You and the whole fireteam can help too! I don't want to *leave,* I want to keep you safe too. They could use you guys against me."

"Come on, do you really mean that much to these shitheads?"

"They killed my father, Maeve. They tried to scoop me up in Dayton and they followed me to Peru. Yeah, I really think I do mean that much to them."

"But why?"

"That's the last piece in the puzzle. I got Dad's backpack and I know what they wanted from him and what they want from me. I just don't know why yet." She does—sort of—but she's never told Maeve about that little burglary she did for Dad back when. It will take too long to explain.

"You're being so cryptic! What was in the fucking backpack, Sura?"

"A key. Only, Maeve, you have to see it to believe it." Her words catch in her throat. "It's so much more than just a key and I can't just tell you about it, I don't *want* to tell you what it is unless you can *see* it." The mesh will only give them a voice connection right now; it's maddening. As she's talking she comes away from the window and sits on the bed. She gazes at the thing she found in the orange backpack. In a way it explains everything. It's a gut-punch every time she takes it out.

In other, important ways, it explains nothing. "Let's try again in a bit, I'm told the mesh traffic goes down after nine. Anyway, I have to phone Graciella. If we're in luck she'll have the last puzzle piece."

"Well, fuck. All right then, get on it. Love you, girl."

Sura blows out a heavy breath as she rings off. She turns back to the bed, and the miraculous, terrifying, and oh-so-obvious-now-that-she's-seen-it thing that leans on the backpack.

It's her. More precisely, it's sixteen-year-old Sura Neelin, as scanned by Dad and 3-D printed in the form of an eight-inch-tall figurine. She's always been amazed at how exquisite the details are, right down to a pimple on her chin. Not seeing the thing in years has refreshed it, as though it (and her younger self) is being revealed for the first time.

I get it, Dad. You put me next to your bed all these years, just like I put Ganesha next to mine. I'm your ultimate trophy, that one thing you did that worked. Why not use that trophy as a biometric key, the way Vaughan made a squashed can into one?

When did Dad realize that she hasn't changed that much since he took the scan?—That given the right makeup, shorter hair, and maybe a little cinching around the waist, live Sura could pass for scanned Sura? Real for *in virtua*? No wonder Jay, when he first caught her, delivered her to a biometrics lab.

"Making me your key was a really, really dumb thing to do, Dad." And flattering, and touching, weird, and infuriating.

Infuriating because, like Britt Birch, he seems to have had more of a relationship with this thing than he did with his real daughter.

"Fine." She turns away and calls Graciella Perea.

* * *

"I'm glad you're well," says Graciella after Sura recounts a heavily edited version of her adventures in Loreto. "I've been busy while you were away! I sent one of my students around to the address of your Norris Trading. Do you know what he found?"

"Tell me." This doesn't sound promising.

"A scanning company! One of those ones that will take your mail and scan it and email that to you. I thought 'how odd' and phoned Norris's number. I reached a very nice lady with an Indian accent who told me she works for a call center in Kolkata. It seems that Norris Trading is an entirely online affair. Another of my students called it a D-A-C. Do you know what that is?"

"A DAC. Yeah, I know. Thanks, Graciella."

"So did visiting where he died bring some, what do you call it, closure? Between you and Jim?"

"I-I don't know. I'm still pretty emotional about everything."

"Time is the only healer, Sura. You'll be fine, I saw that when you sat down in my little garden. You have the heart of a lion, did you know that?"

"No one's ever told me anything like that."

"I dare say most people are not that perceptive." She can hear the smile in Graciella's voice. "I hope you remain in touch, Sura. I want to know how your adventure ends."

"So do I. And I will stay in touch, thanks, Graciella."

Afterwards, sitting alone with her miniature self, she wonders what someone with the heart of a lion would do at this point. There's no reason to stay in Lima now; Norris isn't really based here. They're not based anywhere. The *D* in DAC stands for Distributed, after all.

What's more worrying is what the *A* stands for. An autonomous corporation is just a set of dApps and smart contracts, maybe administered by an AI. All the functions of CEO, CFO, of HR, Legal, they're all automated. There needn't be any humans in the loop at all. Just shareholders, extracting money from the DAC as if it were some sort of vending machine.

She laughs, amazed. So anyway, if she were the kind of person who had the heart of a lion, what would she be doing now? For starters, she would coldly, carefully retrace the chain of clues, drawing lines between the photos on her mental murderboard until it all added up.

Say she does. The lines start with the burglary she did for Dad. It could be something else, but this all feels personal; so say it was that. He did have her steal a computer hard drive, after all. He at least felt there was something very important on that drive. Not necessarily valuable, at least not in the conventional sense. He didn't get rich off it. But something that would be paramount to an environmentalist.

That "something" could be a digital key. The fact that it was stored on an air-gapped computer means that was probably the only copy. Likely, it was the password to a blockchain address, or the coordinates to the same. That address has something to do with spoofing an environmental sensor network so vast that it covers most of the planet. And just about this time last year, Dad went to a place where there were lots of such sensors, and got murdered. Before he died he hid the key to the network, and whoever killed him didn't find it. Unfortunately, he'd led his personal Judas Remy to think that Sura had a copy; so they came for her.

"Well, hello, you," she says to her figurine.

And that's it, she thinks. Or, almost all of it. All she needs is names to go in the blank squares that all the arrows point to. Who are Norris's shareholders? Who hired Summit Recoveries? And Jay.

In short, all she has to do is find answers to the very same set of questions that she started with, and all will be fine.

"Fuck." She slumps back on the bed, and waits for the clock to tick past nine p.m.

"Oh, so much better!" It's Sura's turn to ride Maeve, who's gazing out the condo's front window at a Michigan winter night. "Although, it looks like crap there."

"Oh shut up. I wish I was somewhere warm right now." Maeve laughs. "Enough of that, show me your thing! What's got you so worked up that you can't even tell me what it is?"

Sura fades Detroit and turns so Maeve can see the figurine. She's perched it next to a vase with some fake flowers in it.

"Ooooh." There's a long silence while Maeve digests the implications. "At least there's a silver lining," she says eventually.

"What?"

"They want you alive. Think about it! If they can get the doll, great, or your Dad's 3-D file of it, even better. But if those are gone, you're the closest thing they're going to get. So you better be in one piece. I doubt corpse-you will work on whatever key-scanner they want to put this in front of."

"It might. They could pose me, wire me up like a store dummy." That's too gruesome a prospect to continue thinking about. "You're right, actually. I hadn't thought about it that way."

"So you stay one step ahead of them. Or—" Maeve cackles suddenly. "Get a face-lift. And a boob-job. Walk right in and show them. It'll be too late, they'll have no reason to keep after you then."

"Gee. Great."

"I know. It still sucks to be you." There's a longer silence, then Maeve says, meekly, "I still want you to come home."

"Me too." Sura goes to sit down, and fades up Maeve's perspective. "Hey. You and Malcolm, huh?"

"Uh . . . Well . . ." Maeve's sounding guilty. "He is incredibly hot, you gotta admit. And you and me . . ."

"Were never a thing. I know." Sura laughs. "I can still be jealous."

"Oh, no!"

"Not in a bad way. Just in a 'he fucking well better appreciate what he's getting' sort of way."

"Oh." There's some kind of noise from the street, like a car backfiring. Maeve looks over from her position on the couch, but the windows remain dark. "I don't know what Malcolm and me are," she goes on, "but I do know it doesn't affect what you and me are. I told him about us, he's cool with it."

"Wait, what? Does that mean—" Red letters suddenly obliterate her view. *GENERAL ALERT,* they say. *PLAYER DOWN.*

Maeve jumps to her feet. "What the hell?"

"Players get into trouble all the time," Sura says doubtfully, but Maeve's running to the window. Fractured red light slides around the walls and ceiling. Something's going on outside. There's shouting.

Another horrible noise echoes around the neighborhood. Sura's only ever heard this kind of buzzer at basketball games. The jolt of it forces you to move. It's followed by a voice saying, *"This is not a drill. The emergency overlay is loading, please evacuate the building and gather at your designated assembly point."*

Maeve throws on her jacket, swearing; Sura's forgotten she's in Peru and is trying to assemble the fireteam. "Vaughan? K.C.? Rico, are you awake, we've got a situation in Not in Service."

There's no Rico; doubtless he's safely asleep in silent Pittsburgh. After a few seconds, though, Vaughan responds with a simple, "Here."

"K.C.? Where are—"

"Hang on, Sura, I'm trying to contact the larpwrights." Behind his voice Sura can hear an echo of the same buzzer that's biting her own ears.

Through Maeve's glasses she sees the condo hallway fly by. Sura's bed is empty, and so is Compass's—empty and made. "Maeve, where is she?"

"I don't know, haven't seen her in days." Now Maeve runs through the living room and downstairs. As her rider Sura can see the arrows and icons of the emergency overlay, more clearly than Maeve who keeps tripping on her way out the door. There's a stream of people racing by in the street, nearly all of them wearing glasses. She starts to follow them.

"Maeve, stop! We need to find the others. Everybody, pop up a flag!"

Maeve fumbles off her gloves, draws signs in the air as, thousands of miles away in Peru, Sura does the same. Three flags jut up in the city that's half-visible through Maeve's glasses.

One of those labels is close by and approaching. "There you are!" says Vaughan as he runs out of the shadows. "What the fuck is going on?"

The streetlights go out. At the same time, the urgent voice falls silent. Somebody shouts something about an EMP and someone else shouts back, "No, my eyes are still working." Then, through Maeve's ears, Sura hears a pop-pop-popping sound coming from somewhere nearby.

The crowd is surging in that direction and Maeve gets swept along. "Vaughan, stick with Maeve, where's she going, stop her." Maeve's view twists; Sura can see that a silhouetted figure has grabbed her arm. "Don't you hear that?" shouts Vaughan.

"Fuck, look at the overlay, Vaughan, we gotta go this way."

"Maeve, stop!" It's too late, she's twisted out of Vaughan's grip and mixed herself into the shifting body-shapes.

An awful certainty settles onto Sura. She looks at the emergency overlay, and all the green arrows point in the same direction. But there it is again: *pop-pop-pop, coming from that way.*

And now she hears screaming.

"Maeve, stop, it's a trap!" Maeve reaches for people as they surge past, but they're all following the overlay and whatever they're hearing through their earbuds is drowning out the gunfire, at least at this distance. "Vaughan, can you see her?"

"I've got her flag, she's near K.C."

"I'm with Pax and his team." K.C.'s finally back online. "We're trying to get out."

"But you're running *to* the guns! Guys, the emergency overlay is lying! Turn around. Turn back!"

The chaos up ahead is absolute, and seemingly invisible to Maeve and the onrushing crowd. As her helpless rider, Sura is suddenly, uncontrollably there, panicked and mindless as the rest. Vaughan's voice floats in—"They gamified a trap," she hears him saying. "They must have played it out, figured out how to spoof the security system . . ." She can't speak, and neither does Maeve as she runs and dodges down a street where red and blue flashes are sliding across the rooftops. The man next to her says, "Gotta help," and breaks into a run.

Sura finds her voice. "But how can he tell?" she yells. "Maeve, how can you tell it's not a trap?"

"Shit," says Maeve, slowing. "Shit, shit shit."

"Just breathe. Take stock. Where are you, what's happening around you? I'm riding you, I'll be your eyes if you need. Just—ignore what the sky's saying."

Like magic, Maeve is abruptly alone. Sura can hear people, see movement up and down the street, but there's nobody near her. Somewhere, a fire is waving an orange hand over the sides of a building, lighting up stop signs and hydro poles and the bellies of dozens of incoming quadcopters. She's all turned around, it could be their house burning.

"Police drones," says Maeve. "They seem real. Look! There's K.C." She walks up to him; he's standing with Nile Abbott and three or four other people. "Where do we go?" she asks.

Abbott nods decisively. "This way!" He's got a commanding presence, and everybody follows.

But Sura's looking up again. "Guys, I don't think you want to—" Maeve turns a corner and, in the light from a burning house, she beholds a street strewn with bodies.

There are men with guns standing among the fallen people. They are wearing the camo and boots of the doxers from the troll factory.

Her earbuds erupt in noise and Sura's view judders strangely. Then the world is turning on its ear. Sura herself falls over on the couch. She sits up, muting just long enough to make sure she hasn't knocked anything over, then returns to Maeve.

—Who is on her side on the ground, looking at the ankles of running people.

K.C. enters the shot. He's got a gun, and he's waving for somebody to get behind him. It's Pax, looking confused. K.C. stands still, one arm behind his back, straight-arms the pistol and aims. He fires once, clinically and carefully. Then again, and again as he walks backward into shadow.

Something blows up off in the other direction, and the windows of the houses go from mirroring fire to black as red splinters of glass are knocked inside.

"M-Maeve? Maeve, talk to me."

"Fuck this," Vaughan says in her ears, as clearly as if he's standing next to her. "Fuck this, fuck this." His voice joggles; he's running.

"Vaughan, find them! Get help!"

"Fuck this, fuck—" He's gone, suddenly.

"Vaughan? Maeve? K.C.?"

Maeve's glasses are still on the ground, pointing at a curb and fallen bodies. Sura can see her right hand, which has caressed the asphalt and is unmoving.

The view doesn't change. Seconds pass, a minute, and only the dance of fire in the windows says that this is not a photograph.

"Jay? Is that really you?"

"Are you okay?" His voice is the same as always. Solid. Sura's knees buckle and she collapses on the couch.

She's been running back and forth, jamming her few things into her backpacks while in her glasses, buying a ticket on the next hyperloop out of Lima. It's used up all her money.

"I'm, I'm fine," she tells him. "But the others, they're all alive but nobody's answering! Maeve's down, she's hurt, but her tattoo says she's still breathing—"

"I got a call," he says. "Woke me up, that there'd been an attack. It's all over the Net now . . . Were you there, what—?"

"I—I wasn't there, but the rest of the team—Jay, I don't know. None of them are talking to me, and I can't *go* there, I—I'm somewhere else—"

There's a silence. Then, "Where are you? I'm driving up."

She strangles a hysterical laugh. "From Pittsburgh? We might just arrive at the same time."

The bags are ready. She takes a deep breath, looks around, then notices that in the upper right field of her vision there's a discreet 43. That's the number of text messages waiting for her. "Just a sec," she mumbles, and looks at the senders.

Most of the texts are alerts from the emergency system. None is from Compass. But one is from Bill Duchene, and it's only minutes old. She opens it.

Shit going down internationally. Coordinated attacks on the frameworlds. Are you safe? I can shelter until it blows over. Let me know.

"Bill?"

"What's that?" says Jay.

Sura calls up a virtual keyboard and taps out a reply. *Can you send someone to friends?*

Jay: "Sura, what's going on?"

"It's okay. Just trying to get help to Maeve, I don't know I—"

The notifications number turns to 44. Duchene's reply is, *On its way.*

Sura stands up. "It's okay," she says to Jay. "I'm out of town and you'll get there before I do. But thanks for calling, for, uh, thinking of me and all." She reaches up and flips down a menu for local services. Finds an overlay for available cars and flags one down.

She summons Vesta's confident voice. "I've got it covered, Jay. Thanks for calling. I'll update you when I get there."

"But—"

She hangs up.

CHAPTER NINETEEN

"Who sent them?"

Duchene holds his hands up, palms out. "Whoa, good morning to you too! Are you okay? You weren't picking up."

Sura's only just opened her eyes to find herself propped up on bolstered pillows in a big, anonymous bedroom in an equally big, anonymous house. Her glasses still on her face. They'd unmuted when they registered her waking, and images and lists and chat windows had blinked open everywhere, like eyes of Sauron. She'd shouted and thrown the glasses across the room. Ever since then, she's been pacing around the house, trying to find out how Maeve is, and the others. But among the police, paramedics, hospital staff, and news, who can she trust to tell her the truth? Or to help rather than hinder?

She vaguely remembers a long, terrible drive from the airport to the gated bedroom community visible out these windows. She'd been so exhausted and broken at that point that she has no clear sense of where she is.

Bill steps across the white marble-tiled foyer. He is haloed by Vaporous white-curtained windows' glow from the light of a front yard plated with untouched snow. She follows him to the blond carpet in the family room, whose only distinguishing feature is an actual television above the gas fireplace.

She chose Bill over Jay. It hurts, but she's been telling herself that she had to make a command decision: Who had the most resources to help in the situation? And Bill had offered. It was one of his cars that picked her up at the terminal. This is one of his houses.

"Who set the doxers on us?" she asks again, gnawing her thumbnail as he sits in a leather armchair. "Who would do such a thing?"

Bill shakes his head. "It was more than just the doxers; this was a coordinated attack, worldwide. Who's behind it? Hell, I know who Pax is blaming. He's got a real easy target, I mean, sixty percent of the world's assets are owned by just five people. How do you think they feel about the frameworlds eating those resources from the inside out? They wouldn't even have to lift a finger, just rev up the fake news cycle a bit for the far right. The militias have been stockpiling weapons for decades and losing touch with reality the whole time. They expect an apocalypse and are just itching for the trigger. Maybe Pax is right. Maybe it was the trillionaires who set them off."

She gazes out at the snow-covered lawn, digesting that. Then she realizes that this is *him*, live and in person, and sees how patiently he's waiting. "You gave me this house to stay in," she says. "And you're here now. That's . . . incredible. Thank you."

He looks away. "I still have nightmares about that fucking room those assholes kept me in. Then you burst in like some Jedi . . . How could I not help? I mean, I've tried to pay you back, over the last little while. Nothing seemed adequate. Is it ridiculous to say that I jumped at the chance last night?"

"I suppose not."

"Listen, have you eaten? 'Cause I haven't."

She's starving. "I dunno what's in the fridge but there might be tea—"

"Coffee," he says. "I can afford it, you know."

"Coffee! Haven't had that in years!" She heads for the kitchen but he's faster. "Oh, no, you don't have to," she protests, but secretly Sura wallows in the attention. Bill seems to know where things are, and soon he's cooked up an omelet, made some actual coffee, and even set a proper place for her at the table. Meanwhile her brain is slowly grinding back to life. As she sits she says, "I guess you own this place?"

"Company guest house. Yeah, I own it. Why, you want it?"

"Don't joke."

"Sorry." She barely tastes the coffee, real though it might be, and doesn't taste the omelet at all. Her eyes are faraway, she knows, and finally she says, "Fuck. I have to catch up." She takes a deep breath and unmutes her glasses.

Friend status: The fireteam are all listed as active players—even Maeve. Sura had tracked the ambulances and news reports during her loop, and then in the air. She's been told that Maeve is in the Detroit Receiving Hospital but has no idea what her injuries are.

Compass registers on the player boards, but the only messages are from Sura and Rico. She remembers the thread from last night; it was like she and he were in a black room together, calling the others' names, to no reply. It was heart-wrenching and exhausting.

She mutes, and sits again on the stool at the counter. "Right, sorry, I had to check the fireteam's status. They're all, they all made it out alive. My friend Maeve, she's been shot, I think, but I don't know how badly she's hurt . . ."

"I'll get my people on it." She goes for more coffee and when she comes back he says, "I think I know what happened to one of your other teammates." He goes to the family room, gesturing the TV awake.

He flips through channels and lands on the news. It's live, but allows rewind, so he zips back a bit. "Here."

And there he is, spread across half the wall: K.C. He's smiling grimly at the camera. Under him there's a red banner with the words, HERO OF ONEOTA.

"I was just exercising my second amendment rights, like any good American," he says to a reporter. His backdrop is Brush Street at dawn. It's packed with emergency vehicles. "I had my pistol, so I used it, and with God's help I was able to get a few good people out of harm's way."

He windows to the top left of the studio shot, and the news anchor says, "K.C. Kinney was a prominent talk-radio personality in South Africa before coming to the States. Already a rising star in the frameworlds, he's quickly gaining an online following after his heroic actions last night."

"Aw, fuck, K.C." She turns away.

The rest of the news is no happier. Bill's right, there were multiple attacks, worldwide, and they're still going on. Different groups are claiming responsibility, but it's pretty clear that a planned, violent backlash against the frames is happening.

"You said you knew who Pax is blaming," she says eventually. "The one percent, or above that. But you think otherwise?"

"What I think is that Pax is an agent provocateur. He didn't start the frames, and he doesn't run them. He's the self-appointed star of the larpwrights, but they mostly disown him. I wouldn't be surprised if he pushed the militias to this deliberately. As of this morning, the whole planet's polarized. There're countries in Africa and Asia that are trying to ban framing or nationalize it somehow, but you can't do that. The frameworlds live on the mesh, they're open-source, trustless systems, and those governments have no idea how they work. They want to turn them into companies or state-owned industries, but they're post-state, post-monetary, and post-market, and we're becoming dependent on them. Any economy that tries to ban them is going to collapse. I think that's Pax's plan. He's tipping over the dominoes."

"That first night when we met, you thought you could privatize them."

"I was naïve."

"Yet you think there's some shadowy conspiracy behind it all."

"Wake up, Sura! Maybe the frameworlds aren't owned by anyone, but they were *designed* by somebody. Nobody knows who invented Bitcoin, but blockchains have upended the whole economic order. It's the same with the frameworlds, but this time, it's someone who learned from Bitcoin. Somebody who understands that code is law. Technology is legislation. They know they don't need to act in the open, politically, at all. All they have to do is put the right tech out there, and the world will change. Yes, it's happening."

An absurd possibility pops into her head. "AI."

Bill doesn't laugh. "That's certainly part of it."

"You had a name for this conspiracy. *The Rewilding*. Where'd that come from?"

"It's something the doxers talked about. *Not* like they went on about their other crazy conspiracies, that's the point. They didn't have any elaborate theories about the *Rewilding*, it was exactly because they couldn't figure it out that they were scared of it."

He shakes his head. "Things're gonna spiral out of control unless we do something. We have to find out who's behind the frameworlds. And we've got to get ahead of Pax and his apocalyptic rhetoric. He's just feeding the fire."

It's like he's gotten taller somehow—a real superhero moment. Sura knows she's falling for it, but really, she's never seen Bill like this. The last person in her life to speak with such passion and conviction was—

Her dad.

"What are you going to do?" she says, even as she finds herself flooded with conflicted feelings.

"This is all about governance," he says as he waves the TV off. "Only an idiot would deny we're plunging into an economic revolution. It's about to become a political one too and this time it's global. So who comes out on top? It can't be the fascists or the communists or the dictators. It's got to be us, We the People."

"But how do we do that?"

He hesitates, seems about to say something when the arm of Sura's glasses vibrates faintly: somebody's calling her. *It could be Maeve.* "Hang on. Hello?"

"Hello, is this Countess Vesta?" It's a voice-only connection, and the caller sounds like an older woman.

Sura frowns. "This is she."

"I hear you have a detective agency in Oneota. There are people missing after last night's attack. We'd like you to help us find one of them."

Her heart sinks. This would break her spirit, she knows it, so she has to say no; besides, her team has shattered. "I-I don't know," she stammers. "I don't think . . ."

"We think you might know her, that's one reason I'm calling.

"She calls herself Compass . . ."

Her eyes track the Detroit skyline as Bill's car takes her home. Her whitelisted status should let her walk in and out of Not in Service, even if it's crawling with cops. She's done nothing, after all. She never did anything. She has to go home anyway. Dad's urn is there.

The skyline is a mix of epic modernist ruins and airy new towers, mirrored by burnt-out houses next to fresh condos and half-real, half-virtual popup stores. The place is working again, but in a weird schizophrenic way that nobody yet understands. It kind of makes sense in Mixed Reality, where you can see the city's shifting circuit board of relationships etched on the sky. Poorer, older, and less-educated people don't have glasses and can't see that, but they do see the revival of the community. They've been finding out that food, clothing, and lodging are available, whether they have a traditional "job" or not. Lately, the mood on the streets has been shifting.

Somebody is very, very angry about that.

She takes off the distracting smart glasses and summons the magic of the *fuck-you*—trying to look past the tech and the people to what's really going on. For a shimmering moment it seems like the utility poles and crumbled curbs, buried sewer pipes and tottering fences have all somehow woken up. The physical infrastructure of the city is coordinating its own reconstruction, thinking for itself, just like the apples that found their own way to the people who needed to eat them.

The glasses vibrate in her hand. It's Rico. "Hi!" she says with relief.

"Have you found out anything? I know all about K.C." *And I don't want to talk about it.*

"Malcolm found her. She's at the Receiving Hospital. They wouldn't let him in to see her. It's the family, they've driven up from the South. All piled into her room and they're keeping anybody else out. They broke her glasses!"

"Oh, shit." Maeve's crazy, bigoted relatives are the last people she'd want finding her right now. They're backwards and afraid of the modern world—and now she's trapped with them.

"But how is she?"

"Out of danger. Bullet did a through-and-through near her right kidney. She's still asleep, but she'll pull through."

"Thanks, Rico. When she's better we'll stage an extraction. Anything about Vaughan?"

"Ah. Well. Yeah. He sent me a text. Said the frameworlds are no safer than anywhere else, so why shouldn't he go for his money now, and get out? I think he meant, get out of the country. 'Cause he's gone."

She nods, crestfallen. His tattoo still registers, but its location is muted, as are all means of contacting him. He might still have a tiny fortune, and maybe he'll be able to set himself up on some South Seas island. She says this to Rico, and he snorts.

"More likely he's gonna get himself killed. Either way, he's run off, Vesta. What about you?"

"I'll be fine. Thanks, Rico. I'll track down Compass and let you know when I find her."

She tries not to see the bullet damage, or smell the sour taint of housefire as she walks up Brush Street. Nothing here's been touched—or so she thinks until she reaches her own building. Its door hangs open, the lock and doorknob blown out by what must have been a shotgun blast. "What the—?"

There are two women standing by the door. One says, "Countess Vesta?" They're instantly tagged in her glasses as *Constella* (the older one) and *habit_former.* Sura recognizes Constella from *Diminuendo.*

"You're the ones who called me?"

Constella, a stout black woman in orange and brown, says, "You are a friend of Compass's, aren't you?"

The younger, a mousy blonde, blurts, "We're really worried about her! You know how she is."

"Compass can take better care of herself than anybody I know." There's a big *however* attached to that, though, she has to admit. She ducks her head. "I'm concerned too. But it hasn't even been a day. The whole town's dispersed, half the population's gone to ground somewhere else and the other half are hiding in subworlds, pretending like nothing happened."

"Yeah, we seen the lists and follow the finder boards. Most people are accounted for. But Compass ain't most people. Come on! You know that."

"Yeah. I live with her, actually. But I don't really know her. I don't think anybody does."

Constella nods. "That's Compass all over. Girl's got problems. Who's gonna look after her at a time like this?"

"I'm trying." Then Sura looks down. "I guess I'm not doing a very good job."

She pushes the front door and it wobbles and falls. "Come on in," she says, aware of the heavy irony in her tone. She half expects to find Compass sitting on the couch with her headphones on, oblivious to everything. But the couch is on its back with its stuffing out and its arms slashed. The whole place has been efficiently tossed. Thankfully, there are no bodies in the beds. She checks her bedroom; everything's strewn about, but while Dad's urn is on the floor, it hasn't been broken into. They were looking for something in particular—like, maybe, a 3-D–printed figurine of a woman, about eight inches tall?

She walks around dispassionately assessing the mess, while Constella and habit_former huddle together in shock. Sura goes in the kitchen. "Huh. Funny thing. They left the beer."

"No," says habit_former distractedly; "Yes, please!" says Constella.

Sura rights some chairs and they talk about Compass. Both knew her *in virtua* before she moved to Detroit. She's been so many people in so many worlds, they hardly know where to start in describing her exploits. Soon all three are laughing and shaking their heads. They've been living with their own trickster goddess. If she's gone, the loss to the frameworlds will be immeasurable.

Everybody leaves, Sura reminds herself. It doesn't help. "When's the last time you guys saw her? She told me she was working for this out-of-frame company, Brim I think it's called, modeling clothes."

Habit_former laughs, a kind of uneasy bark. "Compass, modeling? Last *I* saw she was trading spice under the noses of the sardaukar."

"She gave up the Brim job," says Constella. "Said something about turning it inside out. She told me she'd been doing side jobs a few months now for some mystery group, what were they called . . ."

Sura's suddenly alert, but Constella says, "The *externalities*, that's it."

"The what?"

"It's the flip-side of business." Constella's voice shifts; she sounds like a business professor. Maybe she actually is one. "An externality is whatever your business affects that you don't take account of. So pollution, that's an externality. Or displaced garment workers in Asia or wherever. Externalities are affected by what your company does, but don't have a say in it."

"How could she be working for something like that?"

"There're these things called actants that speak for them. She told me she was NPCing for them, or being ridden by them . . . ? I guess they're not really NPCs, they're players. Just . . . not human."

Sura remembers Tamshiyacu. Was she an actant? "Do you know if these externalities, do they have a, like a union, or a clubhouse? How do I get in touch with them?"

They draw a blank. "Is there anything else," Sura presses. "Anything at all? It might be small . . ."

"Well," starts habit_former. "I don't know if it means anything, but I did notice one thing lately."

"Yeah?"

"You know how she dresses." Habit_former wrinkles her nose. "It's Salvation Army all the way, and totally gender-neutral. Never seen a piece of jewelry on her nor any makeup. But, last few times I seen her she's been wearing a broach."

Sura sits up straight. "A what?"

"A, a kind of broach, like on the front of her jacket here." Habit_former cups her hand above her left breast.

"Like this?" She pulls the bird ornament that Binesi gave her from her inventory and clips it on *in virtua*. "Did it look like this?"

"A lot like it, yeah," says habit_former. "Does it mean anything?"

"It might." Sura vanishes the broach. "It just might."

She reassures them that she'll follow this clue, and then they share more stories about Compass.

With the front door fixed (sort of) and the sky full of neighborhood-watch drones, Sura finally feels safe enough to sleep in her own bed. Apart from the buzz of the quadcopters there's an eerie silence on the street, and many of the houses are dark. Maybe their owners will be brave and come home tomorrow. Maybe Compass will be one of them. Sura keeps texting her, and Vaughan, but neither reply.

For some reason tonight's loneliness reminds her of her old place in Dayton. There were times when she'd felt free there. Just as often, she'd been like an abandoned doll, akimbo on the couch, a book open and unattended, music playing and ignored. Now, she opens the window to let in some fresh night air. Despite the date, autumn refuses to let go, and the temperature's gone up, melting most of the snow. For a while Sura sits looking at the last smudges of the sunset, gingerly testing memories of Mom and Dad to see what hurts. The bright promises of childhood are unfulfilled.

Something black lands on a tree branch, blotting out the peach line of sky at the horizon. It's a crow.

"I've seen you around," she tells it. It's a good thirty feet away and probably can't hear her; it wouldn't understand her if it could, any more than she knows its language.

This is clearly a sign. *Get off your ass and try it.* She hunts in the heap of junk she collected off the floor until she comes up with the amber stone Binesi gave her. It has powers too unsettling to dare. Yet Compass has been wearing one, a broach like hers. Putting on her glasses, she holds up the amber and looks past it at the crow. "How do I . . . ?" The camera in her glasses should recognize the glyph on the stone, use it as a key—like her figurine.

A name bubble appears over the crow. *Bob 3455* it says.

"Well, hello Bob," Sura whispers.

This is silly, it . . . She blinks. "Holy shit." Bob's not alone—*so* not alone that her glasses are struggling to keep up with the data flooding into them. In leaps and washes from left to right then right to left, thousands of other tags spring up. They recede in perspective, becoming a sea of dots on the tree-lined horizon. Some connect by spidery-thin lines that jut up like flags to meridional junctions in the sky. One line joins Bob to Alice 6754, Judy 3298, and a couple too distant to read. Metadata says that these are members of Bob's family.

If she looks up she can see the ID and FAQ for this overlay. Such notes are usually written on the zenith, out of normal line-of-sight. Sura expects something of mythic Cahokian significance, but the overlay's title is EXTERNAL STAKEHOLDERS—DETROIT.

External, as in *externality*? Only some of the labels are attached to animals. Many are trees, or groups of trees. Some are empty lots, some are buildings. Some have human names.

There's a menu; the overlay lets you see more than just family connections. One option is *owned by.* Sura selects that and nearly all the lines vanish. Nobody tells Bob what to do, apparently. A few threads knot together overhead, but others send thin runners arcing off over the horizon. One runner is labeled *Proudly Eagle Owned!*

Maybe the taxi service really is run by some Pacific Northwest eagles, in the form of a DAC running on the decentralized protocol stack, outside of any national jurisdiction. It'll own the cars, paying some money for AI business and legal services. Profits could go to suing Washington State loggers and hiring ornithologists.

This network of AIs is such a batshit crazy idea, but so totally unlike the *Terminator/Matrix* vision of AI Sura grew up with, that she can't fault herself for not guessing it was here. It's hiding in plain sight.

And that could mean . . . She examines the menu options available for the city's external stakeholders.

Among other things, they can have Matters of Concern. Detroit's raccoons are worried about a new hair gel that's poisonous to them but tastes great and is ending up in recycling bins. The birds are concerned with the ever-growing drone population. Various of the raw material resources used in Not in Service are complaining that they're being depleted. One of the options available to them is to hire human avatars to lobby on their behalf. Avatars such as Compass, maybe?

She filters the view for avatars, and finds a couple dozen on the move in the city—and a thick concentration, nearly twenty, all in one building on the edge of town. None moving.

She's suddenly sure of it: she's found *The Rewilding.*

Even if Compass isn't in that building, if she's been working for the externalities, then the people in that old warehouse are Sura's best bet for locating her.

Sura's tiredness hasn't exactly evaporated, but she remembers this spiky energy. It's how sadness and anger used to mutate into the drive to burgle. She's felt it recently, when she rescued Duchene, and then again in Peru. It's irresistible. It's the *fuck-you.*

She closes the window and grabs her backpack.

CHAPTER TWENTY

"Hi, Bill? It's Sura. I know you're asleep, but listen, I've got a lead on this *Rewilding* game, and I'm going to check it out. I'll be in touch."

It's done. At least now, if something happens to her, there's some trace of what she's done.

She turns her attention to the impending break-in.

Warehouses are easy, in principle. Tonight, she's tired, worried, distracted by continued alerts that speak of ongoing attacks on the frameworlds. Shit's hitting the fan all over the world. The freezing cold is her friend, keeping her alert as she finds a dark corner of the parking lot and releases some microdrones she borrowed from the Oneota Art School. They're on the lookout for cameras and other drones.

As they rise along the windows, Sura goes back to her frame overlays. In the view unlocked by the amber, the five-story brick building is like a sun, almost invisible behind countless tags. Each tag corresponds to an environmental sensor of some kind. It seems the warehouse stocks IoT devices.

The only lights are on the top floor. She sends one drone up there and makes it circle the building, watching through its eyes. Looks like people are living up there. Two are walking together down a broad, brightly lit corridor. Another can be deduced from the mound of blankets in a bed. One room has old-fashioned workstations, like big draftsman's tables. There, one person is drawing carefully on a screen.

Next door, there's a small bedroom with one light on. Somebody's sitting there, a woman, perhaps, judging from the broad fan of frizzy black hair spilling over her shoulders.

Sura nudges the drone closer to the glass, risking discovery. She recognizes the clothing, even if she can't see Compass's face. She also knows that posture; the first time she saw it was the time Compass broke her glasses.

All right. She needs no technology to figure out the layout of the place. There are cameras on the front door, and some around the periphery, but there's an approach that avoids them. At the end of that invisible path some trash is leaning against the wall; the ground-floor windows start eight feet up, they're classic multipaned affairs. Sura darts across the parking lot, scales the junk until she can reach one, and by working up the frame square by square, manages to grab the bottom of a fire escape ladder. If she pulls on that, it'll descend, so she just uses it for balance as she climbs the window. Her feet are braced against the frame, if she falls it's going to hurt a lot . . . She reaches for the lowest of the fixed fire escape steps, and just manages to grasp it.

Here's where all the time on climbing walls pays off. She's able to haul herself onto the steps. From there it's easy. She walks up a couple of flights, but pauses on the level below the lit one. Curiosity is prodding her.

Finally she curses under her breath, and slips her shiv under the dark fourth-floor window. She needs to know what's in here.

It's a world of silhouettes, blocky squares and tall rectangles. She doesn't use her flashlight but waits for her eyes to adapt, then moves cautiously between the stacks. She's feeling for an open box. When she finds one, she uses the light to look inside.

The crate holds sensors almost identical to the ones in Peru. They're nestled in foam, five by five at a time, in layers of at least a dozen.

A few rows down, the boxes have even smaller ones—chip sized, the sort of thing you could attach to a leaf, or the back of a fox. She moves on.

Near the open door to the stairs, she finds a box labeled RED EYE CAPS. Fine. Whatever; it's time to go up.

Her drones are watching, and she's set a timer in Purrloin that will call the cops if she doesn't regularly reset it. She eases into the black stairwell. Up above, white light outlines a rectangle, and past that is Compass.

Sudden doubt: Is all this sneaking ridiculous? Just to be sure, she tries calling her one last time. There's no answer.

She goes up.

It's easy to navigate the fifth-floor halls; she's always had a good sense of direction. Sura passes the open door where the man at the workstation is still drawing with painstaking slowness on his screen. The next door is Compass's. She knocks.

After waiting a decent interval, she tries the knob. It doesn't turn. The lock is electronic and invisible, but the mechanics of door latches haven't changed. She knows how to run a shiv in, and how to lean hard on it to move the bolt inside. It makes a cracking noise, and the door opens.

The room's about ten feet wide and twenty long; it looks like a wide entryway that's been repurposed as a bedroom. The far end is all glass, but there's an open doorway to the right.

Compass has pulled out her braid; her hair fans down her shoulders. She's sitting with her eyes closed, listening to music that's pouring out of a pair of speakers under the window. It's one of her guilty pleasures, an old seventies-era electronic group called Tangerine Dream. Seeing her calmly rocking to the pulsing sound, Sura is suddenly sure that all this has been a gigantic mistake. She has no business being here.

"Hey! Who're you?"

The man in the doorway still has his tie on, though his collar's been loosened; his black hair is tousled, and he's holding a square glass with some amber liquid in it. He's of some darker-skinned ethnicity than the usual white supremacist. Her glasses don't recognize him.

She struggles to breathe. "I'm Compass's roommate. She hasn't been home, I've been worried about her."

He takes a step inside; she can see that he's wearing glasses. "How'd you get in here? The doors are locked."

She moves between him and Compass. "Do you know what a distributed persona is? Look." She points at the window. "Drone outside watching us. I'm that drone, and down in the street, there are people. They're me too, listening to us right now. If you try anything I've got a flash army that'll storm this place faster than the cops can get here."

He blinks, hesitates, and takes a quick sip of his drink. "You're Sura. She talks about you."

"Yeah? Then why hasn't she invited me up here?"

"It's . . ." He looks for somewhere to put his glass. "Complicated. But you don't need the army."

"I'm taking her home."

"Well that's entirely up to her, don't you think?"

Sura carefully moves to a place where she can bolt to the hall if she has to. She looks at Compass, who's still got her eyes closed and is nodding in time to "Tangram." "Compass? Hello?"

The man has a label over him now: *Mikom*. He tilts his head, puzzled. "You've never seen her like this?"

"I have. She usually comes out of it on her own."

"Yeah. Where are her glasses?" He points. "Give them to her."

Sura retrieves a pair of glasses from a bedside table. "Compass, put these on."

Compass opens her eyes, blinks at Sura, and slowly reaches for the glasses. As soon as she puts them on there's a shift, like recognition. She sits up. "Oh. Hi, Sura."

"Compass, I've been worried sick! What the hell are you doing here? Don't you know what's been happening, out, out there?"

Compass shakes her head. "We been trying something." Suddenly herself, she stands and goes to gently punch the man in the shoulder. "Me and Cuz."

"This man's . . . your cousin?"

"Sura, meet Mike. He's family."

Carefully, Sura reaches for Compass's hand. "You should have called. I was worried sick. Compass, a lot has happened—" Behind Compass, Mike is shaking his head. Frustrated and confused, she changes her tack. "Can you tell me what you're doing here?"

Compass withdraws her hand, smiling coolly. "Cuz and I have been looking."

"For what?"

"For me."

"Come on," says Mike, picking up his drink. He goes back the way he came, into a much bigger space. The warehouse has a twelve-foot ceiling, making the giant square room with its thick wooden pillars somewhat cathedral-like. There's a fridge, stove, and various tables clustered around power outlets on the main posts. The place is heated by steam so it's too hot, and the windows are open.

"Vesta!" It's Binesi, rising from a threadbare couch that's part of a rough circle of furniture huddling under some standing lamps. Smiling widely, she comes to close Sura's hand in hers. "You made it! Was it the raven led you here? Or the coons?"

"A crow."

Binesi tosses Mike a look. "Told you."

"What's this all about? Those things you twinked me—they were *lures*?"

Binesi nods. "More like clues, for the right kind of mind to follow. Truth to tell, I give out lots of them, but I seldom hook a fish."

"I'm glad you're okay. I don't know if the others—"

"The larpwrights are fine," says Binesi. "But let's talk about that later."

Compass appears at Sura's side. "Would you like a beer?"

"S-Sure."

She heads for the fridge while Mike and Binesi sit in the furniture circle. Sura joins them, landing in a burnt-orange armchair whose upholstery suggests a history with cats.

She turns to Mike. "So Compass is your cousin?"

"On my mother's side. We're Anishinaabe. I grew up in Ontario; Anwaatin is from this side of the border."

"Anwaatin?"

"It means 'it is calm.' She was always the level-headed one. Somebody nicknamed her Compass when she started playing the games, and it stuck. Most of us do that—adopt a settler name. Not Binesi," he adds with a shrug. "For me, my real name's Mikom, but you can call me Mike."

Mike smiles fondly at Compass as she hands Sura an open bottle. "I asked Binesi to check up on Compass a few weeks ago. We all look in on her when we can. She said she was starting to drift again."

"We used to think she was hiding," says Binesi. "She got snatched when she was twelve and the bastard headed out on the road. A thousand miles later they cornered him in Texas and the truck rolled over. Anwaatin had a head injury, and she couldn't remember what happened to her. After that she was anxious all the time."

"The doctors said she had a brain injury," Mike says. "Said there's two kinds of memory, factual and episodic—or historic. Compass has no problem with facts, but there's a hole where her episodic memory should be. She recognizes us, but she can't remember growing up. She has trouble remembering who she *was*, but not who she *is*.

"It's like your blind spot. You can find it if you hold up a pencil and wave it back and forth over here." He raises his finger in his left field of vision. "There's a hole there, but your brain knits the sides of it together to make it disappear. Compass would do that with her past if you asked her about anything. She'd make shit up, but she didn't know she was doing it. She thought she was remembering when she was actually inventing. The doctors call it 'confabulation.'

"She was okay, but aimless, you know? She had no past, so why imagine a future? Then this one time a white friend of Binesi's comes over and shows off her smart glasses. There was a game, one of the early MR larps. When Compass put on the glasses she was transformed. She became somebody. It wasn't anybody we knew, but she could tell us anything we wanted to know about the person. And the thing was, she was more that person than she'd been herself since the injury.

"We bought her a pair of glasses and let her play."

"Are you a relative too?" Sura asks Binesi. She's acutely aware that Compass is curled up in one of the threadbare couches, listening to all of this without comment.

"I'm not blood, no," says Binesi. "But I help watch over her." She waves a hand impatiently. "Point is, Compass is always someone other than herself. She always has been, since that day. It worked, for a while."

"But it's not working anymore," says Mike.

Sura takes a drink, eyeing them both. Not working? It's true she hasn't seen Compass since before Peru. What she had been seeing then, though, seemed a more competent, more focused woman than she was when they first met. "Maybe she's . . . not herself in a new way," she says carefully. "But that's not a bad thing, is it? She's not sleeping in cars anymore . . . Hey, did you know she was doing that?"

"Yes—"

"And you *let* her?"

Mike looks puzzled. "They were high-end cars."

"The p-problem was who I was playing," says Compass.

Mike nods. "How does it help her to play people so different from the soul she used to be? To play a *store*? A store, for Christ's sake! We've been encouraging her to play people more like who she was before. Hoping to bring her back to herself."

Coldly, Sura says, "And how's that been working out for you?"

"Not well," Mike admits. "I mean it wasn't, until Binesi suggested we let a truly powerful spirit ride her."

"A what?"

"A deodand," says Compass.

"A what?"

"The stone I gave you lets you see the deodands' world," says Binesi. "Compass always knew that world was there, but she had no way of playing them until just recently. Now we've got the resources to give the people of the woods and waters their own voices in the colonists' world. They can be players at last. And when they play by riding her, she becomes . . ." She turns to Compass, who laughs again, spreading her arms.

Is that all they've done? Made Compass into a mouthpiece for some local copy of Tamshiyacu? She can't reconcile that idea with what she's seeing, and she can't reconcile what she's seeing with the Compass she knew. She wants to back away slowly from this version of her—so carefree, so opposite the dark-eyed, fathomless, and serious woman she lives with.

"But she's still not—you're still not yourself."

"Would that be a problem," says Compass, "if the person I'd turned into was *better* than who I was before?"

Sura stands up. "Come with me. You need to get out of this place."

Binesi nods. "We all need to get out of here. It's not safe in town right now. Pax has exposed us to every reactionary force that might want to take us down. The other night was just the start of it."

"I'm going with them," says Compass simply, but with finality. "What about you?"

Sura has no answer to that. The condo is trashed, the fireteam broken. Supposedly Jay is in town, but she hasn't heard from him. And what are his connections and contacts going to be like? She imagines an extended family of tattooed truckers, carnies, and droopy-eyed motel operators. Is she going to stay with them?

"We're driving up to Wequetonsing," says Binesi. "In the morning, during rush hour—such as it is these days. If we left right now, we'd be easily spotted."

"You can stay the night," Compass offers. "There's plenty of room."

"Thanks, no." The condo may be a mess, and maybe all her worldly goods can be rescanned and uploaded to populate some other place—but Dad's urn is there. And the figurine. "Where's this Wequeh . . . tonsing? What's there?"

"It's one of those places," says Mike, "where the Rewilding touches our Earth."

There's too much to ask, and Sura doesn't know where to start. "If I came up to Wequetonsing with you, could I meet this Rewilding?"

"There are deodands," says Binesi. "We could introduce you. You've already met one of them, you've just never been properly introduced."

She nods slowly. "What time are you leaving?"

Rush hour; early, in other words. As Mike is escorting her downstairs, Sura calculates that what with getting home and packing, she'll maybe manage four hours of sleep tonight.

She could just call Bill and tell him *The Rewilding* is based in upstate Michigan. But she doesn't even really know that. And Compass is in play now, something she hoped would never happen. No, she needs more information, and she has to know Compass is safe before she does anything.

As she treads down the well-worn wooden stairs, Mike says, "I know Anwaatin isn't herself. We're trying, I promise. We'd never do anything to hurt her."

"You let her be possessed by an AI."

"The deodands . . . they're different. They're not terminators or *Westworld* androids or anything like that. People think of artificial intelligence as cold and calculating. But it could be anything; so why not innocent and pure?"

Sura barks a laugh. "You're shitting me."

"Come up to Wequetonsing. You can see for yourself."

They descend another floor in silence; then Sura says, "I'll be here."

"We'll see you at eight."

I call bullshit on this, she thinks as she flags down a car. She's tired, and cold, and feels hurt that Compass never told her anything about this. She could have helped; she would have wanted to help, and Compass should know that.

I call bullshit on all of it.

Maeve's out of danger and has been moved to a private room. She never talked about her family having money, but they must. It's the wee hours when Sura finds her. The nursing station is busy as always; she's come armed with flowers and a box of chocolates for the staff. That and Britt Birch's signature get her in, though visitors are technically not allowed.

There are two people asleep in chairs in Maeve's room. They might be her parents; the woman, who does look a bit like her, has her hands folded over a Bible.

Now that she's here, Sura doesn't know what to do. Maeve is asleep (she hopes that's all it is) and looks very small in the big plastic-railed bed. Her heart monitor shows a steady beat, but she's very pale, and there's an IV drip. Sura gnaws her knuckle, feeling truly helpless for the first time since the attack.

"They're going to take you away, aren't they?" she whispers, glancing around at the parents. "Take you back? They don't want you to see me—any of us, anymore."

There's no reply from the bed. "Maeve, I'm so sorry—" She catches herself. This isn't right. Maeve needs a power-up, something to let her know she's still got allies and friends in the frameworlds. She needs a talisman . . .

Sura puts the flowers in a vase and then heads back to the nursing station, where she's left her backpack. She digs through it, comes up with something. "Can I leave this on her table?"

The nurse looks up, laughs. "Sure, go ahead."

Sura goes back to Maeve's room, finds her right hand, and gently closes her fingers around Ganesha.

"You get better," she says. "I'll see you soon."

"You gotta have friends in the area," explains Mike as they head up the 75 toward Flint and Flushing. "People to say that you've got reason to be there. Nobody goes sightseeing in the country anymore; do, and you'll get pulled over by the militias or run into a farmers' blockade."

"That's just crazy," says Sura. She's in the back with Compass.

"When people had no idea who might be driving by, they trusted each other," says Binesi. "Now that you can know exactly who's out there, everybody's paranoid. Even though you can see they're no threat at all. Knowing nothing forces you to trust. Knowing a little makes you doubt everything."

The countryside north of Detroit looks like a war zone. Rate payers and farmers have set up no-go zones, sunset rules, and drone sentries. They've bought off the highway patrols and installed cameras along all the major highways. Sura can see all this in Mixed Reality—flags stand above properties and roads, signifying red, yellow, and green zones. Hunkered down in their bunkers, former farmers monitor car IDs by satellite, insisting on a right to filter who can and can't approach their now-fallow fields. Other flags show injunctions by civil rights organizations and hardcore libertarians and the occasional socialist collective. Roadside stands offer sousveillance services, free bodycams for travelers, and off-season corn.

Somebody's been shooting down neighborhood-watch drones, and the police have finally cornered a driverless that's been cruising 24/7, flashing lasers to blind mailbox cams as it goes by. They can't figure out who set it going because it was stolen in Florida, hacked, and given its own NotchCoin charge-up account before being let loose. It's been driving steadily for months, like a *Proudly Eagle Owned!* gone wild.

Where there are no virtual flags, there are gap-windowed houses on overgrown lots that used to be family-owned farms. Towering concrete grain terminals dot the horizon; everything agricultural is corporate run, except for the compounds and estates of rich retirees from the city. Drones rise to watch the car as they drive past these. The people in the mansions refuse to pay for the roads' upkeep, so the car constantly steers around potholes, and avoids the crumbling shoulder.

Efficient as the factory farms are, they're losing out to the vertical greenhouses in the cities. The countryside is hollowing out. The people that are left are the people who refuse to leave, and they live hand-to-mouth, watching over their shoulders in a red hinterland hostile and suspicious toward the blue of the major centers.

Sura knows she should be wary too. She's driving into the middle of nowhere with strangers. In any previous era she'd be vulnerable. She has Purrloin, though, who's got satellite connections and partly lives on the Global Processing Blockchain. If she disappears, her tattoo is programmed to send Bill and Jay her last known position. She's no more isolated here than she was in the city.

She emailed Constella to let her know Compass is all right, but didn't say anything about Wequetonsing.

Outside, public MR shows place names, virtual plaques for historical locations, and nearly as many ads as there are trees. The frame overlays are sparser, just a few English tags interspersed with glyphs and stars and targets, though the sky is carved into zones by gauzy walls that shimmer like the Northern Lights, signifying different realities. Looking back, she sees Detroit as a solid pillar of light, drowned in detail. There's a promise of beautiful countryside past all that, and when she takes off her glasses she can see open farmland interspersed with billowing treetops. Autumn was late this year, and some trees still sport red, orange, and yellow hairstyles, their background amber fields.

"Oh!" says Binesi suddenly. "Look there. In the larpwrights' overlay."

Something vast with legs like pillars of cloud stands over Flint. You can put anything in MR and Sura's seen it all, from the Stay Puft Marshmallow Man stomping on cities to clouds painted with confederate flags; in commercial MR the whole world is a billboard. This thing, though, has a different feel to it. It seems to be walking, slowly and majestically, south through town. "Is that a deodand?"

"It's an actant. The Flint Michigan water table, to be exact."

"Holy crap! It's terrifying."

"That's because it's something real," Mike says dryly. "I bet you haven't seen one of those in a while."

"What do you mean, real?"

"*Real* player AIs—the ones with power—persist outside the frames. Some are immortal."

What the hell? She doesn't have a clue what to say to that. She sits for a while, thinking about self-owned objects and talking groceries, and has a moment of dreamy reflection—a glimpse of a world where giants stride the horizon, cleaning up humanity's mess.

They pass Saginaw Bay, invisible off to the right, and head northwest on the 75. Compass eventually pulls off her headphones and starts working at her braid, a ritual during which she seems closest to being herself. "I'm sorry about where we left things," Sura says to her. "I didn't know what you were going through."

Compass smiles. "Neither did I. But, apology accepted. How's Maeve? You said you snuck in to see her."

"I don't know." She tells Compass how she hid Ganesha in Maeve's hand.

"That's good. But once we're done upstate, you and me have to rescue her."

"Yeah! We'll do it together." There's a little pause, then Sura says, "I miss our place. Listening to you play in the evenings."

"The piano, the music . . . it was important. B-But it wasn't enough. It was another way of searching for myself, I get that now."

"How do you mean?"

"You asked me once why I liked certain composers—Schumann, Beethoven. Some pieces, like the *Brandenburg Concertos*. I didn't really get why, but . . . they were p-p-puzzles. I thought if I could solve them, I'd come back carrying, I dunno, treasure."

Beethoven's Ninth, the *Brandenburg Concertos*—neither were ever heard performed by their composers. They were imagined paradises, never experienced by the very people who made them. "So the question was, how could they make music that they would never hear? And you wondered, for you, how—" *How could you make a life for yourself that you would never remember.* Sura can't say it, but Compass nods.

Those composers, present only in their music, hinted at but never quite seen dancing in the distances of history—it all makes sense now. Just like the hole in Compass's memory, that she fills with confabulations in an effort to have something there. All these years, Compass has been running after one will-o'-the-wisp hoping to find the other.

"Is that why you were playing the games? To discover clues to who you are?" Again, Compass nods.

"And now? When you play these 'actants'?"

"I let the actants ride me for a while. But I do better with the deodands. I have good days and bad days. Sometimes, I'm myself and it's okay. But it fades . . . it's like treading water. One reason we're g-going to Wequetonsing is I need an upgrade, so I can experience thalience firsthand. Mike says he's seen it and he th-thinks it'll work for me."

Thalience . . . Sura's heard that word somewhere; it comes freighted with mixed emotions, but she can't remember what it means.

"Once you find yourself, is there something you want to do? Somebody you'd like to be?" This has never been a possible question to ask. Now Compass tilts her head and frowns a little.

"I still like to play the piano."

Sura smiles in relief. "Then we should find a way for you to do that."

The car turns onto 68 West from Indian River. There's more forest than farmland in Tuscarora, and it's all gorgeous gold and fire; you can tell there are spirits partying in the woods because here and there the wind lofts handfuls of leaves into the air. The amber's overlay hints at that version of reality. Instead of complex relationships between labor and machinery, it shows landscapes painted by flows of energy and water, phosphorous and nitrogen. The players here are deer and raccoons, crows and ospreys and now-dormant bees. Oh, and humans too, but they're not presented as special in any way. Just part of the overall pattern.

West of Conway, where the road is walled with forest on either side, Mike spots a side road on the left and says, "Pull in here." A single-lane gravel drive meanders south under a dense ceiling of gorgeous color.

Sura rolls down her window, and after a moment Compass does too. "Have you been here before?" Sura asks; Compass nods.

"Just once."

Sura forgets to be jealous, because the trees outside are glorious, their canopy half-denuded so shafts of light fall to highlight toppled logs and the myriad shades of bark and moss surrounding them. The air is crystalline and brings back childhood memories of crumbling dried leaves in her hands. Then she realizes that there are no tags in sight and she has to touch her glasses to make sure she's still wearing them.

The car pulls into a little gravel lot that just has room for some sun-tracking solar panels and several other vehicles. It isn't staying, apparently; after they climb out and take their bags out of the trunk, it trundles back the way it came.

A cut through the trees shows an A-frame cabin and a few other buildings, plus what look like the white shrink-wrapped shapes of three large boats. As they walk up to the A-frame Sura realizes that the boat-shapes are fake, just wire frames with weather-resistant plastic stretched over them. Each stands about eight feet above the ground, and under them are large satellite dishes. She just has time to notice that cables snake throughout the clearing and that there are more solar panels and big portable batteries. Then the A-frame's door bangs open and a large, blousy woman steps out.

Sura stops and drops her backpack. "Oh, fuck."

"Hi, Sura," says Marj.

PART IV

A DOLLHOUSE IN THE SNOW

CHAPTER TWENTY-ONE

Marjorie Cadille, AI researcher, her dad's new partner. Famously critical of the idea that any disembodied system can exhibit actual intelligence. Dropped out of academia about four years ago, some time after meeting Jim Neelin. And here she is, giving Binesi a big hug.

Like tumblers clicking in a lock, the realizations come to Sura:

Marj knew how to find her in Oneota. Aside from Jay and Bill, the only people who know her frame identity are in her fireteam. Them, and Compass.

Who knows Binesi. Who knows Marj.

Marj wasn't just her dad's lover. They were working together on an investigation into corporate spoofing of environmental sensors. In the note she left with his urn, she said something about Dad doing *a test* when he got killed.

And then, whoever murdered him came after Sura, who ran straight into Compass's arms.

Her head's suddenly throbbing. "So. How far does this little conspiracy go?" She squints at Marj. "Let me guess: it was actually you who hired Jay, so he could introduce me to Compass who—" No, it's absurd, and Marj is shaking her head.

"I dropped off the urn the same day I found out where you were," she says. "Sorry I was radio silent, but I've had to hide, too."

Sura's feeling woozy despite the fresh air. "Hide from who? Whom? Shit, Marj, what the hell?"

"You'd better come inside."

They step into the main room and Sura has time to register how rustic it is (lower level all open, with kitchen, seating areas, and lots of overlapping Persian carpets; a loft that takes up half the building's length) when suddenly her glasses activate. There are public overlays in here, and she's being invited to join.

She does, and the A-frame's walls fly away. What's revealed is similar to the agricultural mapping she'd seen on the drive here, but this informational skyscape seems to go on forever. It's full of vast, slow-moving entities, like walking thunderheads. They're like the thing she saw looming over Flint.

Something soft bumps her ankle; there's a meow at her feet. "Ah, Bargain wants to get to know you," says Marj as Sura reaches down to stroke the broad head of a gray and white cat. "Bargain's our mouser."

"Aw." She mutes the distracting MR overlay, and kneels to scritch Bargain's ears. The others are moving around purposefully, except for Marj who's waiting. When Sura stands, she looks in the direction of the steep stairs to the A-frame's loft. Sura nods, and they go up. As expected, there's a sleeping platform here with a bed and a dresser, separated from the rest of the place only by the stairs and a railing. Sura leans on that for a moment, gathering her thoughts and watching Compass and her cousin work in the kitchen. When she turns, Marj is sitting cross-legged on the floor. Sura joins her.

"So how do you know Binesi?"

Marj shrugs. "Through your dad. He had connections with the Water Keepers, always ran in the same circles. I had a strong interest in Gwaiicoin and smart economies. There were probably five or six ways that your path and mine were inevitably going to cross. I hear you've been working with Bill Duchene and Trey Saunders?"

"You know them too?"

"Also run in the same circles." Marj hesitates. "Don't even know where to start. What do you know about what happened?"

It's a thin skein of deductions, but Sura has to believe it's true: "When I was a kid I burgled an office for Dad. I stole a hard drive for him. It contained a cryptographic key, which unlocks some backdoor that lets you spoof Internet of Things sensors. He had it for years before you guys found the lock it works in. Back in June he went to Iquitos to test whether you were right about the lock. They were waiting for him, or they found out somehow—"

"They flagged a suspicious transaction," says Marj. "He'd done another test two days earlier, and they picked it up. They had people in

Iquitos and somebody bribed Remy. That was all it took. They staged it so it looked like he was pulling some kind of publicity stunt that went wrong. But Remy knew, and so did I."

"So I'm right? You were trying to prove you had the right lock and key? A key to the sensors?"

"Not the sensors, but the blockchain they report to."

Sura sighs, looks out at the ceiling beams. Happy conversation drifts up from below. "The snark. And there's this company, Norris Trading," she continues, "that's been using the backdoor to manipulate the data from pollution monitoring systems to save some oil companies a whole whack of money. I get it. There was a lot on the line. You wanted to expose them, and they wanted to stop you. So they came after Dad. You went into hiding, and they came after me because they found out he imprinted the key on me before he died."

"It's something like that," says Marj levelly. "But not quite. We're not interested in exposing them. There's way more at stake here than just a few trillion dollars."

Sura tries to think about that, but she's too tired from late nights and trauma. She shakes her head.

"Do you know why I stayed with your dad?" Marj asks. Her voice is gentle for the first time; Sura looks up.

"I've always had a thing for strays, and Jim was a stray." Sura barks a laugh in agreement. "He started out as an idealist," Marj goes on, "and got lost in the politics of it all. When I met him, he'd completely lost his way. He was bound and determined to save the world, but he never went *out* in it anymore. He had this office in Flint, and he spent all his time on the Internet, campaigning. I knew him for six months before we took a walk in the park! There was a time when he had a personal relationship with the natural world. But he'd forgotten all about it, forgotten that it was what he was trying to save. He wasn't fighting *for* anything, anymore. He just fought against things."

"I think he'd gotten that way with all his relationships," Sura says.

Marj nods. "I wanted to shake him up—show him what he'd been missing.

"So, I showed him the deodands."

Sura unmutes her glasses and can again see the gigantic beings that stand astride the horizon. "They look like gods . . . but they're not. I met one in

Peru, it was cagey but it was no robot overlord. They're *externalities,* right?"

Marj shakes her head. "The original actants are externalities—negative spirits. Deodands are positive. Do you understand?"

"Not really."

"Nobody gets it at first," says Marj mournfully. "There's an 'aha!' moment. I designed them and *I* have trouble explaining them. People usually don't have the 'aha' until they meet one.

"How they work is easy; they're online, autonomous self-owned corporations with an executive that's operated by an AI or two. They make smart contracts with us and each other. Computer-driven companies, right? Institutions not run by or for humans."

"DACs," says Sura. "Sure."

"And that's basically how the commercial world uses AI right now. But it's a failure of the imagination. The corporate world put a lot of time and money into designing AIs that behave as rational economic actors, because you can attach them to DACs. Your autonomous online corporation will then buy and sell and compete with any human-staffed company, because it's got similar motives. But that's just trying to fit these things into the categories we already have. What *I* saw was that the most important thing about AI isn't how smart it is, it's *what* it thinks it is. You and me, we identify with our bodies. We are these." She waggles her hands. "But an AI—you can make it think it *is* anything you want. If you can add intelligence to virtual corporations, you can also add it to things that aren't accounted for by current economics."

"Like externalities?"

She nods. "If you can make an AI believe it's an online company, you can also make one think it *is* all the negative impacts of that company. In the first case, I could attach an AI to a DAC that manages the Flint water supply. Make the AI a rational economic actor, and it'll hire people and buy equipment, enter contracts and do work, all for the benefit of the water system—because that's what it thinks it is. But I could just as easily design that AI to think that it's all the citizens of Flint that're still suffering from the pollution and mismanagement. Sure, it can be a rational actor, but it's no trick to flip its motivation from defending and promoting itself to making itself go away. It's not alive, it doesn't have a natural drive to live. We can design it to want to cease to exist—meaning, it'll try to make the pollution, the kids' brain damage, the poverty and despair, all go away. Programming a disinterested AI—an actant—is just as easy as making a self-interested one. It's the kind of AI I was designing when I met your father.

"Sura, he instantly understood them. He *got* them—and it made me sick to realize it. He understood them because he no longer saw life in the world, he only saw our negative effects on it. The actants are just like him—they fight against something. I wanted Jim to see *life* again, Sura, so I made the deodands.

"They're a kind of actant, they're AIs that don't work for us. But their drive is not to extinguish themselves. They want to live. Each one thinks it's some particular nonhuman stakeholder, like an ecosystem or geophysical process. Watersheds and forests and pods of whales can all have deodands working on their behalf. Even the atmosphere. But where actants want the thing they think they are to go away, deodands want it to persist. They want balance. They want to sustain all the little things that live in them. Things like us.

"That's the technical description, anyway. But it turns out that's not really what they *are*." Marj smiles enigmatically. "To understand that, you have to meet one."

Sura stands and goes to lean on the railing. "Compass is channeling deodands now. What does that mean?"

"I think she's the best person to show you." Marj waves at the floor below.

"Compass! Why don't you take Sura to see our friend?"

Compass picks up her stuff and indicates that Sura should grab her own pack. They head outside. Compass sets off purposefully, and catching up, Sura says, "Have you been here before?" Compass nods. "What is this place?"

"A data center. Marj calls it a heavy lab. She's got all kinds of high-speed c-connections to the mesh from here." She lifts the tarpaulin that's draped over one of the satellite dishes.

Compass enters a kind of tunnel through the underbrush that leads into the bright gold of the late-autumn woods. Sura keeps looking back at the A-frame, which shimmers in a cloud of tags. She's not sure what she thinks is going to emerge from it—dragons? A team of anime girl warriors with giant swords sworn to slice and dice her? Marj being here has turned her world upside down; it feels like anything could happen.

She nearly bumps into Compass. "Cabin Three." It's a classic shotgun shack, complete with a decrepit rocking chair on its tiny porch. Buried as it is under the trees, it must be pretty dark here in the summer. Now, the denuded branches are letting plenty of light down to its corrugated roof.

"Well," Sura says. "This is cozy."

"I've stayed in this one," says Compass as she opens the front door. "There's bunk beds."

"I call bottom!"

Compass doesn't smile, but when they reach the tiny back bedroom, she heaves her backpack onto the upper berth.

Then she turns. She's taken off her glasses. "You came to find me," she says. "You broke in!"

Flustered, Sura fumbles with her pack. "I was worried about you! After the attack, I thought—well, anything was possible." She opens the pack; nestled in with her clothes are Dad's urn and the tissue-wrapped figurine of herself. For an instant she wants to take out the urn and say something disarming and silly, like, "See, I brought Dad along!" But she doesn't.

Instead, there's complete silence. Without all the distraction of Oneota, there's nothing to fill the space between them but a tension that's been there ever since Sura watched Compass attack a piano in *Diminuendo*.

The moment lengthens, rife with possibilities. Sura clears her throat, but Compass puts on her glasses again and says, "Come on. I want to show them to you."

They leave the shack and Compass takes off into the denuded woodland. Stands of brush crowd together between upthrusts of gray bedrock, and overhead the sparse canopy has become a galaxy of yellow dots, like a pointillist's vision of Heaven. The ground rolls in solidified waves, with browning leaves instead of whitecaps. Tall straight tree boles form a kind of maze without walls. With the sun playing hide-and-seek behind clouds, distant tangled tableaux of branch and trunk are suddenly spotlit, as if the forest were some crowded endless theater, the play unfolding in front, behind, all around.

Sura's got her glasses on, and they're registering signals—lots of them. "I guess every tree's got a smart nail in it? And there's sensors all over the ground? The animals are tagged?" Compass shrugs.

"Don't think of it like that." She's pulling ahead, starting to descend behind the lip of a miniature hill. Sura moves to catch up.

"This deodand I'm going to meet. What does it do?"

"Do?" Compass looks back and laughs. "What does anybody do?"

"Well . . . can I talk to it?"

Compass waits for her to catch up. Then she smiles again, and says, "Ask me anything."

Sura stops. "You're channeling it now?"

"You don't want that? It's what I do."

Sura stalks on ahead. "I just thought . . . you wanted to walk. With me." Feeling stupid and betrayed, she turns to look for the cabins, but they're lost in the maze.

Compass's hand touches her shoulder. "This is a gift."

"You retreating behind another player is a gift?"

"This is important to me. I want you to understand where I live now."

"Where you live?"

"You'll need the k-key Binesi gave you."

Sura slowly draws out the stone, keeping her fist closed over it. "You've done this, right?"

Compass shakes her head. "I've met them, like you're going to. But I haven't seen through their eyes. Marjorie says the upgrade will let me do that."

But now this is getting silly. There's nothing mystical going on here, however otherworldly these woods might look right now. Sura blows out a breath and opens her hand to reveal the amber.

Little telltales come on, like fireflies in her lower visual field, indicating that new overlays are activating and connecting to some local mesh of sensors and processors. That's all. "What the fuck?" She looks up.

The forest is gone—no, it's there, it's just flickering weirdly. She blinks, shakes her head, tries to focus on something neutral—the nearest tree.

Her vision skitters around its edges. She can't see it properly, but she sees *something*. When she looks at it, the world narrows somehow so the tree's background is other trees—certain, specific other trees.

"I don't like this. I wanna go back." She reaches up to mute the glasses, but in doing so looks down.

Below her is a vast network of tunnels, tubes, and fissures, and what was solid earth and stone has been replaced by a vast, unending tumble of shapes, jostled together like sleeping giants. It's the bedrock, and atop it, the warrens of shrews and voles and moles. Fuck, she can *see* them, curled up down there, and when she looks at one—

"Ohmigod!" Lines of relationship have sprung up. She's seen these in the frameworlds, many times, and knows exactly how they work. That particular shrew is connected to those two over there, fifty feet away. It's their son. The older ones are related too, but to something else: smears of nutrient in patches of soil, runnels of sap in nearby trees. The dead.

"Compass, what's going on? I can't see right—"

Her hand is on Sura's shoulder. "Me too. You must have got the upgrade when you switched on. I could see the relationships and the whole before. This is new. It's thalience."

Carefully, Sura raises her eyes. She's ready for chaos—and she gets it. Gradually, she realizes that when her eyes focus on anything, her glasses rearrange *everything else* in her visual field; the objects around it are no longer ordered in terms of their spatial position, but by relationship.

It seems like chaos because everything here is related to everything else, and as her vision darts about, the forest expands and collapses over and over, combining and recombining to keep up with where she's looking. She tries to study one thing at a time, and the relationships gel when her gaze is still, revealing the dazzling complexity of just one tree, stone, or leaf.

All the signs and symbols she's learned to read in the frames—signifiers of resource, need, politics, and affiliation—they're all here, but knotted and wound together by inhuman hands for inhuman actors. There are people in this tangle—she can feel the impact of the houses, power lines, and roads, see the slow echoes through the ground, ripples years in spreading from the laying of concrete slabs, the digging of holes for septic tanks. Humans are agents too, like the stones and the sunlight. But the thing they're a part of is so much more vast than they, that Sura finds all her cynical words have abandoned her. She's literally speechless.

This tiny slice of woodland, bordered by roads and threatened by development on all sides—the complexity of its flows and resources, production and consumption dwarfs all human schemes and ambitions. There are more organizational principles at work in just this one forest than humanity has invented in ten thousand years, and seeing them all working together, Sura starts to laugh. "Ohmigod, Compass, look at it! It's huge! It's practically fucking infinite!"

Compass is the center of a mandala of possible links to everything around them. Sura hears her say, "Can you see the deodand yet?"

She shakes her head. All she understands right now is that the economy of Nature far outstrips humanity's. For half her life Sura has crept about with the weight of a lie on her shoulders—the lie that her species has overtaken the world. Hell, it hasn't even conquered this little park.

She can hear herself laughing like a maniac but she can't stop. "It was always here! Right here, all along!" She just hadn't been able to see it. She'd only had human eyes, after all.

"We better sit down," says Compass. They mute their glasses and Compass leads her past an upthrust of grizzled, moss-covered rock, to where a pillow of bedrock forms a kind of natural bench looking out over a dell full of birches. They're mostly nude now, so the few remaining leaves are startling bursts of gold among the white trunks and dun-colored branches. Compass sits cross-legged, so Sura does too.

With the glasses muted, she sees the spatially organized forest—as she evolved to see it. She's had a brief glimpse of another way of understanding, though, and it's sensitized her—for now at least—to the details. She spends a while admiring the uniqueness of the pattern of fallen leaves at her feet, then notices the grizzled face of that rock over there. She knows how to see like this. It's how she saw as a child, but a year ago she couldn't have done it. Learning how to play again, and how to reframe what she sees—to *re*-see—has exercised long-dormant muscles. This forest—you could *perform* different versions of it—

"Oh."

Her heart's pounding. "Compass! I thought I saw but it couldn't be real—in all that craziness—was there something *dancing*?"

"I think you're ready to meet it," says Compass.

This isn't like crossing a threshold, the way that her first step into the games was. This is like jumping off a cliff. The terror she feels comes from realizing how much she longs for the freedom of the fall.

She unmutes the glasses.

Like an opening flower, the deodand reveals itself.

The A-frame glows up ahead; right now, for Sura, it's just another actor in the network, no more or less significant than the water in the soil. She delights in how this water gets moved around by the fungal networks that connect the trees. The trees trade nutrients, and the elders will give sustenance to young growing within their boundaries, even if those saplings are of different species. This landscape of fountains returns lifeblood as humidity breathed from the loam, sap sucked in by aphids, in animals dying, and leaves dropping back to the fungal carpet. It's just one of many closed cycles that make up the systems-in-systems of the woods.

She doesn't just see them; Sura hears these loops as music, the deep running water setting the beat. Within that, beetles and birds and foxes improvise.

It's like a drug, but she can stop the trip, and she has to because there's something she needs to know. She closes her eyes and mutes her glasses, then steps into the homey A-frame, with its musty smells and herbs hanging above the gas stove.

"So?" Marj starts to say.

"Did he meet them?"

"What?"

"Did he meet them? My father!"

Marj's expression softens. "Yes. Yes, he did. Actually, you've got the same look on your face as he had, that first time."

"They're incredible! Did he *see* them, I mean, really—"

Marj is laughing. "Oh, he did. Why do you think he gave up the desk job? He went back into the field because he remembered what he was fighting for." Serious suddenly, "That's also what got him killed, and maybe it's my fault."

Sura shakes her head. "No, you can't blame yourself. I went through that after he left Mom and me. It's a dead end." She pictures her dad out in these woods, moving between the human sensuality of touch and scent, and the awareness of the vast powers at play all around him. She knows exactly the smile that would be on his face.

The rational part of her mind is saying that it's all just sensors and software. But with their help, she's seen something real. In fact right now, the deodand seems like the most real thing she's ever seen.

Compass has been rooting in the fridge and comes back with two beers. Sura gratefully takes one, and they go to sit on the couches. With her glasses unmuted, Sura can see the local deodands and distant actants, vast presences spreading away to the horizon.

Marj points them out. "There's Flint's water supply. That's the Great Lakes watershed. They're not monolithic, they can split apart and recombine, or nest inside one another. Each one is an AI that manages smart contracts for some ecosystem or externality. They help the larpwrights organize frames and games, that's how they get paid, so far. The plan was to have them pay for themselves eventually. We've been letting them spawn for the past couple years. There are thousands now, they're everywhere."

Sura contemplates the vista. "But I don't understand. Why did Dad feel he had to go out again? Why Iquitos? That stupid wellhead sensor in the middle of fucking nowhere? It makes no sense."

Taking off her glasses, Marj slumps back and presses her hands to her eyes. "Oh, I wish . . . It all looked so perfect, the frameworlds, the sprites, the actants . . . Post-economics in service of the whole planet, not just humanity . . . but there was this little problem. Your dad found it; actually, *you* found it for him."

"The break-in? Did he know what he was getting me to steal? He never told me."

"It's the Achilles' heel for all this. He didn't understand that, didn't even tell me about the sensor backdoor until after I'd shown him the first deodand.

"Sura, the framing AIs are only as good as the data they get. Like us, deodands and actants have to trust their senses. If there's a way to spoof those senses, then they can be manipulated. Controlled, even."

It's clear to Sura that the local deodand only exists because of the thousands of environmental sensors embedded in tree trunks, strewn on the forest floor, and lying in the streams. "You're not gonna tell me all these sensors use the same protocol that Norris Trading cracked? That they could sell fake data about this ecosystem just the same way they sell fake well emissions for Bolivarian State Oil?"

Marj shakes her head. "Oh no. It's much worse than that. That same protocol is used by the frames' sensors. Mixed Reality larping depends on spatial-mapping and positioning IoT devices too. So do the wear monitors in the beams that hold up half the country's bridges. Furnace temperature regulators, nuclear reactor control systems. Sura, in the early days this was the most trusted protocol for IoT. It became the standard. By the time better, quantum-encrypted methods came along, the protocol was embedded in trillions of devices worldwide. Replacing them would take decades, cost hundreds of billions. It can't be done."

"And we stole it?"

"What you stole was a cryptographic key. Jim knew he had something he could use to blackmail the companies, but he didn't know what it was exactly, not until he showed it to me and we worked it out together. Norris freaked out when they lost it, but luckily they never traced the robbery to you guys. As long as Jim never used it, they couldn't find him. The thing was, though, without testing it, we couldn't be sure that it did what we thought."

"And . . . does it?"

Marj nods. "The key controls a gate to a gate. It lets you set permissions and capabilities for another set of keys—keys to a backdoor into the

IoT reporting protocol. It makes you the broker who can sell the permissions to, say, a failing oil company. With those they can target specific sensors, or whole groups of them up to any size, but only according to the rules you've laid out. They can alter the data and nobody can prove they did it. And you can revoke that right at any time. So you can *rent* access to it and charge whatever you want."

"This is what Norris does?"

"Yeah, but they've been frustrated. They'd kept a single copy of the master key because, well, this was before the self-sovereignty tech, the homomorphic encryption that we use. They thought an air-gapped computer would keep them safe from hackers. They didn't reckon with a human burglar. They were only able to sell an initial set of sub-rights before Jim—before *you*—took the only master from their office."

Sura thinks through the implications. "Their whole business stalled out. I guess they could keep demanding rent from the oil companies, as long as nobody called them on their bluff. 'Cause they can't revoke the keys they sold, can they? Not without the master?"

"Right. More important, though, is what they can do if they get their hands on it again. They know Jim had it, they figure I've got it, and you're on their radar too."

"They won't stop, will they? Too much is at stake . . . Do you know what form this, uh, key takes?"

Marj just looks at her. Sura clears her throat. "It's me. I'm the key."

"Jim didn't tell me he was going to change the master into your biometrics. Sura, I wouldn't have let him do it if I'd known. By the time I found out, he was in Peru."

"Why didn't you go to the FBI? Or Interpol or somebody?"

"Well, here's the thing. Who are you going to trust to keep something like this?"

"Why not copy it back out of me and then destroy it?"

"How do we prove we've done that?"

"Oh. Shit."

Marj stands. In MR, this places her at the bottom of a vortex of tags and signs and connecting lines, with gods walking in the deep background. "It's all going to hell. The frames are out of control. They're working beyond our wildest dreams, but they're a problem precisely because they're using resources more efficiently than ever. They have no limits, so they'll overload the planet's carrying capacity even faster than capitalism did."

"Yeah, I've seen the numbers."

"The actants could be advocates for our limited resources. But they have no power, and practically no voice. Sure, you found them compelling, but you needed a whole education in framing interfaces just to understand what they are!

"Anyway, none of that matters if Norris gets hold of the key. Then they can control the reporting from every single one of those shared resources we trade in. What's to stop them from demanding an arbitrage fee every time the games do anything with the data? Or every time any device, anywhere, accesses the IoT pool? Imagine having to make a micropayment every time you turn on a light, open a door, or, hell, tie your shoes! It can easily go that far.

"At that point, for all intents and purposes, they own the world."

Sura's too exhausted to take in any more, so while the others talk about supper, she wanders back to Cabin 3 and collapses on the lower bunk. It's cold, so she turns on the baseboard heater, which makes pinging and cricking noises that she thinks are going to keep her awake. But she falls asleep almost instantly and only wakes when Compass comes in and flips on the lights.

"Wha? What time is it?"

"Time to eat." Compass smiles. "And there's a shower in the lodge. You might want to play a human being tonight."

"Very funny." The water in the A-frame is either scalding hot or freezing cold; both help her wake up. By the time she's wrapped her hair in a towel and dressed, her mind is sharp. It feels like the first time in days that she's really herself.

And yet, when she enters the main room and sees Mike ladling some pretty standard spaghetti onto chipped old plates, the cynical part of her brain fails to kick in. She grins and says "That looks great!" with no irony whatsoever.

As she watches herself through the meal she's aware of the difference; so she's not surprised to find herself asking Marj about her dad. "How was he? I mean, this last year or so? I got a couple of emails from him. He said he was going to visit—but then, he always said that."

"I think he meant it this time. Being out in the field woke him up. He remembered what he was fighting for."

"There were kids in school whose parents told them to stop being my friend, because we were communists. They truly thought that the 'environment' was just a code word for 'workers' or something, and it was the same international Bolshevik conspiracy behind both."

Mike guffaws. "Capitalism, communism, what's the difference? They're just excuses to take our land."

"Is that what this is about for you?"

"I used to think so. It's still about the land. But it's not ours. We never owned it, the way you own things."

"I guess that makes you communists too. So who owns deodands and actants?" she asks Marj.

"That's the whole point. They were supposed to own themselves. They do, actually—they're digitally signed, only a majority voting together can spawn a new one."

"But why? They're—well, awesome in the genuine sense. But what are they for?"

"Think about the larpwright toolkit," says Binesi. "You can simulate an entire country with it, right down to the behavior of individual people. It's awful likely that the Chinese are doing this with their whole population—based on surveillance of those very citizens. We know the Republican National Committee do it with voters. Their NPCs are all based on real census data. Advertisers data-mine our lives and run simulations of us to see how to sell more junk to us. And the big corporations are trying to game the whole economy the same way.

"Now. Remember Pax's speech? Where he talked about gamification and next-gen economics and all that?"

Sura nods. "It was pretty amazing, even if I only heard half of it."

Binesi shakes her head. "That speech. What shortsighted bullshit that was."

"Uh, what?" Sura's spent a lot of time thinking about Pax's ideas. All the players she knows were floored by his vision—and here's Binesi kicking it over like an anthill?

"I mean, really. He's only holding half the solution. Take, say, a hammer. In China's smart economy, or the US's, the hammer knows what it is and what it can do. It can advertise its services; it can buy and sell its time. If you own it you can even take a cut. But look: all it is, and all it can ever be, is a hammer. Because your economy may be smart, but it's not creative. It can't see other possibilities for the use of that particular thing. Its identity is defined in the system, locked there, and it's forever condemned to be that one thing. And if it's not a hammer? If it's a human? Same thing. And that's the very definition of totalitarianism, right there.

"You were there for Pax's speeches about how the frameworlds make us all free. His ideas are all about tool-consciousness—the idea that, as long as the hammer works, you never really see it. It's just an interchangeable piece of your plan. Just like, say, an individual human being . . . You never really encounter it until it breaks, and then suddenly, it reveals itself to you as unique. As *this* not-hammer. As *this* person, standing in the town square and howling at your injustices. A distinct and unnamed piece of the world, waving at you and proclaiming, 'Hello! I'm here!'

"It's only when the hammer breaks—when a thing no longer fits in one of our preconceived categories—that something completely new can enter our world.

"The frames exist to break the hammer.

"Pax understands this and he's running with it. That's the real answer to why the *frames* need the *games*. By reframing things, situations, and people—by strange-making the world—we can discover new opportunities, move past roadblocks and entrenched dilemmas. By gaming, we take a merely smart economy and give it the heart of an artist."

"So what's wrong with that?"

"The frames are a vision of unlimited potential—unlimited freedom. A kingdom of the imagination! It's incredibly exciting and seductive. There's just one problem: on this planet, at least, not everything is possible.

"Capitalism, communism, fundamentalist religion, and Pax's frames—they've each made up their own version of the world. In the case of the frames, it's a version where 'reality' conveniently doesn't exist. So, like the others, it's not taking into account the *real* world, the one outside all our stories. So they plunder, they waste, they destroy. Climate change, mass extinction on land and sea—I mean, do I really have to spell it out here? I don't, anymore than the scientists were really the ones arguing that global warming was real. The climate won the argument on its own.

"Sura, this is about what's *real*. The actants take one step past the frames: they give voice to things that are real but not accounted for in our models. In frame terms, whatever's *not made up* about a given situation."

"I call 'em the leftovers," says Compass fondly. "They're the things we left out when we made a reality."

Marj nods. "They are that which is still there, even when you stop believing in them."

"Now I remember!" Sura hops in her chair. "Thalience! That's your idea, thalience, right? It's about making an AI that doesn't just use our worldview, but invents its own."

She laughs, feeling a bit light-headed. "You're saying we need these guys because *we*," and she jabs her finger at her own chest, "aren't smart enough to tell the difference between what's *really* real and what we just made up! We literally can't do it on our own."

"Yeah. Something like that. We turned away from the other life forms on our world. They used to help us stay grounded but we can't see them anymore. The actants were supposed to take over that role, keep us from screwing up and wrecking everything." Marj grins. "—Shall we retire to the 'drawing room'?"

On the couches (which, Sura realizes, mirror the layout in the loft in town), they sit beneath a galaxy of actants. "Did you just go into hiding after the 'test'?" asks Sura. "I mean, do you have a plan?"

"Well, finding you was top priority. It helped that you ran straight into the games, but it still took us all summer. We were in damage control most of that time anyway—"

"Stop. Who's this 'we' you're talking about?"

"Global network of larpwrights. I've been introducing them to the deodands; so far, all the larpwrights who've worked with deodands have been indigenous. They tend to get the idea of dealing with nonhumans as equals better than white people. We've got some South Asians, too, who're used to negotiating with gods. But those metaphors don't really capture the world of the twenty-first century. Anyway, the plan: find a way to seal Norris's backdoor, then figure out how to get the world to pay attention to the deodands."

"Huh. That one . . . I don't know."

"That's where you come in," says Binesi. "You and the other larpwrights we're training. We need new games, where actants and deodands are accepted and listened to."

"Oh!" Sura can see the possibilities. (After all, says the ironic part of her, it's just gamified participatory economics with self-aware forests and fisheries as equal citizens!) But it really is simple, if you frame it the right way: everybody plays and everyone has a stake—human or not. This time there'll be no pile-up of carbon in the atmosphere, because the atmosphere is going to say nuh-huh to that. There'll be no overfishing because the fishery knows itself and will trade its knowledge only to those players who'll abide by its codes of conduct. But to do that—

"But who enforces the rules? Why should governments and corporations pay any attention to the actants?"

Marj and Binesi exchange a look. "That's the real problem," says Marj. "If it's some human agency, like the UN, then there's still the possibility of corruption. Hidden agendas, like the communists your friends' parents see under every bed.

"We've managed to give Nature a place at the table. But we haven't figured out how to give it any *power.*"

The rest of the evening is a blur. Sura learns more about Binesi and Mike, and Compass's childhood as Anwaatin. Binesi tells these stories, as Compass doesn't know them and laughs at them as if they're anecdotes about some other person.

It's late when Sura and Compass go back to Cabin 3. As soon as they step outside, the darkness swallows them. Sura's breath must be frosting with the cold but she can't see it; if she looks away from the A-frame's windows, the world is absolute blackness. Luckily, the path's been tagged in MR; even the low-hanging branches have markers. Sura's had this experience before, but usually there are visual cues to the real world behind the tags. "It's like we're in a video game," she half giggles, reaching for where she knows Compass to be.

The cabin is a wireframe with a huge neon-yellow 3 hanging over it. After taking two steps up to its tiny porch, Sura takes off her glasses. Compass is already through the door and moments later a table lamp clicks on. Back to shabby reality. She laughs again.

The baseboard heater ticks and crickles. Compass is changing into pajamas, unself-consciously revealing her gorgeous body. Sura admires her, then shakes her head. "What are we? To each other?" she asks suddenly.

Compass pulls on a blue flannel top with little square-headed robots printed on it. "I don't know," she says simply.

"Roommates? Friends?" Ever since she met Compass, she's felt something, which at different times she's thought was love or lust. It's neither really.

Compass sits down on the bed next to her. "Why'd you come find me?"

"I guess I feel responsible for you."

"Maybe we're family, then." Compass rises and climbs to the top bunk.

"That would be nice," says Sura. But it's not quite right either.

Compass's head appears over the low rail. She wrinkles her nose. "You're overthinking again. Maybe there isn't actually a word for it." She disappears.

Sura opens her mouth to say something clever; closes it again. It's true: they have a relationship. It's important. That's all she knows.

"Turn off the light," murmurs Compass. "And for God's sake, turn off your brain."

"All right, all right."

She does.

When chilly dawn comes Sura finds herself wide awake, practically vibrating. Rather than wake Compass with her restlessness, she carefully retrieves her clothes in half-light. Then she reaches for the orange backpack that contains her figurine and her dad's urn. The tiny bedroom seems like the only warm place in the world. Sura adds another layer of coat on her way out, but she's determined to experience the forest at daybreak. She brisk-walks down the path they took yesterday, filled with a complex of emotions she can neither control nor name.

Meeting the deodand feels like a breakthrough, really a break-*in,* as if she's burgled her way into a possible new future. It's really quite simple: if things like the deodands exist, then she can't hide behind cynicism anymore. She's been called on her own bullshit.

Now that a suffocating lid has been lifted off all the possibilities of her life, Sura finds herself thinking about things she'd set aside years ago. Old ideas become new again, of a home, a place in the world. Maybe, someday, her own family . . . Having broken her way into a new perspective, she can look back on the old one. It's not pretty. God, what a beige existence lies behind her! The plodding sameness of the days after Mom, the shallow relationships with old school- and workmates. All these years she's been presented with this or that offer of happiness or meaning—friendships, jobs, careerism, art, religion—and every time some deep instinct in her has said *not that.* Her whole life up until this moment has been an endless recitation of *not that.*

It's all too intense to dwell on right now. She tunes the glasses to the right overlay and can see that most of the locals are still denned down. She walks quietly, so none of the animals will have to avoid her.

This little strip of forest is just half a mile wide and seven or so long.

It curves halfway around the north shore of Little Traverse Bay, interrupted on one side by Harbor Springs, on the other by an airport and Round Lake, and hemmed in by highways. Here and there gravel laneways penetrate it, seeding houses among the trees. It's hardly the wilderness, but that makes it more representative of Earth in the Anthropocene than any untouched woodland could. Sura can trace the arcing lines of its friendship with the Boyne Highlands to the north, and with the vast lake just out of sight to the west. They exchange energy, trade birds, deer, and foxes. The animals have brought in seeds from upstate that next year may germinate a new generation of trees. The humans do their part too, tracking in mud from distant locales that introduce new worms and bacteria. It's dynamic, balanced on the edge of chaos, and even now at the cold end of November, busy.

She has a right to be here. That's the real triumph. The deodand isn't just a representative of the animals and plants. Walking, therefore, in the mazeways of a friend, she draws a deep, icy breath, and says, "How are you today?"

"We are well." It's a voice in her earbuds, machine-generated. There's no mystical spirit giving rise to it. No bright artificial mind living on the Internet either; instead, the million monitors of the smart dust have reported in, and the limited AI focused on the forest has summarized their collective status. Those words were the report of something real, not an opinion about some disembodied entity's inner state. And that means they were authentic, their message more genuine than the introspection of any artificial consciousness could be.

There's a logical step for Sura now, and she takes it. "Hey. What do you think we could do for one another?"

The forest reveals its riches. There are so-and-so many deer, groundhogs, crows, and mice, all co-owners like her. Each has its own history and relationships. They are also resources, just as she is. The woods know how much potential fertilizer there is in her body and what could grow here if she were to drop and die on this spot. It knows which birds are likely to leave for the day and how many might not come back. The place has its budget and can tell her what it needs for the internal thriving of its lives. It shows her what it can spare if she needs to take something from it.

This accounting extends past the roads and legal property lines. The forest doesn't have a firm boundary, but is itself part of a greater deodand, Northern Michigan, and then the Great Lakes themselves. The question Binesi asked her last night was "I don't think your father was unusual.

Most people will be able to see actants. They understand decay, collapse, and how to fight against things. How can we make a frameworld that shows people what to fight *for?*"

She believes that Sura, with her burglar's sense of how to upend conventional rules, might know how to reframe the deodands so people can see them. That won't be easy, if it can be done at all. Sura also has to admit, now she's alone, that she's not convinced she wants to share.

Smiling at herself, she takes the path she thinks leads to the spot where she met the deodand yesterday. How to frame this relationship? It's not like the gods woke up and are speaking to humanity at last—tempting as that metaphor is. The AIs are not really humanity's children, either. People will want to treat them like wise parents or ancestors—oracles and spirits. But deodands are as naïve as anybody else. They're equals, so the word for them that keeps coming to mind is *spouse.*

Engrossed in these thoughts, she finds herself on the southern edge of the woods. Beach Road cuts left to right, and past it the ground slopes down for a hundred feet or so to the lake. Little Traverse Bay is spangled with diamonds as the sun lifts over the far shore.

There are lots of cottages along the lakeside, all private property, but there are gaps, too. One is just in front of her. Sura strolls across the road and down to the pebbled strand, and there, she opens her pack to retrieve the urn.

This is a personal moment, so she takes off her glasses and stows them in her jacket pocket.

"I have no idea if you'd want me to do this," she says to the urn. "We never talked about it. God knows Marj didn't know what to do with you." She unscrews the lid, hesitates a second, then digs her fingers into the ashes of her father's body.

"It's up to me now. So, here you go, Dad." She tosses a handful of gray into the clear breeze. The tears are starting to come. "Goodbye." She says it with each throw, watching ash touch down on lapping water, on gleaming rounded stones, and on sand. She cries unashamedly and, afterward, perches on a big rock to watch the sun crest the distant treetops.

How different she is, how different this moment. She hugs her knees. Last night Compass said she was family. It's true, Sura has no intention of leaving her again. Once everything's sorted out, they can get another condo together, and work for the deodands. They can get Compass a proper piano, and Sura can help her become who she is.

Compass is so damaged; but then, so is Sura. Just like the whole goddamned country, and the burning world. Right now, she's prepared to give all of it a second chance.

The tears are done, and she dwells for a long while in a silence broken only by the talking of the waves. The cold won't leave her alone though, so eventually she has to move. Distant sirens remind her that this isn't really paradise. Creaking in anticipation of age, she rises slowly and digs out her glasses. They'll guide her back.

The gulls are out, she notices, as she puts on the glasses and calls up an overlay. Everything looks fine, there's a local map, though *The Rewilding* isn't visible from here.

That's odd.

An icon she rarely sees is twirling slowly up in the sky. She squints and it reveals its label: *No Signal.*

"Shit. Oh shit." Her body gets it before her mind; she's flushed with shock, gasping, but why? Signals drop, that's normal with mesh networks. In the city coverage overlaps, dropouts rarely happen, and if she had a repeater in her pocket it wouldn't matter at all. Purrloin could find a satellite or something.

But she had a fine, clear signal when she walked down here. Between her taking off her glasses and now, something happened.

"Shit, oh shit oh no." She runs for the road, plunges through frost-whitened grass into the trees. Still no signal. She knows things are coming across the bay, things she stupidly thought were gulls, but they're not. She never *sees*, she paints whatever she wants to be over what's there—so she saw the drones but didn't *see* them.

There's one thread of hope. Purrloin has an online component, and it hasn't been able to contact the tattoo on her calf for half an hour or more. Her usual safety triggers are up; if she doesn't check in it'll send an alarm to her trusted circle. If she disappears . . .

The sirens are louder, coming from up ahead, and converging from both directions. Something casts a quick flickering shadow across the grid of sunlight on the forest floor. There's another, and a third. They're circling the A-frame, which is lit intermittently by red and blue flashes.

Whump! Orange flame mushrooms up from the clearing next to the A-frame. Sura stops as the pressure wave rolls over her, gaping at bits of solar panel that are twirling against the serene azure sky. She imagines all the forest people scattering, panicked, pictures *Rewilding* labels bouncing and receding. She should be doing the same, but Compass is up ahead so she starts running again.

Somebody steps in front of her, a black cut-out against the orange. Firelight crawls around the silhouette, revealing Binesi in a bathrobe, carrying a shotgun.

"Where's Compass?" Sura shoulders past Binesi and Binesi hits her, backhanded. Sura falls into clawed bushes.

Binesi's kneeling next to her. "Who did you call?"

"What? Me, I wouldn't—"

"Then they tracked you! How did you come to us? Did you take the *White Rose*?"

"I didn't have to, I—I'm . . . whitelisted?" As she says it she realizes what happened and sees the same understanding on Binesi's face.

"I got no choice," says Binesi. "Marj said 'see to the key' and you're the key. Gotta keep the key safe—or destroy it." Sura backs away. Binesi looks disgusted. "Go!"

Binesi whirls and there's a sudden startling shotgun thud. One of the drones tumbles onto the path near Sura. Men in tactical gear are piling out of a van next to the A-frame.

Sura scrambles back under a thorn bush as the squad encircles Binesi. "In the air! Now!" The cops sound scared, they're carrying assault rifles and the drones are converging, twitching and buzzing like saws. Marj and Mike are being pushed out into bleary daylight. Sura hears a sound behind her—and there's Compass, coming up the path with her hands on her head while a black-helmeted man shoves her with every other step.

Her glasses are gone. Her wild eyes are darting around; they land on Sura and look through her as if she's as anonymous as the trees. Sura stifles a scream.

Vesta takes over, or her burglar self, she'll never know; she dances back into the confusing shadows of the trees. The A-frame is burning, men are shouting, Compass and the others are kneeling in a line in front of the fire; she should be running, but Sura has to know.

She finds half of the drone that Binesi shot out of the sky and turns it over.

SUMMIT RECOVERIES is stamped on it in military stencil green.

Nobody follows as she weaves drunkenly through a gauntlet of tangled branches and stabbing brambles, making for the road.

CHAPTER TWENTY-TWO

She meets Bargain at Beach Road. She's winded but says, "Here, puss-puss," and gathers him up. He's wet and his little heart is fluttering as he sinks his claws deep into her coat. Sura stands there, holding him, blinking at the silent highway.

Her panic's receded just enough for her to remember the last time she felt this kind of shock. It was the day Jay rounded her up. Then, she went along passively, her head empty of strategies. It can't go that way this time.

She turns right, cradling Bargain, and walks in the direction of Harbor Springs. After she's been at this for about twenty minutes, a big black van pulls up beside her. There's a click from the passenger door as it unlocks itself. She looks inside, expecting the thing to be packed with soldiers like some fascist clown car, but in fact it's empty. Driverless; but there's an old-fashioned smartphone lying on the seat.

She gets in and drops Bargain in the driver's seat; the van does a U-turn as she's doing up her seat belt. The doors lock as they speed up. She tries to open hers, but it doesn't work. Neither does the manual override on Driverless mode.

Sura yanks on the review mirror to look back. There are no other vehicles on the road. Off in the distance she can see a helicopter rising from the Wequetonsing woods, but by now the van is well on its way to Indian River, and from there, it can make Detroit or Chicago in four hours.

She tries the phone; it lets her dial, but none of her calls go through. There's no Internet.

With nothing to do but think, she watches upstate Michigan slide by. Bargain curls up in her lap, demanding a hand on him before he'll settle. Eventually they turn south, and she speculates on which city she'll end up in. The morning sunlight has been replaced by a wall of slate-gray cloud—the deodand promised snow, and here it comes. At least that'll drive the copters and drones out of the sky.

A few white scouts explore the highway and declare it safe; the vanguard of an invasion follows, winter's cavalry riding down to take the forest. She's mesmerized by the onrush of white streaks, they make a kind of tunnel through the corridor of trees. The adrenaline's worn off and she's exhausted, starting to doze, when the phone rings.

She fumbles it, picks it up, forcibly relaxes herself.

"I was never whitelisted, was I, Bill?"

"Hi, Sura. Well. You were, for the feds and the tax collectors.—Look, are you okay? You haven't been hurt or—"

"Oh, fuck off. Do you really expect me to be all chummy after you raid Wequetonsing with the very same people who killed my father?"

"I had nothing to do with your father's—"

"Imagine how little I care. You're in with them now, that's all that matters."

There's a pause. "I didn't have much choice."

"I bet you didn't. After Trey unwrapped the sensor I gave him, it would have started broadcasting—all the standard stuff it was supposed to monitor, like humidity, benzene levels. Location. How long did it take before the goons showed up at your door?"

"They were businessmen, actually. Very polite—"

"But firm. I can see it, clear as day: you and Trey caught in *flagrante delicto* with one of the Iquitos oil well sensors whose data had been hacked. It did something that they can no longer do and they want to know how. You told them you don't have the key that unlocked the magic box, but they don't have any reason to believe you, do they?"

"No, they don't. But listen—this only just happened."

"Well, obviously, because otherwise you would have rounded me up for them days or weeks ago. Months. You were clueless about me, but you weren't innocent about what's going on, were you? Why did you really go to the troll factory?"

There's another long pause. "Sura, these people, they've got Marjorie Cadille now. If she has the address they want, you have nothing to worry about."

"Unless Dad made me a copy. Right? You know they can't let me live."

"But I can keep you safe! That's why I'm calling, why I sent the car. I don't want anyone to get hurt. Cadille—I don't know if I can save her. You're a different story."

"And then what? I hide for the rest of my life? As your toy girl, that you own? You'll have to stuff me in a dollhouse somewhere, you know. Otherwise, how can you trust that I didn't make my own backdoor key, to sell to somebody else?"

"Why would you? Stick with me, you'll be the richest woman on Earth. I'm not without my resources—that's why I'm a partner with these assholes, and not roadkill. Oh, shit, I'm sorry, I didn't mean—"

"No, you're right, Dad pretty much was roadkill when they got through with him." He must be able to hear the naked rage in her voice, because he doesn't even try to respond to that.

Up ahead, a single car is approaching through the swirling white cyclone. She pays no attention until suddenly it swerves into her lane. "Whoa—"

The van honks, veers, and starts to slow, but it's too late—the oncoming car slews sideways, blocking both lanes.

The van skids into the left lane—

—And here comes the ditch.

Bargain flies out of her lap and her head hits the side window. Then the airbags go off.

"Oh . . . shit . . ."

"Sura?" It's a faint voice, somebody she recognizes. Coming from far away.

She realizes she's pinned by the airbag; it's in her face, blinding her. She still has the phone in her hand and can hear Bill shouting, asking if she's okay. Bargain is yowling. She cranks her head around to look out the side window and sees that they're still in the ditch; the van is spinning its wheels and trying to rock itself out. As it's struggling a man in a green army coat walks down from the road. He's got a big pry bar in his hand.

Haloed by snowflakes, Jay grins and waves, then attacks the door.

Sura squirms, managing to raise the phone to her mouth. "Sorry, Bill, something's come up. I'll call you later, 'kay?"

She can hear him protesting as she drops the phone. The door bangs open. Jay stabs the airbag and cuts her seat belt off with a ridiculously big knife. Then she does the inglorious thing and falls into his arms.

* * *

Sura wakes to an absolute silence she's only ever experienced once before—in Peru. It's such a luxurious thing that she savors it for long minutes, burrowing deep in her blankets. Bargain is a dead weight against the small of her back. She finally opens her eyes when she hears Jay moving about in the next room.

She remembers an epic drive through threatening darkness and hurricanes of dense snow. They took side roads south, using a printed map that Sura read by dashboard light. When the squalls made whiteout conditions, Jay got her to roll down her window so she could keep an eye on the shoulder. "You're drifting," she'd say. "Left. No, the other left." The drive was slow, but faster than she thought was safe. He refused to turn on the car's navigation and self-driving systems, and that decision, at least, she agrees with.

Her very first question to him was "How did you find me?"

In the dim light, his half smile had seemed both ironic and a little sad. "Seems you never took me off your trusted list. You had a trigger set in case your tattoo went offline for too long. I was in Detroit looking for you anyway, so when I got a last-location ping I headed up here. While the car drove I talked my way onto the local rate-payers' chat board. You know there're houses all along that strip and they were not pleased to have their power and Internet knocked out by some military contractor's EMP. They'd been videoing the whole incident, so I got a nice clip of you climbing into that black van. Wanna see it?" She shook her head. "Well, anyway, when I spotted it coming at me through the snow, I just reacted."

"I'm glad you did." They shared a grin.

Now, her room's one window glows white with winter light, revealing plywood walls and a chipboard floor. Her little cot has a side table, and there are pegs on the wall where she hung her clothes. Sura teases back the curtain and beholds a rolling landscape of purest, untouched snow, framed on the left and right by stands of trees and brush.

She remembers more. Jay refused to go back to Detroit; instead, they passed it and curved around Toledo, heading southeast. The storm was epic and they didn't stop except to pee at the side of the road. Shivering, she snuck a peek at him over her shoulder; he was standing, legs apart, sending his stream downwind. "I used to squat like this in the woods when I was a kid," she said to his silhouette. "But we never went out in winter."

"Shame. You haven't lived till you've been winter camping."

The car's charge was dangerously low when they finally eased past a chevroned NO ENTRY sign and onto a narrow track leading into denuded forest. Nearest Sura can tell, they were somewhere east of Columbus. "What is this?" she'd asked. "A hideout? Your own little prepper compound?"

"Naw," he said as he steered like crazy, slaloming them through thick drifts of snow. "Uncle's farm. I've got a deal where I pay part of the taxes in cash, and the cousins don't talk about me coming here."

It's not clear whether he actually parked the car, or if it just ran out of road. There was nothing in sight as they got out, but Jay hoisted a huge duffel bag on his shoulder and stalked off into the dark. She and Bargain caught up to him as he was unlocking the side door of this little farmhouse.

Once she's dressed she meets him in the kitchen. He's in jeans and a white T-shirt, humming as he cooks something. "I have a funny feeling we're off the grid."

"Oh, there'll be satellite service," he says. "But why the fuck would you go online when we have that?" He points out the window. Sura goes to take a second look.

Forest surrounds two square fields that are joined at one corner. The farmhouse sits on the diagonal point of the shape, so what she can see is an inviting white plain shielded by trees, with a tantalizing gap in them at the far end that leads to more white. There might be more past the second field. "Do you snowshoe?"

"Cross-country skiing's better. There's a snowmobile."

"Cool!" Except she wonders what the local deodand would think of it. Too noisy for the deer and foxes, probably. She says that and instead of laughing, Jay nods. "The snowmobile's for working, like when the pump at the spring seizes. If you want to actually see anything, take the skis."

There are four pairs in the closet by the door. She eyes them hungrily, but the impulse to go online is too strong. She fires up her glasses, does a quantum-encrypted handshake with one of the libertarian CubeSat Internet providers, and checks her accounts. A flood of emails and alerts pours out.

First of all: K.C.'s checked on Maeve, and she's doing okay but her family have had her transferred somewhere. South, apparently. Vaughan's in the wind. Rico's been arrested, along with a slew of other Pittsburgh activists.

She widens her focus a bit. The frameworlds are under full-out assault, not just here but in many countries. The excuses differ. In some places, they're being branded as seditious, in others, as tax cheats or religious apostates. Here at home they're being blamed for a wave of insurrection that's consuming the Midwest and South. It's really the preppers and ultranationalist militias, finally seizing their moment and using the frameworlds as cover. The result is that places like Oneota are burning, the players scattered. Nobody can stop them communicating and organizing, though, and already games and countergames are being run to help them.

Sura's inbox is full of appeals for assistance, a lot of them from K.C. He's put himself in the eye of another storm, this time with Nile Abbott; they're calling on players to swear allegiance to the cloud country of Zomia. "The Westfalian nation-state is dead," Pax shouts in a clip that's gotten millions of views since yesterday. "Security, health care, a stable identity, and work—*we* can give you those things! *They* no longer can." She sees shots of tear gas, riot police kettling mobs, tanks and APCs in the streets chasing down militiamen who fire back with rocket launchers.

"Oh, fuck." She mutes the glasses and stares at Jay. "Can you believe this shit is happening?"

He sets two plates down on the table and sits calmly across from her. "We all saw this coming years ago."

". . . And all started stockpiling guns and bombs in our bomb shelters?" She expects an ironic reply, but he just nods. "Fuck."

Half the country was raised on a diet of apocalyptic prophecies and warnings about outsiders. They've been primed, they know exactly what to do when the Signs appear. Somebody's put up those signs, so naturally they're going berserk.

Jay examines her as they eat. "Are you gonna tell me what happened?" he asks. "That was a serious amount of firepower came down on that little strip of lakeshore. I hope it wasn't all for you."

She sits back. "It pretty much was." It takes a while to tell him the story, mostly because he refuses to believe anything until she shows him the amber stone and shares the *Rewilding* overlay. When he boots it up he's quiet for a while, then says, "I have no idea what the fuck I'm looking at." But he stops interrupting while she finishes.

"So you're saying it's a hostage situation. They've got Compass and your dad's girlfriend, and you've actually got the thing they always thought you had, but that you didn't have." She nods, then frowns.

"You just framed it!" Suddenly restless, she goes to stand at the window. "You framed it, the way they'll be framing it. As a hostage situation. They'll expect me to offer a swap. That's what you do with hostages, isn't it?"

"Um, yeah. What else would—"

"That's the point! What else? How can we reframe it to our advantage? If it's not a hostage situation, what is it?"

Jay stretches, clasps his hands behind his head. "Is this what they taught you in wacko school?"

"No, I'm serious. We need help. We need to see what's really going on here. And I know who we can ask." She heads for the closet.

"Your cousins ever have any girls up here? Looks like." Turning, she holds out a pair of cross-country skis that look like they'll fit her. "You want to give me a lesson, Mr. Outdoorsy?"

He laughs. "Now you're talking."

Cross-country is both easier and harder than she expected. After twenty minutes of effort, they've made it about fifty feet past the windbreak trees. Behind her are uncertain, wobbly lines in the snow, punctuated by Sura-shaped craters here and there. She's giddy from laughing, but they've gotten to where she wanted to be. "Just look at it!"

The sun is intense, washing everything in whites and blues, and a haze of intense sparkles dances on the field. At the rate she's going it'll take her hours to cross to the far gap, but who cares?

Jay slides up next to her. "I hate to be a griefer, but how does this help us with your little problem?"

"Just wait, you'll see." She unmutes her glasses, and raising a mittened hand, shouts "Helloooo!" into the white.

"Unmute, Jay. There's a good reason, I promise."

Her greeting echoes across the field, is taken up by the trees. Even if there are no sensors in the area, the farm is assayed for its carbon by satellite; regional monitors can tell which animals have gone in and out; the state of the water table is known. Jay's land is part of some deodand or other—and here it comes, rearing up in her display like a giant tossing aside its white blanket. The glasses reveal where the deer are, and that there's a bear about a mile south, and crows, and bedded-down badgers and mice digging tunnels under the snow that the owls are trying to find.

"Crap," says Jay.

"This is nothing. Deodand, show me the state of the planet."

She hasn't tried this before, but she's certain it's possible. Marj wouldn't have left the deodands without a way to pool their knowledge.

Globes and maps and charts blossom around them, and at first it seems that it's not all bad news. CO_2 emissions are declining; afforestation means that global biomass is actually growing for the first time in a century. On closer inspection, the Caribbean Dead Zone is clearly visible, as is the growing desert that used to be America's breadbasket. Almost all whales are extinct; all rhinos are, except for a few clones in zoos.

"It's depressing as hell," admits Jay. "But there're people trying to fix it."

"Sure, but they're isolated and there are never enough of them. Believe me, learning that was my whole childhood." The dead zones, the dying cores of the continents, the unbearable heat—they're forcing mass migrations. "Look at the deserts," she says. "If you think of them as political players, it's pretty fucking obvious how they're feeding our diplomatic, religious, and ethnic tensions. The deserts are attacking us, driving us out. They're causing wars. It's not a metaphor, Jay, that's the point. Give them a voice, and you see it."

"All right . . ." He's clearly not getting it. "So what?"

Sura frowns at the global display for a while. "You're right. Too abstract. You know, Marj is a programmer. I don't think she thought about interfaces much when she designed these things. Not very exciting right now.

"Hey though. I just happen to have another toolkit here." She opens the larpwright overlay and copies the view to Jay's glasses. "See, there's this library of characters you can build based on roles. Maybe Marj does get it, 'cause it turns out that's what the word *actant* means: it's a role, like hero or villain, sidekick, you know. So I can take all these systems' reports on their relationship with humanity, and call those *attitudes*, and . . ." She grabs databases, slips a translator bot in between them and feeds the result into the larpwrights' Chernoff character generator. A little dramatics isn't out of place here, so she raises her arms and shouts in her best Vesta voice, ". . . Deodands! Personify!"

The tags flicker, turning from columns of data into characters: knights, maidens, sly thieves, cardsharps and pirate captains, rusted robots, cartoon fish, neon-shaded hookers, and haloed nuns. Clouds around their ankles, they stretch, look around, and then as one, turn their gazes on Sura and Jay.

"Huh," says Jay. "It's fuckin' Cloud Cuckoo Land." He's shuffling his skis as if he wants to back away.

She raises an eyebrow. "Aw, you like *The Lego Movie*? That's sweet, Mr. Bounty Hunter."

She turns to the teeming, hopping mob. "Deodands! My name is Sura Neelin. My father was James Neelin. Ask Tamshiyacu about me and then tell me if you trust me."

There's a momentary pause, then the local deodand (a farmer in overalls with a corn-cob pipe) scowls at her and says, "We'd trust your father. Don't know about you."

Now Jay actually does jump back. "Crap! They talk?"

"They're just reading my Promise Theory score," she asides to Jay. Then, to the actant: "Trust me enough to do some framing for you?"

It cocks its head. "Sure. But it'll cost ya."

She and Jay exchange a glance. "Uh, okay. Cost me what?"

"Money," says the deodand impatiently. "Playing in the frameworlds takes computing power. We need Gwaiicoin to pay for it."

"I'll give you all I have. Then can we talk credit?"

"Maybe." It scratches its stubble. "What's the frame?"

It takes a while for her to describe her idea. To keep her feet from freezing she starts skiing again; they cross the field slowly and when they reach the gap that leads to the next, even more lovely one, she says, "Good. If we're agreed, then commit, and play until my money runs out." Turning to Jay, she says, "Hey, let's mute."

They do. The new gods disappear, leaving behind snow with real rabbit tracks on it, trees that still wear white hats, and stands of brush that lend yellow accents here and there. It's silent, except for a sigh of wind through the forest.

"That was crazy," says Jay. Sura is smiling at the gorgeous white field, the furze of undergrowth below the trees, and the black lines on the pale birches.

"Funny," she says. "We worried that this world was an illusion—some kind of mask with the gods hiding behind it. But it's the other way around, isn't it? Everything we just saw, that was the mask." She draws a breath of cold, crisp air.

"This is the truth."

* * *

"Hi, Bill."

"Sura, thank God! They thought you'd cut and run, they were about to—"

"Don't! I—I know the situation I'm in. I mean, I thought about running, starting over—but we both know I tried that already. It only works for so long. And I'm tired, and I, well, I don't want Marj and the others to die because of me."

"Believe me, I get it." He sounds relieved. "I know you won't understand this, but you and me are in the same boat. I can't back out of the deal I'm in either, or the same thing happens. Sure, I've got resources, but they're like your hiding tactic—they only work until they don't. Listen, is Jay with you?"

"Jay who?"

"I only ask because my, uh, business partners are willing to extend the same amnesty to him as to you—and even a bonus—if you can turn over the key."

"Huh." She looks over the table at Jay. It's taken three days for the actants to get back to her. That's given her plenty of time to think about how this conversation is going to go. Naturally she's recording it and loading the recording onto a provenance blockchain that can prove when and where it occurred. Since the whole discussion could be spoofed by any good game engine, right down to voice-prints, whatever she and Bill say is still not going to be admissible in a court of law.

"Here's the thing, Bill. I might trust you, but I don't trust your 'business partners.' If we're going to make an exchange, I need guarantees, but you can't give them, can you?"

"It is what it is, Sura."

"No, actually, it's not. Because I'm not doing this without those guarantees. Luckily there's a way to get them that I think'll work for you."

"Oh? And what's that?"

Things are never quite the same in reality as you imagine they'll be; for instance, Sura's side of this negotiation is happening as she sits in front of an electric space heater in Jay's kitchen. Its round little red mouth glares at her while she wriggles her toes in the radience. She's wrapped in a blanket and has a cup of cocoa in her hands. Outside, the evening is mauve touched with orange horizon light. Hardly an underground volcanic-island lair or executive suite.

"We're going to make a smart contract," she says, "executed in a mutually acceptable subworld—one where I get to walk away alive and free at the end, and you get the key and the anonymity your business partners need. I mean, I can't stop them hunting us all down later in life, but there'll be a dead-man switch on me that'll at least send the whole story to the press. Fat lot of good that'd do, but it's something."

"Let me relay your proposal. My offer still stands, by the way," he says. "I can keep you safe."

"I'm . . . considering it," she says, but she makes a face at Jay.

"Tell your friends, Bill, this is a take-it-or-leave-it proposition. I don't expect to get out of this alive if I play by their rules. They can threaten to kill Marj and the others till they're blue in the face, but I'm just assuming they will anyway if they pull any ultimatum shit on me. So this is it: a smart contract, in a world where what's real and what's not is decided in such a way that both you and I get what we want. I'm a larpwright, and I'm sure you've got one or two in your pocket by now."

"Oooh . . . kay. They're asking where you want to meet."

She rolls her eyes. "These are old farts, aren't they? They have no idea what I just asked for. All the better.

"I'll tell you what," she says, trying to make it sound like she's just thought of this. "Why don't we do the exchange on neutral ground?

"Say, where you and I first met."

CHAPTER TWENTY-THREE

Sura walks to the south end of the Zug Island railway bridge. It's one of only two ways on and off the place if you don't want to swim. The other approach is on the north side, near the doxers' compound. There used to be a rotating truck bridge on the west side, but it's been frozen sideways for years now.

Last week's snow has mostly melted, revealing a grim vista of stripped bushes and struggling brown grass. Across the span the color of the landscape changes; bizarre purple-gray humps have stained the ground. The island was actually an Indian burial place back when the Cahokians were building their mounds. These piles are not monuments to gods or the dead, unless steel is a god. There's an actant for it, so she supposes it is.

Two huge yellow pipelines cross the bridge and point the way into the interior. Sura takes one more deep breath, mutters "fuck you," and starts across. Halfway, she unmutes her glasses.

Part of her contract with Bill is a geofence. The glasses show green, amber, and red zones up ahead: places she can walk, places that will put her on notice, and areas that, if she enters them, will void the agreement. The contract doesn't actually specify what happens to her if it's voided. She knows.

As she starts up the road, dozens of drones lift off the ground, forming a dome a hundred feet over the island. They're triangulating on her, listening for any signal she might send. If she emits anything that's not on the prearranged frequency and using the protocol they agreed to, that too breaks the contract.

The island's smokestacks rear above the twin yellow pipes. Silent an decaying now, the foundries once fed steel to the automakers of Detroit and clients all over the world. That work was not without consequence; something on the island—no one now knows what—produced a constant, maddening hum that only some people could hear. It could drive men mad, and it could be heard fifty miles away. People living in the adjacent neighborhoods, and across the water in Windsor complained of nausea, headaches, foul air, and tainted water. If anything could claim to be the actant of Detroit's industrial legacy, it's Zug.

Ironically, there have only been environmental sensors on the island since the plants shut down. They're scattered everywhere, measuring the chemicals leaching through the soil and the health of the struggling scrub grasses. There are very few inside the padlocked buildings—so to Zug's actant, and to the frames, the mafia, the police, and anybody else taking an interest, the island's covered in blind spots.

Or anyway, it had been. As soon as she'd proposed they do the exchange here, Bill's people swarmed the place, planting cameras and motion sensors everywhere. Sura's own spies monitored the whole operation. All volunteers, they're an eager bunch, some of them former interns with her investigative agency, others loaned as a favor from K.C. and the larpwrights. They watched as the blind spots were found and filled, and Zug Island turned from a hole in the world to a panopticon, surely one of the most surveilled spots on Earth.

The pipelines turn down a rough road that leads to one of the big blast furnaces, but Sura continues on to the next turnoff, where a blackened track undulates across long-dead ground to a jumble of squat buildings, round oil tanks, and glossy refinery stacks. More drones hang over this region, brass buttons on the embroidered sky.

An SUV is parked under one tall and complicated stack. Bill Duchene is standing next to it.

She takes this road and there are no more choices now; the only green path leads up it. Behind, all is red.

They don't speak as they climb the metal stairs that circle the silvery tower. Bill and Sura won't even meet each other's eyes. As they ascend, the mile-wide River Rouge slowly emerges past the leaning walls of the blast furnaces. Its far shore is LaSalle, a suburb of Windsor, Canada. As they reach the top of the refinery tower (Bill winded, Sura barely breathing harder), they turn as one to look at the water. They're on a ten-by-ten-foot square platform pierced by the wide offgassing stack. The thing looms another fifteen feet overhead; Bill puts his back to it, understandably because the vertiginous sense of height and slight swaying are nauseating.

Sura's the first to break the silence. "Can you see *Carol*?"

Bill shakes his head. "This was clever," he gasps. "Doing a hostage exchange as a smart contract." He's wearing some kind of Arctic expeditionary parka over what looks like an expensive suit; of course he's got his glasses on. Sura's interface to the circling drones tells her he's not sending any suspect signals. That doesn't mean he isn't packing a pistol under his jacket. She certainly is.

"There was no fucking way I was going to trust your new friends," she says, but there's no heat behind her words. She worked through her anger in Jay's woodpile, an ax being a wonderful thing. Events are in motion now, they've done the Commit, and her mind was always this crystal clear and calm mid break-in. In those years between that night she burgled for Dad, and the day he died, she'd been ashamed of this version of herself, but now she feels like she's discarded every other Sura—even Vesta—like so many old clothes.

"The only way this works is as an escrow transaction through a neutral third party." She nods at the river. "It took a while to figure out what that arbitrator could be, granted how many hooks your friends have into the police, the government . . ." She knows that Summit Recoveries' goons are lurking just on the other side of Zug. How could both she and Bill's associates have trusted any legal firm, militia, or gameworld to act as their intermediary? Either of them could buy off any supposedly neutral third party, with money or moral suasion. It seemed like an impossible dilemma—until she remembered Zug and thought of *Carol*.

"I'm sorry that you have to be here," he says. He's shivering despite his coat. "They insisted. I think they're worried you'd abandon your friends."

"Because it's just what they would do?" She puts her back to the metal railing, crosses her arms, and gives him her undivided attention. "Bill, who are 'they'? That's all I ever really wanted to know."

His shoulders slump. "Ah, Sura. I'm sorry, but here's the thing. There is no 'they.' Not in the way you're thinking. There never was."

"What do you—it was *you*?"

"No, fuck no!" She's taken a half step toward him and he holds up both hands, turning his face away. "I don't mean it was *me*. I mean there was never any 'they.' I mean it was nobody. Nobody killed your father. Nobody sent Summit Recoveries after you.

"I investigated. You know I've got the resources. Once I had your name, I had a thread I could pull, and I pulled. Hard."

With obvious reluctance he comes to join her at the rail. He points at the mad Looney Tunes architecture of Oneota, hovering *in virtua* on the skyline. Detroit's core is dissolving in the acid of possibilities unleashed by frame thinking. "Look at that," he says. "Half the companies in those office towers have abandoned their charters and let go their workforces. All the ones that're trying to stay alive with a traditional structure are failing. Their CEOs can be replaced with AIs that make better decisions, and the guys in the loading dock are gone because the bots can load and unload. Accountants, order processing, legal; they're gone too. Workforces and business plans and supply chains can be summoned into existence for a day, dissolved the next morning. The only function the corporation has anymore is to *own* things."

She gives him a long look. "DACs," she says. "You're talking about DACs. Say, didn't you make your fortune from DACs?"

He ignores her heavy irony. "I saw this coming. That's how I made my fortune. And *this* is a world where, soon, there'll be no humans in the workforce anymore. In a world like that, the only question that counts is, who do the robots work for? Not who *does,* but who *owns.* It's the age of the shareholder. If you are one, you'll have a future. If you're not . . ."

"Norris Trading is a DAC," she says. He nods.

"Lots of people were involved with the original plot to spoof the zk-SNARK. Most of them have moved on. What's left is a distributed autonomous corporation—and its shareholders. Sura, do you think any of them give a shit how it conducts its day-to-day business?"

Sullen, she turns back to the river. "I thought DACs were transparent. They have to follow ethical rules and all that."

"Not if they're designed to cheat from the start by people with very deep pockets."

"You're saying nobody's responsible. My dad was murdered by a fucking algorithm?" He doesn't answer; Sura shakes her head. She wants to kick something off the platform, but there's nothing handy so she rattles the railing. He steps back and she laughs cynically. "But he was killed by someone. Some person."

"Summit has two assets on retainer in Iquitos."

Two. Now she too retreats from the rail, has to put her back to the stack for a moment. It seems she's already avenged Dad's death.

"I'm sorry, Sura. This is how it is now. Haven't you been watching the news? I've been pulling a lot of strings with Congress. If our bill passes, and it looks like it will, it's soon going to be illegal for frame assets to not be owned. The frames are great, as long as all the stuff they play with is somebody's property. Once it is, we can make sure that every single action in every game, in every world, has a transaction fee attached to it."

"Like they did with the Internet. The fuck, Bill, you're smarter than I gave you credit for. This is why you went into the games to begin with, isn't it? Not because of some asinine bet with Trey Saunders. But because you saw an opportunity to own *everything*. A tax on every event, a slice of everybody's pie. You weren't in *Lethe* to play, you were doing research."

He shrugs modestly. "But totally by accident, you led me to something potentially bigger: Norris's arbitrage system. Can you blame me for jumping at the opportunity?"

She has no answer to that, but just stares past her feet, through the grid flooring at the ground a hundred feet below. Then she glances up and points to the river. "There's *Carol*!"

In one of their early talks on larpwrighting, Binesi had said, "If you think about it, any game is a contract. You the player can do certain things, the characters and landscape and timings can do another. The agreement is that the level gives the player a challenge so tough that he'll *almost* fail at it, and then a big reward for the achievement. All we do, as larpwrights, is turn our real-world social contracts into game levels."

The trick to designing this specific level was to make it seem just hard enough for Bill and Norris Trading. It's a very particular game, but one they can't lose, and all the pieces are logical, predictable, and vetted by both sides. They think they have Sura Neelin where they want her. She has to make sure they continue to.

The *Carol* is a boat. It's self-steering and has room for four or five people; right now, it's moving south on the River Rouge, a few hundred feet offshore. From this distance she can just make out several human figures seated in it. She knows they'll be tied hand and foot, and that they're alone on the craft, because those details are part of the contract.

Sura takes a deep breath. Another rule concerns proof that those distant dots are who they're supposed to be. "Compass?" she says. "Can you hear me?"

There's a long pause. They should have given her glasses, damnit. And those glasses should be connected to the Zug mesh.

Then she hears Compass's voice: "What's the game?"

Sura wilts in relief, though she has to smile, too. "Are you okay?"

"They hurt us, Sura. They wanted information, b-but none of us could tell them what they wanted to know. Th-They went at Marjorie worst, I think. But. Yeah. We're okay."

"Can you pop up a flag from your location?" There's no way to spoof the self-sovereign tattoos, so when she spots Compass's identifier icon hovering over the boat, Sura's sure that's where she is. "Binesi, Marj, and Mikom are with you?" Compass says yes.

"The game is called hostage-exchange. See, there's this company named Norris Trading that's been watching an online backdoor into the global environmental monitoring sensor network. Their key was stolen years ago; once somebody uses it they own the system. Norris's monitors showed that somebody—my dad, actually—unlocked the door, so they figured correctly that the first thing he'd have done is change keys. They want the new one, I have it, but I can't just give it to them. And why should they hand you over? Neither of us trusts the other.

"So, our smart contract goes like this: I send the key to the contract, and Norris gives you to it as well, by putting you in that boat, which the contract controls. It's just a dumb algorithm, but it can steer. It'll try the key, and if it works, the contract transfers the key to Norris and sends a signal to the boat to steer left, to Canada. If the key I give it doesn't work, the *Carol* steers right, back to the people who put you in it to begin with. And they come for me."

She's received a verification that her people inspected the *Carol* before it launched, as did Summit Recoveries' thugs. There are no bombs in the *Carol*, and its control system has not been tampered with. Its hardware and sensors are very old, and for that reason, well known and trusted by both sides.

"Moment of truth, Sura," says Bill. "The key, please."

She laughs. "That's the irony. It was actually right in front of you all along." She does an extravagant curtsy.

"What do you mean. You're—?"

"A version of me, anyway." She digs in her pocket and brings out Dad's figurine of her. She holds it up in the wan sunlight and turns it around. "In all my teenaged glory."

He gapes at little Sura. "Well, shit. So I, what? Just scan it?"

"Yep. Here, I'll rotate it for you."

"Uh." He looks uncomfortable. "Why don't you just give it to me."

"Why? Afraid I'll toss it over?" She mimes doing that and he flinches. With another laugh, she plunks it into his waiting hand.

As he's turning it in the sunlight, she walks a little around the curve of the stack, frowning as she examines its smooth curving surface. She undoes her coat and reaches awkwardly to her mid-back. Bill's too busy admiring the statuette to notice her uncoiling 150 feet of climbing rope; when he does a double take the look on his face is priceless.

"Transactions are always delayed at this time of day," she says. "It'll be a few seconds before your friends realize I broke the contract." Her heart's pounding. She's pretending to be oh-so-casual to cover the fact that she's terrified of seeing what's happening on the river.

A faint sound of rolling thunder drifts from the opposite direction, and they both look over to see little puffs of smoke in the Detroit streets on the west side of Zug. High overhead, flashes signal the separation of dozens of small gleaming objects. Bill stares at them. "Fuck! Sura, what did you do? You know I can't protect you . . ."

She stares at the approaching drones. "I think those are called slaughterbots. They're not supposed to be legal on American soil." She tosses her line over a post at the top of the off-gassing stack and takes several deep breaths, summoning her nerve. Then she looks back at the river.

". . . I know they're not legal in Canadian territory."

Bill runs to the rail. "The boat! It's not, why isn't it coming back?" He turns to her, bewildered. "How could you hack a smart contract?"

She starts up the rope; she only has a few seconds before he realizes that Sura Neelin's hostage potential is the only card he has left. Far below, on the River Rouge, the *Carol* is steering resolutely for the Canadian shore. It's supposed to be going the opposite way; after all, she did cheat by scanning the figurine when she held it up to the light prior to giving it to Bill—and by opening the Norris Trading backdoor herself just after.

She reaches the top of the stack and throws a leg over the side of the now-empty metal shaft that used to contain some expensive piping. He staggers over to stand beneath her. "What are you *doing*?"

"I found this on a drone fly-over of the island. Goes all the way to the ground! Bye, Bill."

She's dropped her line inside and is clipping a rappel device to it when he squeaks, "How?"

Sura pauses. "Aw, come on, Bill. You know perfectly well that smart contracts are incorruptible. Obviously, the only way you're going to fool one is by fucking with the *oracles*!"

Down she goes.

The cliché thing after cross-country skiing would be to sit before a fire, wrapped in a blanket with a cup of hot cocoa. Jay's cabin doesn't have a fireplace, so Sura had to make do with the little space heater, which glared at her while she wriggled her toes in front of it. The cocoa was real if a little out of date. This was where she and Jay conspired to keep the key and save her friends.

"Looks like you've got four choices," he'd said after they listed all the players and the stakes. "The obvious one is that you can give Bill your key in exchange for Compass."

She shook her head. "I know about the exploit, including its basic architecture. I could go public with that or blackmail them with it at any time."

"Didn't you say Bill promised to cut you in? Make you rich?"

"He might trust me, but his partners won't. They won't trust him, as a result. He knows that perfectly well. So he's playing nice right now, but we both know I can't be allowed to live."

"What if you make a dead-man switch? You die, the information about the exploit gets posted on the Internet for everyone."

"Then they just have to make sure I never 'die' in a way that'll trip the dead-man. Doesn't mean they can't render me brain-dead or hold Compass hostage for the rest of her life."

He nodded. "So your second choice is publish the key. Let the world decide what to do with the backdoor."

"Sure. Except then Bill's friends get snippy and kill Compass out of spite."

"Third option: destroy the key."

She laughed. "Nobody can ever, ever prove that I did that. They'll assume I memorized it or hid it and torture me forever to get it." There's a little pause, then she said, "What's plan D?"

"Doesn't matter," he'd said. "It's impossible."

"Out with it."

"Find a way to free Compass and the others. And don't hand over the key."

She'd snorted bitterly; obviously he was right. It was only later, when they were talking about the necessarily incorruptible nature of online smart contracts and how one would make the perfect intermediary in a hostage-swap, that she'd remembered a lightning-soaked moment in Peru:

Her, crouching among sensors, all kept in wire cages that would block their signals and keep them from radioing home—

—And seeing that the old lady who played Tamshiyacu was standing over a tarpaulin piled with older ones, all out in the open. Sura had thought those ones were broken, but Tamshiyacu shook her head. They worked just fine, but their GPS readings were being spoofed. Reading about it online, Sura had learned that it was, really, the oldest trick in the book.—An old spoof and one so rarely used that the first few generations of IoT sensors hadn't been protected against it.

The *Carol* thinks it's facing north. It's following the smart contract perfectly. Sura broke that, so the boat's supposed to steer west, back to the American shore. Instead, several thousand dollars' worth of radio antennas planted on the Canadian side by Mikom's friends are putting out false timing packets (the software courtesy of Tamshiyacu's indigenes) that's swamping the real GPS signals. They've flipped the boat's older-generation navigation compass so now *Carol*'s going east, and any second now it'll be in Canadian waters and protected by drones, anti-bullet lasers, and if need be the entire fucking RCMP because, well, American refugees cross the river all the time, often with hostile natives on their tails. There's a protocol for this sort of thing.

Compass, Marjorie, Binesi, and Mikom will be safe.

Sura's a different matter.

She's rappelling in the dark, down a chimney that has dozens of broken bolts, jutting rusted spars, and bristles of cable to avoid. The plan had involved a miraculous video-game swoop to the ground and then life-saving parkour, but instead she almost freezes three times, and does cut her arm badly before she makes it down. "Shit, shit." She staggers into daylight from the access hatch only to find Bill waiting. He's beaten her down by quite a margin; she should have just taken the stairs.

She glares at him, considers reaching for her gun. "What?"

"You've got a plan, don't you?" He looks scared. "Tell me you've got a plan?"

"Why should you care? And yes, yes I do." She pokes her head out from under the steps and it's not good because a dozen or so slaughter-bots reached the intersection and now they swivel as one, aiming their low-slung machine guns—

"Run!" She bolts across the road; to his credit, Bill's right behind her and it's a good thing as there was no real cover under the stack. As bullets tear up the ground and ricochet off the stairs, she ducks into the open maw of another access hatch, this one leading into an empty oil tank the size of a house. In the light from the doorway, Sura waves at Bill to help her roll a smaller but still heavy tank in front of the opening.

That blocks this door, but there's another on the opposite side of the tank, letting in a flood of daylight. She points and they run that way.

"Why are you following me?"

"If you broke the contract I was liable too! That was in *my* contract with them."

"Oh Bill. Try to imagine how little I care."

"Are you just gonna abandon me? They'll kill me!"

"See if you can keep up." She sidles up to the other hatch, leans to look out.

"It's not a hopeless situation," she ventures. "I had some friends stash a few things around the island before I suggested this place to you. Nothing that a bomb- or EM-sniffer would be able to find. Come on!"

They run out the other door and make it into a long windowless shed with cinder-block walls. Emerging from the far end they're facing one of the tall, imposing foundry halls. The sky's momentarily empty of slaughterbots, but she can hear the gritty rolling of heavy tires. "That'll be Summit's ground force," she says in a falsely cheerful voice. A tactical view of the island would be useful right now, and Sura's just caught the edge of a mesh signal when she sees something fast launch from the direction of the approaching vehicles. It bursts far overhead and her glasses are suddenly burning her ears. "Fuck!" She pulls them off.

Bill's snatched his off as well. "Same thing they used at Wequetonsing," he says. "EMP grenade. They've killed everything electronic." Another shot goes up, higher, bursting the same way.

"That way!" They run down an avenue between giant rusting machines; behind her she can hear shouting. There's a T intersection about sixty feet up ahead, and it's a clear sprint to the water if they go right.

Bill starts to run but she grabs his arm and points into a cul-de-sac that dead-ends against the foundry's outside wall.

"But we can't—" He spots the heavy iron door there. "Wait? Do you have a key?"

"It's hilarious actually," she puffs as they reach it. "My boys watched your boys search the island. I saw footage of somebody checking this door. It's smart-locked, right?" She hauls on the Internet-connected padlock to no avail. "They checked its contract and they know I don't have a key."

Bill looks at the blank seamless barrier, a hopeless expression on his face. "Fuck, they're right *behind* us!"

Sura pulls on a piece of duct tape that's sticking out near the hinges, and the door opens from that side. She pushes past it as it wobbles drunkenly, held up only by the padlock. "My boys took out the hinge pins. Come on!"

They restore the door and now they're inside a set of storage rooms painted institution green; a flight of steps leads down into darkness, and a door opens onto a vast indeterminate space lit by windows high up. "Down!"

"How the—" Bill is pointing back at the door.

"Game levels," she says as they clatter down the stairs. "I knew Summit would scan the whole island and run a million or so simulations of the exchange. Basically, turn it into a game. I did the same thing with the doxers' place when I sprung you. No matter what we do, they'll already have a countermove. The EMP won't have taken out the military-grade tactical glasses they're wearing.

"But all their scenarios will be predicated on us using the landscape as it's officially configured." She taps her temple. "Burglar-mind says, 'Why go through a door when you can go through a window?' I rigged a few things here and there, just enough to change how I can move. Right now Summit's boys will be going round that corner back there, or hunting on the riverbank."

It's almost pitch-black down here; she crosses a grit-spalled linoleum floor to another heavy steel door and hauls it open. "There's flashlights and stuff in here. We'll bolt it from the inside."

Bill shakes his head as he walks in ahead of her. "They'll just keep searching. Eventually they'll find us."

"Goodbye, Bill." She slams the door on his startled face and bolts it from the outside.

Back up the stairs and into the open interior of the foundry. The blast furnaces are a couple hundred feet away across a huge open stretch of concrete floor with iron rails embedded in it; cranes and chains and huge metal bins are jumbled everywhere. Large sections of the wall are grimy industrial glass. There are stairs here leading to a gallery above the storage rooms, but Sura ignores them and climbs the rusted, riveted beams. She's about halfway up when a Summit Recoveries team bursts in through a side door. Glancing down she can see they're wearing exoskeletons to enhance their strength, and other expensive military gear. One looks over as she's swinging onto the gallery. "There!" he shouts, and they head for the stairs.

Wait for it. Two seconds. Sound of feet on metal steps. Three. More feet. *This isn't going to work.* Four.

The stairway collapses with a rending sound, taking most of the team with it. "The beams're cut!" somebody yells. There's a lot of cursing, but she doubts any of the bastards have been badly hurt.

The gallery is an obstacle course of oil drums. Several are on their sides next to spots where the rail's been removed. Sura gets behind one and uses all her body weight to roll it. Then she has to sprint and dive behind another because some asshole's tossed up a grenade.

The sharp explosion is a diaphragm punch that half deafens her, but she can hear the scream a couple seconds later as her barrel lands on somebody. She's on her feet again, racing to a wall ladder that's ringed with safety hoops. "Come on, come on," she mutters. She knows the sight lines here as well as they do but taking out the stairs has changed their game level just enough that it takes fully eight seconds before they start firing.

Their budget must not cover smart bullets because nothing hits her before she can make it to a catwalk that parallels the crane rail. Once she's there she pulls the pins as instructed by the players who set up this route; the ladder leans out, then falls away with a grinding noise and a crash.

The crane rail is a massive metal beam that runs the length of the building. It shields her on the left; the catwalk floor is solid steel. She runs, bent over, as bullets dent the surface under her and spark off the railing.

The shooting ends. She's frankly amazed that she's still alive; she snarl-smiles with a savage sense of satisfaction. She might not survive, but Compass and the others are safe. And the other thing that only Jay knows about so far, her only hope is that she'll know whether that worked before they kill her . . .

"Sura!" It's Bill's voice, coming from almost directly below her.

She stops, drops, rolls on her back panting. "How many times do I have . . . to say goodbye to you!"

"Listen, these soldiers know who I am! I've just made them a better offer. You can come down."

"As if."

"At least tell me why you broke the contract. You had no reason to!"

"S-Sorry 'bout that. I just couldn't give you the key. Not after what they did to Dad."

"Is that what this is all about? Revenge for your father's murder?"

She hauls in a deep breath, then another, while imagining them lining up a rocket on her position.

"No!" she shouts. "That's *not* what it's about. Say, Bill—what exactly is it that you think I just did?"

There's a pause, some angry discussion. Summit's boys have their shot and want to take it. She has to hope Bill's curiosity—and money—will hold them back.

"You gave the key to the people, right?" he says. "Uploaded it to some public account. As soon as it's out, half the oracles that all smart contracts rely on are gonna be junked. Hackers will have exploits by nightfall. So will dictators, the mob, wackos with grudges—and you haven't warned the Internet security groups that this is coming! I'd have seen the notifications. Kids will dox ambulances and people will die; hell, you can fuck with people's pacemakers with this stuff! It'll be chaos!"

"You think? Have you looked outside lately? Assuming you can borrow some glasses."

There's another angry discussion; he's asking one of the goons to lend him a pair of tactical lenses. Then—silence, and . . .

"Sura?"

"What do you see, Bill? I'm not wearing, I can't tell."

"Sura. Where's Detroit?"

She smiles. Trailing her hand up the iron flank of the crane rail, she realizes it's thick enough to shield her from a rocket. Quietly, she climbs onto it. She's fifty feet off the floor, it's crazy high up here and all she wants to do is cling to the metal.

"I didn't give the key to the people, Bill. You're right, that'd be bad."

"Who'd you send it to, Sura?"

"See, Bill, it's all about trust. I didn't keep it. I didn't give it to anybody else. 'Cause I can't be trusted with it, and neither can the public. So that leaves you, or somebody like you. And if *you* can't be trusted with it, who can?"

The silence is longer this time. "You destroyed it?"

"Oh, you wish! You know that's not one of the transactions permitted for that object."

She carefully rolls on her back. "Trust," she shouts. "That's what it's all about. I stopped trusting Dad when I learned he was a total hypocrite about his whole 'love of nature' thing. When I lost my faith in him, I lost faith in anything. Everything since, I've said fuck you and moved on. Because there wasn't anything solid to believe in. It's all just somebody trying to play you—religion, politics . . .

"Whatever I was shown, I wanted to see it differently. That made me a good burglar. It also meant I could never commit to anybody, or anything. Pretty sad, huh?"

"What did you do, Sura?"

"You tell me, Bill. The whole reason I led your goons on this little chase was to buy time—time enough for the key to get into the hands of its new owners, and for them to set in motion the plan we agreed on.

"Any second now, you should be seeing something on the horizon.— Not the sensor systems of Detroit, they're owned now, and not by you or me."

"—What the fuck?"

"Do you see the actant of Zug Island yet, Bill? 'Cause I'm pretty sure it's walkin' over here. Not coming to kill you or me, mind.

"But to offer us a deal."

She lies there for a while, weariness saturating her. If they stroll up now to shoot her, she's not going to have the energy to resist. She can hear Bill talking. Sometimes he's shouting. He's scared, and really confused.

Sura imagines Zug Island standing over him, an imperious giant with sinews of rebar, muscles of rusted iron, and a fat gut full of blast-furnace coke. Zug's not going to be happy with the contract Sura made with the deodands, but there are compensations. Bullying Bill Duchene will be one of them.

Of course, she's personifying. Zug's not thinking like a human, if it's thinking at all. Still, the reverie satisfies her until she becomes aware of a growing murmur from beyond the foundry's grimy windows. She sits up when she hears Malcolm's voice echoing from the end of the hall.

"Sir, do you really think you can stop us coming in there?" She's never heard him sound angry before; he's impressive.

"We have orders to secure the area—"

"Duchene, what have you done? Where is our Sura?"

Some muttering ensues. Then Malcolm calls out. "Sura! You can come down! It is okay."

She laughs. "I've heard that one before!"

"Truly! Through my glasses I see . . . well, I'm not precisely sure what I'm seeing, but whatever it is, it seems to have stopped these gentlemen cold, as you say. Come down, please, it's not safe up there."

Levering herself up, Sura frowns at the line of broken bolts on the wall where the ladder used to be. "I don't know how."

"The far end?"

"Ah." She rolls onto the catwalk, peers down the length of the furnace hall. "There might be booby traps, I can't remember. That's kind of why I stopped where I did."

Shadows are moving past the dust-covered windows that span the south wall. Lots of vehicles are pulling up outside and the muttering sound is getting louder. She's not sure what to make of it until she hears Jay's voice; he's talking to Malcolm. Smiling now, she walks to the east end of the hall, where an ordinary set of stairs leads in zigzags to another gallery. She passes old black blast furnaces on the way: Zug's heart, cold and congealed.

Players are pouring in through all the hall's entrances and by the time she reaches the ground they're everywhere, shouting, laughing, pointing at her. She runs up to Malcolm and hugs him; he stiffens in surprise, then laughs and holds her tight. Over his shoulder she can see K.C. and Pax, talking to some floating camera drones. Bill is off in a huddle with the Summit team, but nobody's paying any attention to them. Past the crowding people, at first just a silhouette in a side door, is Jay. He's carrying her dad's orange backpack.

She's got tears in her eyes and a flutter in her stomach; he's a bit uncertain too as he stops a few feet away. He rummages in the pack. "Glasses?"

"You must have been a Boy Scout." Sura takes a pair from him but is afraid to put them on. "Why are we safe?" she asks him. "Is it . . . ?"

"*Not* because Duchene's side got what they want," he says. "Quite the opposite, actually. Go on. Look."

She grips his arm tightly with one hand as she slides on the glasses.

For a while she stares at the windows; then, with one uncertain step after another, she walks to the loading doors and looks outside.

They stand astride the Earth, great angelic forms made of light. The larpwrights clearly suggested something better than Sura's first set of skins—or did the things choose these guises? She can't sustain such an analytic attitude for more than a couple of seconds; it dissolves in wonder, a prickling up her spine and across her scalp as she realizes—intuits, *feels*—what the deodands are.

There's a flicker next to her, and Compass and Marj appear *in virtua*. Somebody on the Canadian side must have given them glasses, but it still feels miraculous. "Are you okay?" She emotes a hug, and Compass smiles.

"We're g-good."

"Is everybody seeing this?" Marj asks. Jay nods.

"Least as we can tell, most of the planet's got these things on their TVs, phones, and glasses, live. The buggers called every phone on the planet, about ten minutes ago. They've got a—" He stops because Sura's raised a hand to shush him. They're talking to her.

Hello.

"Hi," she says. "So you took my suggestion? You went self-sovereign with all your data?"

Yes.

"Jay says you wanted to talk to us. About what?"

All the things that abide on this Earth are now awake; you are just one of them. We, your brothers and sisters, promise that you will never want for food, never want for shelter or the freedom to enjoy your lives, and we extend this guarantee to your children, and your children's children, down all the ages to the very end of the Earth.

In return you will agree that you are not the masters of this planet, but just one tenant, as we are. You and we will work together to heal the world that we share.

The cynic in her won't shut up, it's saying, *It's just a smart contract speaking through a game-NPC driver, laying out one of the scenarios you had the deodands play.* But now that the deodands own themselves, she knows their commitments are inviolable. Contract code is open to anyone to read and verify, but it's unchangeable by any human agency. These awakened spirits of the Earth, advocates for oak and stream, air and sea, are absolutely incorruptible. "You've just . . . just made this offer to everyone in the world?"

To every person we could reach, yes. And every government, every religious authority, and every corporation.

"Because we can't do this on our own," she whispers. And then she's crying, and she's not the only one. Her imagination lights and shows her humanity—all of it—standing as she is, hands loose in the air, streaming tears of surprise, and terror, and joy.

CHAPTER TWENTY-FOUR

Far too late, the former rulers of the world—nations, armies, religions, and businesses—react. Where Sura is, things get loud and crazy as throngs of framers and gamers descend on Zug, along with police and news drones. The island's overrun, though Pax's old code kicks in and food, water, and porta-potties arrive by apparent miracle, conjured by reframing. Zug's the perfect place for a riot, or celebration, or ceremony—she has no idea what this is—but soon enough big men with FBI printed on the backs of their jackets appear. Maybe that's the army securing the bridges. Everybody's arguing and shouting, MR is full of speech balloons and emotes and talking heads and Sura just drifts through it all.

But not for long. The volume on Sura Neelin is being turned up and up, and by the end of the day she's apparently the most famous person in the world. Bill and his thugs, on the other hand, have disappeared.

Eventually an FBI agent comes to her under the lengthening shadow of the refinery and says, "We'd like you to come with us, ma'am." Sura shrugs. "Oh, I dunno," she says. "I need to eat."

The agent isn't used to people saying no to him. "Ma'am, I'm afraid I must insist." She smiles at his stiff politeness, and simply walks away.

And so it goes, as people who used to have power suddenly discover that someone or something has their bosses by the balls. Emergency plans are kicking into motion all over the world, only to be stopped by frantic calls from prime ministers, CEOs, and dictators. The deodands are playing a global game of "keep your hands where I can see them," and one of the rules is *don't fuck with Sura Neelin.*

This would all be great fun if Sura could afford to pay attention to it. The Canadians have Compass and Marj and the others, and she's just now learning what they've been through. All of them were interrogated by Summit's goons, including Compass. They used sleep deprivation on her until she suffered a seizure, then backed off a bit, merely resorting to abusive interviews intended to break her down. They didn't get that Compass is already broken.

Worse is that she's been offline for days now. Without a persona to play, she's retreated into herself. As night falls on Zug, Sura's physically on her way back to her condo, but *in virtua* she's in Canada, seeking answers. The Canadians intend to deport Compass and the others (all except Mikom, who's from there) but they're also inclined to make them wade through a mountain of paperwork first. Sura puts her newfound status behind a demand, and two days later, an unmarked car drops Compass off at her newly repaired door.

She's listless and doesn't say much, so Sura just cooks for her, does her laundry, and fixes the piano. Gradually, with focus and effort, Compass starts to notice her. Sura arranges for a deodand to ride her, and she starts to brighten.

The FBI return a week after Zug, as the general hysteria's starting to settle down. She's upstairs with Jay and Compass; Marj has pulled another disappearing act, and Binesi and Mike are off somewhere playing the larpwright's version of *The White Rose*. When Sura opens the door this time, it's very clear that she can't say no to the summons.

She's assigned Agent Geraldo, who's apparently very important. He treats her like she's made of plutonium and might go off at any moment. Luckily, he knows something about the government's position, and has been ordered to be open with her.

"They're scared," he says at the downtown hyperloop station. The station's been cleared for them, and she and Geraldo are moving slowly through a mass of hypervigilant agents to a Washington-bound pod. "They've had the rug pulled out from under them—we all have. They need someone to say it's all going to be okay and they'll have a job tomorrow."

"It's not up to me," she says. "Really it isn't." They enter the pod's forward compartment, which has two sets of seats facing one another. They're alone, with four agents taking up the aft and others queuing up for the next pod. As the door closes with an authoritative thud, the silence of isolation descends. Sura finds herself relaxing, and Geraldo even flashes her a little smile as he settles opposite.

"You got an offer, I assume," she says.

He grimaces. "Is that what you're calling it? It was more of a weird questionnaire. They wanted me to promise not to do some things. Like, 'Never move to Fresno.'"

"Were you thinking of doing that?"

"No! That's what's so bizarre. None of it made any sense."

"I'll tell you one thing about the deodands," she admits. "They suck at reassuring people.

"Look, about the 'offer'—they're really just putting boundaries on what they know about you. What you might or might not do. They have to do that to add you to the simulations."

"So it's true? They're modeling the behavior of everybody on the planet?"

"Come on, Geraldo. You know perfectly well our government does that already. So do the corporations—and they've got better data than you do. Except for a few big holes in the dataset, like China, simulating the planet's standard practice. The deodands are just refining theirs. Then they play a few moves ahead, a million or so times, and figure out a strategy that's optimal for all of us—humans and nonhumans, planet-wide. The output's a set of constraints; for us humans it's resources we shouldn't use, things we shouldn't do if the ideal strategy's going to work. They'll tell us what *not* to do if we don't want to fuck everything up, but they're not going to tell us what *to* do. That's up to us. It's freedom under constraint, which is the only kind of freedom we can have on this Earth. You might have had the illusion of free will before because the nonhuman constraints on your behavior couldn't talk. Now, they can. That's the only thing that's changed."

"You see, that's not very reassuring."

"How 'bout this, then? If you follow the plan, the number of things you can't do is going to steadily drop, and the number of things you can do is going to grow.—Throughout your life, and your children's lives, and theirs. Is that reassuring?"

As they slide into the hyperloop tube, he shakes his head. "I wish I could believe you."

Sura smiles again, and this time she's not pretending to be nice. "Our belief," she says, "is not required."

Two days later she finds herself, Binesi, and Marjorie Cadille testifying before a congressional committee in Washington. The city itself is a revelation: it runs on as it always has, apparently untouched by games, frames, deodands, or international crises. People here still have jobs, and they own houses in neighborhoods where everybody they know has a job too. It's a perfect bubble, a mirror-world that thinks it's still the twentieth century. If you lived here, you might be forgiven for assuming that the deodands are just another crisis to be managed and set behind.

After all the virtual chambers she's been in—from Cahokian sweat lodges to the palaces of Balkan Europe—it's just as easy for Sura to pretend that this is yet another game. So she does, going full Vesta on the committee members. When one proposes "outlawing" the actants, she laughs out loud.

"You can try it," she says. "But you'll be pulling the plug on the entire economy. I'm not the expert here, but what the actual experts are saying sounds about right. Cutting the actants and deodands out of world trade would have roughly the impact of a full-scale nuclear war. And why would we want to do it, anyway? We're so much better off this way."

"Maybe you can clarify that," drawls the rep from Arkansas. "Because it seems right now like we're in the grip of a catastrophe."

"This is just like the carbon bubble. I remember when I was a kid, and renewables got so cheap so fast that the whole fossil fuel economy collapsed practically overnight. Boom!—And a hundred years of economic dominance is gone. Same thing now, only on a way bigger scale. 'Cause this time it's *economics itself* that's obsolete. I can't really blame you folks for freaking out over it. But it's not a catastrophe.

"All the actants are doing is asking that we take responsibility for the downside of our actions. And the deodands, all they want is for us not to overrun the Earth's carrying capacity. We all know we've done that. My whole life we've been fighting this battle, with international treaties, carbon-trading schemes, emissions reductions, recycling, urban redesign, you name it. All haphazard as hell, reactions after the fact. Sir, we were fully in the grip of a catastrophe before the deodands came along. They're our one and only hope of getting out of this situation alive. We can't do it on our own."

"That's all very well," says the congressman, "but then what? What do we become if we let them win? Their pets?"

"No, their partners. If we'd thought of ourselves that way to begin with, we wouldn't be in this situation."

Later Marj testifies, and she's even more blunt. The press are far more forgiving when she acts that way, because she's already a minor celebrity and knows how to sound like the expert she is.

"Gentlemen," she tells them, for all the world like a lecturer addressing a class of inattentive first-years, "you've all been briefed about the sprites and the games. If I must, I'll review: the frameworlds reimagine local economics to suit some social situation. The actants live life in reverse—their whole purpose is to make themselves go away, so they're no threat. And the deodands are like Japanese *kami*: spirits of places. For them, growth and reproduction don't even make sense as ambitions. All they want is to be in balance, to function and thrive.

"These AIs exist only to fulfill a smart contract. This deal offers humanity two things. First, certainty. If we work with them, they can guarantee us a core of predictable prosperity—basically a guaranteed income for the whole human race, as long as we don't overrun the key environmental constraints that are necessary to keep us all alive. They can enforce the arrangement because, at least right now, they control enough of the planet's sensor data to invalidate most of the world's other smart contracts. They can come through on the deal because they represent our resource providers; they own the tap. We can know with absolute certainty that they're not going to shut it off, as long as we play nice."

"But why should they work with us? Why not go their own way?"

"Because we're part of them." Marj has said this about ten times, but it's clearly not getting through. "Look, they're not separate beings. We're just as much a part of them as the oceans and forests. Our success is their success, why would they screw themselves over?

"Second, we can do whatever we want within the limits they've set. This is our chance to reframe everything. They'll even help—I mean, after all, they're players too."

"You're talking about the 'frames,' now?" The congressman frowns skeptically.

"I know the popular meme around here is that the only reason the frameworlds are growing is because the world's in a depression. You're living in a dreamworld if you think that. The economy's not going to 'recover.' There will never, ever again be a business as usual.

"Frankly I'm amazed none of you saw this coming. I mean, once we had computers, why wouldn't we develop better systems for coordinating production, supply, and demand than old-style markets? Those were based on paper and printing-press tech! Mail, for God's sake! Trusted third parties like banks and notaries. Money—as if money were the only possible way to transmit economic information! We spent nearly a century using computers to just do the old stuff faster, while all the while new possibilities were there to be taken. It's ridiculous. Of course something like the frameworlds was going to happen. Now that it has, there's no going back.

"The second thing they're offering is *possibility*. Unlimited reinvention of ourselves and what we can do, as long as we keep one foot on the ground."

At the end of her own testimony, exhausted and out of patience, Sura shrugs. "I know you folks like sound bites," she says, "so how about I sum it all up in one? It goes like this: Up until now, economics has been about making people into things. We're just reversing the process.

"If that frightens you, I'm afraid there's nothing I can do about it."

As it turns out, that's not what frightens them.

The moon is lowering over Jay's farm, and Sura's contemplating going out when she spots headlights playing hide-and-seek through the trees lining the drive. "Oh, visitors," she says. She goes to the cabin's window, cupping her mug of bhang, and watches as two black limousines pull into the yard. "More FBI," she mutters in disappointment; then, "Hey! Is that—?"

She jumps into her boots and doesn't bother lacing them up but bangs the door open and runs into the bitter cold. "Maeve!"

Maeve laughs in delight and they hug; behind her, Compass smiles uncertainly until Sura drags her into the mosh. FBI agents stand in the snow and watch, and Jay leans in the cottage doorway, arms crossed.

"Where's your coat?" asks Maeve. "It's freezing out here!"

"Yeah, spring seems to have given us a miss this year."

The formerly peaceful cottage explodes with noise as they stomp inside. Jay shakes his head and retreats to the kitchen while Maeve stares around at the faux wood-grain panels, the acoustic-tile ceiling, and linoleum floor. She kneels as Bargain comes to see her. "Whoa, this is *not* what I expected," she says. "I figured on an underground bunker."

"Oh, that's still an option," says Jay. "Some security perimeter, huh?"

"They fucking X-rayed me! What *is* this?"

"It's for your protection, ma'am," says Geraldo from his post by the door.

Sura grimaces. "Don't mind him, he has to say that.—So you're on the mend? Compass said your folks still wouldn't let you talk to anyone. When she left she just said she was going to 'fetch Maeve.' How'd she get to you?"

"I recorded the whole thing," says Compass. "B-But they wouldn't let us bring it in." She taps at her temple, where the frame of her glasses would normally be.

"What about that?" says Maeve. "Nothing electronic? Not even a radio? What the fuck?" She suddenly looks exhausted and sits at the table.

"Compass didn't tell you? Okay, but you first. Did you have it out with your folks, or what?"

Maeve laughs, and shakes her head. "Oh, it was a lot more dramatic than that."

She tells how her family's been keeping her locked up in their compound in LA. They're a lot richer than she ever let on—and a lot crazier. Just like here, she's been cut off from the mesh. Her folks believe in television and radio and the social media; anything else is suspect. They would only allow her to watch religious programming—"God, the last two months have been one long string of interventions!"—and by the end of it, she half-believed what they were telling her. Because they believe it.

"They wouldn't tell me what happened! They said it's all come apart, that it's the end of the world."

"You mean you didn't get an offer from the actants?"

"What's an actant? Compass tried to explain, but . . ."

"Shit. Your folks are real dicks. So how'd she get to you?"

"They let me out for walks, as long as the cousins came along to chaperone me. We were on Mulholland, where it looks out over LA, three days ago. And this jogger runs up."

She's never seen Compass wearing a track suit, so it wasn't until she zigged and Maeve's cousins zagged, and she bumped into Maeve that Maeve saw the ponytail. "Oops! My bad," the jogger said as she pressed something into Maeve's hand. Then she kept going.

Once the cousins settled down, Maeve slipped on the glasses while their attention was elsewhere. Compass appeared before her, rather cartoonish *in virtua*. "Wotcher, Knife Fairy," she said as she fell in step beside Maeve. "Anybody notice the hand-off?"

"Compass," Maeve hissed, "get me *out* of here! They're, like, praying me to death!"

"A car'll pull up in about a minute. Get in. Hey—can you lend me your feed? I wanna see the looks on their faces."

"Sure." Her crew-cut cousins in their starched white shirts were talking and laughing—well, it was just a family outing, after all—and didn't look her way until a black car came to a halt right next to her. Maeve made her break for it as its passenger door self-opened.

"Maeve, what are you—somebody stop her!"

"So I'm in," she says now, gesturing broadly and almost spilling the cocoa Jay's handing her. "The door closes and I'm frantically trying to fasten my seat belt because the car won't move until I do. My cousins are yelling and pounding on the trunk and then I'm just . . . waving bye-bye as we drive away.

"Picked up Compass a couple blocks away, and we've been on the road since then."

By the door, Geraldo shifts uncomfortably on his feet.

Sura grins at Compass. "That's badass!" Compass shrugs modestly.

"It's what I d-do."

Sura frowns at Maeve. "But you should have got an offer. We all did."

"When I logged back into my account, there was this mountain of emails and texts and clips waiting for me. Somebody calling themselves 'Us' was trying to get ahold of me."

All that Maeve had heard was a wild-eyed epic, distorted through filters of conservatism and twentieth-century understandings of AI, and fundamentalist expectations of history's aim. Servants of Satan crafted demonic computers that have hijacked freedom and the monetary system, enslaving Mankind. "That can't be right, can it?" Maeve asked.

"Sure it is, well except for the Satan part. And the enslaving part. And the hijacking part. The economy was already hijacked, the actants just grabbed the ball and ran with it. Maeve, it's okay. They aren't the robot revolution."

"Well, I did read the offer on the drive up. I just can't believe it, is all."

The actants have found a way for Maeve to go back to school if she wants. They can see that the supply of female philosophers is low; they're encouraging education across the board, particularly in the humanities. Since the University of Pittsburgh campus is a deodand, it's in on the planning process. Maeve can't wrap her head around how the professors and students and maintenance staff can all be part of the thing; after the past season's adventures, she's not sure she wants to go back.

"You're in charge now," Sura points out. "Where do you want to go?"

Maeve frowns at the FBI agents. "Some other world." Then her smile falters and she winces. She presses at her side. "Except it has to be a world that has good health care."

"Ha! Haven't you heard? Health care's been reframed. It's a right now."

Compass smiles and says, "Some other world? We can d-do that—but you also know we can do better.

"*This* world is yours now, Maeve."

When Maeve gets tired and they settle her in Compass's room—the same room where Sura first slept—Sura announces she's going out. "Look at it," she says, pressing both palms and her nose against the glass. "It's never going to be like this again."

"Do you want company?" asks Jay. She shakes her head.

"That goes for you too." She waggles a finger at Geraldo. He shrugs; he doesn't like cross-country anyway, and by now he knows she's not going to try to escape. There are FBI drones ringing the property, nobody's getting through their cordon, either in or out.

So, she bundles into her ski suit one last time, laces up her boots, and plants the giant toque she borrowed from Jay on her head. "Back in a bit."

It's crisp outside but not unpleasant. She spotted a V of geese heading north yesterday, and the forecast says that an onslaught of warm air is advancing from the south. Winter is about to cave; the snow will be gone by the weekend.

The moon is low now but throws enough light to navigate. The land's a pearl scattered with diamond dust, and just as her own breath makes the only clouds, her skis make the only sound as she leaves the yard. This perfect silence is a gift and she's determined to take it.

Jay has skip-tracing work and Maeve has prospects with Malcolm, so they're both talking about heading back to Detroit. That's wonderful, and she knows they'll come back to visit. What's harder is that Sura is encouraging Compass to go with Maeve, because as beautiful as the farm is, Compass can't live without her link to the deodands. For her the silence is not a healing thing, and Sura wants her to heal.

Those fucking congressmen. They know they don't understand the technology; their eyes glazed over whenever the experts used terms like *directed acyclic graph* or *quantum onetime pad*. Knowing that they don't know, their caution is probably perfectly reasonable.

These deodand things won't tolerate us executing you or imprisoning you, they'd told her. *But while we believe that you gave the backdoor into their data to them, and the experts say that they will never abuse it, we can't be sure that you did not create another backdoor by unknown means. For that reason, we've decided to prohibit you from using any digital technologies, until such a time as we are convinced that there's no threat of you taking control of the deodands.*

The whole point of blockchains is that there can only be one copy of the damned key! And she gave it away. Provably. But the congressmen don't get math, and they know they don't. They have to be cautious. And so she is here, with no devices, no TV, no electricity. The FBI took out the power lines and now the place is heated and lit with gas. They did bring in a library of books, the printed kind, but every damned one has had its NFC tag cut out.

Jay and the others can come and go, as long as they submit to a thorough and humiliating search on the way in and out. As of now, this little Ohio farm is probably the only dark spot on Earth, digitally speaking.

She loves it here.

The fields are more overgrown than they look from the house; Sura weaves around upthrusts of brush and young trees. Jay's uncle doesn't mind that she's wintering over, as long as no new development happens while she's here. It turns out he's making more money selling the carbon credits from rewilding the place than he made from farming.

She pauses to look up near the gap to the back forty. The black is perfect and the Milky Way is God's scarf flung across the sky. The stars are elusive, always balanced just on the edge of clarity. She'll never fully capture them for memory, which means she'll have to come out here again and again, each time meeting them anew.

Maybe Congress will let her out of her exile someday, maybe they won't. It doesn't matter. She has a right to be here, in this world, and it's bigger than America, or humanity.

In this moment, she can open her heart a little and feel close to Mom and Dad. This is what they wanted to show her, Mom through her music, Dad through their trips together; this is why they drew her into being in the first place. You see such a sky, you want to grab someone and bring them under it. Wonder is to be shared. What with the thousand details of life, and money issues, and sickness and bickering, they just forgot about the wonder. They got distracted, like everybody does, and lost faith and confidence in themselves. She understands that now.

"Well, you tried. And I am here."

She skis on. It's been a long arc from awe and curiosity to cynicism and doubt; to a retreat into the imagination; to new worlds, and then back again. Like this land, she's had her try at being civilized. Like it, she's come home to what really matters, with a rewilded heart.

The back field opens out before her. There might be foxes but the deodands told the FBI that there are no bears nearby. It's safe for her to be alone; still, she pauses to look back. The little cottage is a dollhouse in the snow, its lights amber and inviting. Sura smiles and moves on into the field, the deodand, the self-owned world.

She reaches the far end of the trapezoid as the moon is cresting the trees. Long blackness leans into the fields, matching the darkness of the sky. It's silent, eerie, and wonderful, this immortal nonhuman world. And while there are satellites in the heavens, and billions will be online and in VR right now, while there will be space colonies and robots and biohacking and flying cars and the whole snowballing technocratic future that Bill and his friends always wanted, she knows now that this will remain.

If she unleashes her imagination here, what perfect world will it show her—what else, than this? She closes her eyes, summons her inner vision, and imagines a sky crowned with stars, a bowl of land cupping all care. In the center of it stand two companions joined in the simple awe of being—one a woman, defiant and proud, the other a forest, slowly rousing to the dawn of spring.

She opens her eyes, and beholds a sky crowned with stars, a bowl of land cupping all care. In its center stand two companions—one a woman, defiant and proud, the other a forest, slowly rousing to the dawn of spring.

A laugh rises in her.